AN EMPTY HOUSE DOESN'T SNEEZE

ALSO BY DAVID SCOTT RICHARDSON

River's Reach: Coming of Age Amid the Fish War

AN EMPTY HOUSE DOESN'T SNEEZE

DAVID SCOTT RICHARDSON

ISBN: 979-8-9886479-5-9

Dedication

The story is dedicated to Val Richardson (Aunt Val in the story), a real-life "Rosie the Riveter," who riveted B-17s at Boeing's Seattle plant in the 40s. She has been a tireless champion of women's and gay rights her entire life, inspiring all who know her.

Contents

1. Breaking the Blackout

EVERY STORY HAS MANY plausible beginnings. Where each starts depends on who's telling the story and who's doing the listening. If this story was told by adults, they might say it began when Germany invaded Poland in 1939 or when the Japanese bombed Pearl Harbor in 1941. War historians allege that the table was set for WWII with the Treaty of Versailles in 1918—at the end of the so-called "war to end all wars." Still others argue that it never would have happened if the Great Depression of the 1930s hadn't intensified the storm clouds of conflict. But none of that matters now. The tendrils of history mingle, often weaving too tightly for us to unravel.

…which brings us to the present…

If WWII simply *wasn't*, the Johannsens would probably be enjoying a peaceful evening gathered around the Philco, after which fifteen-year-old Scotty Johannsen (our storyteller) would retire to his room where he'd leaf through *Life Magazine*, learning what he could about the ways of women.

But there *is* a war on, and Scotty is huddling with his family in their basement bomb shelter during a Seattle air raid drill. This small story is nested in a much larger one that engulfed the world and raised mushroom-shaped clouds over Hiroshima and Nagasaki in 1945. Scotty will leave that part of the story to the adults and tell us instead what he experienced from his front door.

The battlefields were thousands of miles away, but the war settled into every pore of the country, including Seattle. Automobile companies began rolling out tanks and designing army Jeeps. Shipyards cranked out Liberty ships at a pace that boggled the mind. Seattle revved up to meet the challenge, bustling with war activity that kept the Boeing aircraft plant humming around the clock. New rationing measures restricted gasoline and groceries, compelling heroic adjustments from everyday people to maintain a semblance of normal at a time when things were anything but.

Concern grew for friends and family members deployed in the military. Neighbors eagerly devoured news from the front and anxiously gossiped about those who wouldn't be coming home. Posters urging the purchase of war bonds proliferated, and those blaring "Uncle Sam Wants You" were plastered nearly everywhere. Luxury goods were particularly scarce, and local task groups formed to lead scrap drives and plant victory gardens. The country was on a war footing and people did their part, telling themselves, "We're all in this together."

By 1943, Americans had done their best to adjust as shortages and rationing increased and nightly blackouts were imposed to protect cities from air raids and coastal shelling. For the most part, they adopted Winston Churchill's advice to "Be calm and carry on," but there was an underside to this comforting picture of patriotism.

The flash flood of government money to fund the war was tempting, and many took advantage. Graft wormed its way into military contracts, and a black market of rationed goods soon emerged. Not everybody supported the war—some for political or religious reasons, some because they didn't want to participate in humans killing humans, and others who were simply scared shitless at the thought of entering combat.

Many initially believed the U.S. shouldn't get involved in foreign wars. "Let them fight it out over there," they complained. However, the attack on Pearl Harbor shook many out of their isolationism. The government made accommodations for those who wanted to serve but eschewed combat roles. Some were given conscientious objector status if they met certain conditions. The vast numbers of men entering the military yielded opportunities for women to enter the workforce as never before, and thousands took jobs in factories, construction, and trucking.

For Scotty Johannsen, the war spawned concern for everything and everybody he loved. It also meant that good chocolate was scarce. War games entered the fantasy repertoire he and his friends shared, and battles against the "Jerrys & Japs" replaced those between "Cowboys & Indians." Imagination primed, he'd find himself at the controls of a sleek fighter plane taking off from a carrier deck or looking through the bombsite of a B-24 while crossing the English Channel for a raid over Germany. "Playing his part in the fight," he always returned safely to base.

He'd never considered the possibility of somebody *not* going along. After all, everybody he knew was doing their bit to support the war effort. He'd heard the rumors of "spies in our midst," but he couldn't conceive of anybody traitorous enough to set fires during the blackouts, risking the horrors of war invading the home front. But Scotty would soon discover that there were such people, and that one of them roamed his own cozy neighborhood nightly.

The firebug later said he'd never intended to hurt anyone, nor was he making a statement against the war, although many thought

13

otherwise. Why else would anyone light fires during the mandatory blackouts? One fire might have been an accident, but several, all begun during a blackout, strained credulity to think they were unrelated. When questions later arose, the authorities would say it didn't matter whether there was intent to injure someone. There was an intent to break the blackout, which was a serious crime. More importantly, there was intent to commit arson, and the facts proved this beyond a reasonable doubt. Arson is against the law, war or no war.

Some were certain that the firebug planned every fire, but the truth was murkier—he operated primarily on instinct. Thoughts of fire had long consumed him, like a siren call he found impossible to ignore. Fire-riddled fantasies entered his dreams, roused his curiosities, and inevitably steered him to his next incineration. Fire was like an unsolved mystery, and as an essential element of survival, he felt it was important to gain control over it. It warmed the hearth, cooked the food, and helped forge things necessary for existence, including the implements of war. Some believed they'd mastered fire, but flames weren't so easily enslaved. Fire had a mind of its own and could outwit the well-intended in a flash. Sometimes, it was angry and unpredictable, and at others, it brought campfire comfort, keeping frightening creatures at bay. Nothing could withstand the determination of fire for long, not even the rocks deep within the earth.

What distinguished this night from any other since the blackouts began was the crystal-clear sky and the firebug's growing temptation, now at a fever pitch. All in all, it seemed as good a night as any to let fire have its way with him. Like a security blanket, the blackouts gave cover for the city to hide from the prying eyes of an aerial attack. They likewise armed the firebug with concealment for his secret pursuits. He was eager to put his stealth and planning to the test.

He'd waited patiently, enjoying the anticipatory thrill even before the fire was set. When the setting sun gave the OK for the blackout to take full effect, he zeroed in on the task of starting his fire. If he'd been asked what he expected to gain from his act, he wouldn't have known what to say. A vague answer lurked somewhere in his bones, but it was a secret he kept even from himself. It was action, not words that drove him. He'd light the fuse, and after a breath-holding moment, the fumes he'd come to know so well would ignite with an exhilarating whump. The beacon would be set to burning and he'd look back over his shoulder as he ran. As his fires lit a path, he could do nothing but follow.

Striking a casual gait, he sauntered down the nearly pitch-black alley with a Mason jar half full of rationed gasoline, siphoned from a neighbor's car. His eyes darted from side to side, but nobody saw him on the lonely street lined with blacked-out windows. The jar was secure in a jacket pouch that was probably designed for some sort of survival gear. Caressing it, he thought how strange it was that something so cold could burst instantly into searing heat. He felt no reluctance at what fire had asked him to do and was powerless to turn down its sinister invitation.

There was always risk. A chance the blackout wouldn't keep his secret. A few people were out and about—those with crucial tasks to complete, others without a care in the world, and those seeking escape from their cloistered homes. Roving air raid wardens checked to see that everyone was in compliance: Were their windows covered? Did they have fire suppression materials? Did they have any business being out and about?

He'd walked this alley many times and thought he knew what to expect. But the unexpected is the enemy of certainty; like gravity, it never sleeps. Still, he played the favorable odds that he wouldn't be seen. He'd studied the routines of the authorities for weeks, and surprise was his ally. The act itself would be quick, taking only several seconds. He could always forgo accomplishment if the risk was too great, but as he got closer to the pile of splintered wood, a primal excitement rose inside him, like a prelude to a symphony. He hadn't seen anybody since turning into the alley, and light from the gibbous moon was nearly obscured by clouds.

He'd experimented extensively with various ways to start fires. He'd read about elaborate timing devices and planned to devise one in case it was needed in a difficult circumstance. Tossing a lit match might work, but chances for success dwindled in the event of wind or rain. Pouring a trail of gasoline and lighting it with a match would probably work, but gasoline was scarce, and he hadn't been able to obtain much, even by illegal means. He explored other methods, but they all seemed too complicated, unreliable, or risky. Eventually he settled on a homemade fuse, which he'd light at a distance, using a match he'd stolen from his dad's pipe-smoking supplies. His practice fuses had worked flawlessly, even in rainy conditions, and he had no reason to believe tonight would be any different. He didn't need to toss the Mason jar like a grenade. All he needed was to quietly douse the debris with a little gasoline, run the fuse away from it, touch a match to the fuse, and run. If it didn't light, it didn't light, and the lingering smell of gasoline would be the only evidence of his failed attempt. There would be other opportunities. Neither the war nor the blackouts would end anytime soon.

2. Home Sweet Home (Seattle 1943)

WHEN MY FOLKS BOUGHT the house next to Ravenna Park it wasn't for its luxury bomb shelter potential. It was, they said, because it had such architectural charm, the right number of bedrooms, and, as I later found out, it was the right price. I fell in love with it for the circular stairway that snaked up the castle-like tower, not to mention the possibility of finally having my own room. Our backyard spilled into the park across an invisible property line that separated the world of wartime shortages and air raid drills from the forested wilds where I imagined war was too busy to visit.

Making sure we were prepared in the event the sky fell in the form of Japanese bombs, Dad converted our basement into a bomb shelter, doubling its duties as a haven for spiders and the occasional mouse. As the local air raid warden, Dad took his responsibilities very seriously. In one short week, the cold dark den of spiders was outfitted for basic air raid comfort. He'd given little thought to how stifling it might become if the *All Clear* didn't sound in an hour or so. In the absence of a real air raid, the basement practiced sheltering our family of five from the prying eyes of Japanese aircraft.

It was less than two years since the surprise attack on Pearl Harbor, and things weren't going well for our forces in the Pacific. Most adults assured kids that nothing like that would ever happen here, but most of us could tell they weren't sure. Even so, our bomb shelter gave us the illusion of a safe harbor when the sirens screamed and the sea rose in anger. So far, the storms have remained distant.

While the basement did its part to make us feel safe, my sister, Greta, and my older brother, Erik and I did our part by entertaining ourselves without too much of a ruckus. This wasn't always easy no matter how hard we tried. Often a ruckus would erupt and take us all by surprise. Greta said that the person who invented board games must've been thinking of life in a bomb shelter. Just how many times can you play Chinese checkers and still care about winning?

Whatever the basement lacked in cozy decor, it made up for in sardine-can togetherness. With our small, improvised dining table holding center stage, it was a tight fit, but each of us had carved out a niche. Mine was near the old coal bin where Dad kept tools and wardening supplies and Mom's was a worn-out chair in front of the pantry shelves. She looked like she was guarding the hard work of last year's victory garden. Erik's room had been in the basement since we first moved there, and it was more-or-less teenage comfortable. It wound up being our makeshift living room whenever we had to shelter. Recently, he'd even turned his "Private. Keep Out!" door sign around and rearranged things so Greta would have a comfortable place to sit. Both Mom and Dad tried to lighten up these wartime gatherings, saying they were a family bonding opportunity that we wouldn't have had in peacetime. They'd say things like, "When you look back on this, your hearts will warm with fond memories." As it was, I thought I'd bonded quite well with everybody already, even limited as we were to the first and second floors of the house. Bomb-shelter bonding left a lot to be desired.

I was the middle kid, in between Greta and Erik. I answered to both Scott (Mom's preference) and Scotty (Dad's choice), as well as a few other names. I didn't particularly like being called Scotty. Scott just sounded more dignified—something Mom said I should aspire to. She said dignity was "like a suit of armor that would carry me through tough times."

A few of my friends called me "The Hankie" whenever I was a pain in the butt. Mom usually made sure I carried a hankie, and my friends would sometimes pull out theirs and make like two foghorns blowing a duet. We'd all double up laughing, and then I'd pull out mine to make it a trio. We called ourselves "The Hankies."

Seattle and other West Coast cities initiated the blackouts and air raid drills about the time Pearl Harbor was attacked. The goal was to make targets hard for the enemy to see from the air and to prevent ships from being silhouetted against city lights. Windows had to be covered and outside lights turned off. Train engines, and some cars, were even issued little eyebrows so their headlights wouldn't shine upward, giving them away. Not everybody took the warnings or penalties seriously. Some dared to drive without headlights at night, giving parents yet one more reason to keep their kids from running around after dark. My parents never seemed concerned about that though.

During the blackouts, I sometimes met up with my friends after sunset and we'd discuss important teenage matters. We fancied ourselves as authorities in the art of talking with girls who weren't our sisters. Some of us even thought we understood what kissing was all about, although reliable information from experienced participants was hard to come by. In the absence of actual data and in the interest of science, we planned kissing experiments to test our hypotheses. But even the most brilliant scientists among us never carried them out.

We'd joke that the blackouts were the best weapon the enemy had. Every day we'd hear about someone who'd tripped, fallen, or crashed in the dark. Some of these accidents ended up being fatal, so I guess it really wasn't something to joke about, but gas rationing kept most sensible people at home and the death toll limited to single digits. Kids knew what parents only suspected, that blackouts were made for mischief of every kind imaginable. I won't go into details. Just trust me, I had nothing to do with any of it.

Sometimes air raid drills occurred during school hours. Teachers would yell, "Get Out and Get Under," meaning get out and under your desk. I was getting so big that it was hard to fit, and I entertained myself by imagining I got jammed in and would have to spend the rest of the day wearing my desk around, stuck on my back. We understood the reasons for these drills, but after a while they made it seem like the adults just liked to cry wolf.

Not only had the Japanese nearly destroyed the U.S. Pacific Fleet at Pearl Harbor, but they'd established a foothold in the Aleutian Islands. In a daring, submarine hit-and-run attack, they'd even shelled Fort Stevens down on the Oregon side of the Columbia River. Who's to say they didn't have their sights set on the big Boeing aircraft plant running three shifts a day in preparation for what might be coming right here in Seattle? The revved-up riveting at Puget Sound shipyards undoubtedly sent out a similar invitation.

Maybe the British had the right idea by sending kids to the countryside so they wouldn't get bombed in the cities. Dad once threatened to send me to the English countryside—not to save me from a bomb, but just to get me out of his hair. In reality, if we had to go anywhere for our safety, we'd probably end up with Mom's

20

folks near La Conner in the Skagit Valley. If the British had the chance, they'd probably send their kids there too. Except for missing my friends and not having Ravenna Park as a backyard, I wouldn't have minded. I loved my grandparents, and the farming country of the Skagit Valley did seem safer than the city and all its tempting targets.

3. The Family Dungeon

AS BOMB SHELTERS GO, ours was hardly ideal. Even if it was, nothing could protect us from the finality of a direct hit by a lonely bomb that took a shine to us. People assured me the chances of that were one in a million, but when the lonely bomb thought snuck up on me, it grabbed on so tight I needed a major distraction to wrench free. I took some comfort that our neighborhood wasn't a very juicy target for the enemy. But my comfort dimmed when I considered how easily mistakes could be made on foggy or rainy days, the kind we have much of the year. Frightened pilots might care less about accuracy than just unloading so they could get back to base in time for supper. Sand Point Naval Air Station wasn't that far away, and adults said the Japanese spies knew all about it. I took pride in identifying planes by silhouette or engine sound, but occasionally, I'd hear one I didn't recognize, and my stomach would tighten.

We had what was called a daylight basement, for the unsurprising reason that it let daylight in from one side where it opened up at ground level. The other three sides were dug into the hill. We'd boarded up the daylight side to prevent being showered with glass if a blast came from that direction, but what would've been a bright and cheery space was now dark and dank. I suspected it was a little like being in a coal mine. Seattle was short on sunlight anyway, and a dimly lit bomb shelter was like just one more cloud in the sky.

Initially, the security I felt when we were all together made it easy to ignore the vulnerability of having a thick cement foundation on *only three* of the four sides. The basement wasn't meant to be a bomb shelter though, and with one wall open to whatever the world had to offer, I still found room to worry. Our coziness slowly faded, only to be replaced by the stress of squishing together in a space that was designed more for projects than getting to know each other in ways we'd rather keep to ourselves.

The basement wasn't designed for commodious living, especially for a family of five with some of us given to sudden bursts of grabbing each other's stuff. Greta and I were usually the guilty ones. Feeling trapped and bored, we'd break into a commotion that eventually required parental intervention. We'd get antsy, Mom said, and the ensuing hullabaloo would draw her ire. I wondered if a hullabaloo was brewing inside Mom and Dad as well.

From time to time, we found evidence that rodents sheltered in our basement alongside us. Dad joked that the air raid drills scared the bejesus out of them. We didn't remind him that they'd left their bejesus anywhere they felt like since long before air raids, wars, or bomb shelters. For years, Erik had tried to negotiate a peace treaty, but with all of us cooped up as regular visitors, he was forced to take a harder line. The startling snap of a mousetrap would send Greta into a tirade about how all animals had a right to live. But when fresh signs of rodenthood appeared, she agreed to limit their rights to the outdoors. As a precaution against being called a murderer by his own sister, Erik checked the traps when Greta wasn't around and flung the beady-eyed cadavers into the ravine to feed and fertilize whatever needed them. He claimed that a properly functioning mousetrap was instantaneous and not a bad way to go.

We all knew that spiders took over completely when nobody was there. Greta and I were freaked out by even the tiniest creepy crawly, but Erik was fascinated by them. He'd set out little spider snacks of dead insects, taking care not to damage the webs, which he never tired of gently jiggling, just to see what the spiders would do. He always got their attention and convinced himself he could communicate with them on their terms. Nobody argued the point. Once, he tried to expand the spider's diet by sticking some precious cheese in a web. What a waste of cheese, I thought. Cheese was such a rarity it made sense that cheddar was yellow, like gold. Months had gone by since we'd eaten any.

The only finished room in the basement was likely predestined for wartime togetherness long before sirens began ordering us around. Erik's bedroom included a fireplace, but the rest of the basement was bare cement walls. Erik complained that the fireplace was designed to suck heat out of the room and freeze the occupants to death, so he cobbled together a cover for the opening out of old shiplap and cardboard. It was hard to tell if it helped or not.

A stash of extra light bulbs saved us from injury in the event of an indoor blackout, and candles sometimes made it feel like we were camping out, but aside from Erik's room, the basement was essentially one large dungeon with an old coal bin off to the side. Dad did his best converting the coal bin into a workshop, but all it was good for was storing a few tools. Now it kept our extra cots, one of which I used during the air raid warnings, plus first aid supplies that Dad could grab quickly as his duties required.

Erik and Dad built some racks to store our bedding and extra clothes, along with dry food and our canning harvest from the victory garden. Tin cans were a rarity on the shelves, since most canned goods were shipped to the troops, but Erik finagled two cans of SPAM from somebody. They'd collected dust for so long that I'd given up waiting for them to become SPAM fritters, which some considered a wartime delicacy. We must have been saving it for a SPAM victory celebration when the war was over.

Erik decorated one wall of his bedroom with a poster reminding us to save grease so it could be used for making explosives. On the opposite wall, he'd hung his all-time favorite defense bond poster, "You Buy 'em. We Fly 'em!" Anything about airplanes was a hit with Erik and me. As if the drills and blackouts weren't reminder enough of the uncertain path ahead, Dad put up posters as well— "Remember Pearl Harbor" and "The Walls Have Ears."

Everywhere, especially in public places, war posters wagged their fingers at us, reminding all who passed to do the right thing. Dad's role as a warden gave him access to posters that others didn't have. Greta begged and begged till he brought home a Red Cross recruiting poster, which she promptly displayed on the inside of her bedroom door. She insisted that if Mom and Dad ever let her grow up, she'd join the Red Cross and go to work helping our soldiers. We all believed she would, but I hoped we wouldn't need soldiers by that time.

Mom didn't much care for the posters plastered all over the place, but she often commented on the quality of the artwork, saying, "People contribute to the war effort in different ways, and perhaps we could do more with a paintbrush than with a gun." She ruminated over the inevitable destruction of irreplaceable art and speculated whether artists would be the ones to put us back together again when the war was over.

Erik was especially fond of one poster with a quote from President Roosevelt saying how the war effort took people from all backgrounds and nationalities. I wondered if the quote really applied to everybody or if it was just for show. It certainly didn't apply to Japanese Americans—that was clear. I can't say much for the cartoony artwork though, which featured a gray army tank. The washed-out design made me wonder if color itself was being rationed.

We all admired President Roosevelt though, even before the war, and Mom had a special affinity for Eleanor Roosevelt. She wasn't simply the first lady, wife of the president—she was a woman of substance, "with a mind and doings of her own," Mom liked to say. Once, when Dad remarked that he'd like to have dinner with Winston Churchill, Mom accused him of secretly wanting to drink whiskey and smoke cigars with the British Prime Minister. Mom would rather have breakfast or a mid-morning snack with Eleanor. "Most things worth doing get done by lunchtime," she jibed, repeating something that Eleanor had supposedly said.

The previous owners of the house had upgraded the coal furnace to an oil burner and installed a cement sink in the basement for laundry. With oil rationed, we had to rely on blankets, extra clothes, and the heat-sucking fireplace to chase away the chilly damp that basements specialize in. We were the only family I knew of that gave their furnace a name. Erik called her "Medusa" after learning about the character in Greek mythology, and over time she came to seem like a member of the family. One look and it was easy to see how she got her name. The pipes twisting out from her head rose in serpentine fashion to connect with the heat registers upstairs.

Medusa's warmth, when we could afford to feed her, was life-giving. We spent enough time with her to get to know her quite well, even addressing her in the first person on occasion: "Quiet down

Medusa, we're trying to have a conversation." Medusa answered in her native tongue, creaking and groaning from the expansion or contraction of her heating system and humming the soothing notes of her oil injector. She had a sinister aspect to her, as well. Hunkered in a dimly lit corner, her dusty green complexion wasn't exactly inviting. She had a way of startling us with ominous-sounding clanks and creaks that made me think she might turn on us. Even so, the basement had become our home away from home.

As often as the air raid siren went off, we still hadn't completely adjusted. How do you get used to the blaring reminder that everyone you love might be obliterated any time, day or night? Even after more than a year, that shrieking siren still gave me goose bumps—the sandpapery kind that don't go away when you rub them. Uncertainty wedged itself into every corner of our lives. In a split second, the siren call could be the real thing. What if we weren't all together in the basement's safe harbor when uncertainty made up its mind to come get us?

4. Taking Cover

WE'D BONDED THROUGH AT least a half dozen air raid drills, but I wouldn't say they'd become routine. There's one drill that sticks out in my mind because it unsettled the neighborhood in ways that nobody could've predicted. It was near dusk on a Wednesday when the siren began yelling at the city to pay attention and take cover. Dad had just gotten off the bus from work, Mom was home fixing supper, Erik was working on a model biplane in his room, and I'd just finished my paper route.

"Where's Greta?" Mom asked nobody in particular.

"She's probably over at Jen's again," I answered.

"Well, she should be here in a few minutes then."

Mom and I went down the narrow spiral stairs single file, and Dad arrived a few minutes later, out of breath after his sprint from the bus.

The standing rule was to hightail it home if you were ten minutes or less away when the siren blared. It was like the rule at school. If you thought you could get home in twenty minutes, you went. If not, you stayed. Depending on where we were, especially if we didn't hear any planes droning overhead, we bent the ten-minute rule as far as it would go, occasionally misjudging the line that would bring on a scolding from Mom or Dad. Most ordinary reprimands came from Dad, the stricter of the two, but being caught unsheltered during an air-raid brought Mom to full attention as the general in charge. Unlike Dad though, she gave a wink to let us know she was glad we'd made it home, safe and sound. Since there was nowhere we'd rather be than home if the drill was more than a drill, we seldom bent the rule too far.

Soon enough, Greta clomped down the brick stairs, nearly falling several times, but managing to hold onto her Nancy Drew book and several well-worn *Wonder Woman* comics.

"Where were you?" Dad challenged in a gruff voice, muffling his relief at her arrival. Besides being late for the air raid drill, Greta knew she'd violated yet another rule—being home by five every day, regardless. She offered a timid excuse with charming innocence and thwarted further questioning.

"I was over at Jen's."

Mom began barking orders. "OK then but get those wet clothes off before you catch your death of cold down here. It'll be a while before this place warms up. Erik, get a fire started. Who knows how long it will be before the *All Clear* sounds?"

"Sure Mom," Erik said, "in just a sec. I need to glue this piece of fuselage."

With her hands on her hips and a clenched jaw, Mom's smoldering glare followed Greta over to her cot in Erik's room. "How many times have I told you to take those wooden shoes off before coming down the stairs?"

"I know Mom."

"Well then, why don't you do it?"

"I just forgot."

"I know you think you're a ballerina in those things, but you won't feel so graceful when you fall down the stairs and break a leg. Besides, you have an old pair of saddle shoes you could wear. They might save your life."

"Jeez. OK, OK."

Greta and her friends had taken to wearing wooden clogs as a matter of necessity since most leather was going to the troops. They were all the rage for a while, and many turned them into personal statements, decorating them with wild and fanciful designs. One class even used them for an art project. Clogs weren't very popular with boys, who took great care to make their raggedy shoes last long after they should've been declared dead.

Once everybody was accounted for, we all gathered at the table and instinctively went silent, as if the preacher had said, "Let us pray." And that's really what it was, a silent prayer, a bow tied around our familial sense of safety and wellbeing. We weren't sure if we could hear planes overhead while down in the basement, but we couldn't resist straining to listen anyway. The absence of rumbling airplanes or explosions didn't mean there wasn't anything to worry about though, just that things got off on the right foot and we could relax for the moment. Nearly as soon as we were settled, Mom rushed back upstairs to check on the biscuits and gravy she'd been preparing when the siren went off. Since the only lock confining us to the basement dungeon was the remote possibility of being blown to bits, we occasionally paroled ourselves, dashing upstairs for things that eased our imprisonment.

Though biscuits and gravy are a faithful belly-filling favorite, Mom apologized for not having any vegetables. By this time of year, most of the canning had been used up, and it would be several months before our victory garden produced new green beans and tomatoes.

Nobody complained though, especially after Mom revealed some freshly made custard. We knew we had more food than most, and we knew there were good reasons for the rationing and shortages.

Usually, the *All Clear* sounded after about twenty minutes, but since nobody had heard it yet, we wondered if we'd possibly missed it. Five pairs of ears straining to be set free don't miss much. Nonetheless, it made us wonder if this was more than just a drill, till Dad joked that "practice makes perfect." He'd known ahead of time that it was a scheduled drill.

Greta piped up, "Mom, make Scotty give me back my comics. He's got his own."

You could almost predict that Mom would suggest a compromise. A devoted negotiator, she probably could've prevented the war if the officials had had the good sense to give her the chance. Perhaps not though. Wars aren't prevented by kindness, consideration, or melt-in your-mouth biscuits. They're more like storms that sweep up everything in their path.

"Can't you two share?"

But Greta went on, "He wrecks my comics and folds the covers over. He's already ruined a bunch of the *Wonder Woman* issues I was saving for the G.I. care packages. Besides, I think he just likes to look at girls dressed that way."

"Dressed? That's a stretch," said Mom. "How about if he agrees to open and close them carefully? You could read them like a hardcover book—not folding over the corners of pages you like to revisit and making sure to return them." She turned her hopeful gaze on me. "How about it, Scott? Can you do that?"

"I'll try, but she better not mess with any of my stuff either."

"Right. What's good for the goose is good for the gander, or in this case, what's good for the gander is good for the goose." Mom laughed, letting us know she was proud of her little witticism.

"Know what else Mom? I think he stole my last copy of *Radio Stars*."

"Well, if you did, Scott, give it back.

"I didn't. She must've loaned it to one of her friends so they could go goofy over pictures of the radio stars."

Though we didn't notice anything remarkable about this particular air raid drill at the time, we'd soon learn about a disturbing incident that took place as we huddled in our shelter, and it would rock our neighborhood's fragile sense of wellbeing, leading some to believe that the war was on our doorstep.

5. News of the Day

DAD HAD TAKEN TO using the bomb shelter for something besides safety. In the confines of the basement, he routinely lectured his captive audience on whatever occupied his thoughts. We'd heard it all before but the tiff between Greta and me launched him into a vent about one of his pet peeves for the umpteenth time.

"I wish you kids would fight over actual books instead of comics. They're not real, you know. They aren't news. They're just fairy tales for people who want to stick their heads in the sand. Besides, the way Wonder Woman dresses is a disgrace. You think anyone actually fighting the Nazis would dress like that? They teach you bad habits and they're a waste of your allowance."

Trying not to giggle, I thought that Wonder Woman's attire might be the perfect thing to make the Nazis forget about taking over the world. Who would've thought? One wonderful woman instead of an entire army might save us all. I had to stick up for myself about not reading though.

"But I do read real books. I've read *Flash Gordon* and *The Witch Queen of Mongo* several times. Grandpa sends over *Railroad Stories* when he finishes with them, and I read the newspaper too."

Dad didn't buy it. "Those Big Little Books are simply comics made to look like real books. Just because they have a hard cover doesn't make them any better. And don't try to tell me you read the newspaper. All you read is the funny papers, and you probably don't even read those. You just look at the pictures and tell yourself that's reading. Tell me, what have you learned from Blondie or Tarzan lately?" His voice rose as he lectured and when Dad got red in the face, I didn't argue. I didn't tell him the soldiers loved to get comics in their packages or how Captain America is always reminding kids to save for war bonds and collect stuff for scrap drives. It wasn't always easy for my mouth to obey though.

Erik went back to his model making after dinner, positioning the wing struts of the biplane. He fancied himself as some sort of expert on biplanes and the aircraft of WWI. Even though he might soon be required to fight in this war, I planned to be the family expert about the war planes of WWII, ones made from aluminum instead of wood and fabric. The government recruited high school kids and Boy Scouts to build scale model planes for use in pilot training. I was too young and not in the Scouts so I couldn't participate. But here was Erik, who loved all those rickety outdated planes, and he gets to make models of shiny new metal planes from my war. I could hardly stand it.

Aside from the silhouettes in the spotting guides, there wasn't much information on the capabilities of these modern planes. All we really knew was what they looked like from a distance. I guess that made sense. You wouldn't want the enemy to be able to read something in *Life Magazine* that gave them an advantage, after all. Even so, I scoured every article I could find, looking to become a WWII airplane expert.

Planes were a regular topic with my friends, and any scrap of new information was always worth lecturing on. Listening to a speech from one of my friends was almost as good as giving one; it made us feel like we were participating. Truth was, we made up most of it but soon came to believe it as truth ourselves. Being convincing was partly what made a good lecture, and if you pulled it off, it was almost like hitting a homerun or catching a fly ball that ended the game.

Dad stuck his nose into Erik's biplane factory and held his breath when the glue vapors flared up his asthma. He didn't care that much about the latest airplanes, but he did care about the British. Like many of his jokes, his British airplane story was one we'd heard before and probably would again if the war didn't end soon. It began the same way every time: "The Brits, you know, had the smarts to make a plane out of wood."

"We know," protested Erik.

"Guess what they did when aluminum became scarce?"

"I don't know," I said, playing dumb, like I hadn't heard it all before.

"They set their woodworkers to task and came up with a wooden plane called the Mosquito. Good name for it too. Does a bit of everything and drives the Germans crazy. Oh, the British, what will they do next?"

"Planes that run on beer," teased Erik.

Erik's joke wasn't as goofy as it sounded. We'd heard a story that the Brits outfitted some fighters with special belly tanks, filled them with beer, and delivered it to the troops. Maybe somebody made that up, but it was a good story anyway.

Pops thought so highly of the British, we had to wonder what side he would've been on during the Revolutionary War. Funny to think there was a King George on the English throne back then and now there's a new King George sitting on the same throne. Erik liked to mock what he thought the British sounded like using his fake Cockney accent, "The Brits had a rough patch with the monarchy, a spot of trouble several years back keeping a king on the job. Guess they didn't pay King Edward enough, so he simply up and quit."

The rough patch was now much more than just a blemish though. It was more like a blot, getting bigger every day, with the Luftwaffe overhead, the German submarines lurking out at sea, and the French across the Channel already under the Nazi thumb.

Dad didn't care about any King Georges, past or present; he had a new "pal," Winston Churchill. He was the guy in charge now and I guess the British only had a king because they felt better for having one. Dad joked about sending letters to Churchill full of advice on how to win the war. We were almost sure he wouldn't actually do something like that, but you never know what lengths adults will go to when they think they're onto something. With the Mosquito story buzzing in our ears for the umpteenth time, Dad paced the dungeon as he awaited the *All Clear* before heading out for his warden duties.

"Why does Dad get so worked up about comic books? Does he ever read them?" I asked, wandering over to Erik's desk.

"I don't think so, but I know he's looked at a few. It's like this. In the comics we're always winning the war. Do comic-book heroes ever get defeated by the enemy?"

"No, I guess not," I conceded.

"Well, he knows the war hasn't been going well, neither in Europe nor the Pacific."

This kind of news made me jumpy, but I knew it had to make Erik even more nervous with the draft closing in on him. "What's really going on with the war?" I asked.

"Well, the Germans now occupy France, Poland, Belgium, Holland, Norway, and a bunch of other countries. At night they're bombing the hell out of London and people have to use the subways as bomb shelters. Our boys in the Eighth Bomber Command are getting butchered over Europe because they don't have enough fighter escorts to defend themselves from the Luftwaffe. German U-boats just sit out in the Atlantic and pick off whatever we ship out to keep Britain alive."

"Does that mean we'll lose the war?"

"We're a long way off from anybody winning or losing. We may be providing a lifeline for the Brits but it's a slaughter out there from what I hear. There's the "air gap" out in the middle of the Atlantic that the planes can't reach to protect the ships. It didn't take long for the Germans to figure that one out. There're subs in the Pacific too, Japanese ones. They've even driven us out of the Philippines. Not to mention, how can we ever forget what happened at Pearl Harbor? It's not just that Dad doesn't like comics. He's worried. It's why he's so tense and serious most of the time. And don't forget, Uncle Ted is in the Navy, and we haven't heard much from him since he was deployed. God knows what he might be going through."

"I thought that after the Battle of Midway we were winning."

"Well, that was certainly a victory. But even though we surprised the Japs and got some revenge for Pearl Harbor, Midway was just one naval battle. The Japanese still occupy most of the islands in the Pacific and we've learned the hard way that they rarely surrender when defeated. Instead, they fight to the death, and that means many more Americans die trying to root them out."

"What about Doolittle's raid on Tokyo? That must have done something. I saw a newsreel about it over at the Neptune a couple of weeks ago. Pretty impressive, flying all that way knowing they wouldn't be able to come back."

"Well, it got their attention, I'm sure. It showed them that the home islands weren't as invulnerable as they thought. From what I get, it didn't do much actual damage. It was more of a psychological victory and a morale booster. Might've had something to do with the outcome at Midway though. The Japs probably kept more of their forces home for defense after Doolittle's raid."

"Do you think they'll try to bomb us here in Seattle?"

"I don't think so, but who would've figured on Pearl Harbor when it's so far from Japan? We're much farther from Japan than Hawaii. You never know, though. Submarines are designed to be sneaky."

"You never know, though" seemed like the chorus to everything about the war. "How come you know all this?"

"If you were seventeen and there was a war draft going on, you'd pay close attention to this stuff too."

"Does that mean you're gonna have to join up and fight?"

"I don't know. I guess I'll have to decide soon if the draft doesn't decide for me. I'll have to register, at least."

Silence stared us in the face and the fumes from the model airplane's glue began making it harder to breathe, so we moved away and closed the door. It was hard to imagine how things would change if Erik went to war. I remembered how he'd been there for me when every other kid in the neighborhood knew how to ride a bike, but I still didn't. He ran alongside me, steadying the bike as I tried to balance. I still have the handmade certificate he drew up after letting go for the very last time. If Erik did have to join up, I hoped he'd have somebody there to run alongside him.

6. All Clear

THE *ALL CLEAR* FINALLY sounded just as Dad geared up for his wardening rounds and Mom called for help with the dinner dishes. The upstairs shades were drawn tight, so we felt free to turn on the lights while cleaning up. At first, eating in the basement was fun, like going on an indoor picnic, but it hadn't felt that way for some time. Dinner went faster when Dad wasn't there. We still said "please" and "thank you" and waited to be excused, but things weren't quite as formal when he was gone. The first rule of mealtime was "No eating till everybody is served and ready." It just seemed rude to do otherwise. Another rule was, "No elbows on the table." Though enforced upstairs, house rules never made it to the basement. They were relaxed in our bomb shelter even if we weren't.

After helping clean up, Greta and I charged off to the second floor. Trying to outrun each other, we fell down laughing when we reached the top. With my room lights off, I peeked out to see if the pencils of lights still swept the sky. Greta and I had turned it into a game to try and figure out the exact source of the searchlights. They seemed powerful enough to light up the moon on a clear night, and I guess they needed to practice just like the rest of us. They were off now though, and it was pitch black. Thank God they hadn't found anything that might've found us.

There was one thing I didn't understand about the searchlights: As good as they'd be at lighting up aircraft during a real air raid, wouldn't they also be like beacons, guiding the enemy to its target? I guess by the time the planes were overhead it wouldn't matter. You'd want to light them up so the gunners could see where to shoot. I wasn't hoping for an actual air raid to help answer this question though.

As far as I could tell, our neighborhood remained obediently blacked out. Then just before letting the curtain go, I spotted a fire-like flickering several blocks away near the Boucher's house. It wasn't large, but it was bright enough to draw considerable attention, and if I could see it, so could others. Dad would probably have a lot to say when he returned from his rounds. There were plenty of opportunities for accidental fires, what with more people heating with wood and the liberal use of candles when they weren't ready to draw the shades. But what if this wasn't an accident? Who would violate the blackout? Curiosity made relaxing difficult, so I settled in with one of Greta's *Wonder Woman* comics in silent defiance of Dad's lecture. It felt good to believe in Wonder Woman. She was definitely on our side and dressed to get every boy in the country doing anything she said.

We never knew how long Dad would be gone during the blackouts. Sometimes he just made a quick spin around the block and was back in a jiffy. At other times, he had important business to attend to. He recently had to write up the Bouchers for leaving their back porch light on, and it wasn't the first time he'd had to talk to them about blackout restrictions either. He was committed to doing the best job he could, but he was uncomfortable policing a close neighbor, especially having to do it more than once. It made me uncomfortable too since I walked to school nearly every day with Burr Boucher. Some called us best friends. I wish I didn't even know about the porch light, so I pretended I didn't and never brought it up.

Dad's role as an air raid warden may have been one of the reasons Burr almost never came to my house. Dad said leaving the back porch light on was probably an innocent mistake, but that didn't change the fact that it could result in a fine or even jail. As the posters reminded us, "Blackout Means Black!" Dad would almost certainly check the Bouchers' house again tonight. Sometimes he checked to see if people had buckets of sand and enough firefighting tools, but his main job was to make sure everything was completely blacked out. He was like a parent tucking in his kids, only his kids included the entire neighborhood.

Mom and Dad seldom argued, even though they had their differences or, as Erik said, came at things from different angles. They might raise their voices a bit in the heat of the moment, but it wasn't their style to yell at each other. They were both so strong willed it probably wouldn't have solved anything anyway. But the harsh slam of the front door followed by Dad's heavy footsteps got everybody's attention, including those of us who were upstairs pretending to do our homework. It was half past eight and, as I'd anticipated, Dad was riled up about something after returning from his rounds. He seldom swore, but his report to Mom started with a curse. "Damn. If I find out who did it, they'll wish they were in a German prison camp."

I made sure my door was open just far enough to hear without having to creak around on the wood floor and reveal I was listening.

"What in God's name is going on honey?"

"Somebody set two trash cans and a pile of garbage on fire over by the Bouchers."

"Who would do something like that during a blackout?'

"That's what I want to know. It's a federal offense if it's intentional, and this just doesn't seem to be an accident. It's sabotage, that's what it is, and it's only two blocks away. Are we living among the enemy?"

"Calm down. Yelling at me isn't going to catch them and you'll upset the kids. What did you do when you found the fires?"

"I went up to the nearby houses and banged on the doors."

"What happened?"

"Well, Mr. Boucher and I put the fires out, but nobody had even seen the flames because of their blackout curtains. Nobody heard anything either."

"Do you think they were telling the truth?"

"Come on Anna, we've lived here ever since Erik was little and know everybody pretty well."

"How about the Gottenbergs? They're German and they've only lived in the neighborhood a few years."

"It's not like you to say something like that, Anna. You know we see them at church all the time. They're good Lutherans, and if it's them, I'm a really bad judge of character. I can't believe you'd even suggest that. It can't be the Japs either. The executive order sent them off to inland camps far from the coast."

"Please don't call them Japs. Most of them are Americans. It upsets me when you talk like that about the Japanese. Nobody from this country attacked Pearl Harbor."

"All right. The Japanese have all been sent away to camps, like that family Erik was friendly with. What was their name? Forget it. I can't remember those Japanese names anyway. They all sound alike. Maybe it is them, though; ancestry runs deep. How do we know if we've cleaned all of them out?"

"You know Harlan, I think fear mongering has gotten the best of you. Is this what we stand for, a country that rounds up citizens just because we *think* they might do us some harm? That's not the America I believe in. What's more, it doesn't necessarily have to be somebody who lives in the neighborhood, does it? Could be enemy sympathizers from somewhere else and they just happened to light a fire near us," Mom protested.

"No way to tell. We'll have to organize watches to see if we can catch them in the act if they do it again. That's the only way to be proof positive. It's no use being suspicious of everybody. I just can't believe anything like this is happening right here. What are they trying to prove? Maybe it's those conscientious objectors who don't believe in the war."

"That wouldn't make much sense. Why would they light fires during a blackout? I don't think they take sides. They just believe war is wrong and they don't want to be part of the killing. Have you ever seriously talked with one?"

"No. I just think they all suffer from muddled thinking, so who knows what they might do. By the way, where are the kids?"

"In bed or doing homework like they should be."

"Erik too?"

"No, he went out again right after dinner and the *All Clear*."

"Where to?"

"He didn't say."

Greta snuck into my room. "What's going on?" she asked.

"I'm not sure of the details, but it sounds like somebody set a fire during the blackout."

"Jeez. Who would do that?"

"That's what Dad wants to know."

"Kids?"

"Could be. Kids do stupid things sometimes."

"So do adults. I don't think kids started the war."

Slumber was hard to come by for the Johannsen household. Whatever comfort we'd taken from the fact that the fighting was a long way off was shattered, and we tossed and turned till sleep finally won out. Maybe circumstances weren't what the news told us they were. Maybe things weren't what they seemed to be. Maybe our preparedness routines didn't prepare us at all. Held hostage by the grip of uncertainty, I didn't know.

7. Unexpected Suspect

SPREADING LIKE WILDFIRE, NEWS reached every house in our neighborhood by late the next day. The fire didn't do any real damage, but conspiracy theories started coming out of the woodwork. Some thought it was set by Japanese spies and saboteurs and were overheard muttering, "Those dirty Gooks." Others supposed it was some sort of protest by conscientious objectors, and still others excused it, saying, "It's just kids screwing around." Sherlock Holmes took up residence in every house. I had no idea who might've started the fire, but I did have a burning desire to visit the scene. Even though I'd heard Dad describe it in great detail, I thought an overlooked clue might be visible to a sharp-eyed Sherlock.

Turned out that Burr shared my desire to visit the scene, so we made plans for a look-see on Saturday. There'd been a little rain since the fire, but we doubted it was enough to destroy crucial evidence. When I got to his house, Burr was still in his PJ's and almost forgot to put on street clothes as he headed for the backdoor. That was so like Burr. It was as though he needed a personal assistant to make it through the day. "Did you bring any sleuthing gear?" he asked.

"No, like what?"

"Like a magnifying glass or evidence bags. We're crime solvers today."

"I thought we were just going for a look-see."

"We are, but we might find something everybody else has missed."

"Well, the cops and the military have already gone over the scene with a fine-toothed comb."

"Yeah, but they probably overlooked something."

"OK. What did *you* bring?"

"A pad and pencil."

"Swell. I'm sure that'll be a big help."

A charred mustiness hung in the air as we neared the garden shed several houses down from the Bouchers. Between the shed and the plot that would later be tilled for a victory garden, we saw some ashes and partially burned trash cans.

"Doesn't look like much does it?" I observed. "I'm surprised you haven't already checked it out since you live right nearby."

"Well, it wasn't much as arson fires go," said Burr, sounding a bit too knowledgeable.

"You know about arson fires?"

"Some."

"Doesn't look like there's any evidence here…at least not enough to figure out who did it."

"I bet I know," announced Burr.

"How do you know?" I asked, wondering if this was just more grandstanding from his attention-getting side.

"I just know."

"Well then, who is it?"

"The Millwater gang."

"Did you see them?"

"No."

"Hear anything?"

"No. I just know."

The Millwater gang was known for all sorts of mischief in and around our neighborhood: Whenever something went missing, the Millwater gang stole it; if there was a broken window, the Millwater gang broke it; when a garden was trampled, the Millwater gang trampled it; and every time something was defaced, the Millwater gang defaced it. The thing was nobody ever caught the Millwater gang in the act. In fact, nobody ever saw them at all as far as I could tell, but everybody had opinions. All the kids I knew were confident that the gang was behind any skullduggery in the neighborhood. But adults sometimes joked, "The devil made me do it...or was it the Millwater gang?" They thought all this mischief was done at the hands of teenagers.

"Let's get out of here before somebody sees us," Burr warned. "Somebody might decide they saw something and that something is us."

"We're not doing anything."

"Well, they say some arsonists come back to the scene of the fires they set after the fact, or even come back to watch while the fire is still burning."

"You know everything, don't you? Doesn't a gang need a rival gang to justify its existence?"

"Don't know the answer to that one."

"You're kidding. What did you write on your note pad?"

"Nothing."

I'd barely hinted at it, but I'd begun to question the very existence of the gang. There'd be a price to pay for even making the suggestion. Many kids in the neighborhood were true believers, and they didn't want to hear about it if you thought otherwise. Burr was among them. Neighborhood gospel proclaimed the Millwaters spent years recruiting new members from kids who showed promise—promise of what I didn't know. Then they held initiation ceremonies in the park's hideaways, or so the story went.

I didn't have any proof for my growing skepticism, but things just didn't add up. My parents always cautioned me not to go off half-cocked about things. "Look for evidence and base things on the facts," they'd say. Their advice made sense, especially to my science-minded sister, but if there wasn't any hard evidence, did that prove something didn't exist? It seemed like beliefs were stronger than facts, or the lack of them in this case. I asked Burr to let me know if he came up with anything more concrete. There was nothing left to see here, and we'd been gunning for a slingshot shoot off in the park.

We crossed the footbridge spanning a finger of the main Ravenna Park ravine, a route I was fine taking with Burr but tried to avoid when I was alone unless there was no choice, like when I was late for my paper route. Worried about running into the bully who seemed to know whenever I crossed into his kingdom, I sometimes took the long way around for my paper route or when Mom sent me to the store. No bully in sight today though. At the end of the bridge, we slithered down the muddy tail into the ravine and hiked to one of our favorite spots for slingshot practice. Burr was rattling on about how we could set a trap for the Millwaters when I interrupted his tirade.

"Listen, we don't know anything about the firebug. Is it a one-time thing, an accident, or part of Emperor Hirohito's strategy to defeat us by getting everybody riled up so the Japs can take Seattle without firing a shot?"

"We'll get to the bottom of it," he responded optimistically.

"We'll see," I said. "Just forget it about for now and get your hands limbered up, OK?"

We stared at each other in puzzlement as a faint smell of smoke clouded the air at the bottom of the ravine. "You smell that?" I asked.

"Sure do. What do you think it is?"

"Smoke, you idiot."

"You'll make a great detective someday," Burr shot back.

"Seriously, why would we smell smoke this far into the ravine?"

"Let's follow our noses and find out."

It was a cool, overcast day, the kind that makes chimney smoke go sideways. Less than thirty feet above us drifts piled up in waves like smoke signals. "You think some yokel's having a barbecue?" I asked, knowing there weren't any barbecue pits in the ravine and that fires weren't allowed.

"I think we're heading in the right direction. The smell is getting stronger."

We heard him before we saw him but couldn't make sense of what sounded like a cross between chanting and poetry. A balding, chubby man about my father's age came into view. Seated on a bare patch of earth under some leggy Madrona trees, he rocked back and forth over a smoldering pile. Every once in a while, he'd shout and fall back laughing. Once he got up and did a wobbly dance around whatever was burning like it was some sort of ritual.

"Jeez. Is he just some sort of crazy person?" I asked.

"Yeah, maybe just escaped from the asylum," said Burr—the person who was *absolutely sure* that the recent neighborhood fire was set by the Millwaters.

"I don't think we should get any closer," I cautioned.

"Maybe he's just drunk."

"Even if he is, it's still mighty strange behavior. This guy just seems like he's nuts, doesn't he?" You think he could be the arsonist? Does he look like he belongs to the Millwaters?"

"Nah, too old."

"You sure? Maybe the Millwaters are a bunch of old guys with a heap of axes to grind and they do all that stuff to keep their axes sharp."

"Well, you can't prove they don't exist," Burr challenged.

"You're right, I can't. "Maybe he's drunk and crazy."

"Could be."

After about ten minutes, curiosity gave way to fear, and we ditched target practice and hightailed it home before the blackout was in full effect. Dad was very interested to hear about the crazy man worshiping a pile of smoldering debris.

Three days later, a larger fire lit up the ravine in a flickering dance through the trees, but the fire petered out before I heard any sirens. Dad said that the fire department arrived after some people from the far side of the ravine scrambled down and put out the fire with water from the little creek. Nobody saw the firebug.

8. Behind Enemy Lines

I RAN HOME AFTER my paper route and burst into the kitchen so fast that I forgot to let the screen door bounce off my butt like I was supposed to. As loud as a gunshot, the door's slam announced that someone was on their way to the cookie jar without washing their hands. Before my hand was even out of the jar, Mom appeared, seeking volunteers for a mission to the Tastie Home Bakery.

When we were the only ones around, she played along with my game of using army talk. She was Sarge, and I was PFC Scott Johannsen. She was damn good at it too and seemed to enjoy hamming it up. I thought she must practice army talk when nobody was around because she sounded very military. We mostly used our rendition of army talk, but sometimes we tossed around some navy lingo and threw in an "aye, aye captain" for good measure. On special occasions we adopted roles from the bomber command unit helping the Brits across the pond.

"Do we have a volunteer for a mission to secure a loaf of French bread?" she asked. I understood she'd issued the kind of order that only pretended to be a question, and for an instant, I wondered what she'd do if I refused to volunteer. You don't refuse a request for volunteers when you're the only other person in the room. I'd have to obey, or risk being court-martialed. She knew I had no intention of refusing an opportunity to return in triumph though. Being the hero and succeeding against all odds was in my interest after all. Mom and I had an understanding about things like this. My fee was one slice for an easy mission and two slices for an especially dangerous one.

"Sure Sarge, when do I go?"

"Immediately, Private. And be back by seventeen hundred hours. Be aware, PFC—you know I'll find out if you buy any jelly-filled doughnuts for the troops. Just a loaf of French bread, understand?"

"Yes Sir, Sarge."

The Tastie Home Bakery was on the other side of the footbridge that Burr and I used the day we sniffed out the crazy man in the ravine. The bridge straddled a huge black pipe and a trickling creek at the bottom of the ravine, about fifty feet below. The structure was lashed together by big timbers that fanned out wider at the bottom, like an old railroad trestle.

Without the footbridge, a trip to the bakery would span about eight blocks and an extra fifteen minutes. Of course, if it wasn't there, most of us kids would simply slide down the slippery bank into the ravine, cross the creek, and scramble up the other side. That's what kids do. We trespass through private property, trample victory gardens, leave gates open, and traipse through alleys, spying all manner of activities through curtainless windows. It's from this kind of freedom that stories are born and repeated throughout the school year. I tried to picture an adult crossing the ravine without the bridge, but it seemed they'd all become slaves to sidewalks and cars, a fate us kids thought we could outrun.

Besides being the shortest way to the other side, the bridge was famous in neighborhood lore. It's where kids went to prove themselves in search of immortality. While adult history focuses on civilizations, kid history highlights feats of derring-do: Who can kick a football the farthest? Who can hit a homer clean over the fence? Who can make a substitute teacher run for the hills? And who can clean whose clock…or thinks they can? Just like with adult history, the average kid is rarely there when history is made, and this is where the neighborhood historians come in—those who don't make history themselves but claim to know it all, even if they weren't there either.

Burr was our neighborhood historian. He was odd in a benign way that was hard to put your finger on and was routinely teased about his name and his glasses. Although we might've become friends anyway because he lived at the end of my block, I rather liked his peculiarities. It was a good thing too because he didn't have many friends.

Neighborhood parents were leery of him too. His untidiness made adults wonder what kind of parents Burr had that they'd let him leave the house looking like he did. Although he often looked a mess, he never smelled bad, and he didn't waste his time thinking about girls. Some of my other friends couldn't think about anything but girls. They tried to dress, walk, and talk the way they thought girls would like. All this posturing probably made them unrecognizable to their parents, and their obsessive preoccupation made me wonder: Did girls want boys to be themselves? Or did they want them to be like actors, scrambling to deliver their lines?

I suspected Burr simply felt uncomfortable around most people and that was why he kept to himself most of the time. In other words, you went to his house; he didn't come to yours. He'd eased into a space with neighborhood kids that only he could occupy, and most of them respected the boundaries he claimed for himself.

Besides being our neighborhood historian, Burr had earned a reputation as a scientist. His experiments usually involved destroying something. He then cobbled the remnants together into contraptions that were absolutely ingenious but did nothing useful. His research fascinated all of us, and we understood that someday he'd have a major breakthrough. When he eventually became famous, we reasoned, we could say we'd known him in the old days.

Burr maintained there were only two people who'd performed the ultimate neighborhood feat of derring-do. Simon Lashbaugh, from the unshaven neighborhood that stretched between the footbridge and the bakery, and Natsumi Fujiko, from up by the truck farms, had both performed the feat and lived to tell about it. Even better, they each had a credible witness.

According to Burr, Natsumi gained her notoriety in seventh grade, years before she became my brother's girlfriend. The path to neighborhood immortality was a balance-beam walk across the entire length of the footbridge on the narrow two-by-four railing. Some kids practiced privately with two by four's arranged on the ground and periodically boasted they were almost ready, but their bravado inevitably evaporated when it came time for prime time. Close examination of the discouragingly narrow railing and the probable drop to oblivion ensured the neighborhood hall of fame would never get very crowded. No amount of backyard training could dull the vision of whiplashing off the bridge timbers as you screamed your way down to the shallow trickle of a creek below.

I can't remember ever crossing the bridge without my own rail-walking fantasies. It wasn't so much about technique as it was about the accolades and a longed-for confident strut from defying the odds and the doubters. Today's fantasy dissolved in the face of the party crashers from the other side of the ravine. Just as I skip stepped down the twelve stairs to the bridge deck, there was Simon Lashbaugh and two of his eighth-grade buddies at the other end. He flicked his Zippo lighter open and shut with a menacing click. Even pretend missions to secure French bread for the troops back home had their risks.

It wasn't like I could just cross to the other side of the street. The bridge railings fenced all of us in like the ropes of a boxing ring. I'd gone too far to casually turn around and pretend I was distracted, and I knew the worst thing I could do was show weakness to someone like Lashbaugh and his lieutenants. Even though he was a ninth grader, his buddies were always eighth graders. Perhaps he wouldn't be so intimidating without his sidekicks, but nobody on our side of the ravine could remember ever seeing him alone.

I never understood the cloud of anger that engulfed Lashbaugh. Menace oozed out of his pores, clearing the path ahead of him like motorcycles paved the way for dignitaries. If there was a way to avoid him, you did. As far as I knew, we had no history of a family feud. What did he get from his boot-stomping swagger? Maybe it was a health problem or something as simple as an ingrown toenail that pained him with every step. I told myself it wasn't personal. He was generous with his anger, showering even those who clustered around, like the self-appointed emperor of the unshaven neighborhood.

A winter wind settled in my stomach at the very sight of him, squeezing my tense muscles into a tight ball. My pounding pulse joined in as the rhythm section, drowning out the weak huffs of my shallow breathing. Lashbaugh had never beat anybody up as far as I knew. But whoever came up with that sticks-and-stones garbage never faced off against Lashbaugh's mouth in the middle of a six-foot-wide bridge. Hemmed in by railings and two of his buddies, I had very little hope that we could pass by in silence with a quick, "Hi, how ya doin'?"

"So, Hankie Head, what brings you across the bridge? Aren't you afraid of the trolls? Maybe you came to practice on the railing." Simon took a long slow look over the railing to the body-mangling support timbers while I fished for a clever comeback that suggested I wasn't to be messed with. It was risky to be too clever in these situations. Erik's advice was to remain calm and keep your wits about you. My pulse throbbed, my throat narrowed, and I wasn't far from hyperventilating. I had the crazy thought that fainting might be a way out of this situation, but I kept my silent chuckle to myself.

"So, Hankie, you'll never even try it? What if you fell and popped a few too many pimples and all your puss leaked out?" His buddies grinned back at me while Simon did the talking. He always did the talking and they always did the laughing. As my awkward silence became even more awkward, he turned his menacing expression on his buddies and told them to shut up.

His next question brought expression back to my frozen face mask, almost like he'd decided to be a little friendly. "How's that big brother of yours? Has he joined up yet?

"No, he's registered at the U of W for this fall, and he wants to go out for crew."

"Really? When there's a war on, he wants to go rowing?"

"Well, that's what he said anyway."

"I hear he's afraid to join up. I hear he's one of those chicken shit objectors, a C.O."

"What's a C.O.?"

"The 'C' stands for chicken, like you're chicken to walk the railing. Go ask him what it means. I bet he dresses up in a zoot suit when nobody's looking. Maybe he'll let you wear it when you're doing your paper route."

My stomach relaxed a bit and the pounding lessened. "I'm not chicken. I just need more practice."

"That's what everybody says. Well then, you'd better start practicing. What're you doing on the bridge anyhow?"

"I'm just going to the store for my Mom."

"With ration cards?"

"No, just for a loaf of bread. I don't need any for that." I said, revealing the secret of my mission.

"So, you've got money then?"

I put the grin mask back on and breathed deeply. Oxygen to the brain is supposed to help.

"I asked you a question."

"Yeah, just enough for a loaf of bread."

'Well, hang on to it tightly. You never know."

His buddies stopped laughing long enough to chime in and chant the chorus. "Yeah, you never know. You never know. You just never know."

Simon got off one final shot to accompany our retreat. "Does he still have that Jap girlfriend?"

"No. The government sent her family away."

"That's good. We won't have to worry about another sneak attack."

The trio laughed as they made a show of finger-walking down the railing. They made an even bigger deal of pretending to fall off the railing, hollering that there was more than one way to make history on the bridge. One of them went so far as to flop down on the bridge deck, writhing in slapstick pain till his last convulsive jerk. They finally left their stage, and the curtain came down as they climbed the stairs and disappeared into my neighborhood. Once off the bridge, my vital signs resumed their leisurely pace. Even though

I was now in Lashbaugh's stomping grounds, I felt safe knowing that he and his buddies were stomping in mine.

Basking in relief at surviving the bridge gauntlet, I passed the haunted house in Lashbaugh Land with barely a glance. I'm not a believer in hauntings, but nobody could deny the spookiness of the place. The withering two-story dilapidation lurked behind the family of neighborhood houses like it had been cast out of the community. The house looked lonely and desolate, and it was hard to imagine it had ever been a *home* with pleasant cooking smells or the excitement of Christmas mornings.

The paint was largely chipped or weathered away and it wouldn't be long before all the siding fell off. Glass was missing from most of the windows, giving free reign to whatever the wind and rain had in mind. The chimney had crumbled away, there was a pointless patch in the roof, and a spotty forest of weeds framed the structure. The blackberries that crept up from the ravine discouraged anyone from getting too close, and behind the hulk, several ominous-looking fir trees completed the unsettling scene.

The stories of someone living there under such impossible conditions made the house seem even more sinister, leading some to believe that it was inhabited by a witch. There was probably nothing haunted about the place, but it was as good a word as any to describe the state of decay. People had tried to rid themselves of the eyesore for years, hoping someone would build a new house on the property to enhance the entire neighborhood. But the only way they'd get their wish was if the decaying hulk fueled a fire that reduced it to rubble.

My buddies and I jacked up our fears whenever we walked by the house together. "I bet you're afraid to run up and look in a window," we'd taunt one another. The glass had long since broken, and all but one of the windows were covered in tattered blankets that merely pretended to keep the weather out. Sometimes we'd torment each other with the dare of dares, "Why don't you go knock on the door to see if a witch opens it?" The more of us there were, the wilder the dares. As brave as we all thought we were, nobody was ever willing to risk a face to face with the haunting.

Over the years, the ramshackle residence took its place in neighborhood mythology. Some said a woman's husband died while they were building the house and without the money to finish it or relatives to care for her, she went crazy. Our neighbor, Mrs. Watkins, blamed the sad state of the house on drinking and the likelihood that a witch lived there. It was never clear whose drinking she was talking about or how she would know such a thing. "Could even have been her own drinking," Erik said. Another neighbor, Mr. Philips, came up with the far-fetched idea that the woman had murdered her husband, but as far as anybody could tell, there wasn't a shred of proof for his theory either. I didn't have any theories of my own, but I confess to having repeated these stories and a few more, no matter how far afield they seemed. Funny how if you repeat something often enough, it grows branches of truth, some sturdy enough to withstand the seasons.

Just to be safe, I took my usual precaution when passing the haunted house. I crossed to the other side of the street, tried to imagine the aroma of fresh baked bread, and strained to forget what Lashbaugh said about my brother being a C.O. Despite my best efforts, I couldn't help glancing across the street, hoping I wouldn't see anything unusual. Once your imagination gets going on something, even your basic senses join in and start making things up. Thankfully, the only signs of life were the blackberries. They'd advanced even further and looked ready to smother the house by the middle of summer if they kept going.

With the first whiff from the Tastie Home Bakery, my worries about the bridge encounter and the haunted house evaporated. "Take a Number," the sign said. They were now serving number sixty-three, and sixty-nine was the next card on the hook. I had plenty of time to locate the jar of broken cookies while my fingers came in from the cold. The jar was on the counter all right, but aside from a few crumbs, it was empty. The wait grew longer.

The clerk called out, "Number sixty-nine," and I heard a cheery, "What can we do for you, Scotty?"

"How about a loaf of French bread?"

"Sliced?"

"Please."

While the blades of the chrome slicing machine chattered up and down, I tried to come up with a no-cookies sad face. Trying to sound like I was just making conversation, I asked, "Didn't break any cookies today?"

"Actually, we did, but this late in the day the jar is usually cleaned out. I suppose we could find a few broken pieces around somewhere, though."

I knew she was in the back breaking a few perfectly good cookies for the jar. She came back to the counter with a big smile on her face and a few crumbs on her lips.

"We can't sell these, but there's no law saying we can't give them to a hungry soldier."

"Swell, thanks."

Before the door closed behind me, I clamped the crinkly bread bag to my nose, inhaling the deliciousness released by the slicing. The heel of bread disappeared before I reached the corner of sixty-fifth and twenty-eighth. That was OK with Mom. She always said the heel was my delivery fee. There's no smell more wonderful than the first whiff of fresh-baked bread, and the heel was just a tease for the comforting softness I knew was buried deep in the loaf.

This hadn't been the ordinary uneventful trip to the Tastie Home it usually was. It had been a trial by fire, escaping the dragon from the other side of the ravine and living to tell about it. I was behind enemy lines, after all. Surely, I deserved more than the end crust—perhaps even a warm slice from the middle of the loaf. I ran my fingers between the loaf and the bag and pulled out a lucky card from the deck. Mom would either not notice or understand when I filed my report back at headquarters.

I didn't know where Lashbaugh and his buddies were by now, but I had no intention of getting trapped on the bridge on the way home. The longest way home seemed like the shortest route—no bridge and no bullies. Over three blocks on sixty-fifth to the light, then down the two long blocks on twenty-fifth to my street. There weren't any haunted houses on this route, only the house where the Fujikos used to live, standing empty and waiting. The arms of the pot-bellied Buddha on the porch were still raised in a frozen celebration of the happiness that lived there so recently. The statue seemed to guard the house—maybe hoping, like Erik, for the Fujiko's return. The few cars on the street scurried for cover before the blackout went into effect, and I scurried along with them.

9. Table Talk

"SCOTTY, GET DOWN HERE. Dinner's ready."

French toast for dinner was one of my favorites, and we had it about twice a week. Finding something to sweeten it up was a challenge with all the shortages. I tried sprinkling it with chopped-up raisins once but that just reminded me that French toast needs something gooey to achieve its Sunday best. While it lasted, we had some jam from the raspberries that Natsumi gave Erik last year when he stopped by their farm for a couple jars of honey. Turns out, honey in jars wasn't the only sweetness Erik found on the Fujiko's farm.

Before the war, Erik routinely visited the farm to buy honey and whatever vegetables Mom wanted that we didn't grow. I guess they didn't trust me to do it, probably figuring I'd eat everything on the way home. Anyway, that's when Erik got to know Natsumi, and he'd make dumb jokes about her being his honey.

Since the Order, he sometimes talks with Mom about where Natsumi and her family might be. He knows they were taken first to the processing center in Puyallup, but where they were now, he could only guess. Natsumi could be anywhere. He'd heard about the inland camps in Idaho and Wyoming, even down in Texas. He didn't know where to write or if that was even allowed. Visiting was probably out of the question. Nobody knew. Occasionally, Erik would go by to check on their family farm, and it was clear that someone was still growing something in that rich black bottomland. He didn't know who; he just knew that for now, there was no Natsumi and no honey.

With nothing to put on the French toast, I tried pretending it was meat. Mom used her home-baked bread most of the time, but sometimes she broke out the Tastie Home Bakery French bread, and its golden, crunchy crust tasted like birthday cake.

"Hurry up," I hollered at Greta, "Dad wants to listen to Murrow after dinner."

Edward R. Murrow's radio broadcasts and Ernie Pyle's newspaper reports from the front were Dad's window on the war. While I relied on *Life Magazine* for news of the war from the comfort of my mattress, I don't think Dad ever missed one of Murrow's broadcasts, certainly not for French toast. Of course, he never missed one of FDR's "fireside chats" either. I don't know how it was for other families, but in ours, it was as if the world stopped while the President chatted to us right there in our living room. He was somehow inside the radio, but not really there at all—a kind of electro-magic that everybody quickly took for granted but few understood.

At some point in the dinner conversation, I could count on the same old question from Dad. It had several variations, but the thrust was always, "How's that long division coming?" "It's algebra," I'd remind him, and the corners of Mom's mouth would betray her amusement at Dad's mistake. It was like long division was the only kind of math he'd ever heard of.

Their reactions said quite a bit about the differences between them. Dad was straightforward, logical, and blunt to the point of seeming rude when he didn't mean to be. Nobody could put you on the spot like him. It may have been good for an air raid warden, but I didn't like it one bit. Mom could read between anybody's lines and understood things that Dad's logical mind missed. I got the impression Dad thought if I could master long division, everything else in life would be a piece of cake. I graduated from long division last year but all I got was algebra instead of cake. Maybe that's what the end of the war would be like—no more algebra, no more shortages, and cake anytime we liked.

"So, how's that algebra coming?" Dad pressed.

I wanted to ask him how he did in algebra, but it was time to bite my tongue. "My teacher says I understand the process but keep making stupid mistakes in calculation."

"It doesn't do much good to understand the process then, does it? You get that algebra down and doors will open for you. We need good math people to stay ahead, especially these days."

That may have been true, but I didn't seem destined to be one of the good math people, even though I came from a family of them. Erik and Greta—even my friend Burr—were all good math people. Presumably Dad was too, and I suspected that Mom was secretly a math genius. I'd have to rely on other strengths to open doors, and I could only hope they paid well.

"Better not spend so much time reading comics and playing war games in the park. Studies come first," Dad rattled on.

It was time to change the subject. "Hey Dad, since there's French bread, is there American bread?" That did the trick but ran the risk of a long fact-filled lecture. Greta rolled her eyes at me.

"Well, I don't know. I guess Americans eat all kinds of bread. We're a country of bread bakers from around the world." I raised my eyebrows at Greta in surprise at Dad's mercifully short lecture.

With Mom serving as a block leader and Dad an air raid warden, there wasn't much about our neighborhood they didn't know...or thought they knew. Mom was a full-time volunteer, organizing the community victory garden and scrap drives. It's a good thing there are only twenty-four hours in a day and that some are for sleeping. Otherwise, she might've volunteered for something around the clock. She's inevitably at the center of many things besides our family.

Some people had enough space for their own garden, but our neighborhood was lucky to have a vacant lot where everybody else could plant. It doubled as a convenient place to pile our collected scraps as they accumulated.

"Dad, do you think the government really does anything with all that scrap we collect? I can't see what they could make with any of it."

"Of course, they do. It's for the war effort. Why do you ask?"

"Some of my friends say they just have us collect stuff to make us feel like we're making a difference."

Dad set down his fork, closed his fist, and clenched his jaw. "Hell no, who told you that lie? I'd like to set them straight. Saying something like that could be considered sabotage by rumor," he said, sharpening the edge in his voice. "Who said that?"

"I can't remember, I just heard it somewhere. Well, what do they do with it then?"

"Don't believe everything you hear. The metal can be melted down to make equipment, and the leather goes to make boots and belts for soldiers."

"What about the silk?"

"That's for parachutes, and the rubber is for tires and other things the military has to have."

"I heard that grease and sugar are for explosives. How do they make that stuff blow up?"

"I don't know how it works, but it's true. Take some chemistry and you'll probably find out."

"That's good, we're showering the enemy with sugar to sweeten them up…so they forget they're trying to kill us?"

"Don't be smart, you hear me?"

"Yeah."

Most canned goods went to the troops, but fresh vegetables and fruit had kept us in hog heaven through the end of harvesting season. Till the garden withered and browned, our fresh bounty meant we could give away as much as we dared, and home canning got us through the dragging months when the sun was low in the sky.

Victory gardens were encouraged wherever there was good soil and enough sunshine. Though our neighborhood had plenty of space, there was barely enough sunshine to make things grow. On top of that, our sandy soil needed all the help it could get, so we composted our kitchen scraps and dug them in.

The Order sending Japanese away to inland camps rankled Mom, and as a practical matter, she argued, "it's just plain stupid. Not only is it inexcusable for the country to suddenly treat some citizens like the enemy, but much of the fresh produce grown and sold around Seattle comes from Japanese truck farms. Here we are making our shortages even shorter by casting out the people that feed us." Just one more invention from the world of frightened adults, I thought.

Mom wasn't merely the one in charge of the community victory garden; she believed in it like she believed in God, and she was determined to make everyone a believer. With so many serving in the military and others moving from farms to work in defense plants in the cities, she warned there wouldn't be anybody left to work the farms. I wondered why war prisoners couldn't work on the farms. They'd probably like that better than the alternative. I didn't know how much we needed to worry about all this, but it did sound logical, and Mom was very serious about the whole garden thing. I tried to sound serious too and do my part, especially the eating part.

"We're having a little trouble getting enough muscle to spade up the soil in the victory garden," Mom complained. "We'll eventually get it done, but it sure would go a lot faster if we had some help," she hinted, looking my way with a charming smile. Ever helpful, Dad pointed out that we had major muscle power wasting away right here at the table…mine. I guess if I didn't have a math brain, muscle power would have to do.

Mom's challenge interrupted my thoughts. "How about your friend Burr and his buddies? They don't have anything better to do than read comics and play games the way I heard it." Mom's eyes lit up. "But what we really need is Erik and some of his burly friends. Where is he anyway? He's hardly ever here for dinner anymore. I bet if Natsumi was assigned to the job, he'd be right there next to her, digging dirt like a prairie dog."

I didn't know where Erik was either but felt compelled to make an excuse for him. "I think he's helping somebody put up war-bond posters." Maybe he was and maybe he wasn't. I just blurted it out to give him some cover for whatever he might be up to. I wished he was here. I could really use some good math help, and even though Greta had a math brain, she hadn't done algebra yet.

While Dad navigated shortages of rubber tires, gasoline, and hardware supplies, Mom managed our food shortages, a challenge she solved with creativity and ingenuity by inventing alternatives for anything that wasn't available. Dad's only contribution on that front was his gift of *The American Woman's Cookbook*—a compilation of recently revised recipes for rationing. Mom was famous for her chewy carrot-molasses cookies and home-baked wheat bread. I'm not sure what she was saving the can of SPAM for though. Perhaps she just forgot about it. Dad never tired of joking that SPAM was ham that had failed its army physical. He rarely risked a new joke that might backfire or draw blank stares.

Mom's least favorite new task was saving grease before it went rancid and stank up the place. "Thank goodness meat's expensive and hard to get. Less meat, less grease," she said, basting her sunshine on everything she did. Oh, how I longed for several strips of bacon to go with the French toast. Dad was quick to remind us that saving grease for explosives was our patriotic duty. I suppose a true patriot would have bacon for every meal if they had a friend with a pig farm. Carrots in cookies and grease and sugar for bombs—who comes up with this stuff? It reminded me of one of Burr's experiments, but of course it wasn't. It was the adults who believed that science and sacrifice would win the war.

Except for the cookbook, Dad didn't make things any easier for Mom. He had no idea how resourceful she had to be with strict limits on basic things like flour, sugar, and meat...or how much work the victory garden was. He had a full-time job at the post office, after all. I kept my mouth shut for fear of opening a can of worms. That was their business.

Ration stamps weren't always a guarantee of getting what we wanted either. The store had to have it in stock, and they often didn't. Thanks to our backyard chickens, we were never short on eggs. The whole neighborhood was alive with clucking chickens, which occasionally got loose and roamed the streets like a pack of dogs before we corralled them. We had something with eggs at least three times a week, often in the form of French toast, whether we had something extra to smear on it or not.

If there was an upside to what the country was going through, it might be that the shortages brought neighbors together. We learned things about our community that we might never have known. Mrs. Braithwaite had a collection of dolls she said were worth thousands. Mr. Kelley played the cello with Rudolph Serkin at the Metropolitan Theater in Seattle. The Abernathy's son had mental problems and hardly ever left the house. The Bronson's daughter had recently married but moved back home to save money when her husband shipped out just before the baby came. Having recently earned her pilot's license, Mrs. Jensen's sister was just dying to fly for the military, but they wouldn't take her. She'd heard about the women pilots who flew new planes from the factories to the battlefield, and she was looking into that. The Greenberg's lost their son in a military training accident at Fort Benning, Georgia. He never even saw action.

Neighborhood kids helped keep things stitched together too, serving as runners to borrow a cup of this and a pound of that. Nobody kept a formal accounting of what was borrowed, but everybody understood the need to keep things fair and balanced. People still had their differences, but the differences just didn't get in the way very much. We liked to think that the glue holding us together was something grand, something more than the war, and this allowed us to cross over rather than hunker down.

"So how about it, Scott? You want to help dig? Get your friend Burr, and it will go faster. You're good at pretending. You could pretend to dig fox holes and latrine trenches." It was another one of Dad's questions that really wasn't a question.

"Oh, that sounds like fun," I said sarcastically. It just slipped out.

"Watch your mouth, son."

Should I say I had to study algebra for the big test coming up? Not a chance. He'd see right through that. This was a you-betcha, no-excuse situation. "Sure, Dad. When?"

"Ask Mom. She handles all the paperwork."

Mom chimed in, "I'll show you what to do on Saturday. Then you can work on it after school till it's done."

"Will there be cookies involved?"

"There might be."

Might be? There were always cookies. Maybe it wouldn't pay well, but cookie currency was a darn bit better than nothing. "Don't bring us any powdered milk to wash them down with though, OK? It might make good biscuit gravy and all, but I just don't like to drink it."

"How about plain old water then, you should take some with you and you should drink more water anyway."

"Fine."

"You know Scotty, you might not like powdered milk, but at least you have milk. Maybe you should think about that before you complain."

"I know Dad. I'm sorry."

"It's a done deal then, right?"

"Right. Dad, what's this business about the blackout fires? Learned anything yet?"

"Not yet, but we're not taking this lightly. We're keeping our eyes peeled and ears listening. If you hear anything, be sure and tell me. Promise?"

"Yeah, I promise. Hey Dad, you hear anything about Uncle Ted lately?"

"Well, not much of anything; he doesn't have room to say much in those tiny v-mail letters. Besides, the military limits what he can say. He's stationed somewhere in North Africa and I'm guessing he'll join the invasion of Italy when that gets going."

A sudden and ferocious banging on the front door brought us to full attention. Dad threw open the door to Mr. Merten, who looked panicked as he tried to recover after the run from his house to ours.

"There's another fire, and it's bigger than the first fire by the Bouchers. This one's over by the Fosters," he said, trying to catch his breath, "and it's lighting up the sky right now. Better get over there."

Dad had yet to finish his dessert but tore off his bib and wiped his chin. With one arm in a coat sleeve, he ran out the door while his other arm struggled to catch up. I followed suit before mom could object.

The glow from the fire lit up nearby houses and the border of trees at the park's edge. Smoke drifted low to the ground and blew in our direction as we ran. Despite the blackout, several neighbors lifted their blinds to see what the commotion was all about. Most were careful enough to keep their indoor lights off. Others stood on their porches or out in their yards, seemingly unsure how to respond.

The fire had nearly consumed the Foster's prized garden shed. We heard the crashing of rafters and saw a shower of sparks as the rafters gave up their purchase on the studs. Several neighbors arrived with buckets of sand while others ran empty buckets to the closest spigot and heaved bucketfuls on the growing bonfire. Matt Foster had stretched a garden hose far enough to shower the flaming pile of debris, which responded with angry hissing and even more smoke.

"It's no use." Dad yelled over the hubbub. "The shed's a goner but we need to protect the house. Splash the shrubs next to that arbor, and then hit the side of the house. Scotty, get that pile of lumber as far away from the house as you can."

Shielding my face from the heat, I got close enough to grab the ends of the planks and drag them away. Maybe they'd end up being used to rebuild the shed. With the shed reduced to a pile of embers, danger to the nearby structures receded, and the fire brigade slowly morphed into a somber and anxious block party. Quite a few neighbors had shown up by then and talk mostly turned to whether the fire was intentionally set. While his tearful wife lingered in the back doorway, several neighbors made a point of shaking Mr. Foster's hand and expressing their relief that nobody got hurt.

Dad set about talking to everyone there and asking if they'd seen anything. Nobody had. He asked Mr. Foster if any of his recent projects in the shed could've ignited the fire. Mr. Foster said he didn't think so, but noted he'd forgotten to lock the door to the shed. By the time the excitement was over, the Seattle Fire Department showed up with a pumper truck.

Old man Foster's garden shed hadn't been a little box in the far corner of his yard. It was as large as a single car garage, which may have been its first assignment back in the twenties, and it had housed a lifetime of tools. When the embers cooled, he could probably salvage the business end of a few shovels, rakes, and hoes and later replace the wooden handles. Behind Mom, Mr. Foster was second in command of the victory garden and spent much of his spare time planting, cultivating, and weeding. This fire would make things more difficult for everybody.

Dad muttered to himself as we walked home, but I only caught the occasional word. Finally, he turned to me and asked, "Where's Erik?"

I shook my head. "I really have no idea." I wondered why Burr hadn't shown up either.

10. Digging Ditches

SATURDAY BEGAN AS ONE of those April days that warns you to be ready for any kind of weather, from hailstones to a heat wave. Neighborhood moms would remind kids to wear layers so they could adjust to the weather's fickle moods, and kids would answer, "I know, Mom, I know."

I rounded up enough duds to satisfy Mom and gave her a quick hug on my way out the door. "I'm headed over to get Burr, and we'll meet you at the diggings as soon as he's ready."

Burr was slow to get going, the kind of kid who might take all day to eat breakfast unless somebody noticed he was late for lunch. An avid reader, as any neighborhood historian should be, Burr's practice of reading while eating was what made his meals sometimes drag on for hours. He'd get so interested in the words on the page that he'd forget about what was on his plate. I'd even seen him set his book right down into his food and never notice. Yuck. Today he was engrossed in an article in *Popular Mechanics* about some new-fangled firefighting pump engine they used at airfields.

"What's that other book on the table there?" I asked.

"It's a story about spies and sabotage. I just read some stuff about making timers from wristwatches and alarm clocks. It sounds simple. For a wristwatch, you just put a little screw through the clear face, attach a wire to it, then run the wire to a battery and a fuse. When one of the hands comes around and touches the screw it makes a complete circuit and the current from the battery goes to the fuse."

"You wouldn't think there'd be books like that around telling people how to make timing devices."

"Yeah, you wouldn't think so, but it's a free country. It's an old book of my Dad's, and he thought I might like the story."

"Have you made one?" I asked, as Burr licked his fingers clean.

"You mean a timer? No. I don't know where I'd get a fuse. I don't think anybody can get batteries these days, and who would want to give up a working clock?"

I could almost see the wheels for his next experiment turning in his head. Burr's research usually began by taking something apart to see how it worked. Getting it to work after he put it back together again was another story. Often, his experiments seemed like just an excuse for destroying things. He had boxes of bolts, pulleys, springs, gears, switches, and more—parts left over from things that sort of worked and others that were completely dead but awaiting a proper burial. "Never know when I might need some of this," he said. One highly polished wooden box was labeled, "Wizard's Warehouse & Parts Department—Keep Out." It contained his most prized parts for machines of the future. Burr's efforts required an assortment of tools, and luckily, his dad encouraged "the scientist" by letting him use almost everything in his shop. He even contributed to his son's own toolbox with cast offs and the occasional shiny new tool.

Hoffmans' Hardware was the hub of every neighborhood project ever attempted or completed, but it had recently closed. Wartime rumors mushroomed, and suspicions held that the Hoffmans were sympathetic to the Germans. Suspicions fueled retribution, and sometimes, when the Hoffmans opened their shop, they'd find a broken window or sign saying something like, "Krauts Go Home." At great inconvenience to themselves and thinking of it as an act of patriotism, most people stopped shopping there, and some even talked like the Hoffmans' store was a Nazi garrison. But when it came right down to it, people who saw the enemy in every foreign-sounding name did more harm than good, and in this case, they managed to shoot themselves in the foot. Now, the nearest hardware store was no longer within walking distance, and gas rationing made driving anywhere a fraught calculation.

Fear clouded people's thinking. Dad said the Hoffmans had been sending money back home for years, and it had nothing to do with the war. "What would we expect them to do when they started making a little?" he fumed. It was sad to see a closed sign on what had been much more than a hardware store. Till somebody new bought the store, it was boarded up and the windows were plastered with posters to remind us of our patriotic duties on the home front. Somebody even posted a hand-scrawled sign, reading "C.O.'s Can Go to Hell." Lost in thought, I fretted about the implications for Grandma and Grandpa Keister, Mom's folks who lived up near La Conner. Like the Hoffmans, my grandad's parents had also emigrated from Germany.

Burr took so long to finish breakfast, we had to run. The morning air was cold, but it didn't keep us from stripping off our top layers when we were halfway there. Fully layered and with a shovel at the ready, Mom was already on site with spade in hand, eyeing the weeds of early spring.

"Morning, Burr. You ready to work for a living?" she asked.

"Sure, for a cookie or two, Mrs. Johannsen."

"Here's what I want you to do. The idea is to turn over the soil, loosen it up, and bury the weeds. The rows start here and go down to those stakes over there. Each row needs to be turned over twice. We'll dig in that juicy-looking compost after we have a funeral for the weeds. You can decide how you want to work it. One of you can use this spade and the other one will have to use the shovel. I'll come back and check on you in a couple of hours, OK?"

"Sure, Mom. Remember, no powdered milk and don't forget the cookies."

I had no idea if the spade would be easier than the shovel or the other way around. Burr, always the expert, even on things he'd never done before, grabbed the curved shovel while I was still mulling it over. "Want to race?" he asked in a challenging voice.

"I don't think we should turn this into a race. What if we do a crappy job? I'm the one who'll get a talking to and have to do it over."

"OK, have it your way, but it seems like the older you are, the more fuddy-duddy you get. I think I even see some gray hairs. That'll be your new nickname—I'll say, 'Hey Fuddy' instead of 'Hey Buddy.' Better do something about all your wrinkles before they mistake you for a mummy."

"And I'll start calling you 'Burp.'"

"Wouldn't be the first time."

"Cut the crap and just get to work, OK?"

Being a first-time spader fooled me into thinking we'd be done before Mom arrived with the cookies. By the end of the first row, I knew that was hopeless. The soil was wet and heavy. The weeds knit everything together, adding to the effort it took to lift each spadeful. Burr didn't say anything, but it didn't take a math brain to realize he was thinking the same thing. Finishing the first row, he groaned, "How many cookies do you think this job is worth?"

"I don't know. I guess it's worth however many she gives us."

"How high can your mom count?"

"In your dreams."

By the end of row three, we started making up silly stories, and by the end of row five, we imagined we were digging a latrine trench long enough to circle the globe. It was hard work though, and even two revved-up imaginations couldn't change that fact. We'd have made more progress if Burr hadn't been distracted by everything his shovel turned up. Pieces of glass and rusty metal caused his digging to halt. Unearthed insect larva brought him to his knees as he peered closer in curiosity and wonder.

"Hey, Burp. Stop that. You're wasting time—mine and yours." Taking careful aim at a nice big juicy earthworm and slicing it in half with his shovel, he didn't even hear me. "Mom says worms help the soil by drilling holes in it and digesting things."

"Digesting things means pooping things. I'm not eating anything from this garden if you don't mind."

"You will if you're hungry enough."

"Is it break time yet, boss?"

"I'm not the boss. The real boss is Mom, and she pays in cookies. But you're right. Let's knock off for a while."

My arms grew even heavier as I scanned the fifteen rows yet to go, and I groaned at the extra punishment of doing every row twice. There was a reason Mom said we could work on it after school, and it was the same reason she had us rather than the adults doing it in the first place. It was really boring real work that didn't require a real brain. Could we even finish in a week? Seemed like a shovel was as important as a gun in the army.

The sky rumbled and a roar enveloped us. A giant shadow passed over the garden plot as two tired soldiers leaned on their tools. Four radial engines faded to a murmur, the B-17 got smaller and smaller, and birds emerged from their hiding places as the roar and its shadow thundered into the distance. Jolted out of our exhaustion, we looked at one another in wide-eyed exhilaration. Burr's eyes bugged out with excitement—the kind of excitement that bubbles over when you've been in the presence of great power.

"Wow, I've never seen one fly that close overhead."

"Me neither. I didn't think they were allowed to fly that low."

"Maybe not, but they just did."

We saw B-17s all the time, but not like this. This one was close enough to read the tail numbers. The "Flying Fortresses" were built right here in Seattle and my aunt Val worked on them at the Boeing plant. Burr and I thought of ourselves as expert plane spotters, but it didn't take an expert to spot a lumbering B-17. Anybody with an ear and one working eyeball could make a positive ID, either by sound or silhouette. As far as I knew, they were the loudest, largest, and grandest sight to fill Seattle's skies.

The surprise visit from the B-17 fired up our flying fantasies and spilled over into other thoughts. "Burr, you ever think about this air raid thing?"

"What do you mean?"

"I mean, do you ever think it might be the real thing when we have those drills and the sirens wail?"

"All the time. How can you tell if it's the real thing or not? Isn't the point to make them seem real?"

"Sometimes I think about what it would be like if there wasn't any warning, like what happened at Pearl Harbor."

"I know. We didn't even hear the Flying Fortress sneak up on us till it was almost overhead. And there are so many planes flying around here. What if the spotters mistake the attackers for friendlies?"

"What? You think the Japs can fly all the way across the Pacific to attack us?"

"You know what I mean. They used carriers to get close to Pearl Harbor."

"That's not going to happen again."

"But yeah, sometimes when I hear a plane, I get this knot in my stomach, and it sticks with me till I'm sure everything is OK and it's one of ours. You know what we should do? Let's go see where the Corsairs hang out and maybe even watch one take off over the lake. Can you ask your dad to take us down to Sand Point to see them? It should be easy for him to get us in since he's an air raid warden. It just makes me feel safer when I see a flock of our birds."

"OK, I'll ask, but he's awfully busy." The idea almost made me forget we were still waiting for cookies and had rows to go before our digging duties were over. Just listening to a Corsair fire up and taxi around was like beautiful music. I could picture myself at the controls with the enemy centered in my sights just before I blasted them out of the sky. I liked the Catalina rescue planes too. They were like guardian angels. They could land in water and then waddle up a ramp onto land like a duck. "Know what else I'd like to do?"

"What?"

"I'd love to take a ride over that new floating bridge. I just don't see how heavy cement can float on water."

"It's just physics. Anything can float if it doesn't weigh more than the water it displaces."

"What's that mean?"

"I can show you with a simple demonstration sometime," Burr bragged.

"I just don't get it. We all know that a chunk of cement sinks."

"Well, it's not a chunk of cement. It's a pontoon—a box made of cement, so it's hollow."

"Enough, science man, I'll take your word for it. I just want to ride on it." I asked my Dad if he'd take us for a ride on the bridge, but he says gas is too precious for a silly pleasure trip like that. Of course, he had to tease me about how Tacoma's Galloping Gertie ended up on the bottom after a windstorm. He says it should've been called 'Galloping Girder.' Hey, maybe your dad could take us. He doesn't seem to worry about gas. Does he get it on the black market?"

"What are you saying? I don't know how he gets gas. I never thought about it. I'll ask him if he can take us though. Seems like a fair trade, a visit to Sand Point for a trip across the floating bridge."

Gasoline was one of the most strictly rationed items. Everybody's car had a sticker identifying how much gas they could get each week—to keep people from lying, I guess. Regular folks received four gallons a week with an A sticker. The B sticker authorized eight gallons. Ministers, mail carriers, railroad workers, and doctors got more with their C stickers. Truckers had a special T sticker, and some people had an X sticker that I suppose meant they could have as much as they wanted. Rubber was in such demand that the authorities even periodically checked vehicle tires for wear and tear. As for Burr's dad, he had an A sticker but seemed like he drove anytime and anywhere he wanted. Seemed fishy to me, but Burr claimed to know nothing.

Just like the B-17 we never saw coming, Mom snuck up on us too. She appeared suddenly, like the Cheshire Cat in *Alice's Adventures in Wonderland*.

"You boys look like you're done for the day. Here's your cookies, and those rows look darn good, by the way. Mrs. Thomas and I will dig in the compost and rake everything out before planting when you guys are finished. Think you can be done with the rest by next weekend?'

"Easy squeezy, Mom. Thanks for the cookies."

The day had warmed up and so had we. We spotted a few more planes high overhead on the way home, another B-17 and a pair of DC-3s. This was one time I didn't have to worry about a scolding for coming home covered in mud. I glanced down at the filthy layers I'd shrugged off. Boys digging in the dirt seldom come out clean. It was just one more thing for Mom to take care of and make right.

As we ambled home, our talk turned to comic books, a topic that often tilted toward argument. I'd been thinking about a comic-book trade for weeks. Burr was a hard bargainer, and this was serious business. Comics, which issues and how many, were a measure of wealth and prestige in our group of friends. Erik said our strutting and grandstanding wasn't all that different from adults. Burr went easy on me this time, and we struck a deal—one *Sub Mariner* for one *Captain America*, and we agreed to a separate negotiation over my *Green Lanterns*.

"You want to dig some more on Monday after school?" Burr asked.

"Tuesday would be better. Remember, I have my algebra test on Tuesday."

"Oh yeah, I forgot about helping you study," Burr replied. He then veered off on a tangent like he frequently did. "What do you think would happen if I focused a magnifying glass on a slug? Do you think it would melt?"

"Cripes. I don't know. I keep forgetting to ask you something my Dad was really worked up about this morning."

"What's that?'

"Last night's fire. It burned down the Foster's garden shed. You know anything at all about it?"

"No, why would I?"

"Well, you seem to know quite a bit about the fires. I went over there last night with my Dad, but we should go look through the rubble and see what we can see."

"I guess. If that's what you want to do."

"How about tomorrow after lunch?" Burr smirked and gave a quick salute before he headed off to his house on Twin Maple Lane.

"Hold on," I said. There's one more thing I forgot to ask you. Lashbaugh says Erik is a C.O., and it has something to do with being a chicken shit. I'm pretty sure it's about not joining up, but what exactly does it mean?'

"It stands for somebody who doesn't believe in war and refuses to fight."

"Is war supposed to be something you believe in, like a religion?" Burr shrugged his shoulders and turned back toward home.

Even though the Sunday paper was fatter and heavier than weekdays, I hardly ever minded starting my paper route early when the weather was nice. But the next day, my sore muscles complained as I got out of bed. Nonetheless, I was off to start my route when the sun was just a warm glow in the east. It had fully risen by the time I got to the newspaper shack near the Tastie Home, and it blazed briefly before a billowy white blanket of clouds enveloped it. I made it back home for breakfast about the time everyone else was rubbing the sleep from their eyes. I even had time after breakfast for a short nap before we all headed out for church. As Pastor Nyland droned on, I drifted away from the sermon, much like I often drifted off at school. I thought about the war and the latest fire, wondering how they fit together.

Surprisingly, Burr was ready and waiting when I arrived after lunch. He'd actually remembered our planned visit to the scene of the fire. This burn was farther away than the previous one, and I took some comfort in that. There wasn't much of a scene except for a stinky pile of ash and the charred ground where the shed had been. Burr didn't say much, even when I asked him who he thought did it. All he said was, "Next time it'll probably be a house."

I went home to algebra, and Burr went home to whatever experiment he had in the works.

11. Testing, Testing

BETWEEN SATURDAY'S VICTORY-GARDEN slave duty, Sunday's visit to view the latest firebug carnage, and war games in the park, my plan to have Burr help me study for the algebra test over the weekend fell by the wayside. Now I'd have to fall back on my time-tested study plan: asking for divine intervention. Divine intervention is how adults explain things when something good happens and they don't know why. When something bad happens, they just make something up, chalk it up to fate, or point out that the powers that be work in strange ways. Ain't that the truth?

The divine had saved me during a test before when I couldn't remember why the colonists were so mad at King George. The genie whispered that it was because of taxes, earning me five of ten possible points and contributing to my barely passing score, but I knew that seeking help from the heavens posed certain risks. What if the divine was like the proverbial genie in the bottle, and I was limited to three wishes? The genie might not give a damn about algebra. Worse yet, what if I was on my last wish and needed it *in the future* to save my life or the life of someone I loved? Of course, with the war on, the divine undoubtedly had better things to do. The bell rang, and students began funneling into algebra. I pleaded with the genie, "Just one more time, please."

There was nothing divine about Simon Lashbaugh. But here he came with several new members in his choir. They pushed and shoved their way through the hallway multitudes, and given the speed we were all traveling, I figured they'd reach me before I reached the safety of the math class door. Wrong-way-hall traffic had sent people to the hospital, but that didn't stop Lashbaugh from crossing the center line and plowing a shoulder into the side of my head. It would take several growth spurts before my shoulders lined up with his, and hopefully we'd both be long gone by then.

"Say 'excuse me,' snot rag, and watch where you're going. Oh, I'm sorry. You're that famous Mr. Hankie Head, aren't you?"

I wanted to give him a traffic citation for swerving across the center line into the oncoming flood of students but thought better of it. God help us all if he ever got a driver's license. Unfortunately, there weren't any citations for pushing and shoving in the halls. Not only was it expected, but fighting upstream was often the only way to get between classes.

"I told you to say, 'excuse me,' cripple brain."

His choir closed in, jeering their favorite barbs, and even though Marty and James were with me, I felt as vulnerable as when we met on the footbridge. "OK, I'm sorry. I've got a math test to get to."

As the choir parted and opened a path for escape, Simon barked, "Be sure to check your locker at lunch."

Math class was filled with the sweet chemical smell of freshly mimeographed tests and the last-minute chatter of students drilling themselves on the order of operations. Monsieur Beret hadn't given up on getting us to call the process an algorithm, but he must've recognized that he was outnumbered twenty-eight to one in a battle he wasn't going to win. Without reinforcements, he'd need to become as mean as a drill sergeant to achieve victory, and there was no way he could pull that off with his French accent, bowtie, and beret beanie.

"Everybody take your seats, please."

Inwardly, I rolled my eyes. Just how many seats can one person take? Whenever I had to take a test, I got so nervous my mind would fixate on some trivial thing and take off for parts unknown. Today was no different. My mind was off, wondering about the metal inkwells that some of the desks still sported from prehistoric times. Imagining them filled with ink, I pictured an angry mob storming the school and demanding that ink be banned because the parents couldn't afford to keep replacing ink-splattered clothes. Who on earth thought kids could ignore a little pool of black ink on every desk? I guess outstanding penmanship was the primary goal of public education in the old days.

"Once you're all quiet, I'll pass out the tests, and remember, keep them face down till I give the signal to begin. I'm still waiting. I said 'quiet' Mr. Johannsen. Remember to keep track of the time. Double check your answers and bring your test up to me when you're finished. Once you hand in your test, you can't have it back, even if you think you made a mistake. Just take the time to double check. If I catch you copying or talking, I'll take your test, mark a zero in the grade book, and call your parents. Everyone understand?"

Mocking his repetitive lecture, a few students nodded their heads in slow motion. Even though 'once you're all quiet' sounded like a challenge, we slowly complied, and the din died down. Monsieur Beret passed the tests out and we nervously awaited the signal to begin. Some of us sniffed the mimeographed pages, making a show of breathing in deeply, rolling our eyes with an "ooh yuck" face, and feigning fainting.

"Any final questions? No? OK, you may begin."

Four whole pages. While the math brains might finish by the end of the class, it was sure to take me a month. "Dear divine," I begged. "Can we have an air raid drill right now, or could you draft Monsieur this minute?" Page one looked easy. No decimals or metric units to worry about, and I worked out the first few problems without any hitches. The second page must be for university students though. Jeez. Filled with story problems, sloppy reading could trip me up as much as sloppy calculation. Monsieur even livened up the test by using names of actual class members, and this just seemed like a dirty trick to grab the attention of those of us who'd already drifted off task. Naturally, he threw in a few problems about the metric system to reinforce how ridiculous it was that Americans didn't use it. "The metric system is the measuring unit of the future," he routinely said.

By the end of page two, it began to look like I'd at least finish in time to sleep in my own bed. Unbelievably, I completed the test with a minute to spare. Just enough time to resume wondering whether whatever Lashbaugh had put in my locker would explode in my face. I wondered if the divine intervention that allowed me to finish the test could be stretched to a different purpose without submitting new paperwork. Of course, whatever was in my locker was probably quite undivine. In fact, I might need witnesses or backup. As soon as I made it into the hallway, I collared Burr and two other friends to join me as we headed to my locker. No time for an explanation before the next bell rang. Just saddle up and ride. I'd answer questions later.

I half expected to see Lashbaugh and his friends hanging out nearby, already congratulating themselves on whatever cockeyed scheme they'd cooked up.

"Hey, nobody's there. It looks OK from the outside," said Burr. "Hurry up, we only have a few minutes left before social studies."

Everything appeared to be as I'd left it early this morning, but just as I thought the divine must've intervened, Bobby pointed. "What's that down at the bottom?" he asked.

"What?"

"It looks like a note is sticking out of your baseball glove. Open it."

"OK, OK."

An ordinary piece of three-ring binder paper was folded into fourths. I unfolded it to reveal a message scribbled in pencil:

Meet me on the footbridge at four o'clock today. Do not bring your friends! — S.

12. Alone & Unarmed

FRETTING ABOUT MY FOUR O' CLOCK appointment with Lashbaugh consumed the rest of the afternoon. I'd typically be in the middle of my paper route then, and doing it later wasn't an option since I was the station manager. The only solution I could think of was to tack a note to the bridge railing saying I'd be late, and hope Lashbaugh would see it.

His demand of "no friends" meant no reinforcements, but that was a risk too great. I needed somebody there as a witness at least, and my first choice was Burr. Even though he was sometimes a loose cannon, I asked for his help anyway because he was always willing. Besides, he was my best buddy. If he agreed, I'd be alone when I met up with Lashbaugh, but not completely alone.

Burr's response came as a huge disappointment. "I can't today," he explained. "Mom says I have an eye appointment. Why don't you ask one of your other friends?"

James would've been the next best choice, but I knew he had to do his own paper route after school. That left Marty, who seemed to have gone missing. Burr hadn't seen him since lunch and figured he must've gotten into some kind of trouble. Probably smashed into a teacher while walking and thinking about girls at the same time. Things were getting desperate. Even if I could find a guardian, it probably wouldn't be a certified angel.

What if I had a lookout instead of a companion? They could hide in the bushes, with a clear view of the bridge. Then, if things took a turn for the worse, they could nonchalantly appear, as though they were just on their way to the Tastie Home Bakery for a loaf of French bread. Now there's a thought. And if the worst of the worst happened, they'd be able to testify that I hadn't fallen to my death by rail walking.

Crumbs on the counter told me that someone had beaten me to the cookie jar today. It could only be Greta, in a rush to do her homework as soon as she got home. I wondered if all girls were as studious as she was—and whether they were just trying to make their brothers look bad. It was unusual for her to be the first one home after school, though. Giving in to my dire predicament, I went upstairs to ask for her help, hoping I wouldn't have to beg, or that the bribe would be something I could afford. No time to waste before heading off for my route.

"Gret, I've got a big favor to ask."

"Don't call me that. Can you wait till I'm finished with my homework?"

"Actually no. It's something that has to be done right after my route, as close to four o'clock as possible."

"OK. What's the deal?"

"I've got a problem."

"You usually do. What did you do now?"

"Cut it out. This is serious. You know that Lashbaugh bully from across the ravine?"

"Well, I've heard a little about him. You aren't friends with him now, are you?"

"No, but he wants me to meet him on the footbridge at four o'clock."

"What's wrong with that?"

"He wants me to meet him alone, and I don't know what he's up to."

"So, what do you want me to do about it?"

"I don't want you to do anything about it, just watch from behind some bushes at the top of the ravine."

"What am I supposed to be watching for?"

"That's just it, I don't really know. Just watch in case something happens."

"Like what?"

"Like pushing and shoving or something, I don't know. I just want you to watch in case something does happen so you can tell somebody. If you do see him pushing me around, just come across the bridge like you're going someplace, real casual like. A witness should make him stop."

"What about running for help? Is that an option?"

"I really don't know. I hope it won't come to that."

"OK, I'll do it, but I don't want to be part of any trouble."

"Thanks. You won't be. And please don't be late."

We lived only four houses from the top of the footbridge stairs, but I still had to make sure Greta knew the best place to hide.

"So, tell me exactly what you want me to do."

"Cut through the Reddicks' yard and go around the back of their house. They've got lots of shrubs along the edge of the ravine. Just hide behind the bushes and watch for me to show up on the bridge."

"What if the Reddicks see me?"

"They won't. They're never home till after five."

"You hope."

"Don't forget to be there a little before four, OK?"

Having completed my paper route in an adrenaline rush, I tensed as I approached the footbridge. Greta didn't have much experience sneaking around behind people's houses, and I could see where she was hiding. She reminded me of a soldier on a scouting mission or a cougar waiting to pounce. Lashbaugh could probably see her too if he knew where to look, but time had run out and the die was cast. I waited till she was settled before descending the twelve stairs to the bridge deck. No Lashbaugh in sight. Maybe it was all a game, and he wanted to keep me in a state of impending doom. Maybe it was his way of saying, "You may live around here, but I'm king of the jungle." Or maybe he just forgot. The comfort I found in this thought vanished as Lashbaugh and his shadow paraded down the stairs on the far side of the bridge and joined me in the middle, uncomfortably close.

"So, I didn't think you'd actually show up. At least you're not a chicken shit like your big brother," he began.

"Leave my brother out of this. What does he have to do with it anyway?'

"More than you might think." My eyes darted back up in the direction of Greta's hiding place, thankful that I couldn't see her and thankful she was there. "Have you been wondering why we're here?"

"Yeah, of course. What is it? I've got stuff to do."

"I have some information for your dad."

"For my Dad? Why don't you just tell him yourself?"

"It's better this way."

"So, what is it?"

"You've heard about the blackout fires?"

"Yeah, I think everybody has."

"Well, I know who's been setting them."

"Why don't you tell somebody then?"

"I'm gonna tell you cause your dad's the air raid warden. Ever wonder where Erik is during the blackouts?"

"Most of the time he's at home with the rest of us."

"But not always, right?"

"I guess not. What are you trying to say?"

"He's been seen setting a fire."

"Who says?"

"Never mind. He's been seen."

"Who saw him?"

"I said, never mind. He's been seen."

"What am I supposed to do about it?"

"Keep him from getting arrested."

"How am I supposed to do that?"

"Nobody has to tell your dad, and if your brother stops doing it no one will ever have to know."

"I thought you wanted me to tell."

"I do, unless…"

"Unless what?"

"Unless he joins up."

"Why would you even care if he joined up or not?"

"Cuz, we think he's a chicken shit C.O. and we want him to prove he isn't."

"What makes you think he's a C.O.? You don't even know him."

"Well, he had a Jap girlfriend didn't he, and most of his high school buddies have joined up or say they will as soon as school is out this year. So, what's the matter with him? There's a war on, you know. Besides, I've heard he talks to people about whether war does any good. Only a C.O. would say stuff like that, and it would be just like a C.O. to be setting those fires. Did you ever find out what C.O. means?"

"Yeah, I did. It stands for conscientious objector."

"How about chicken objector?"

That was it, conversation over. I went back to my side and Lashbaugh went back to his. Even though it had to be a bum rap, my insides squeezed so tight that I felt like a pressure cooker, ready to explode. When I reached the top of the stairs, Greta popped out, asking, "What was that all about anyway? Anything to report?"

"No."

"Nothing at all?"

"No."

"I went through all that mud and got covered with spider webs and stepped in dog poop, all for nothing?"

"You made me feel better."

"Is that all? Tell me something."

"There's nothing to tell."

"You were down there long enough. There must be something."

I thought I'd have time to think through what to say about Lashbaugh's challenge, and there might've been if not for Greta peppering me with questions. I really couldn't tell her the truth, and I knew her chain of questions would link together faster than I could answer, making it easy to trip and land face down in my own lies. She threatened to describe the entire scene to Mom and Dad if I didn't tell her what was going on, so I had to come up with something. Something fast and believable.

"It was about comic books." Once you open your mouth, you have to live with what comes out, and sometimes it even changes your life, or someone else's. I'd let her questions guide me. It would be a small and innocent lie. She'd never know.

"Comic books? That required a secret meeting on the bridge?"

"Yeah, comic books."

"What about comic books?"

"He wants to buy one. He's a Green Lantern fan and he heard I've got a copy of *Green Lantern Joins the Army*."

"For that he had to meet you on the bridge in secret? I'm not sure I believe you."

"I guess he thought so."

"You have that one?"

"I've got two."

"How much is one worth."

"We didn't talk about that."

"You didn't? You're not much of a businessman, are you? Well, I hope you get rich selling it. You can split it with me for getting all covered in spider webs for you."

I must've sounded halfway convincing, because Greta's questioning petered out and she ran straight upstairs to finish her homework as soon as we were through the door. Mom was intently repairing one of Greta's pleated skirts and, without looking up, she asked how school was. I mumbled something about the algebra test, dashed upstairs, closed my door, and crashed down on my bed. Gradually my heartbeat settled back to idle.

Having raced through my paper route, I'd hoped there wouldn't be any missed-customer calls. At least fate had worked in my favor on that front. What about what Lashbaugh had said though? Could it be true? Was there even a remote possibility Erik could be lighting the fires? And what did he really think about the draft anyway? I'd have to find time to talk to him. If it was true, would keeping my promise to tell Dad be the Judas kiss that sent my brother to prison?

Just the suspicion of such a thing could ruin our family. If I was honest, I'd been wondering where Erik was during some of the blackouts myself. True or not, I couldn't imagine what Dad's reaction might be. Why should I even believe Lashbaugh? He could be lighting the fires himself. Hard to imagine since he was so gung-ho about all the war stuff, but he was just the kind of person who might be doing it for kicks. Adults try to come up with reasons for the mysterious ways of kids, but some of those ways defy logic. Most have no idea why they throw rocks that break school windows or steal candy when they have money to pay for it. Some things just don't have explanations, or if they do, they're buried so deep nobody can dig them up.

When dinner was served, I was both there and not there at the same time. My mental confusion must've shown, because Mom asked if I remembered to go to the bakery to buy the cake.

"What cake?"

"The one for your birthday."

"It's not my birthday."

"Just checking to see if it's only your body sitting here or if your mind is here too. You remembered to do your paper route, didn't you?"

"Yeah."

The soothing deliciousness of Mom's rice pudding didn't linger beyond the last swallow. Back in my room, my mind revved up, questions returned, and I couldn't concentrate on homework or anything else. Like the night before Christmas, sleep kept its distance. I pictured pushing a cart full of questions up the side of a mountain and coasting down the other side on a sled filled with answers. I wouldn't even dare talk this over with Burr. As comforting as the cushy bed usually was, I tossed and turned all night.

13. Rosie Comes to Visit

ROSIE WASN'T HER NAME, but that's what Greta and I called her. Dad knew it was because of the *Rosie the Riveter* song that had recently become so popular, but he didn't think the nickname showed his sister the proper respect. He didn't scold us too much though because Aunt Val really was a riveter, helping Boeing build the B-17s. Dad's younger brother, Ted, had recently become an Ensign in the Navy and was assigned to a minesweeper stationed somewhere in North Africa. His other sister, Ruthie, had moved to Arizona for college, and we'd hardly seen her since she started school. The war disrupted and dislodged all of us in its effort to unite us.

Aunt Val was Dad's baby sister, and she came for a visit every couple of months. In between, we'd visit her at Grandma and Grandpa Johannsens in West Seattle, usually by trolley to save gas. Auntie nearly always stayed overnight because the trip across town took "two lifetimes on the streetcars and trolleys," she said. That was fine with Greta and me. We loved her to death and couldn't get enough of her. She always seemed interested in us and was willing to do whatever we wanted, within reason, of course. It wasn't that Mom and Dad weren't interested. They were just flooded with family activities, work, and their new war-related duties. As our day-to-day people, Mom and Dad blended into the background of everyday life, while Auntie stood out as part of the foreground. Not much older than Erik, she combined the wisdom of an adult with the playfulness of a kid. Adulthood hadn't quite caught up with her.

Given that there was only one of her and two of us, a mostly friendly competition emerged between Greta and me for her time and attention. She was good at dividing it evenly and spent most of her time with both of us. Sometimes she'd take us to a movie at the Neptune or Egyptian theater in the University District. If there was time, we'd walk through the park instead of taking the trolley. Aunt Val was the only adult that ever walked the entire length of the park with us, and that alone told us everything we needed to know about her. She'd even venture into the "wild" parts of the park if that's what we wanted to do.

I had my movie list and Greta had hers. Greta liked kissy movies best, especially if they starred somebody like Bette Davis or Olivia de Havilland. Musicals were her second favorite. I liked war movies, mysteries, and spooky movies, even when they were more stupid than spooky. Thank God for imagination. But if there was a comedy or anything starring "Rinty" as Rin Tin Tin, all three of us gave an enthusiastic thumbs up. Burr said that in the future, all movies would be in color. I don't know where he gets his ideas, but he usually turns out to be right. I'm just happy that movies nowadays are talkies. And if there was a double feature with a newsreel and cartoon, that's about as good as life gets for twenty cents.

Greta and I checked the newspaper listings and flipped a coin before Auntie arrived, and when heads won, the ball was in my court, and I held serve. My vote was *I Walked with a Zombie* at the Neptune or *The Leopard Man*, playing at the Egyptian. Even if it wasn't a double feature, the newsreel, serial, and a cartoon would round out our time together quite nicely. If going to a movie didn't work out, we'd scheme for time in front of the Philco with *Lux Radio Theater*, *The Green Hornet*, or my favorite, *The Shadow*. When Mom and Greta took their turn with our new talking furniture, they'd suggest the *Fibber McGee and Molly* comedy show or dancing to Glen Miller like there's no tomorrow. And for all we knew, tomorrow might never come. When Dad had a say, he'd vote for the *National Barn Dance* from Chicago, unless it was time for the news.

While our kitchen was traditionally like Grand Central Station, our new Philco radio had become the magnet for family togetherness. Mom didn't like it when we wanted to eat in front of the big mahogany box instead of at the dinner table, but there wasn't much she could do when we all ganged up on her. With the invention of radio, "voices and music could sail on a sea of invisible waves," Aunt Val liked to say. She talked poetry like that sometimes. The pull of the Philco increasingly won out as time went on, morphing into a must-have thing for most people. Erik called our living-room gatherings a campfire of sound. We were drawn to this chattering piece of furniture into the light of each other's warmth, and just like at a campfire, it was easy to forget what lurked beyond the flickering flames.

The radio seemed to have two personalities—one that pulled us in and spirited us away to a place of laughter or mystery. The other, like Dad's news programs, spit us back out. Many of its peacetime uses had yet to be discovered, but I suppose it was inevitable that the radio would become a weapon of war. Troops used it to communicate, but the propaganda machines used it as a weapon—spewing out persuasion and confusion. On the home front, it was unsettling to hear how riled up people could get from false information that sounded legit or even from news that was legit.

"How about if we listen to *The Shadow*? It's tonight, isn't it? I love the line, 'Who knows what evil lurks in the hearts of men? The Shadow knows.'"

Whenever Mom overheard this, she cautioned about the dangers of taking radio programs too seriously. "You heard what happened a few years back when they broadcast that program about a Martian invasion, right? It was so realistic that many people thought we were under attack from outer space and did all sorts of ridiculous things," she cautioned.

"Mom, we know *The Shadow* is just a radio program and that people who believed we were being invaded by Martians were just plain stupid."

"Well, don't be so sure. People could say anything on the radio and make it sound believable. How would you check it out? You heard what happened in the little town of Concrete?"

"What?"

"I guess the power went out during the program and some people went around screaming that the world was coming to an end. Bad timing for a storm. There was even an article in the *New York Times* about it. They must think we're all a bunch of ignorant hicks out here."

I didn't exactly agree with her, but she did have a point. Even though I never heard the program myself, I knew the radio-invasion episode caused quite a stir. How would you check out the truth of something that sounded so real like that, especially when the power was out?

There's something about radio that seems more real than the movies. If they tried to portray the invasion in a movie, I'm sure it would look fake. With radio, the movie is in your mind. For all I know, the broadcasters might be in their underwear. Listening to the radio shows, I sometimes feel like I leave my body. That never happens in the movies. Dad likes to say, "radio must be believed to be seen."

Listening to a good radio show could take some doing, especially if it interfered with one of Dad's news programs. Although he'd never admit it, I think he liked *The Shadow* as much as I did. Usually, he'd give in when his baby sister visited and let us listen to the radio for a while, as long she wanted to listen with us. I wasn't sure if Aunt Val was a *Shadow* fan. If not, she was a great pretender. Even though Dad would let one of us choose the program sometimes, there was no doubt that he was the king of radio land, and his favorite chair was his throne. Nobody minded. This was just the way it was. Dad was tough in many ways, but everybody understood he was riddled with soft spots. With both Greta and me poking around, we found most of them and knew exactly where they were if we needed one.

"Mom, what bus did she say she was taking?"

"I think it was the Ravenna bus, and I believe it left at half past ten."

"So, she should be coming down our driveway right about NOW!"

Even though I saw her first, Greta ran past and almost jumped into Rosie's arms, knocking one of her shopping bags to the ground.

"How's my Greta? Getting prettier every time I see you."

"Hi, Auntie."

"And Scotty, you're bigger and stronger than ever. You're getting to look more like your big brother all the time. Give me a squeeze, but don't squeeze me in half, OK?"

"If I do, I'll glue you back together."

"What have you two been up to? Good deeds, I hope."

As the three of us headed for the front door, Greta and I talked a mile a minute over the top of each other, jostling to be heard. We eventually gave up and broke into the *Rosie the Riveter* song we'd memorized from the radio*: All the day long, whether rain or shine / She's a part of the assembly line / She's making history, working for victory / Rosie brrrrrrrr, the riveter.* It was kind of a dumb song but making the sound of the rivet guns was too good to pass up.

Mom calmly opened the door to see what all the fuss was about. "Hi, Val, so good to see you. You didn't happen to notice that Greta and Scott are excited to see you too, did you?"

"Yeah, as a matter of fact I did. They've really got that song down."

"Are you staying over like usual?"

"If you'll have me. I'll just take the streetcar from here to work on Monday morning, if that's all right."

"It's always all right. That will give us plenty of time to get caught up."

"Wonderful. I brought a bag of good wishes from Grandma and Grandpa along with some things from their garden."

With the movie issue settled, at least in my mind, it was time to inspect the shopping bags. They were chock full of garden treats, some fresh and some canned. Grandma and Grandpa were master gardeners long before anybody thought of victory gardens. Auntie said they got their gardening start in Missouri, where it had become a matter of survival during the Great Depression. She said they taught classes at the community center on how and what to grow, even going around the neighborhood and making house calls like garden doctors. The community relied on them for good advice about how to store what they were able to grow, and some families expressed their

103

appreciation with gifts of their own preserves, which often ended up at our house. It was too early in the year for fresh greens but not for root vegetables that had wintered over. Besides the fresh vegetables, there were canned beans, pickles, plums, pears, and a decorated jar of raspberry jam. The problem of bare-naked French toast was solved.

You could tell that wasn't all. We knew it wouldn't be. There was always something special for Greta and me in the bottom of the bag. I spied the corners of a box that wasn't doing a very good job of hiding in the bag, and I'd be lying if I said I didn't expect a non-birthday present.

"Oh, and I almost forgot," Auntie fibbed.

"Here's something for you, and I've got something for Greta too. Hope you like it."

Typical presents included books and comics, and Grandpa often sent *Railroad Stories*. I called them bookazines since they couldn't seem to make up their mind if they were books or magazines. Auntie was a big believer that reading opened doors, "and windows too," she joked. Sometimes there were card games or board games, pastimes we could enjoy together.

"What is it?"

"Unwrap it and see," she nudged.

"I can't believe it! How did you know?"

"It wasn't hard to guess from all the questions you ask."

"Oh thanks. This is hunky dory. I can't believe it. Thank you so much."

"Only one thing...I want to see it when it's done, and don't go setting it on fire and dive bombing it off the bridge like your mom says you did with the last plane you built."

"Don't worry. I'll hang it from the ceiling in my room, or maybe give it to you. That other one was a flying model. This one's just for display."

Dad chimed in, saying, "Read the directions first this time."

"OK, OK. I will."

I was the proud new owner of a wooden scale model of a Flying Fortress. The Strombeck-Becker assembly kit came complete with glue, sandpaper, wood filler, paint, and decals. It was better than Christmas or my birthday—a complete surprise and the rare, perfect present. I'd built several of the older Strombeck-Becker train model kits, but I'd dreamed about this kit for months. I first saw it on display in the Woolworth variety store, and something about the shape and the smooth wood parts fitting seamlessly together reeled me in. I couldn't wait to cruise above the clouds with the rest of my bomber squadron in a "Fort" fresh out of Seattle's Boeing plant. There was work to do.

"Now for you, Greta." Auntie handed Greta an unwrapped package.

"Jeez. It's a microscope and there's a box of science slides too. Where'd you get it?"

"I sent away for it from the Gilbert catalog."

"Last week in science, we scoped out some things at school, and you wouldn't believe all the things we found in dirty old pond water— more little wiggles than we could count. We even made our fingerprints with lead pencil and looked at the patterns. I had two tent arches and three whorls. Have you ever looked at money under one? We did."

"So, you like it then?"

"Oh yeah."

"Well, if you don't become president, maybe you'll cure polio. But I can tell from his look, you'll have to share it with Scotty from time to time." She pulled out one more package all wrapped in newspaper and tied with twine. "It's Uncle Teddy's pea coat, and I thought Erik could get some use out of it, especially with this cool spring weather we've been having." Her shoulders slumped and her voice trembled as she continued, "Teddy won't be needing this to wear for a while."

Aunt Val's well-chosen gifts trumped any desire for a Saturday matinee. It was too early to tell if Greta had the brain of a future president, but we all knew she was headed for great things. I don't think anybody had figured out what kind of a brain I had. Sometimes they acted like I still needed one, like the Scarecrow on the way to Oz. I took some comfort knowing I was older than Greta and always would be. Dad once told me the power you get from being older wears off as you grow up, but he couldn't remember how many years it took for his to wear off.

Upstairs we went with our treasures while Mom and Dad chattered away with Aunt Val. As I emptied the box and spread the parts across my desk, my imagination took flight for a bombing mission over Germany. Time all but vanished till my fantasy ran low on fuel. I headed back over the English Channel, where the lack of sleep from the night before caught up with me, and I landed heavily back on earth.

14. Catching Up

"Dinner's ready," called Mom.

No matter what meal it was, Dad always followed up with, "Soup's on." Maybe that's all they had when he was a kid. As usual, he said grace, thanking the Lord for all we had, and asking for an end to the war. But before saying "Amen," he lowered his voice and asked for help discovering who was setting the blackout fires. It wasn't his usual prayer voice. Thinking the Lord probably already had his hands full on the battlefields, I wondered if it was a good idea to get Him involved in neighborhood detective work. People always talked like God was on their side. But what if he wasn't? Or what if he didn't even take sides? We'd have to wait and see who won the war. The Lord couldn't possibly be on the losing side.

"Dad, are they doing a better job on the blackout requirements over at Burr's?" I asked.

"Sort of. They didn't have any violations this time, but Burr's dad was in a temper when I went over to check. They're just not taking things seriously. He's convinced there'll never be a real air raid and thinks the blackouts are a waste of everybody's time. He says they don't even have them on the East Coast.

"You didn't write them up, did you?"

"No, you can't write somebody up for a bad attitude. I don't know why we all can't just do what needs to be done without causing a problem, especially since it's the law. He's probably right about the likelihood of a real air raid, but it's downright stupid not to be prepared. We all need to pull together like that Husky crew did in '36. They showed that Hitler son of a gun a thing or two, didn't they?"

"Is it true that they don't have blackouts on the East Coast, Dad?"

"Not exactly. They didn't at first, but the Brits convinced us that it was stupid not to after losing so much shipping to German U-boats close to the coast. Does Burr ever say anything about the blackouts?"

"A little. He thinks they're a pain in the butt and kinda dumb too."

"That figures. He doesn't say anything about the fires, does he?"

Auntie perked up. "So, what's this about the blackout fires?"

"We've got some idiot, or a bunch of idiots, lighting fires during the blackouts, but we'll find out who it is soon. Just about everybody but Santa Claus is on the case. Some people around here are so upset they'd probably hang the firebug from the nearest tree if they found him."

"That's terrible. I wonder what would make somebody do something like that," said Auntie. "I understand people being upset, but I sure don't think vigilante justice is the way to handle it."

"You're right. I was just saying."

"I know."

"You're sure it's a 'him' though?"

"Wouldn't you think so?"

"I guess. But you never know." Auntie looked across at the empty chair and asked where Erik was.

"Well, I couldn't tell you for sure," Dad replied. "It's getting to be a regular thing, him not being here in the evening."

Auntie tried to reassure him by pointing out that Erik was *at that age*. "You know how it is—when friends pull harder than parents—and outnumber them, as well."

"I do know, but it still bothers me."

Mom chimed in like she was Erik's lawyer, reminding everybody he had his reasons. "He's most likely studying with friends or putting up war posters." Her words reminded us that he'd always been truthful, and we had no reason to doubt that now.

Auntie turned the spotlight back to Greta. "Your mom tells me your teachers have nothing but good things to say about you, Greta."

"Mom, show her my report card."

"After dinner, honey."

"It's so important to do well in school. It will open doors for you."

"And windows too," I said, just to see if Dad would give me his glare.

He did and attached a little narration. "We've heard that one before and we're tired of it."

Strange comment coming from someone who was on the fiftieth telling of some of his jokes. Should I remind him? Nope.

Greta was so good in school, and most things in general, that I honestly thought she was in line to be the first woman president. She might be, but let's see what happens when she gets to algebra, I thought. Girls, especially Greta, were just better at most things adults seemed to care about. So why didn't we already have a woman president? Something I didn't understand must happen along the way to the White House. I'd never told Greta, but I would vote for her and tell my friends to do the same. Auntie assured us that we'd live long enough to see the first woman president. She was a believer in things like that. To prevent the conversation turning to algebra and my report card, I took the offense by asking how things were at the Boeing plant. "What does Boeing pay riveters anyway?"

"Not enough. I get sixty-seven cents an hour as a riveter, but I'm looking to earn a ten cent raise by soldering wires. It's not all that much, but it does add up."

"I see you still have your teeth." Everybody's face puzzled up and Mom asked what I was talking about.

Auntie explained. "Last time, I told Scotty I might not have any teeth left 'cuz the pounding of the rivet gun would have shaken them loose."

"What part of the plane do you work on?" I asked.

"I really can't tell you details like that. I'd get in trouble. You know, it is a defense plant and we're at war. I can tell you a good story, though."

Just then, the slam of the screen door announced the welcome "intruder" we'd been wondering about. Setting down his pile of books, Erik drifted over to the dinner table and filled the empty chair.

Dad spoke first. "Where have you been?'

Before he could answer, Mom asked, "Didn't you know Auntie was going to be here? She brought you a present, one of Teddy's pea coats for those cool spring mornings."

"Or evenings," Dad injected sarcastically.

Aunt Val saved him from having to respond with her typical greeting, "Good to see you, Erik. You're still sporting those sparkling eyes and that unfurled brow, I see."

"Oh, thank you. I can't take credit for them. I was born that way." Erik squeezed out a smile along with a little nod. At least he had the good sense not to say anything about where he'd been and

110

bring on the third degree from Dad. I reminded everybody that Auntie was about to tell us a good story.

"When you work at Boeing there are lots of rules, different than those you might have at a regular factory. One of them is that you can't bring a camera into the plant. That makes sense. There could be spies. There's a place outside the plant where we check things that can't be brought inside. So, last Tuesday I'd planned to take some pictures after work for a friend of mine, but I was running behind, and rather than punch in late and have my paycheck docked, I slipped the camera inside my jacket and ran on in. There's a drawer near my workstation for purses and things like that, so I stuffed the camera in there. All day I was panicky for fear it might be discovered, and I would be carted off to jail as a spy. But, as you can see, I'm right here for a visit and not sitting in jail."

"We're glad you are," I said, speaking for all of us.

"The food is undoubtedly better here too," Erik joked.

Greta piped up. "How are Grandma and Grandpa doing?"

"Well, you know, Grandpa complains about the coffee shortage and how hard it is to save on heating oil. We tried blocking off the registers in rooms we don't use much, but it didn't make much of a difference. If Grandma would let him, I think Grandpa would listen to the news whenever he's not at work. He still loves his job with Great Northern, and work is the one thing he never complains about. He likes to remind us how important the railroads are for the war effort. And I'd like to remind him how important Grandma is to the war effort. She never stops moving. If she's not cooking, she's working in the garden or canning. She does all the regular cleaning, cooking, and laundry, and still has time to sew and work at the community center. Her motto is, "Mend and make do." She's even talking about inviting a soldier or two for Thanksgiving dinner. Can you imagine what it must be like to be so far from family, ready to ship out to some godforsaken place where they shoot at you, even on holidays? How about you guys? How are you doing with the ration cards, shortages, and all?"

This was obviously a question intended for Mom, and the only person who didn't understand that was apparently Dad, who plowed into a minefield. "Well, by the end of the month we're down to caviar and champagne, but we make do."

His insensitive comment brought a round of glares that set him straight, and he immediately began singing the praises of his wife for making do in a way that made ration cards and shortages seem more like a gift than a hardship. You would've thought she was Helen of Troy, the Queen of Sheba, and the inventor of SPAM, all rolled into one.

Once he'd redeemed himself, Dad turned the conversation to Uncle Ted. His deployment was one of the reasons why both Dad and Grandpa gorged on every scrap of news but were always starving for more. If they just read the comics, I thought, they'd relax a bit. Even better, maybe Dad could enlist Ernie Pyle to track down Uncle Ted and find out how he's doing. Pinning his gaze and his hopes on Aunt Val, Dad asked, "Any word from Ted?"

"He writes every couple of weeks. You know, those v-mail letters are nearly impossible to read, even with a magnifying glass, and I'm supposed to have good eyes. Maybe I should use Greta's microscope."

"He writes to us too, but not that often," Mom added.

Aunt Val went on, "He complains about the weather just like he did back home, only now it's about the heat and humidity and how there's nobody to sew buttons back on his uniform."

"Does he say anything about the action he's seen?"

"No, but they can't always talk about that stuff. It's kind of strange. On one hand, we want our guys to see action to end the war, but we don't want any of them getting hurt. I guess we can't have it both ways."

Changing the topic, perhaps to avoid any news about Ted that sounded like bad news, Mom asked, "What about Ruthie?"

"It's weird, but she doesn't write as often as Ted does even though she's stateside. She's keeping up with her studies and she mentioned something about having a boyfriend who's in flight school. She's doing her part though. The USO connected her with the names of some servicemen, and she writes to them regularly. I've been doing some of that too. The messages I get back are incredibly grateful, and most of them say that the letters mean even more than packages full of goodies. Some of them don't have anybody that writes to them, you know. When I don't get a letter back, I tend to worry that something has happened, but that's so out of my control I try not to think about it. Most of them want pictures of me and I'm not so sure that's a good idea."

"I guess it's safer to have a flyboy on an army base than one on campus," added Erik, thinking everybody would laugh.

Mom furled her brow and looked over at Dad before addressing Erik. "What do you mean by that?" she asked.

"Well, you know the reputation pilots have, right?"

"No, as a matter of fact I don't, so tell me."

"Never mind."

Curious, Greta asked Auntie, "did you actually send a picture with any of your letters?" When she didn't get a straight answer, she shifted gears and joked that Ruthie's new boyfriend might inspire her to get a pilot's license so she could join the WASPs. Drawing a glare from Dad, she said, "Ruthie could deliver a new plane from the factory every time her boyfriend crashed one."

"What are you saying Greta? Why should he be crashing? That's not very funny if that's what you were trying to be."

"Golly Dad, I was just kidding. Sorry."

Auntie reminded us that it wasn't only the guys risking and sometimes losing their lives in planes. "You think being a WASP isn't serious business? Just imagine taking up a brand-new plane for the very first time. They don't all come out of the factory in perfect condition you know. Of course, everyone tries to do their best and the planes get checked out on the ground before they fly. But many things can go wrong, and the WASPs are the first to find out what the problem is. WASPs get killed in crashes too and not because a Messerschmitt shot them down or a flack burst ripped them to shreds. Gravity isn't picky about who the pilot is. It just patiently waits for an oil line to come loose or a magneto to die."

"Or pilot error," Dad chimed in.

Erik hadn't joined in the conversation much, even though I knew the war weighed on him. He used to be the chatterbox of the family, but over the past few months, a change had come over him. Lately, he'd become a mystery, saying very little around the house and spending nearly all his free time with his friends. I suppose it wasn't too surprising, given everything that must be on his mind—college, losing his girlfriend, and mulling over the draft and whatever he really thought about the war. Intuitively, Auntie offered him the opportunity to speak up.

"Erik, what have you been doing with yourself these days?"

"Oh, not much, just trying to get through calculus."

"Do you think you'll make it?"

"Oh yeah, just a question of getting a B or a C."

That reminded me. "I forgot to tell you. I got a B- on my algebra test. Hard to believe, isn't it?" Rather than giving me a compliment, Dad's eyes rolled heavenward. I guess he figured I must've had help from the genie in the lamp. Compliments came from everybody else though, even Greta.

After the brief celebration, Auntie turned back to Erik. "What are you thinking for the fall after you graduate?"

"One thing's for certain, I'll have to register for the draft. I turn eighteen in June."

"That doesn't mean you'll get drafted though."

"No, but it sure looks like I will with the way things are going. Have you been following the news?"

"Yes, even if I didn't want to, it would be hard to avoid, what with Grandpa being such a newshound. I wish you didn't have to worry about things like that. There are already enough decisions to make when you graduate from high school."

"I heard the Allies are getting ready to invade Italy. Do you think Uncle Ted will be involved in that?"

"Probably, since he's stationed in North Africa."

With that, Dad tensed up and I could practically feel the storm clouds brewing. Unbeknownst to me, one of Ernie Pyle's latest reports from the front had left him with a knot in his stomach. The article apparently focused on how combat can change soldiers in ways the rest of us will never understand. I'd seen the article headline, and that alone had been enough to leave me wondering what Uncle Ted would be like when he came home.

During the tense silence that gripped us all, Greta had been carefully standing her green beans on end in a mountain of mashed potatoes, like they were little trees. She poured gravy on the top to watch the rivers run down the sides and puddle up on her plate, making little muddy lakes. Without looking up, and without warning, she pounded both fists on the table, a fork clenched in her left hand and a knife clenched in her right, ominously pointing straight up in the air. "Why do we have wars anyway? Why can't people just get along?" Still looking down at her mashed potato mountain, she pushed herself away from the table and charged upstairs. Nobody knew quite how to react. After a bewildering moment, Mom got up and followed her.

It was Erik who came back to life. "What do you say to a question like that, especially to a ten-year-old?"

Dad dodged his question, saying, "I don't know about other wars, but I do know why we're fighting this one. We didn't start it, but it's certainly one we'll finish, I can promise you that."

Auntie protested that we didn't need his assurances. "We all know why we're fighting this one, even if some of the pacifists say we should stay out of it, especially out of Europe. It seems like when historians look back after a war, they find there were ways it could have been prevented, but these things take on a life of their own. Maybe the generals and politicians should study our history more. I don't know."

Like Auntie, Erik seemed to take Greta's question seriously. "Right, wars do have their special causes, and the people fighting inevitably feel justified, like they're in the right. That wasn't Greta's question, though. She asked why there's war in the first place, not about what caused this war." Even Dad had no answer for that, and I think he knew better than to try and sound like he did, so Erik continued. "When you're working on those bombers down at Boeing, do you ever think that you're helping to build a killing machine and that its bombs can't tell the difference between soldiers and civilians, adults and children, or war factories and people's homes?"

116

I could see Dad's jaw clenching, but he didn't say anything. Auntie noticed Dad's reaction too and calmly responded to Erik in such a way as to prevent an eruption between father and son. "That's a fair question and I've thought about it quite a bit." In fact, I've discussed it with my coworkers, especially the ones with strong religious convictions. I think we all understand what those bombers are capable of, and the last place I'd want to be is underneath one when it opened its bomb-bay doors. A lot of people believe that we *are* trying to stop the killing by destroying the Nazis' war machine though. You know what the Nazis are doing to the Jews and other people they don't like, right? They just ship them off to death camps—no questions asked. That is, if they don't shoot them first. They're aiming for some kind of racial purity and think that anybody who doesn't fit their mold is subhuman. They believe they're part of a superior Aryan race and should rule over everybody else. I wonder what they thought when that 'subhuman,' Jesse Owens won all those gold medals back in the '36 Olympics, with Hitler right there in the viewing stands. I guess they pretended it didn't happen."

I wanted to ask what the Aryan race was, but it didn't seem like the right time to interrupt Auntie. I didn't know if we were Aryan or not and wondered who else the Nazis thought were subhuman besides Jews, Negroes, and Gypsies.

Auntie continued. "You've heard the news about the nightly air raids on London, right? Some of the things they're doing to the people in the countries they've conquered just turns your stomach. In some cases, Hitler has put to death a hundred villagers if just one German soldier is killed by partisans. I don't know what you'd call it, but that's something even worse than war. When things go that far, it seems like there's no choice but to fight. After Pearl Harbor, we didn't say, 'Tsk, tsk. Please don't do it again,' and turn the other cheek. Look at it this way. If somebody was pointing a gun at you or your family and the police came, you'd want them to do something, and that might be shooting the person holding the gun. I believe Winston Churchill when he said, '…but if we fail, all we have known and cared for, including America will sink into the abyss.'"

The mention of Churchill brought Dad back into the conversation. "So many people in this country find it convenient to ignore the utter cruelty of what the Germans are doing in Europe." Dad picked up speed. "After taking over in France, they set up a prison just for hostages, so they'd have a ready supply of people to kill when others rose up or didn't abide by their orders. That's how they control people. They sometimes do more than kill the villagers; they might burn the entire village to the ground and kill all the livestock too."

"Do all the Germans do that kind of stuff?" I asked.

"No. There are good people there too, but the country is under the control of the Nazis who have both the military might and control of the propaganda. Some are bullies, but most are just bystanders. Just like here, people tend to support their country when it's at war, right or wrong. You can't do much against that once it gets rolling. I don't know how it all got started over there. I guess we'll have to sort that out after the war."

I knew there was a third choice besides bullies or bystanders. It was the choice Uncle Ted and many like him had made. It was the choice the country had made—to stand up and fight the bullies.

Erik, like the rest of us, had heard this reasoning many times, but for him it wasn't theoretical. He had to register for the draft any day now, even if he did apply for conscientious objector status. "Well, I suppose working on a bomber is different than if you had to point a gun at another person and pull the trigger while you were looking directly at them. But the idea that you have to kill to prevent more killing sounds like going around in circles and chasing your tail. The bombers may say that they're only killing factories, not people, but how can any thinking person really believe that? We know the bombs often miss their targets."

Despite Auntie's willingness to keep this conversation going now that Erik had warmed up, Dad didn't like where it was headed and tried to put up a stop sign. "What's the point Erik? We *are* at war and we're going to stay at war till it's over."

This conversation and many like it didn't have an end, but it came to an abrupt halt when Mom brought Greta back downstairs and asked who wanted dessert. I guess dessert was the sweetest answer we could find for Greta's question.

That was it for me. I ran back upstairs as soon as I downed my last bite of cobbler. The Flying Fortress needed more sanding on the fuselage before I could attach the wings anyway. Auntie followed me up to the landing to say good night and I blurted out, "What's a zoot suit?"

"Well, it's a kind of fancy suit some guys wear when they go out to party and dance."

"That's it?"

"Some people don't like them because they use too much cloth and we're under strict rationing. Some people even say they're worn by draft dodgers and people against the war. Otherwise, why would they be so extravagant?"

"Oh, OK. Good night, Auntie." I held tight to my secret from the bridge and wondered if I was the only one with a secret.

15. G-Men

BURR AND I NEVER did go to Sand Point to watch the Corsairs or make it across the floating bridge made of magic cement. Instead, we got front row seats for a mock air raid at Husky Stadium, and it more than made up for our loss. As soon as word got out, I begged Dad to let me go and bring along Burr. When I asked Erik if he wanted to join us, he said he didn't want to see things get bombed and burned, even if it was pretend. This would have to be the best Saturday afternoon ever—better even than an outing to the Neptune Theatre for a scary movie with Auntie and Greta.

Dad explained the idea behind the demonstration was to show Seattleites what a real air raid might be like and to help the city be as prepared as possible. They must've hired a movie set crew, because they did a super job of making things look real. They built a small village on the football field complete with special lighting, shops, and cars, plus actors to play the residents, cops, medics, and firefighters. They set a stage of careful realism, all for the purpose of being blown up or burned, and Dad said they planned to make a movie of the whole shebang. There was even a drill team with a band playing before the attack started, sort of like a movie theme song. Then the P-38s came screaming over the stadium while mock soldiers shot blanks at them. They were mind-numbingly loud, not to mention low, close, and lightning fast. Seeing the P-38s was way more exciting than seeing a few Corsairs down at Sand Point or having a B-17 fly overhead while digging the victory garden. The hair on the back of my neck stood up, and Burr exploded after every bomb as though celebrating a University of Washington touchdown.

Despite the attack, the mock civil defense forces had saved the city. People filed out of the smoky stadium, wiping their eyes, and speaking in hushed tones. We overheard enough to know that some were reassured by the demonstration. Still, the fears of some were amplified, and others weren't sure who'd won the game. On the following Monday at school, Burr was sure we'd be the center of attention, reenacting what we'd witnessed using hand gestures and sound effects. But pushing through the school's massive front doors, we couldn't help but notice the gray government car as it pulled away from the curb.

"What do you suppose they're doing here?" Burr asked when we met up with James and Marty at lunch.

James thought maybe they wanted Monsieur Beret's advice on how to win the war using the metric system instead of bullets. Marty, a bit of a flat tire who was usually a day late and a dollar short, said, "Those government people just like to kill time. They're probably here because they don't have enough important stuff to do."

"Not even with a war going on?" I asked. "What if they think a student here is the one setting the fires?"

Burr chimed in, saying, "You hear about the latest fire? A big one in an abandoned building. Everybody thought the Foster's garden shed might be the last, but I guess not."

"Yeah, my Dad's more concerned than ever," I said.

"Could be that the Feds just want to make sure teachers are listening," James piped up. "Ears to the ground, right? You know how kids talk."

"Thanks for the common sense. Yeah, kids talk, but that doesn't mean they actually know anything," Burr retorted.

Kids talk all right, but those who do seldom have anything important to say. Lately I'd seen more and more gray government cars and brown army cars, prowling the neighborhood like hound dogs. After a week of spading the garden toward victory, I was more than ready for a fantasy vacation in the park with my pretend platoon. Our various outposts needed to be resupplied and reinforced, and we could pretend the park had been invaded by enemy soldiers. We might even take a swing or two out over the ravine on the rope we'd attached underneath the Fifteenth Avenue Bridge. It would be a high-flying thrill, with a blissful moment of weightlessness before swinging back to earth.

I wondered if it wasn't Lashbaugh himself setting the fires and if he was just trying to throw everybody off by accusing Erik. In the absence of evidence, I had only suspicions to guide me, nothing that would help me decide what to tell Dad. The best decision for one might be the worst for somebody else. My darkest thought of all was that the G-Men might have been at the school asking about Erik. After pleading to the heavens for my algebra test, I knew I was fresh out of wishes for any genies to grant. I felt like there was a stop sign no matter what direction I turned.

"Hey James, what do you think will happen to the firebug when they're caught?"

"Well, for an accidental blackout violation, it's just a fine or a warning, but this is different. It must be intentional, so I'm sure it will involve jail time. You'd have to go to Mars to find a creature who thinks this is accidental."

"What if it's not an adult? Do they just throw kids in with everybody else?"

"Juvie then I guess," James added, like the authority he thought he was. James always acted like he knew the score whether he did or not. But there was one big difference between him and Burr. James *wanted* to be the big cheese, issuing orders to anyone blind enough to follow. Burr, on the other hand, simply had an endless reserve of ideas that he made free for the taking, no questions asked. If there was a campaign for neighborhood president, James would be the frontrunner. In some ways, it was like he'd already entered politics. He always appeared to be more vigorously scrubbed and immaculately groomed than the rest of us.

"For how long?" asked Burr.

"A year at least."

"Maybe they'd make you join up if you were old enough," interjected Marty.

"I don't think so. They wouldn't want somebody who'd been setting blackout fires. That's sabotage," said James with the air of a military commander.

Impatient, Marty said, "We can talk till the cows came home if we want, but none of us are having any fun sitting around talking. Let's go get some German spies next weekend. The park's full of them."

"You can go if you want," said James. "But I've got a better idea. War games in the park are getting kind of boring, you know, and I think we've tracked down all the spies there are. What if we did something real for the war?"

Marty perked up. "Like what?"

"Like find out who's lighting the fires. We'd be real heroes."

Skeptical, Burr shot back, "What would we do, hand out surveys, asking people if they've been setting fires or if they know who is?"

"No, stupid, we need to catch them in the act," said the big cheese with a frown.

"It was supposed to be a stupid joke. Are you too dense to get it?"

"Sorry, I didn't mean you were stupid, just that it was a stupid idea."

"It was supposed to be. That was the point." Burr still wasn't convinced. "Who do you think we are, the Hardy Boys?"

"Make fun if you want, but we can do this," replied Mr. Cheddar Head.

"What makes you think so?"

"We know every crack and cranny of the whole neighborhood, including the park. If it is a kid, sooner or later somebody will brag about it. Kids can't keep secrets."

"Except from their parents," reminded Burr.

The big cheese in chief was really getting on my nerves, and I was edgy anyway. If he only knew how tightly I'd been holding onto my own secret since meeting Lashbaugh on the bridge, he might not be so sure about kids and secrets. I guess he thought "loose lips" could sink more than ships.

"True," agreed James, but Burr wasn't ready to give up yet.

"Right. So, we live here, but aren't the government people already on it? Those government cars have big spotlights and can cover more ground in an hour than we could in a week. Besides that, they don't have to spend their evenings doing homework."

Marty had been carefully considering this after all. "They might not want to use the spotlights during a blackout, though."

Burr sharpened his point. "What about Scotty's dad? He's on it too, right?"

"Well Burr, I guess you have a decision to make." James said, cutting him off. "Are you interested or not?"

Why just Burr, I thought. Don't we all have a decision to make? None of them could possibly know how hard this was for me. I had the most to gain if it turned out Erik wasn't involved and the most to lose if he was. James went around our circle like the hands on a clock, locking eyes with each of us in turn, waiting for some sort of answer. But two of us couldn't commit.

"Well?"

"I'm in," announced Marty. James advanced to me.

All I could manage was, "Do we have to decide right now?"

"No, but the sooner we get started, the more likely we'll find out who's doing it. So, what d'you say?"

"Tell me how we're gonna do it, first. What's the plan?"

James had already given this some thought as well. "We'll do scouting patrols, just like in the real army."

As Marty got more excited about doing real army stuff, Burr grew even quieter. I would've thought this was the kind of thing he'd jump right into. He always talked about how things are in the real army, or how he thinks things are, like he's been to the front and back and is just waiting to lead the victory parade when the war is over.

"Who's in charge?" I asked.

"We all are."

"That doesn't sound like the real army way. Isn't there always a captain or an officer in charge?"

Interrupting, Marty asked, "Not that it matters, but will we be a squad or platoon?"

Platoon, squad, or a bunch of village idiots, there was no question our leader would be James. Follow the cheese and your belly will be full. If I was in, I guess I'd be giving up whatever choice I had in the matter. That's the way things are in the military, for better or worse. Follow the cheese. Do or die. "OK, I'll do it," I pledged.

We all looked at Burr who looked away, just hating to be put on the spot. James pressed for an answer. "Well, what about it?"

"I don't think so."

"What do you mean, you don't *think* so? You're either all in, or you're out."

"OK then, I'm out. My folks never let me go out during a blackout anyway. They say it's too dangerous, with some people still trying to drive with their lights off and all."

"Aren't you the master of sneaking out after dark, like you're always telling us?" Marty asked.

Burr kept quiet. With his retreat, it was settled. He'd remain a civilian. As James continued to brief us on his plan, it became apparent that he'd been planning this far longer than I thought, probably since he finished the algebra test before everyone else.

"We need to be organized about this. First, we need to make a map of where the fires have been and where any new ones are set, including date and time. This will help us see if there's any sort of a pattern. Scotty, you keep us posted on this by talking with your dad. He should know all the details. Second, we need to make a schedule of when and where we're going to patrol. Let's see if we can get enough information to start on our map and schedule by this weekend. My room can be headquarters, and we can meet there at ten hundred hours on Saturday. Don't forget to keep your ears to the ground."

Marty pumped his fist, "We'll get that creep. We'll get the goods on him before anyone can say 'Jack Robinson.'"

Nodding, I said, "I'll be there with whatever I find out from my Dad."

16. Operation Sneaky

I DIDN'T HAVE ANY fantasies that James' patrol project would make me a hero, but it sure would be satisfying if we could confirm the firebug wasn't Erik after all. I'd celebrate by treating every member of the unit to a warm apple fritter from the Tastie Home Bakery. Without confirmation, I felt like a ping pong ball, slapped between an intolerable state of indecision and the prospect of intense shame for snitching on my brother. But I'd enlisted in this operation believing that one's word was gold. If we weren't the Hardy Boys, maybe we were the Three Musketeers, too young and foolish to be trusted with muskets.

I spent most afternoons that week coming straight home to work on the B-17 before charging off for my paper route. We were best friends, but I'd had enough of Burr after a week of watching him slice earthworms in half. We usually walked to school together anyway, so I knew I'd see him then.

I followed orders, gathering what intelligence I could through conversations with Dad, but I learned more by eavesdropping from the top of the stairs when I should've been in bed. Mustn't be too obvious. Sometimes secrecy is the only weapon you have.

James was the most organized kid I knew. He could give Monsieur Beret a run for his money when it came to thinking things through. But the more I thought about our mission, the more I saw things that James hadn't thought through, and they'd started to pile up like a logjam in a river. We had a lot to discuss at headquarters on Saturday.

Some Saturdays seem like a year in the making and others pop up out of nowhere. This one advanced and retreated like it wasn't sure about things. When it finally arrived, I aimed for headquarters and pictured Burr eating breakfast while conjuring his next experiment. Who knew whether he'd finish in time for breakfast on Sunday? While he might not patrol with us, he was still part of us. He knew what the mission was and who was going to carry it out, even if he didn't know all the details. If captured by the enemy, he could become a pair of loose lips.

James had done his best to transform his room into headquarters. He'd posted a large butcher-paper map of our neighborhood on the wall opposite his bedroom door. It looked like he'd penciled in every house, garage, and shed. Unlike many neighborhoods, ours was easy to map, with the streets all dead ending at the park ravine. The main entrance branched off into four dead ends. Any cars entering the neighborhood would have to park or turn around, but those traveling on foot could keep going right into the park and across the footbridge, like it was an actual border crossing.

Three small notebooks were positioned on the floor below the map. James had scrawled our names on the tops, but it wasn't clear what we were supposed to do with them. The sorry state of his rumpled military garb suggested he wasn't all spit and polish. He wore an olive drab jacket, several sizes too big and decorated with cardboard emblems and campaign ribbons. Marty was bowled over by the garb, but I thought it looked clownish, like someone in a low-budget war movie. It was a shock to see James looking so frumpy. He was the only one of us, in civilian life, who could possibly be called a snappy dresser. Apparently, his reputation was only skin deep, and he had a ragamuffin hiding inside. Even so, he held himself like a man in charge. We had to think that his parents' plan, whatever it was, was working so far. The world would have its say though.

"Nice map," I said. "What'd you do, fly overhead with a pad and pencil?"

"No, I just walked around after school several times and made some sketches. It wasn't that hard."

"What should we call you?" Marty asked. "Are you a sarge or a captain?"

Captain Cheese, I thought, but I kept it to myself.

"None of that. Plain old James will be just fine. Here's the first thing we need to figure out. We need a schedule for when to go on patrol."

Sounding disappointed, Marty said, "I thought we should always go together since we're a squad."

"Well, I was thinking we might have a tough time coordinating that," James replied.

Being out and about during a blackout wasn't encouraged, and I guess it was just in my nature to think of things that might go wrong. It was time to see if James had thought things through as thoroughly as he made out. "Wait a minute. I think we're getting ahead of ourselves. You know, we aren't the only ones that'll be out there looking. My Dad says that the police, the FBI, and the military are keeping an eye out. What if we run into any of them and they think we're the ones lighting the fires?"

"Well, we won't be caught in the act 'cuz we aren't doing the act."

"But what if people think we are?"

"OK." James challenged, "What do you think we should do?"

"We should tell somebody what we want to do and get deputized or something. Get some kind of permission. I don't know exactly what."

"Marty, what do you think about this?"

"Well, when people fight a war, everybody in the country fights it together, don't they?"

"They should, but the whole country can't be in the military. Don't forget, some resistance groups are part of the underground, and they stay out of sight for good reason. We're like the resistance. We're underground."

"You mean like moles?" spoofed Marty. "But what if one group doesn't know what the other one is doing and we mess each other up, like the right hand taking the left hand captive or something?"

As Marty rambled on, I turned to James. "See? That was my point."

"OK. So do we vote on this then?"

"It's really up to Marty to cast the deciding vote, because you want us to act like the underground resistance, but I think we should ask my Dad and get the OK. Our votes would cancel each other out."

"What if the adults say no? They're good at that."

"I think it's a chance we'll have to take, and even if they do call a halt on our plans, we can still look and listen when we're doing our regular stuff."

"So, Marty, what about it?"

"Sorry Scotty, I want to do this. James is right. It's much better than war games in the park. They're just games, and this is real. Besides, we don't seem to be making much progress."

"That's the way wars are," I said, like I knew what I was talking about. "So, you two are going ahead on your own?"

"Yeah, you can still change your mind. The one thing you can't do is tell anyone. Not other kids and certainly not adults, not even the crows in the trees. Keep your mouth shut except to eat, OK?"

"OK, if that's the way it has to be. Want some advice before I take off my uniform? It's free."

"What uniform?" asked Marty.

"It was just an expression," corroborated James.

"What the heck are you planning to do if you see someone setting the fires? I know we're all good with a sling shot, but there's a reason the police prefer pistols. You think you'll be able to scare them to death with last year's Halloween masks? What makes you think you'll even get close enough to see who it is? And the real biggie— what if they're armed, whoever they are? I don't think you guys know what you're getting yourselves into."

"Damn Scotty, you're so pissamestic," James complained.

"Was that some sort of joke? Not very funny if it was, the word is 'pessimistic.'"

"OK, smarty. Spell it."

"Right, I can. It's P-E-S-S-I-M-I-S-T-I-C, and I prefer to call it caution or common sense. I'm not the fool who rushes in."

"So then, are you saying Marty and me are fools?"

"No. Just that this whole thing could go sideways before you know it and you guys could be in real trouble."

"Well, thanks for the advice," James huffed. "I'm glad I didn't have to pay for it."

"I promise not to tell, but what if you guys get caught and someone thinks you're the firebugs?"

"Then we want you to tell. You're our alibi. Agreed?"

"OK."

"So, you can stay, or you can go, but I have a favor to ask, no matter what," said James.

"What's that?"

"Tell us what you learn about the fires so we can put it on the map."

What we knew of the fires was mostly rumor, with very little specific information. I guess it was my job as the intelligence officer to sort the facts from fiction. Wasting time on the facts made a whole lot more sense than wasting time on the rumors.

When we met up at lunch on Monday, I told them what I'd found out. "There actually haven't been all that many fires despite the hubbub. With everybody talking about it, you'd think that the whole place had gone up in flames. What's more, they haven't all been right here in our neighborhood either."

"What do you mean?"

"Well, there've only been five fires over the last two months, but the circumstances were similar. When you look at where they were set, it sort of makes sense. One was set in an abandoned building, and two of them were started in alleys and behind houses. If I was setting fires, that's exactly where I'd do it, because there's usually junk around that might burn easily. There are more places to hide in an alley too, with less chance of being seen."

"I wouldn't talk like that if I were you."

"What do you mean, James?"

"You sound too knowledgeable."

Nice, I thought, now the Big Cheese is calling the kettle black. "You asked me to get the info, didn't you?"

"Yeah, I know. So, what's the scoop?"

"Well, we know the first one was on our side of the ravine, over by Burr's house a couple of months ago. The second one was a tiny fire in the main ravine a few days later, but my Dad determined it was unrelated. The guy dancing around a few embers seemed drunk or crazy and was probably just trying to keep warm. The third was a much larger one in the main ravine about ten days after the first fire. The fourth torched the Foster's garden shed a few weeks ago, and the latest one was about week ago in an abandoned building up by the old folks' home."

"That's not much to go on…not great odds of being there at the right time when the match is lit."

"That's what my 'pissamesticism' was trying to tell you," I retorted.

"Very funny, we don't care what religion you are. Could you be more exact about the locations?"

"The fire near Burr's house was in the alley between twenty-second and twenty-first, but I don't know how close to sixty-fifth it was and you know where the Fosters live. The old folks' home is over in Lashbaugh land, not far from the Tastie Home Bakery. So, are you guys still going to do it even if I'm not?"

"Sure. What do we have to lose?"

"Sleep I guess and a few missing homework assignments. Well, I wish you guys luck."

"We'll need it. We can still count on you to keep your mouth shut, right?"

"Yeah, don't worry. My mouth is zipped tight. See you guys later."

134

The jingling change in my pocket reminded me that I still had a mission to complete for Sarge before heading home. I slapped my coins on the Tastie Home counter and said, "I'm here for a loaf of French bread please, and I'll take that big fat jelly doughnut too." It came with an equally large napkin to wipe up the sticky blotches of raspberry goo I was known to drip down my front.

Moseying home, I mindlessly wandered down the alley that ran between Lashbaugh's house and the old folks' home, the site of the latest fire. Alleys are where houses go to run around in their underwear, and they usually have stories to tell. The remains were riddled with remnants. A charred garbage can was all bent out of shape and looked useless for anything but a tripping hazard. A few new weeds had already sprouted up and would soon erase the browned-out burn spot. The charred earth led like a path to a lump of something about ten feet away that was seared beyond recognition. Several wires stuck out of an old rusty can near an uncoiled spring and a small gear wheel that could be from a clock.

"Hey, Scotty, what are you doing here?"

Lashbaugh's shout soured the lingering sweetness of the jelly doughnut, and I shivered with the memory of our encounter on the bridge.

"I said, what are you doing here?"

"I was just looking around on my way home."

"Looking for what?"

"Just looking."

"See anything interesting?"

"Just the garbage can and some burned grass."

"Yeah, this is one of the places your brother lit his fires. What's happening with him anyway? Is he going to join up?"

"I don't know."

"So, did you tell your dad?"

"No, not yet."

"How come?"

"I'm not sure I believe you. Besides, I don't think you have any proof."

"Believe me, we have proof. See those wires over there? The cops said they were part of a timing device and that somebody really had to know what they were doing to make it work. In other words, it was done by a science guy. Remember when your brother won the science fair award in ninth grade? His exhibit had something to do with how fire and rust were just different forms of the same thing if memory serves. I do pay attention in school sometimes."

"That's not proof."

"Don't worry. We've got more than that on him. Tell you what. I'll give you one more week and then I'm going to the authorities myself. Or, if you'd rather, my friends and I could just handle it some other way. Chew on that for awhile."

Lashbaugh wasn't as intimidating without his chanting buddies and their chorus of taunts, and I was glad to have found courage and comebacks—at least this time anyway. If the firebug was Lashbaugh, why would he set a fire so close to his own house? Even wild animals don't foul their nests. What I needed was the "Lasso of Truth" that Greta always talked about. Better yet, Wonder Woman herself, however she might be dressed.

17. Stomping Grounds

WITH MARTY AND JAMES dedicating themselves to the crime fighting patrol, Burr and I had more time to hang out in the park on our own, and that's exactly what we planned to do today, bringing our slingshots along for entertainment. I waited patiently on the school steps and wondered if Burr had forgotten.

"Jeez. I didn't think you'd ever get here. What took you so long?"

"I had to see the vice principal after Language Arts."

"What happened?"

"Nothing happened. Somebody said I was trying to blow up the toilets."

"Blow up the toilets? That's crazy. Were you?"

"Of course not. You know how school rumors are though. Some people have it out for me and say I'd rather be with books than people."

"How does that make you a bathroom bomber?"

"No idea. The veep wouldn't tell me."

"So how did you prove you didn't do anything?"

"I didn't have to. There was no proof I did anything."

"So that was it, he set you free just based on your innocent looking face?"

"Yeah, but he said he'd keep an eye on me and check in with me from time to time. I guess it's like being on probation."

"He didn't make you swear on a stack of *Captain Americas* or *Popular Mechanics* or anything?"

"No, I think he just used it as an excuse to make me sweat and see if I knew anything about German submarine movements."

"Get serious. He ask you anything about the fires?"

"Nah."

Entering our neighborhood of dead ends, we agreed where to meet in the park after my route. "Well, let me know if you see or hear anything I should know about."

The park was open to the public but kept its secrets from casual visitors. Few knew it like we did and even fewer spoke our language of park geography. Like the early explorers, we named our discoveries: Suicide Trail; Jungle Gym; Boulder Monster; and the Backward Trees. Some landmarks were obvious to anyone, even adults who had their minds on important things. The ball fields, picnic areas, and large wading pool—recently drained because of the polio scare—were near the entrances and easily accessible, but that was about as far as many visitors ever went. A sulfur spring bubbled up next to the little creek near the main trail, and despite the rotten egg smell and a warning sign not to drink from it, some did anyway, hoping the waters would cure whatever ailed them.

We deemed ourselves park natives who could tell the friendly spirits from those who weren't. We explored every twist and turn, knew most of the plants and animals, and, with a map of the park imprinted on our minds, we imagined ourselves being able to hold out for years against an enemy invasion, human or beast.

Drivers using the two bridges that spanned the park probably didn't realize they were driving over an area that had changed little since the pioneer days. The park was an echo of what it once was. Old photographs showed evergreens that were so gigantically impressive that some were individually named. They rose hundreds of feet above the top of the ravine but most of them had long since been cut or died of old age. The little creek burbling along the bottom of the gulley had once been a river in the days of trees with names, or so the story went. Now it had difficulty maintaining a trickle, especially in the summer. Still, even in modern times, the park remained a wonderfully wild place. Despite being city kids, we could slip into a world filled with mysteries as large as our imaginations on a moment's notice.

I was running late today mainly because the advertising inserts made the Thursday *Times* heavier than usual. I was sure Burr would wait for me till sundown. He'd be as happy in the ravine as anywhere, no doubt working to perfect his slingshot accuracy. I came home, grabbed a couple of cookies, and careened down the trail that led from our backyard to mischief in the park. Burr was right where we'd agreed, sitting next to a small pile of rocks—a ready supply of ammunition. I'd forgotten to bring my slingshot, but Burr let me take a few shots with his before he asked for it back.

Minus the slingshot, I picked up a few of the rocks and lobbed them into the trees. "You know, I'm curious about something."

"What? Burr gave me a quick glance but kept shooting at an old snag about forty feet away."

"Have Marty and James found anything out? I haven't talked with them for a few days."

"Nothing I've heard about."

"Did you ask?"

"No, but they've never been able to keep secrets and I think they're too old to start now. They'd want everybody to know so they could be awarded the Congressional Medal of Honor and get their pictures in the paper. Without you, I'm not exactly in their social circle, you know."

"I know, but have you even talked with them about it?" I pressed.

"Well, the other day they did mention something."

"What?"

"It's very black during a blackout."

"I've heard that stupid joke so many times. It hasn't been funny for more than a year. Is that all?"

"No, they said they almost ran into your dad while he was out wardening."

"Good thing they didn't actually run into him."

"Why?"

"He'd ask them what they're doing, and he'd probably tell their parents to keep better track of them at night and remind them that there's a war on." Disappointed and relieved at the same time, I pressed Burr one more time. "So that's it, nothing else?"

"Well, except for one thing. They saw your brother and one of his friends out there too."

"Doing what? I asked.

"Just walking around, I guess."

"Did they talk to him?"

"They didn't say."

"Nothing suspicious, no fires or anything that night?"

"No. There hasn't been one since the one up by the old folks' home."

"That's a good thing I guess, but if there aren't any fires, it's hard to catch somebody lighting them."

"That's like the police saying, 'We like crime, 'cuz then we can catch more criminals.' Seems like it's about time for another one."

"Cripes, what do you mean by that? You know something you're not telling me?"

"Oh, nothing."

"Any sign of Lashbaugh and his friends out there?"

"Not that I know of."

I kept hoping to hear a crumb of information that might help me decide what to do about Lashbaugh's challenge. Around in circles I went like the tiger chasing its tail. If I found a piece of the puzzle, where would it go?

Whether we talked about it or not, everybody wondered how things would be after the war. Would things go back to the way they were, or would they change in ways nobody could foresee? People made all sorts of predictions, and I wondered if they actually knew something or were just grandstanding. Would we have cars that fly or two-way wrist radios? Would gas be so plentiful that we could rent a motorboat the next time we went fishing? Mostly, my friends and I dreamed about an end to the shortages and air raid drills. We fantasized about chocolate and something gooey to put on French toast. I might be sorry to see the blackouts go though. They're kinda fun if you don't have to drive. Thoughts of Uncle Ted found their way into my daydream. Whenever he made it back home, I hoped he could take up with us right where he left off.

"Hey Burr. You ever think about what things will be like after the war?"

"I just hope there's an after."

"No seriously. Do you wonder?"

"Yeah. The skies will be quieter at least. And we won't have to put up with those bogus blackouts or air raid drills. Oh, and we won't have to listen to all the adults talk about the war news anymore."

"I mean, what will it be like for us? I think people's eyes have gotten bigger during the war, and I figure that after the war, they'll get smaller again. And I think that's maybe not a good thing."

"What on earth are you talking about?"

"Well, in war times, it seems like people are thinking about more than just themselves, like they care more about their neighbors and people in other parts of the world."

"Like the ones we're fighting?"

"Them too."

"And more chocolate. I keep thinking about that."

"I had a dream the other night about the war being over."

"What was it like?"

"It was weird."

"Weird how?"

"You know how dreams are. People weren't happy about it."

"You're kidding."

"No, they weren't happy because they were already worrying about the next war."

"The next war…what are you saying? In real life I think people would be about as happy as they could be if this war was over. There won't be another war."

"I know. It was just a weird dream."

As often happened in the park, time ignored us, and we ignored it. Dinner was already on the table when I barged in. With homework, kitchen clean up, and a B-17 in need of decals, I'd have to catch up with Captain Cheese about the patrols tomorrow at school.

18. The Third Degree

FRIDAY MORNING, I SHOWED up for breakfast without socks. Then I noticed an extra button at the top of my shirt and a lonely buttonhole at the bottom. Moms stand guard—on the lookout for just this kind of thing. There's no way to calculate the amount of ridicule they prevent by checking us over before we rush out the door: "Did you brush your teeth? Go back upstairs and comb your hair. We need to get you a haircut. Those pants are too short." We've all heard it. Many of us would end up on the social trash heap without this screening.

"It's only considerate of others to always look your best," Mom often said while slicking my hair down and straightening my collar. She went through this checklist of things that needed immediate attention nearly every school day and twice on Sunday before church. Six days a week was enough for both of us, so unless there was a special occasion, she took Saturday off and looked the other way. Sometimes after the door closed behind me, I'd muss up my slicked down hair. I never told her that I felt like a gangster when she finished slicking me down. Mom looked even more closely at Greta. I guess her fashion errors were so minute compared to mine that they required greater magnification to detect.

By the time I was certified to meet the public, I discovered James had already left for school and Marty was nowhere in sight. Arriving a few minutes before class, I searched the hallway for them, but had no luck. Our next chance to meet up would be at lunch. Lunchroom tables were like mining claims—staked out by early prospectors, inherited from older siblings, or snared by friends with property rights. The others were up for grabs. Our favorite table was off in the corner and secured daily by habit. James and Marty waited with their feet perched on a pair of empty stools, reserving them for Burr and me.

"You guys are hard to catch up with. Where were you this morning?"

"We had to see the vice principal, Mr. Johnson," James responded.

"About what?"

"Well, we found somebody's ration book on the school grounds, and the veep thought we might've stolen it."

"Did you?"

"Heck no. I don't know how it got there. We just found it over by the basketball hoops and turned it in."

"I bet somebody's in big trouble. How'd it get there? Kids don't bring ration books to school."

"Maybe somebody just forgot it in their pocket, or maybe it was stolen."

"Whose was it? Names are on the covers."

"A name I didn't recognize."

"That's weird, I thought you knew everybody at school."

"Must not have belonged to a student."

"So that's all you talked about?"

"No, he wanted to know if we'd seen anything."

"Anything like what? Did somebody snitch on the patrols?"

"I don't think he knows about our unit."

"So why was he asking?"

"Just because we live in the neighborhood, I guess. Maybe the government people thought the veep could find out something about the fires by using his not-so-friendly voice to ask questions, hoping to trip us up so we'd give something away. I don't know, maybe he just likes playing detective and wants to become a comic book hero."

"You mean like you guys? What did you tell him?"

"Nothing. We haven't seen anything. So, nothing to tell."

"That's not what I hear."

"What do you mean?"

"I hear you ran into Erik."

"Not exactly ran into him, but we did see him and one of his friends the other night."

"Why didn't you tell me?" I demanded.

"We would have, but we didn't think it was important."

"It's important to me."

"What difference would it make to you anyway?"

"I'd just like to know, that's all. Did you tell that to Mr. Johnson?"

"Yeah."

"Jeez. You did?"

"Well, Erik wasn't doing anything. We just saw him. That's it."

"Now they'll wonder what he was doing out there and question him."

"Maybe, but why should he worry?"

"He shouldn't. It's just that sometimes things look bad when they really aren't. Suspicion makes people do weird things and jump to conclusions."

"Well like I said, if he wasn't doing anything, there's no problem."

"Ordinarily that would probably be true, but these fires are serious business. They've got everybody riled up. There's a war on you know."

"There's a war on? Where'd you hear that smart ass?"

"Yeah, I am smart."

The bell rang and sent us scurrying to afternoon classes. My efforts to pay better attention in school were failing, and I struggled to steer my thoughts away from my moral dilemma and end-of-the-week deadline. I felt like I was on a runaway train heading straight for a collision with Lashbaugh.

That night the sixth fire erupted sometime after I went up to my room. Dad was late coming back, and he was about as upset as I'd ever heard him. At first, I thought he might stomp up the stairs and take it out on Greta and me, he was so mad. Shortly after Dad got home several government people brought their serious-sounding voices over, and I could hear them talking downstairs. When Erik got home at half past eight, the G-Men were waiting for him in the living room, and I heard Dad make the introductions after ushering Erik in from the kitchen. Their voices were muffled, and I couldn't make out whether Erik was about to be carted off to jail. Nobody was laughing, that's for sure. At some point, it sounded like Dad sent Erik down to his room. Poor Erik was stuck in our bomb shelter while verbal explosions went off right overhead. The G-Men kept talking with Dad for a few minutes and then left, still without laughing. Curiosity kept me awake, but satisfaction would have to wait till morning. I don't think anybody got any real sleep in our house that night. The phone kept ringing half the night as Dad reported what little he knew to the various callers.

The fire rekindled neighborhood concern, which had cooled over the past week. Other than the one in the abandoned building, the fires had been in garbage cans, rubbish piles, and the one shed, and they hadn't posed much danger to houses. But this fire burned a garage completely to the ground, and reports were that it could be seen from miles away. One of our neighbors was convinced it could be seen as far away as Japan. That's how frightened and screwy some people were.

On Friday afternoon, two government cars parked on the street a few houses away from ours. It wasn't unusual for one government car to slowly creep through the neighborhood about once a week, but I couldn't remember ever seeing two. The only time I'd even seen a parked government car was when the Thompsons got the tragic news about their eighteen-year-old son, Roger. Walking past, I saw that the cars were empty, a sign that something unusual was either going on or about to go on. Dad was home early too. Another sign. It didn't seem like a day to visit the cookie jar, even though I might need the nourishment to make it through my paper route.

"Sit down, Scotty. These men want to talk to you."

Talk "to" instead of talk "with" me. Jeez. Yet another clue as to the seriousness of this after-school visit. Mrs. Forbes, one of my big-tipping paper customers, wouldn't find *The Seattle Times* on her porch till quite a bit later than usual today. I wondered what sort of excuse I could offer if she complained.

"How old are you, Scotty?"

"Fifteen, almost sixteen."

"Then we don't have to tell you how important it is to tell the truth, do we?"

"No. I've been reminded of that since I was little."

"OK then. You understand, right?"

"Yes."

"Your dad tells me you hardly ever go out after dark, except sometimes to church or school functions. Is that right?"

"Yes sir."

"You have many friends in the neighborhood?"

"I don't know about many, but I've got three I do stuff regularly with. Why?"

"I'll ask the questions, if that's OK with you."

"Mm-hmm."

"Were you doing stuff with any of them last night?"

"No, I was home all night."

Mom was my alibi, even though I couldn't imagine why I should need one. She interrupted at exactly the right moment.

"Yes, he was. He got home from school, did his paper route right away, and never went out again."

"That's good."

"How about your friends. Were they out?"

"I don't know for sure, but none of them talked about being out last night."

"Would you know if they were?"

"Probably. We talk about everything we do, even when we don't do it together."

"Even if your friends might be doing something they shouldn't?"

"I don't know. I guess. But they didn't talk about anything unusual or seem strange in any way," I lied.

"No? What about your brother?"

"You mean, did he seem strange?"

"Well, not exactly. What I meant was, do you know where he was till about eight last night?"

'No, I haven't had a chance to talk with him for a couple of days. He leaves for school ahead of me most days."

"Does he go out quite a bit at night?"

"Couple times a week."

"Where does he go?"

"Sometimes friends, sometimes the library."

"How do you know?"

"Because he talks about it now and then."

"Does he ever talk about the war?"

"Hardly ever."

"When he does, what does he say?"

"Sometimes it's about the draft, sometimes it's about whether he'll be able to go to the University of Washington in the fall and go out for crew, and sometimes it's about the news."

"What does he say about the news?"

"Usually, it's about how the war is going. We have an uncle in the Navy stationed somewhere in North Africa, so he talks about that. Sometimes it's about something he heard on a radio broadcast or what's going on in the Pacific."

"What's he say about the draft?"

"Just that he'll have to register soon."

"Does he ever talk about the reasons for the war?"

"No."

"Does he ever talk about whether or not he thinks America should be in the war?"

"No."

"Does he ever talk about how he feels about the Germans or the Japanese?"

"No, but he tells me some of the stuff they're doing."

"Like what?"

"Like what they do to the people when they invade their country and what they do to the Jews."

"How about the Japanese, does he talk about them?"

"No."

"Are you sure? Didn't he have a Japanese girlfriend?"

"Yeah, he talks about her sometimes. She's an American citizen, you know."

"We know. Does he ever talk about Japan?"

"No."

"OK, that's all for now. We may want to talk to you again. Make sure to tell your dad if you hear anything about the fires, OK?"

"OK, I will."

Dad waved me off upstairs, where I could hear their mumbling but couldn't make out anything they said. More than anything, I wished I'd talked to Erik weeks ago. I just hadn't found the gumption to ask him some very uncomfortable questions. There were times to confront and times to just watch things work out. As far as I could tell, the worst that could happen never seemed to happen, at least not in my lifetime. Things usually worked out, even when there was a black cloud in the sky. True or not, that's the way I saw things, and it made it easy to drift along, let my imagination wander, and ignore what my inner self said I should do. Mom and Dad periodically warned against drifting along on rumors. They said I might end up hitting the rocks or going over a waterfall. Go to the source, they encouraged. Teachers said the same thing. Kids do sometimes listen to what adults say and sometimes it even has the desired effect.

It was after my bedtime when Erik finally came home, and I could tell he was getting the third degree from Dad. If you asked me exactly what they were saying to each other I could only guess. This wasn't the first time their voices had risen and fallen, duking it out over how much time Erik spent away from the house. It was a kind of duet they'd practiced before, and each knew their part by heart.

The B-17 was nearly finished, but the closer it was to completion, the fewer missions I felt like volunteering for.

19. RSVP

ERIK HAD ALREADY LEFT for school by the time I arrived in the kitchen to doctor my oatmeal with wheat germ and raisins. I headed downstairs and noticed the spidery frame of the unfinished biplane was safely stowed off to the side of his desk. I stuck my note to a tube of glue with a simple message:

We need to talk, but not in the house. — Scotty

Simon's deadline was closing fast, and I was increasingly nervous as the warning whistle blew louder and louder.

Perched on the top step of his front porch, Burr was gazing up at God knows what when I met him for our trek to school. We usually spent more time comparing notes on the latest DC Comics than what we were learning in class. But today, after raving over the new issue of *Green Lantern*, we returned to the latest hot topic.

"Hey, we've got some extra time this morning. How about if we make a slight detour and go check out the alley where the latest fire was?" I asked.

"Nah, I don't think so."

"We might have a problem, but let's go see."

"Problem?"

"Remember when you said that people who set fires often return to the scene? Maybe somebody will see us nosing around and think we did it."

"Yeah, well…that's pretty farfetched, don't you think?"

"Well, it's possible, isn't it? When people make accusations, they raise suspicions, and suspicion can follow you around, maybe for the rest of your life. Where there's smoke there's fire, you know."

Nodding appreciatively, Burr replied, "That's a funny thing to say. Conviction requires evidence though, and I don't think nosing around is evidence of anything."

"I still want to go see, OK?"

"Go ahead."

"What's the problem?"

"We'll be late for school."

"Come on, we've got the extra time. We'll just walk a few blocks beyond the school and then cruise down the alley for a quick look-see. It's not that far out of our way."

"OK then, what d'you think we'll see?"

"Oh, probably just a pile of rubble. The garage burned completely to the ground, you know."

"That must've been quite a fire."

"It was."

"How do you know? Were you roasting sausages on it?"

"I heard it was visible even miles away."

This fire was just beyond what we thought of as our neighborhood. The obliterated garage was in an alley on the other side of the arterial that formed an invisible fence between our neighborhood and foreign territory. Crossing twenty fifth was sort of like crossing the border into Canada. Things might look pretty much the same, but we knew they were different because we didn't know who lived in every house or what their kitchens smelled like at dinner time. Our other neighborhood boundaries were clearly defined—all dead ending at the ravine. Once across the arterial, the streets went off to take up their places in the city's grid pattern. Who knew where they ended up? The willy-nilly design failed to inspire a neighborhood feeling, which, I guess, is why the outsiders never quite understood when we called ourselves "the dead-end kids."

The garage had been reduced to ash. I thought about all the work that went into building it and the treasure trove of tools it must've contained. I had a teacher who once said that fire presented an opportunity to start over. Clearly, nothing here had even begun to think about renewal. Still, I wondered if the garage would ever be rebuilt. "Holy crap," I said, "there's nothing left. Good thing there wasn't a car in there…and it's a wonder the house didn't catch fire. Look at those blisters on the paint. Did the fire department ever get here?"

"I heard that by the time they did, all they could do was save the house," Burr lectured.

I wondered if this was what a real war zone might look like—some buildings leveled while others were left untouched. "You have any idea who might be doing this?" I asked. "It's been going on for quite a while now. You'd think something might've turned up. My question is, *why* would somebody be doing this? Any ideas?"

"No," Burr grumbled, with unusual finality.

"Still think it's the Millwaters? No? Well, I sort of have an idea."

"Good news. Sherlock Johannsen has cracked the case."

"I really don't think the fires have much of anything to do with the war, or even the blackouts. There's been no sign of an actual air raid, so I don't think whoever's setting the fires is doing it to guide bombers to their targets."

"What are they meant for then?"

"I think it's just somebody who likes to light fires and is intrigued by the commotion."

"That's it?"

"Well maybe they have some sort of grudge or something, but I don't think that's the main reason."

"So, are you going to call up the FBI and tell them who it is?"

"I don't know who it is. But I don't think it's an adult. It's just too crazy. It doesn't seem like an adult kind of thing to me."

"Well, that's certainly a big help to everybody. How well do you know adults?"

"Don't be smart."

"Does it make any difference if somebody is doing it just for kicks?"

"I guess not, but it helps to have a theory."

When we finally arrived at the school, Marty and James were hanging out near the main entrance, pretending not to look at girls. More than a few girls got their revenge by pretending not to look back. It was hard to say who was the most convincing in this charade. I'd seen this contest of cat and mouse many times. Every so often, someone would be caught looking by someone who was looking back, at which point they had two choices. They could look away and pretend they hadn't been caught or they could acknowledge they'd been tagged by dropping out of the game and walking away.

"Hey there, what are you guys up to?" I hollered.

"Just trying to picture what we'll all look like in our thirties."

"Really? It looked to me like you were looking at girls while pretending not to look at them. From what I can tell, you're not any better at it than you were last year, especially Marty. He doesn't even pretend anymore. He just looks right at them, and they turn their backs. So, what's this about wondering what we'll look like in our thirties? Do you think any of us will ever reach thirty?"

James, never at a loss for words, said he was planning on it, even if Burr wasn't.

"Who said I wasn't?" Burr challenged."

"Nobody, but sometimes I wonder about you."

Apparently uncomfortable, Burr changed the subject. "Guess what? Scotty thinks he knows who's lighting the fires."

"No, I just don't think it's an adult."

"I don't either," said James.

"How do you know?" asked Burr.

"I don't know. It's just a feeling."

Burr's sarcasm rose to the occasion and blossomed into a shoddy attempt at comedy. "Great detective work," said the judge. "You have a feeling? I see. Well, that's enough for me—that'll be twenty years son, and don't ever do that again."

Even Marty recognized Burr was being a pain in the butt. "I'm heading out. See you guys at lunch."

James was itching to share the latest news. "You guys hear about that bombing in Oregon?"

"No." Burr's eyes lit up as he pressed James for the scoop. "What happened?"

"They sailed a balloon bomb over here all the way from Japan and dropped it in a forest to set it on fire. I heard it went off but didn't do much damage. I guess it was just meant to get people's attention, sort of like that Doolittle raid."

"That's scary. What will they try next?"

Having captured his audience, James resumed his news broadcast like he was Edward Murrow or something. "Did you hear about Marisa's older brother?"

156

"No. What?"

"He was on one of those ships that got torpedoed off the coast."

"Navy?"

"No, the Merchant Marine."

"Any survivors?" asked Burr.

"Don't know." Still in character, James continued, "That's getting a little close to home, isn't it?" He paused for dramatic effect, even though the torpedoing was off the East Coast.

"Ever wonder how it gets decided who survives and who doesn't?" I asked. When no one had a response for that, I fought my way upstream through the turbulent hallways—the alleged river of future progress.

This was Friday, which meant Simon's deadline, if he was serious, would arrive tomorrow. My only backup plan if Erik didn't see my note before I went to bed was to get up extra early for a secret talk in the basement or backyard. I'd procrastinated far too long, worrying that our conversation would be like trying to defuse a bomb, a skill I hadn't been trained for.

I gave the empty cookie jar a sidelong glance as I raced upstairs to see if Erik had answered. He'd left a note on the B-17 box:

Scotty — How about tomorrow at one o'clock, near the Backward Trees? If that doesn't work or in case I don't get home in time, put another note on my desk, and we'll go from there. — See ya, Erik

20. Backward Trees

I CAN'T REMEMBER WHEN we first noticed the Backward Trees, but at some point, my friends and I gave them the nickname. They clustered together, making a handy geographic reference point for our park adventures. Like the early explorers who identified and mapped, we felt compelled to name the Backward Trees in light of their unusual behavior. They were like immigrants from a foreign land. Nobody knew how they got there or why they refused to cooperate with the other trees, but they likely arrived several generations before we happened along.

Their unseasonal behavior is what made them stand out. Unlike the trees that lose their leaves in the fall and play dead half the year, the Backward Trees look like evergreens most of the year. But they'd adopted the backward habit of turning their needles golden in the fall like broadleaf trees, then dropping them onto a pile at their feet. Their bare skeletons survived the winter, sprouted new green needles in the spring, and carried on with their business of being both evergreen and deciduous. If the Backward Trees didn't want to fit in, who was to say they should? Sometime in the past, the park had welcomed these travelers, despite their strange customs.

One day, I became curious enough to look them up in an encyclopedia. Of course, there wasn't anything by that name. After a page-turning treasure hunt and considerable trial and error, I learned they were called tamaracks in some places and larches in others. Eventually, I discovered they weren't evergreens at all, and that technically, they were deciduous conifers. Undoubtedly useless, this little bit of knowledge felt good, and I tucked it away for no particular purpose. Collecting trivial facts was comforting, and I prided myself on the size of my collection. I was sort of like Burr in that way, who said he routinely collected rusty bits of worthless information and piled them up in the junkyard of his mind.

Sometimes when I wandered into the park, it swallowed me up, and I wondered what it would be like to see all the critters who lived there together in one place, perhaps mustered on the lower playfield at sunup getting their orders for the day. The sergeant would say things like, "Worms, you can have a four-hour head start to put some distance between you and the moles. Mosquitoes, look out for the bats at dusk, and Cotton Tails, don't hang out in the open; the hawks and owls are the Luftwaffe of the park. They control the skies, and you'll probably never see or hear them coming. Slugs, stay out of the sun. Now everybody, get out there and enjoy your day."

A pile of fur and a few spare rabbit parts littered the main trail this morning, and I didn't need to be a detective to guess what happened there last night. For the critter kingdom, there had always been a war on, and every species had a system of warning sirens.

Erik was sitting on the ground with his back against a fallen log that sprawled in the middle of the Backward Trees. He greeted me warmly. "Hey little brother."

"Haven't seen much of you lately and I'm not that little anymore, in case you hadn't noticed."

"I know, Dad keeps reminding me. Mom says she can barely stay ahead of your cookie habit and has trouble keeping you in clothes that fit. Speaking of…that looks like an old shirt of mine you're wearing."

"It is. I get some help on the cookies from Greta, and Dad eats a few too, I think. How about you? Are your cookie-jar hands clean?"

"No, I can't resist either. They're so good. With the shortages and all, it seems like Mom must make them out of thin air."

"You'd get more cookies if you were home more, you know. The family that cookies together, stays together."

"Probably true, but there are things in life besides cookies. You didn't want to meet just so we could exchange cookie recipes, did you?"

"Get serious, you never cook anyway. I have to ask you something important, and I don't want you to get mad at me for asking, OK?"

"OK. I figured it must be something important if we couldn't talk in the house."

"You're hardly ever there anyway."

"Yeah, we know. So, what is it?"

I lit the fuse and hoped the bomb was a dud. "Are you the person setting the blackout fires?"

"Jeez, what kind of a question is that?"

"I asked you not to get mad, OK?"

"I'm not. I just can't believe you're asking. I'm your brother."

"That's partly why I'm asking."

"There's got to be more to this."

"There is. Simon Lashbaugh says it's you. He says that he has proof, and that if I don't tell Dad, he's going to the authorities or something worse unless you enlist."

160

"Wow. How long have you been carrying that little grenade around in your head? I don't know what he calls 'proof,' but since it isn't me, he can't have any."

"Can you prove it isn't you?"

"How do you prove you didn't do something? There's a reason the law has to prove you did something and not the other way around."

"He also said he wouldn't tell anybody if you joined up. He thinks you're a C.O."

"I don't get it; I hardly know the guy."

"Maybe it's because you had a Japanese girlfriend."

"Could be. I guess some idiots feel that way about all Japanese, even the ones born here. People have gone more than a little crazy, what with the Order and all. Who knows what Lashbaugh's problem is? Maybe it's just because he lives in a parallel universe on the other side of the ravine. Anyway, I'm not a C.O. I'm just somebody who doesn't particularly want to go off and kill people—or get shot at, for that matter."

"What are you talking about, a 'parallel universe?'"

"Oh, nothing. It's just that some people think so differently it's hard to believe they live in the same universe. Maybe crossing the footbridge is like stepping through the looking glass."

"So, should I tell Dad about this?"

"You bet. We should both tell Dad, like tonight as soon as we get home!"

Although my feet were firmly planted on the exposed tamarack roots, I felt like I was suspended in a hammock, swinging peacefully from the branches. I couldn't remember when I last cried about anything, but tears of relief trickled down. Erik saw them and understood, and we hugged for the first time in years. It felt like he'd hold onto me forever, like he'd done when I was the only kid in fourth grade that couldn't balance a bike on two wheels.

"So, if you don't want to join up and kill people, are you going to apply for C.O. status?"

"Well, I've certainly thought about it."

"What's that mean?"

"That it's not an easy decision. It's complicated. There are so many things to think about, and I still haven't come up with the right thing to do."

"Like what?"

"Well, first of all, could I kill somebody—even in a war? I wouldn't be shooting at Hitler, you know. I'd be shooting at other kids like me who're probably thinking about where they'll go to college in the fall. Then, what about the people who aren't soldiers and just happen to be in the wrong place at the wrong time? If somebody tried to bomb the Boeing plant right here, a lot of other people would get killed too, people who were just too close to the plant. Most of the workers there are civilians, you know, like Aunt Val.

"Yeah, but isn't it kinda late to think about stuff like that once a war starts and your country's been attacked?"

"That's what a lot of people say. What if everybody asked themselves if they could kill people who were pretty much just like they are? Most people would say 'no' if you asked the question that way. When it's a country though, you figure everybody's in it together. You do things you'd never do as an individual. It's like you and your friends. Don't you sometimes do stupid stuff when you're all together that you'd never do by yourselves?"

"Sometimes. How do you know the enemy is just like us? Haven't you seen the posters? You know what the Germans and Japs look like. You make it sound so simple."

"You don't actually think we know who the Germans and Japanese are from the posters and comics, do you? That's all propaganda. They try to scare us by making the enemy all look like monsters. What do you think their posters make Americans look like?"

"Well, they may not actually look like those monsters, but I hear they do monstrous things to people. How does turning the other cheek work in the face of Pearl Harbor?"

It began to sound like we were getting into an argument. Not a knock-down, drag-out brawl, but we seemed to be lining up on opposite sides of the fence. It was hard to tell. Erik's tone changed, and I wondered if he thought I was accusing him of something instead of just asking questions.

"You know, the other day I was thinking about the commandment, 'thou shall not kill.' There's no exception for war, you know. It just says, 'thou shall not kill.'"

"Are you trying to church me now? You never go to church anymore. If you went last Sunday, you would've heard Pastor Wicklund's sermon saying that commandment is often misunderstood. He said the correct translation should be, 'Thou shall not murder.' If you look at it that way, it changes things. Not all killing is murder. You would've heard some great pipe-organ music too."

"Why is he even talking about the war in his sermon? He's a minister, not a soldier."

"Well, the war's a big deal for everybody right now, so it's pretty hard not to talk about it, even in a sermon. What do you think about what the Pastor said?"

"About the commandment or about whether all killing is murder?"

"About any of that stuff."

Erik paused and glanced up at the tamaracks like he thought the answers might be up in the branches, just ready to drop into his head. I wondered if the Backward Trees were like being a C.O. Even though the other trees seemed to follow some sort of rules, the tamaracks were true to themselves and had chosen something quite different.

"I don't know about that translation stuff," he said, "but I don't think going to war should have anything to do with religion, even though it often does. Maybe you're too young to think about the draft, but what do you think about all this?"

"I think it's too late for this war. The choice to fight or not fight was taken away by Pearl Harbor."

"True. Maybe the opportunity was taken away from the country, but the new law says individual citizens still have choice in the matter. That's why you can apply to be a C.O. now."

"But isn't your country like your family in a way? You'd fight to protect your family, wouldn't you?" How could he possibly say 'no' to that?

"If there was a clear threat to the family and there was no other way to deal with it, then I would. But there's always another way in the beginning. Sometimes I think about what I would do in a situation where I had to bomb some of Natsumi's family. They say you're trained to kill to protect your buddy. It's not a political thing at that point—it just comes down to your survival when you're under fire, and sometimes you have to kill to survive.

"What are the chances of killing some of her family? Didn't the Order send them all off to Idaho?"

"She has relatives in Japan too, you know—grandparents and cousins. See, it's like Pearl Harbor flipped a switch on the Japanese in this country. One day they're OK and the next day they're deemed the enemy, without ever having lifted a finger."

"Let's take Natsumi out of it then. Where's the beginning of a war anyway? I heard some people say that the war was on its way long before Pearl Harbor. One thing just leads to another and before you know it the shooting starts. Dad says many say we should stay out of Europe, and not too long ago the President even said that as long as he's in office, he'd never send our troops to fight in Europe again. It's none of our business, and once we get involved, some people wonder how we'll get out."

"Did the President really say that?" Erik asked, sounding doubtful.

"I don't know. But Dad said he did. He also said it looks like we're getting involved little bit by little bit, and he figures we'll be sending troops soon. It's like we're oozing into the conflict. Once somebody starts a war, are there any other options? Did we have any choice after Pearl Harbor?"

"Jeez, Scotty. I didn't think you paid much attention to this stuff. I thought you just read comics and played games in the park. Relax, I never said there was another way after Pearl Harbor. If we were just oozing into war before, Pearl Harbor kicked us in the butt—no more oozing."

"Yes, I've been paying more attention lately. You can't escape it, so you might as well try to understand it a little, especially if your big brother goes off to fight or becomes a C.O. So how do you get to be a C.O. anyway?"

"You have to complete an application and specify a reason."

It was apparent that Erik had done some research and was familiar with the new law. Once he started talking, I hoped he'd give a clue about what he planned to do. Even more important, I hoped it wouldn't be something that drove him further away from Dad. "If you were going to apply to be a C.O, what would your reason be?"

"Well, I guess I'd say I couldn't kill someone, and I don't believe war solves anything."

"Crap, you tell that to Dad, and he'd probably knock your block off."

"Probably right. That's why we don't talk about this."

"What do you think he'd do if you did apply to be a C.O?"

"He'd have a conniption fit, for sure—maybe even kick me out of the house."

"I've heard that a lot of people apply because they're religious. Could you do that?"

"I suppose, but that would be kind of a lie."

"What happens if you apply and get it?"

"Could be different things—some become medics or corpsmen, but they still might have to enter combat zones and carry a gun for protection. Some do what they call a 'service of national importance.'"

"What if you don't want to do any of that?"

"It's the pokey then—Leavenworth, Kansas, I think."

"What if none of us fought and the other side did?"

"That's a bugger, isn't it?"

"Yeah, especially since the other side *is* fighting. Dad is always saying that we didn't start it but we sure as hell will finish it. That's why he calls this a 'good' war. You agree with that?"

"Well, I get what he's saying, but the whole idea that there's such a thing as a 'good' war makes my head spin. I don't think any war is good. What did the last war solve? 'The war to end all wars' wasn't that long ago, and all it got us was a worldwide flu epidemic and another war."

"Maybe they got it wrong, and *this* is the war to end all wars."

"Wouldn't that be nice?"

During our talk, we'd wandered away from the tamaracks, crossing the creek and ambling back under the girder bridge, past the sulfur springs and the bottom of suicide trail. "Do you remember there being fish in the creek when you were a kid?"

"No, but Dad said there used to be before we moved here. I guess the creek was much bigger then, till they hid most of it underground in pipes. Now it's just a jump-over creek. There are plenty of frogs, but I've never seen anything with fins in it."

"Me neither. We used to try fishing. In third grade, Burr and I came down here with strings tied to sticks and dangled worms into several pools we thought might hold a trout. Nothin' doing though."

Nobody who loved the park could help but wonder what it looked like in the old days, when the creek had fish and the monster trees had names. Most of the stories about what it used to be like were probably true and there was enough of it left in a natural state that our wondering didn't have to wander very far. Erik and I fell into a more relaxed tone, but I still didn't have a clue whether he was seriously thinking about applying under the new law.

"It's so hard to understand why this is all happening," I continued. "Maybe that's why most people just do what they're told and let someone else figure out what it all means. You said you couldn't kill someone. What if you and your buddies were being shot at?

"To be honest, I'd probably shoot back if I was being shot at, so it makes sense to think about it ahead of time and do what you can to avoid any situation where someone would be shooting at you."

"Yeah, avoid being shot at. That's the code I live by."

"I thought we were having a serious discussion."

"Sorry."

"That's exactly why some people are objectors. They know they could pull the trigger if someone was trying to kill them, but they also know they could be court-martialed if they were ordered to shoot and didn't."

"What if the draft board asked you that question about being shot at and you admitted you'd shoot back?"

"I don't know what they'd do then."

"What do you think Uncle Ted would say if you became a C.O?"

"He might understand, or he might not like it. I really don't know. It's not a decision that anyone makes lightly. People do it because they believe it's the right thing to do. So, what would you do if you were my age?"

"Maybe that C.O. law says you have a choice, but I don't think there's a real choice on this one. I'd enlist."

"Maybe that's what I will do, but I'm not sure yet. When we talk to Dad, let's not bring up anything about being a C.O. He'll be upset enough about the fire thing."

"Agreed. I only hope that Lashbaugh hasn't already talked to him."

"I doubt it, since he's got to be bluffing," Erik reassured me.

"I hope you're right, but he could stir up a storm of trouble if he does what he says. Maybe you should get married and have a kid to get out of the draft."

"What made you think of that?"

"Some people are doing it, you know."

"Where did you hear that? That's the dumbest reason I can think of to get married or have a kid. It might get you a temporary deferment, but that's about it. Then it would be even worse if you got killed."

Of all of us kids, Erik was the closest to Uncle Ted and was probably the one most concerned about the lack of news. At home though, we hardly ever talked about it. "What do you think about Uncle Ted? Do you think he'll be involved if they invade Italy?"

"Most likely since he's on a minesweeper. They go in before the ground troops and try to clear things out for the landing. I don't think he'll be assigned to keep the Nazis from stealing the pyramids."

"What are you talking about...stealing the pyramids?"

"I was being sarcastic."

"I wonder if he gets to fish off the boat. Did you guys ever catch much when Uncle Ted took you fishing, or were you just out making mischief?"

"Well, it was like fishing always is, sometimes the fish gods smile on you and sometimes they don't. Knowing Uncle Ted, he'll probably rig up some stick and dangle a line to see what he can pull up. The Mediterranean has been fished for years, and I'm sure they had the good sense to save a few for Ted."

"Well, I hope he'll be OK. I'd like to go fishing with him after the war."

"So would I. I've learned a few new spots Ted doesn't know about."

"Hey, you own a zoot suit?"

"No. Why're you asking?"

"Just curious."

The path we'd made slipped from our backyard and into the park like a lifeline to the world above. We approached it, knowing there was still much more to say, but off we went to face the music. Who knew whether Dad would be home yet? I could never keep track of which Saturdays he had to work unless there was some family thing. I tried to imagine what his reaction would be, but there was no telling. He'd demand proof, that's for sure, but I didn't have any. Trust might be the only proof we had.

21. Disclosure

It TURNED OUT TO be a work Saturday, so Dad didn't get home till a half hour after Erik and I returned. He looked a little surprised to see us both in the kitchen talking to Mom.

"Hi guys. What're you doing here?"

"We live here," I said.

"I know one of you does."

"OK, Dad, I know I haven't been home much lately, but let's not go over that again. We have something important to discuss with you. Scotty has something to tell you."

"What is it?"

We hadn't talked about who would say what and it was too late to discuss it now, so I started talking a mile a minute and let it all spill out.

"You know that Lashbaugh kid across the ravine, the one that gives me a hard time?"

"Yeah, the big bad bully you try to avoid?"

"That's him. He told me that Erik is the person setting the blackout fires and claims he has proof."

Dad furled his brow and took a long, piercing look at Erik before turning back and pinning his eyes on me. "What? Who has proof?"

"Lashbaugh himself. That's what he told me a couple of weeks ago, but that's not all he said."

"What else?"

"He said if I didn't tell you by this weekend, he'd alert the authorities or handle it some other way."

"Is that all?"

"No, he said if Erik enlisted, he wouldn't do anything."

"Why would he care if Erik enlisted?"

"I don't know."

"Why didn't you tell me about this when you first heard?"

Erik's glance told me I was walking too close to the C.O. business. I only hoped Dad would be so concerned about the fires, that he'd speed right on by and wouldn't stop to ask questions. "I was afraid to."

"Afraid of what?"

"Of what might happen."

"Did you tell Erik?"

"I finally did. We just now talked about it."

"You waited all that time on something so important?"

"I know Dad. I should have said something, but I was confused."

"Confused about what, doing the right thing by telling me? What about that promise you made a couple of weeks ago to tell me if you heard something?"

"I know."

"You can't just make a promise and forget about it."

"I didn't forget about it; I just didn't know what to do."

"What's that mean? If you make a promise, that's what tells you what to do. You keep it."

Erik had been taking all this in and must've sensed that I felt cornered. He came to my rescue as he'd done so often—like when he took the rap for the overflowing toilet and when he helped me refinish the arms of the Morris chair that I'd wrecked by using it as a sawhorse. He never told anybody when I discovered where Mom was stashing Christmas presents a couple of years ago either. "It doesn't matter now, Dad. Scotty just wasn't sure what to do and in the end he did tell. That's why we're talking about it now."

"Well then Erik, what about it? Are you the firebug?"

"Of course not, Dad."

"So, why would Simon say you were?"

"That's the kind of stuff bullies do, I guess. They don't always have reasons the rest of us can understand. Maybe they don't even understand."

"Maybe it's because he knows Erik is sweet on Natsumi," I said. Lashbaugh doesn't think the Japanese are even human."

Erik wasn't exactly on the hook, but the wrinkles on his normally smooth forehead made me think he was squirming. He had to be pretty upset, having edged uncomfortably close to the C.O. thing himself, plus knowing that Natsumi might have been Lashbaugh's trigger.

The thought of the government ripping Japanese citizens up by their roots and sending them off to camps was one of Mom's biggest aggravations. She frequently said it was history repeating itself, and that it wasn't unlike what we did to the Indians. She said it would come back to haunt us and make it harder for the country to hold its head up. She'd been listening to the conversation but hadn't said anything yet.

Mom and Dad often argued about the government removal of the Japanese, and I felt a steep rise in the tension of the room. They'd usually start by calling each other by their first names, Anna and Theo. It wasn't that Dad completely disagreed with Mom either. He argued that the West Coast was in an emergency situation after Pearl Harbor and that there wasn't time to do what might be the right thing. "That's what war is," he liked to say, "one big emergency." But Mom probably hadn't said anything so far because she recognized that this was a matter that could potentially send her eldest son to prison. For this conversation at least, she wasn't focused on the government's betrayal of the Japanese.

Still, she'd noticed that Dad was keeping his cards close to his chest. In a voice prepared not to wilt, she issued a challenge. "Theo, don't you believe Erik?"

"I'm inclined to, but I need convincing."

"How am I supposed to do that, Dad? The only way I could convince you would be if someone had confessed and that certainly isn't happening."

This exchange brought Mom to full attention and made me feel like I hadn't done a very good job of sticking up for Erik. Mom had more practice, and she must've felt it was time for her to take over. "Theo, there's absolutely no evidence that Erik is doing this, and like I've reminded you on more than one occasion, he's always been an honest and truthful person. There's no reason why we should think that has changed."

"You're right about that Anna," he countered, "and I'm sorry if I gave the impression that I don't believe him, but whether I do or don't still doesn't resolve the matter. If Simon falsely accused Erik about something this serious, that's almost as bad as if it was true. The accusation might even be a crime itself for all I know. It's something that hasn't come up before. There's only one thing to do. We need to go over there and confront him and ask what this so called 'proof' is."

I had to ask. "Who's the 'we' Dad?"

"All of us. All of us except Mom."

"And Greta?" I asked, thinking it sounded sort of funny.

"Don't make jokes. Of course not. She doesn't have anything to do with this. I don't want to let it fester any more than it already has. We need to go right now," Dad ordered.

Ever thoughtful about good manners, Mom prompted, "Don't you think you should phone first, Theo?"

"No. I think we'll be more likely to get to the bottom of things if we just show up. We don't want to give them time to fabricate a story.

But Mom wasn't finished and pinned her eyes on Erik and me. "Before you go, Dad has something he needs to tell you."

Dad was usually very direct. He hardly ever hesitated, and I sometimes wondered if he even had time to think about what he said before saying it. This was clearly different. Even with all eyes on him, no words came out. Mom wasn't about to tell us, so we waited, shifting our glances back and forth till Erik asked, "What is it, Dad?"

"The War and Navy Departments sent a telegram to Grandpa saying Uncle Ted is missing in action."

The gravity of his words blanketed us with a deafening silence. Questions piled on top of one another, but even if we knew what to ask, none of us had the words.

22. Face to Face

DARKNESS SWALLOWED US WHOLE with the news about Uncle Ted. I
don't know when the right time for news like that would've been.
Who knew how long Mom had been fretting over when and how to
tell us? Things that build up demand release, and between Lashbaugh
and Uncle Ted, it felt like we'd opened the floodgates. I couldn't help
but feel for Erik. Aside from Dad, he was the one who was closest to
Uncle Ted, maybe because he was the first born, or perhaps because
of all the times Uncle Teddy took him camping and fishing or gave
him summer jobs when he was younger. Greta and I had a similar
closeness to Aunt Val. I puzzled over the term "missing in action."
Did it mean he might be found soon?

We piled on our jackets, which felt like protection against more
than the rising chill as we crossed the footbridge into Lashbaugh land.
It was around most people's dinner time, so I guessed they'd all be
there—unless they had an evening wanderer in their family too.
Perhaps a courtesy phone call would've been better received than
Dad's idea of barging in unannounced. Too late now—barging was
well under way. Hoping to catch both Simon and his parents at home,

Dad figured there'd be less chance for them to make up a story or for Mr. Lashbaugh to cover for Simon.

Simon's house looked as ordinary as all the other houses in the neighborhood, though on their side of the street, each dwelling was set above the sidewalk level, making them seem more impressive than they really were. Seven concrete steps led from the sidewalk to a short, paved walkway and a series of wooden steps, attached to the porch. The front door was open, letting snippets of conversation trickle out. Whatever was simmering on the stove wafted through the screen door and flowed down to the sidewalk, issuing a friendly greeting, almost as though we were expected. Clomping up the stairs and onto the porch, we sounded like an entire regiment, the wood amplifying the sound of our arrival.

I heard people talking in the back of the house, probably the kitchen, and as Dad knocked, a large man with several days' growth appeared. It could only be Simon's dad. There was no mistaking the physical resemblance or the way he carried himself, even the slightly threatening way he stood.

"If you guys are selling something, we don't need any," he said, in a voice proving beyond a doubt that he and Simon were branches on the same family tree.

"No," said Dad. "I'm Mr. Johannsen. These are my sons Scotty and Erik. We live on the other side of the ravine, and we have something to discuss with you. It involves Simon. Is he home?"

"Tell me what it is first, and then I'll check and see if he's here. He didn't beat up one of your boys, did he? I don't see any bruises."

"No, he didn't. I'd really appreciate it if you could check to see if he's here first. I'd like us all to be hearing the same thing, or reading from the same page, as it were."

"Cut the fancy talk. I don't see what difference it makes, but I'll check."

A woman, who must've been Simon's mom, appeared from the kitchen, and dried her hands on an apron. She wore a simple house dress, but smiled like she was a party hostess. "Why don't you all sit down and make yourselves comfortable?"

Dad thanked her for the offer but declined while Erik and I made for the sofa. It all happened so fast that I didn't even consider whether we should stand with Dad as a show of solidarity. Mr. Lashbaugh returned with an impatient, guarded look on his face.

"Simon will be up in a moment. If you're going to tell me he did something to your boys, you had better have proof. People are always accusing him of things he didn't do, especially at school."

"No, it's not about school. It's about something he accused Erik of doing, and we want to get to the bottom of it."

Simon finally appeared, yawning, as if he hadn't shaken off a nap. He revived quickly when the alarm of seeing us went off.

"What's this, Dad?"

"These people say you accused Erik of something, and they want to get to the bottom of it."

"Bottom of what?"

Dad took over, still addressing Simon's dad. "I'm sure you've heard about the blackout fires, right?"

"I think we all have. I'd say it's the Japs, but they've all been sent away. Maybe they forgot a few."

"Scotty tells me Simon claims that Erik is the person lighting the fires, and that he has proof. Besides that, he said if Scotty didn't tell me, he'd go to the authorities or handle it some other way unless Erik enlisted."

"That's quite a mouthful. So, is your Erik the culprit playing with matches?"

Erik didn't utter a word. "No, we'd be talking to the authorities ourselves if I thought that he was."

"So, Simon, what about this? Is Scotty nuts or trying to get back at you for something?"

"I don't know what his problem is, Dad. I never said anything like that. If I knew it was Erik, I would've told you, so you could've done something about it."

"So, there you have it. It's your son who's lying, not mine."

At this, Erik and I got off the sofa and stood shoulder to shoulder with Dad, giving me the strength to look Simon directly in the eye and fill in some details.

"Remember that note you put in my locker saying to meet you on the footbridge after school and not bring my friends?"

"Dad, I never...he's just saying that to protect his brother."

Mr. Lashbaugh seemed caught off guard by this and turned toward Simon.

"What d'you mean, 'to protect his brother?' Protect him from what?"

"I don't mean anything. Just that there wasn't any note, and I didn't meet him on the bridge."

"Oh yes you did, and that's when you told me Erik was lighting the fires and that you'd tell if he didn't enlist."

"Listen here, Mr. Johannsen, I don't know what your problem is or what Scotty's problem is, but I'm going to have to ask you to leave my house. You come in here trying to sound like some government official, but you have no right to go around accusing people, especially kids you don't even know. What kind of an example is that to set for your boys? We should all be sticking together and fighting for the same thing, not fighting each other."

"I've got that note right here in my pocket."

I had no idea why I'd left the note in my pocket all this time, and it's a wonder my jeans hadn't gone through the wash since they'd been living in a pile of dirty clothes at the foot of my bed. Mom wouldn't approve but I'd have to say my slovenly habits do have their advantages.

"Let's see this 'evidence' then."

"And that's not all. I have witnesses."

A sharp edge knifed its way back into Mr. Lashbaugh's voice as he said, "All right all ready, let's see it."

"Easy, Mr. Lashbaugh, let's not get nasty now," Dad interjected. "Let's just deal with the facts."

"So, let's see this here fact."

"Here it is. It's a little wrinkled but otherwise the same as it was the day I found it in my locker."

"Hand it over. Let me have a look-see."

We all took a deep breath while Simon's dad smoothed out the note. During the long pause before he read it out loud the cooking smells intensified, and I wished this was a friendly family dinner. "It says: *Meet me on the footbridge at four o'clock today. Do not bring your friends! — S.*"

I thought the note might be conclusive proof of Simon's guilt, but no such luck as long as his dad was a member of the jury. He took his time, even turning the note over to see if there was anything scrawled on the back. A puzzled look came over his face, making me think he wasn't quite so sure about things. Several seconds grew to several minutes, and then he seemed to make a decision.

"This isn't even addressed to anyone, and how do we know who this 'S' is? Who's to say Scotty didn't write it himself?" Dad suggested he check the handwriting, and Mr. Lashbaugh took another look at the crumpled note but didn't say anything.

Since talking with Erik in the park, things had happened so fast I hadn't had time to fill Dad in on all the details. He'd have no clue what I meant about having witnesses.

"You said you had witnesses. What's that about?" asked Dad.

"Yeah, James and Marty were there when Simon smashed into me in the hall and told me to check my locker at lunch. And Burr was there when I opened the locker and found the note."

"Is that all?" Mr. Lashbaugh asked, with a dismissive smirk. "You could probably get your friends to say anything."

Sensing that the tone of the conversation had shifted from a discussion of the facts into a tit-for-tat exchange of allegations, Dad tried to steer it back to civility. "Mr. Lashbaugh, remember this isn't a trial in a courtroom, so take it easy."

"It sounds to me quite a bit like a trial."

"I have another witness," I offered.

Dad glared at me for my smart-aleck remark, and I knew I deserved it. "Who's this additional witness?" he asked.

"It's Greta."

"Greta has something to do with this?" quizzed Dad.

"She really doesn't except I asked her to watch my meeting on the bridge in case something happened."

If I thought we had Simon's attention before, this news jacked him up a few more inches—or a few more centimeters, as Monsieur Beret would say. Simon's eyes looked ready to leave their sockets, and Mr. Lashbaugh perked up in unison with his son.

"I asked her to hide in the bushes nearby," I continued.

"So, what did your imaginary girlfriend hear on the bridge?" Simon taunted.

I answered before Dad issued another caution to tone things down. "She didn't hear anything, but she can verify that I met Simon on the bridge at four o'clock that day."

"Who's this Greta anyway? spouted Mr. Lashbaugh. Did you just make her up?"

"It's his sister," Dad replied.

Mr. Lashbaugh still showed no sign of believing us. "Well then, why didn't you bring her along if she knows so much? Turning to Simon, he said, "What do you have to say?"

"Like I told you Dad, I didn't do any of that stuff. It's all lies."

"Well, it looks like we've hit the wall on this. No real evidence, just a wrinkled-up piece of paper and buddies and a sister who would say anything you asked them to. It's Simon's word against Scotty's. What d'you say we just forget everything?"

"It's not that simple Mr. Lashbaugh. I agree it seems like Scotty's word against Simon's, but both allegations are serious enough for my superiors to look into. As an air raid warden, I'm obligated to forward information of this sort."

"Now just hold on a minute Mr...um, what did you say your name was again?"

"It's Theo Johannsen."

"Under the circumstances, it doesn't seem worth making trouble for either of us, does it Mr. Johannsen?"

"I don't want to make trouble any more than you do. It's about doing what's required, about doing the right thing to get to the bottom of all this."

The back door screen suddenly banged shut, like an exclamation point to emphasize Dad's words. Conversation halted, and all eyes zeroed in on the kitchen to see who would emerge. One of Simon's choir buddies burst into the living room. He recognized Erik and me but failed to size up the situation before shooting off his mouth. "Well, I see our firebug has finally been discovered. Did he confess yet or was he caught in the act?"

Simon tried to block his buddy from our view, backing him up to the kitchen door. He held a clenched fist at his side and threw him the smelliest stink eye I'd ever seen. It was just like in a detective story. With a slip of the tongue, the choir boy had blurted out the next best thing to a confession, all but making the closing argument for us.

Mr. Lashbaugh ended this courtroom confrontation abruptly by issuing a gruff order to Simon and his buddy. "You go back down to your room...now. He turned back to us, saying, "OK, I think you can all leave. I'll be having a little talk with Simon about all of this— maybe more than just a little talk."

"Honest, Dad, he's lying," Simon protested as he turned toward the stairs, and the ceiling light caught the first few beads of sweat on his forehead.

"Just go. We'll deal with this in a minute. So help me if I find out you've been lying to me..." His threat blanketed the air like an ominous cloud.

Without any polite goodbyes we spilled out the front door, taking several deep breaths to ease the tension, and headed for home. Dusk had given way to night, but it wouldn't get very dark if the moon had its way with things. Nearly full, it edged to the top of the trees in the ravine. While a rarity for Seattle, I wanted the northern lights to appear, making magic out of gloom. Even though this neighborhood wasn't part of Dad's usual patrol, his wardening habit made him give each house a quick side glance as we went by. I would've paid a hefty price to be a fly on the wall when Simon and his dad had their little tête-à-tête.

Our walk home wasn't a victory lap—no celebration, no high fives, and no back slapping. We all knew it wasn't over. There was bound to be a final act before the curtain fell. Still, my sense of relief was profound. It was as if the northern lights had consented to a private display just for me.

"What now, Dad?" Erik asked.

"I'll have to bring it up with my district supervisor. I don't know what they'll do. They may want to talk to you again. I'm sure they'll want to talk to Simon as well."

"Should I be worried?"

"Not if you haven't done anything."

"Will you be there if they talk to me?"

"If they let me. I want to have a word with Greta too. It's not that I don't believe you Scotty, but I need to have all the facts straight from the source. The horse's mouth, you know?"

"Dad, if you talk to Greta, she'll verify that I met Simon on the bridge, but she'll probably also tell you that we talked about comic books, because that's what I told her we were meeting about."

"Why would you do that?"

"I was worried about what would happen if Lashbaugh's story got out. Besides, the whole thing was such a shock. I just wanted more time to think about what to do."

"If she was too far away to hear anything, I guess that's not a problem. But you need to think about what it means to lie. Even a little white lie can come back to bite you. I'll take your word for it on the comic-book conversation though."

"Thanks, Dad."

As we crossed the footbridge, leaving Lashbaugh to whatever his dad had in mind, my thoughts of Uncle Ted and the war returned. It seemed to me that if you were assigned to a Navy ship and still went missing, things looked pretty bad. It wasn't at all like being lost in the park.

"Do you know anything more about Uncle Ted?" I asked.

"No, they didn't tell Grandpa much, and I don't know what that means. They may truly not know much, or maybe it's something to do with Navy policy, and they have to hold back information."

"How did Grandma and Grandpa find out?"

"They got a telegram from the Navy."

"Do you think they'll find him?"

"I don't know, Scotty."

Dad didn't have to summon Greta from her room or wait for her to get home. She was right there in the kitchen with Mom. I could tell from their expressions that they were talking about Uncle Ted. Aunt Val usually kept her visits to a regular schedule, but I had the sense that things might feel better if she came this weekend. I guess Greta had the same idea, because she'd already asked, and we were now waiting to hear.

Like Lashbaugh's buddy, Dad didn't wait to size up the situation before steamrolling his way into Mom and Greta's conversation. "Greta, I want to talk to you. Up in your room would be good."

"What about, Dad?"

"I'll tell you upstairs."

I wanted to let Greta know that it was OK for her to tell Dad what she saw on the bridge, and that she wouldn't be getting me in trouble. But there wasn't time for that. I hoped she wouldn't try to protect me by making something up, but she was generally as straightforward and honest as Dad, so I probably didn't need to worry. Still, these

185

were worrying times, and I know Dad worried too. He just tried to spare the rest of us by not worrying out loud.

"What happened over there?" Mom asked, curious to know how things went at the Lashbaugh's. "Nobody got arrested, did they?"

"No, Mom. But it was tense for a while," Erik replied. Mr. Lashbaugh didn't believe us till one of Simon's friends burst in and spilled the beans by calling me the 'firebug.' Simon kept denying everything, but I think his dad got the picture. Scotty and I would've loved to be there when Simon and his dad had their little talk."

"So, it's over then?' Mom asked.

"Not exactly. Dad has to inform his bosses so they can look into it and decide what to do."

"Well, I'm glad you all went over there to hear it from the horse's mouth."

"I don't know who the horses were, us or them."

"Very funny, Erik."

Moments later, Dad and Greta came back downstairs, not looking very serious, so I guess there wasn't any reason to worry after all.

"What were you two talking about?" Mom asked.

"I had to verify something with her, but everything's OK."

Except everything wasn't OK. The news about Uncle Ted had opened a gaping hole in the family, and nobody knew if it could or would be filled back up again. The little we talked about it didn't help either. All we could do was hang onto the word "missing." Even Mom had trouble finding her sunshine. In a matter of weeks, we stopped talking about it altogether. We'd all learned that worry only chases its tail and leads to more worry. Mom finally told us she'd let us know if there was any news, and unless there was, we'd already said about everything that could be said.

23. Friends

I'M SURPRISED GRETA HASN'T discovered a cure for polio yet. Ever since getting the microscope from Aunt Val she's spent more time in her room, often coming home with some exciting "discovery" to examine under the eagle-eye of the scope. Our refrigerator now has a special section for her specimens that we've designated "the mold farm." Rotting things hold a special fascination for her, and I have to wonder what her friends think of her yucky hobby. For all I know, the cure for polio is right there in our refrigerator, just waiting for discovery.

The microscope is a portal through which Greta disappears, entering a world of new findings that draw her steadily on. The upside of microscope mania means that I see more of her than usual. Sometimes we wonder out loud about Uncle Ted, hoping he's soon to be found, but fearing we'll likely never see him again. We don't talk about him within earshot of Mom or Dad since they'd made it clear, "no news is good news."

Now that Erik is in the clear and Simon's accusation has been exposed, we discuss the blackout fires too. The Civil Defense people talked with Erik again, but they didn't find any problem. Dad's impeccable reputation as an air raid warden probably helped. Greta speculated that Simon and his buddies were the ones setting the fires—just to see if they could get away with it. I'd thought the same thing for weeks, but there wasn't a shred of evidence. Not even a rumor pointing in his direction, other than his reputation.

After dinner I invited myself into Greta's room.

"What are you looking at under there? See any itsy-bitsy Martians or Lilliputians?"

"No. But come look at this."

Hardly your average scene from a travel brochure, it looked more like a comic-book creation of life on Mars. Teeny-tiny spikes, like trees from outer space, lined up next to a leafless grouping of plant-like shapes. The microscope was like an extension of the mind, turning daydreaming into an after-school career and helping us think our observations were more serious than silly.

"What is this stuff?"

"It's some sort of mold I found on a dead tree."

"Where's that dead tree? I don't want to get anywhere near it. Is it poisonous?"

"I don't think so, but I always wash my hands after handling stuff like this and throw it in the trash when I'm done."

"I don't know about that. Some of it ends up in the refrigerator within poisoning distance of our food, doesn't it?"

"Never fear. Everything in the fridge is sealed up tight—Mom insists on it. Besides, I know she checks the lids when I'm not here."

"What do you do when you see something new under there?"

"I draw a picture of it and record the conditions where I found it."

"You get credit for that at school?"

"No, but I might do something at the science fair."

In addition to the mold farm, Greta had an entire bookshelf full of jars with leaves, mushrooms, dead bugs, bird feathers, and all manner of mysterious and unmysterious things—not the least of which were molds of many colors that made frightening smells if you were stupid enough to unscrew the lid and take a sniff. I couldn't believe she'd talked Mom out of so many perfectly useful canning jars. I guess she was counting on the cure for polio too.

One of the jars filled with gray gunk caught my eye. The gunk was largely unrecognizable, but a couple of dead ants had obviously wound up in the wrong place at the wrong time. "What's this?"

"Oh, I've been meaning to talk to you about that. You know my friend, Agnes? She lives over by the last blackout fire, and she scooped up some ash and gave it to me."

"That was thoughtful. Did she tell you who lit the fire?"

"No, but she did say something very interesting. She said Burr has been over there several times, picking through the ash. I don't know if it means anything, but it's kind of odd, don't you think?"

"Yeah, especially since he was sorta weird about going to look the day after it happened."

"You want to see? I haven't scoped it since she gave it to me. It's just been sitting there on the shelf."

The gunk may have been ash, but it wasn't the powdery sort that blows away with a gust of wind. Still wet from being fire hosed, it looked more like the main ingredient in biscuit gravy. Greta removed a small glob and smeared it thinly on a glass slide. Sliding it carefully under the lens and adjusting the focus she said, "Holy cow, it smells like smoke."

"Not surprising. What's it look like?"

"Well, it doesn't look like anything else I've seen under the scope.

"Let me have a turn." Putting my eye up to the scope, I saw a patch of slimy-looking chunks with something flaky in them. "I don't think this will be the cure for polio."

Glaring at me, Greta took another look and agreed it was one of the more boring things she'd scoped. Even so, she decided it was worth diagramming, including the ants, and jotted down where it was discovered. I guess that's what scientists do, record everything, even when they don't know if it will turn out to be important. I took another look at the jar and noticed some jagged metal looking thing squished up against the glass.

"You have a spoon or something? There's something at the bottom of the jar I want to dig out."

"How about this, is it long enough?"

"I think so. Give it to me." Digging beneath the gray goo and dead ants, I saw something that looked manufactured, like part of a machine. It had little teeth on it and was probably perfectly round before it got torched.

Peering around my shoulder, Greta said, "Let's scope it and see what it is."

I tried to dial in the focus but was immediately frustrated by my clumsiness. "I think I need your help here."

Greta took control and zoomed in immediately, identifying it as some sort of tiny gear. Elbowing her aside, I said, "Let me get a look at it."

I had to agree—it was definitely a gear. So now the question was, what kind of a gear was it? More importantly, where did it come from, and did it have anything to do with igniting the fire? Transported through the lens of curiosity, I began to understand why Greta had been coming home early. "Every day revealed a new surprise and questions to follow," she said. The scope illuminated a hidden world that couldn't be seen with the naked eye. As far as I could tell, microscope questions unveiled even more wonders...the building blocks for a great story and potentially, a miraculous discovery. You could spend a lifetime looking through the eyepiece, and maybe that was Greta's plan.

"It looks like there're some numbers on it," I said. "What're you going to do with it now?"

"I don't know, probably nothing."

"So, can I have it then?"

"What do you have in mind for it?"

"I don't know. Probably take it over and have Mr. Science look at it."

'You mean Burr?"

"Yeah. But wait a sec. There's something else in the jar. Let's spread all that gunk out onto something so we don't miss anything else.

"Here. Will this plate work?"

"Sure. Look here. There's a tiny wire coiled up like a snail shell."

"I don't think it's a wire. Doesn't that look more like a spring that's been unsprung?"

There'd always been things about Burr that just didn't add up. But lately, I had a growing suspicion that he was somehow connected to the fires, and it made me more than a little uncomfortable. I needed to ask him some questions, but I didn't want to do it in a way that put our friendship on the line. It was like a stiff-arm in football—the closer I got to the runner, the harder I was pushed away. I desperately did *not* want to learn anything that would make Burr's life more difficult than it already was, but the strain was taking its toll. On top of that, there was my promise to Dad—that I'd tell him if I found out anything about the fires. There was nothing to do but risk my friendship.

The next morning, I met Burr for the walk to school. His mom had recently adopted a breakfast-in-a-bag approach for his trek up the hill. While talking nonstop and juggling his books, glasses, and lunch bag, Burr regularly missed his mouth with the toast and jam. Looming curbs and parking-strip shrubbery often sent him sprawling, usually face first. The scabs from his last spill were still visible. As his friend, I considered it my job to make sure his face was food free by the time we got to school. We were making good progress today and his face was as clean as the last time it was washed, whenever that might've been.

"I didn't see you on the weekend. What were you up to?" asked Burr.

"We went fishing."

"You don't even have a boat. Where'd you go?"

"We rented a boat—a little sixteen-footer, and we went out on the Sound."

"Catch anything?"

"My Dad did. Got a small king near Mukilteo."

"How big?"

"About twelve pounds. We ate it for dinner with some stuff we canned from the garden last fall. It was pretty tasty."

"Take me with you next time. I've never been salmon fishing."

"Be nice to me then. I'll ask my Dad."

I reached into my pocket for the treasures from Greta's jar of sooty goo.

"Ever see one of these?"

"Yeah, it looks like a gear out of a Westclox."

"How do you know?"

"When one breaks, my Dad gives it to me, and I take it apart. I've got a bunch of them. I can show you sometime."

"I'll take your word for it. What do you do with them?"

"Make stuff."

"Like what?"

"Drive mechanisms, gadgets, and things."

"Gadgets that do what?"

"Sometimes little catapults that throw things. Or sometimes it's timing things. Mostly, I'm just playing around to see what I can come up with."

"Sounds like Rube Goldberg devices to me. Can you show me some after school?"

"Sure."

Over the past few weeks, Marty and James seemed about ready to pull the plug on their patrols. James called it "battle fatigue," but as they began complaining about how hard it was to meet up, I suspected it was really just plain old boredom. Battle fatigue or not, the odds of catching the culprit were exceedingly small, and I guess that had finally sunk in. Besides, there'd only been one fire since they started patrolling. I promised myself not to say, "I told you so" when they finally admitted they were ready to give up, but it was a weak promise and there was nothing in writing.

Thinking Burr might be the firebug wasn't the same as worrying it was Erik. If it was Burr, I'd lose a friend, visit him in jail—if they'd let me—and simply carry on. Burr was younger than Erik, so maybe they wouldn't even send him to jail. If it had been Erik, I'd be living in a family that had raised a criminal, with a dad that had been humiliated by his eldest son. Whether Erik or Burr, I had one concern in common—what if the culprit was never caught and suspicion just lingered on and on?

I figured there was a small chance Burr would come clean to his friends or let something slip while showing off some of his stuff. He always liked an attentive audience, and I thought Marty and James would enjoy the show too, especially if the admission was free. The three of us would have a better chance of prying information out of Burr together. Besides, that would give us four more ears to hear it.

A mission to Burr's to uncover a saboteur wasn't what James had in mind when he began the patrols. But it might shine more light on things than wandering around in a blackout hoping to get lucky. We'd have to give Burr some kind of compliment to get him started, throw in a remark or two about the fires to test his reaction, and then lead him on with some questions. If we could get him rolling, he'd probably build up enough speed to blow right past his own stop signs and let something slip.

Job number one was to get James and Marty to go along, but finding time to talk to them without Burr around was a challenge. Lunchtime might be just the ticket. The three of us routinely arrived earlier than Burr who took so long to waddle out of class, find his locker, and locate his lunch that he rarely had time to thoroughly examine his sandwich and seek a possible trade. I scanned the lunchroom as James and Marty slouched at our table, and Burr wasn't in sight.

"Hi, have you seen Burr?"

"Not in here. He was in art class, though. I think he stayed to talk with Miss Pershawnsky about his project."

"Good, I wanted to talk to you without Burr around."

"What about?"

"Patience please, gentlemen, patience. That's what I'm going to tell you. I want you to help me with something about the fires."

"What? You were the one who opted out of patrolling with us so you could cozy up with your beloved comics and radio programs," challenged James.

"Give me a break and just listen. There are some reasons why I think Burr might be the one setting fires. I don't know for sure, but with your help, we might have a chance of finding out."

"Jeez, Scotty, what are you saying? I thought old four eyes was your buddy."

"Hey, don't call him that, OK? If you needed glasses, how would you feel if people started calling you names? It's not his fault, and maybe they help him see things you can't. Besides, he *is* my buddy and that's why I want your help. I really hope it isn't him, but I don't want to go around thinking it might be and never finding out. And I sure don't want to go around accusing somebody and not being able to back it up, you know, with facts."

"OK, OK, so what's the deal? Why do you think Burr's involved?"

I'd thought things through as best I could, even jotting notes about what made me suspicious. I dug through my memory to make sure I didn't forget anything. If they decided not to help, I might not even go through with playing detective against my odd friend. Who knew if we'd get an actual confession? That's why I needed witnesses, to corroborate the facts and stand firm against any denials. A friendship was on the line.

"So Scotty, lay it out for us," Marty nudged. "Give us the skinny."

"There's a bunch of things that seem to point to Burr and I want you guys there with me when I ask him some things. If it is him, he might just get to talking. You know how he likes to grandstand.

That's probably the only way we'll know for sure—if he actually admits it."

"What makes you think it might be him?" asked James.

"It isn't just one thing, but a bunch of little things, and when I put them all together, they seem like they might point in the direction of guilt."

"OK, shoot."

"The first thing is how he's always bragged about sneaking out during the blackouts."

"Maybe that's all it was, just bragging." Marty sounded skeptical.

"Maybe. Just wait, OK? The second thing is how he's always making gadgets from things he takes apart."

"What's that prove?"

"By itself it doesn't prove anything, but he was reading a spy book once and he told me all about how to make timers from wristwatches and alarm clocks. You remember that first fire? Dad said the Civil Defense people thought a timer was used and I even found some wires in the ashes."

"OK. Keep going."

"Well, the other day, I wanted to stop by and see the fallout from the latest fire on our way to school, but Burr didn't want to go anywhere near the place. He was pretty serious, like he was spooked, but I made him go anyway. He just seemed weird to me. Then there's this. Greta told me he's been seen more than once at that same place picking through the ashes. I didn't think much of it at the time, but it dawned on me recently that he's the only one of us that never talks about the fires. He keeps saying it's the Millwater gang. I don't think they even exist. And remember how he didn't want to be part of the unit? He was dead silent when we talked about it, and it's not like him to be quiet about anything. I even asked him once to see what he could find out about the fires, and he just gave me a funny look and pretended I hadn't asked."

"Scotty, it still doesn't prove anything. Proof is something there's no escape from, and this just isn't it, even if it does point in a guilt-like direction."

"I know it doesn't prove anything, but doesn't it make you really wonder? Here's the last thing and maybe it has something to do with it and maybe it doesn't. You know how my Dad is the air raid warden, right? Well, he's had to talk to Burr's folks more than once about following the blackout rules."

"That's his job, isn't it?"

"It is. But I overheard him complaining to Mom about how Burr's folks are the only people that don't seem to take any of this seriously. So, is Burr maybe lighting the fires because his folks are pissed off about my Dad threatening to write them up? You know, Burr hardly talks about the actual war either. It's usually just military equipment and gadgets, not the war itself.

Here's the last thing. The Bouchers are the only people I know who don't seem to worry about how much gas they have. They always have plenty, and I'm wondering where they get it. I've asked Burr several times but never get a straight answer. Gas is a great way to get something burning, don't you think?"

"I have no idea about the gas, but maybe talking about the war is really your problem," Marty accused. "We're not even supposed to talk about the war. Walls have ears—in case you haven't heard. You should know that with your dad being a warden."

"I know, but what do us kids know that spies would be interested in anyway."

"You might be surprised. They say the most innocent thing can be useful to the enemy. That thing about your dad writing up the Bouchers is a bit of a stretch, don't you think?"

"I know, but it might be a motive or something and it fits with all the other things."

James and Marty grew increasingly agitated the more I talked. You just don't do this kind of thing to your friends, even if you're sure they're messing around in a way they shouldn't. You don't always have to lie to protect them...just keep your mouth shut sometimes. But we're at war, and that changes things. This is more serious than having to postpone a summer vacation to Yellowstone or wear wooden shoes. It's about the future of things.

"You guys want to think about this for awhile or let me know right now? I'm headed over to Burr's after school today. He wants to show me his latest gadgets, and that might be a good time to get him talking if you guys are in."

"I don't know," said Marty, screwing up his eyes and sounding disinterested.

"I don't either," added James in a voice that told me he was thinking about it.

"OK. If you're coming along, meet me on the front steps when school's out. That's where I meet Burr, and we can all walk together. If you're not there, I'll handle it by myself."

24. Snoopers

EVERY SCHOOL DAY AT half past two, the heavy front doors burst open like the breach of a dam. Sitting off to the side, Burr watched the waterfall of kids cascade to the sidewalk below. The faraway look on his face made it seem like he was in another world, with no idea what might happen if he slipped from his bench into the raging rapids just inches away. Anybody wanting to swim upstream would have to wait for the flood to pass. The surge was in stark contrast to the morning arrivals when students dribbled in like drips from a leaky faucet.

The bench was Burr's usual perch and if he happened to be looking the other way, I routinely snuck up behind him shouting "Look out," just to watch him jump out of his shoes. It worked every time. Today I had other things on my mind and decided to keep it light. "You finish your breakfast yet?" I grinned to show him I was just kidding.

"Yeah, but I didn't have time to eat all my lunch. I was talking to the art teacher."

"You promised to show me some gadgets and inventions of yours. Would this be a good day?"

"Good as any. They're not just gadgets, you know."

"Can Marty and James come if they want? They'll show up here any minute."

"Yeah, but I want to stop at the drugstore on the way to see if they've gotten any new candies in. Something with chocolate sure would be nice."

"We'll all go for that. We know what kind of a monster you become when you're on the prowl for chocolate. Here they are."

Marty and James popped out just as the cascade of kids dried to a trickle. Except for the weather, everything was falling into place. It hadn't stopped raining all day and now it started to blow, pushing the rain sideways. We pulled the hoods of our rain parkas tight and plowed through the gusts like ships bucking a storm at sea. I'd been hoping for an easy-going stroll home to help put Burr in a relaxed state. The last thing I wanted was for our questions to seem like an inquisition. A brief stop at Gervais Drug & Variety might be just the thing. We could dry off, warm up, and enjoy a sweet refreshment after our blustery drenching.

"Afternoon, Mr. Gervais."

"What can I do for you boys?"

Marty liked candy almost as much as he liked girls, and he did the asking. "Get any good candies in?"

"Nothing new. You know how it is with all the shortages and rationing. Most of the chocolate goes to the troops. I haven't had any Hershey Bars for several months now, but I've still got some of those penny hard candies. You think they'll do the job?"

"Well, if that's all you've got, they'll have to do," Marty said with a loud sigh.

"You sure there's nothing with chocolate, not even a taste?" pressed Burr.

"Now that you mention it, I might have a few Sky Bars left. They cost a nickel a piece though."

Burr lit up and asked how many he had, and then asked how much money each of us had. We cobbled together eight cents between the four of us, and Burr proposed what he hoped would be a delicious solution. "How about if we put our money together and buy two?"

Skeptically, James asked, "How do we do that with only eight cents?"

"Easy," answered Burr. We ask Mr. Gervais to trust us for the other two cents. He knows all of us and our families too. Besides that, he's a good guy. He was probably candy starved too, once upon a time."

"You think? We'd be buying them on credit."

"If you want to call it that."

"Can kids just do that without permission or a bank account?"

"We can give it a try."

It sounded good to me, so I offered my three cents to Burr. There was nothing better than the caramel-filled section of a Sky Bar. James and Marty ponied up, asking Burr to do the bargaining. I crossed my fingers, hoping we'd be able to work out who got which of the four different fillings. Sky Bars were one of a kind. Each of the four sections had a different kind of filling, so it was more about which filling you got rather than how much you got. Several of us had suggested Sky Bar math problems to Monsieur Beret. It seemed like a natural, but he never took us up on it.

"Mr. Gervais, how about we get two bars for eight cents and pay you the other two cents by this Saturday."

"I might go for that, but what if you don't pay?"

"Ship us off to the army, I guess."

"They'd just send you back till you got old enough. I'll trust you for the two cents, but you know I'll talk to your folks if you don't pay, and you can probably guess what their reaction will be."

"It's a deal." Burr handed over the money and Mr. Gervais placed the bars on the counter. We looked at each other and grinned at Burr's financial wizardry.

The Sky Bars did wonders for our spirits and primed us for what was left of the walk to Burr's house. The rain even cooperated, allowing us to throw back our hoods. Marty's curiosity got the best of him. "Hey Burr, what're you going to show us?"

"Machines and inventions. You'll see. Just wait."

"Sort of like show and tell, like we used to do in grade school?"

"Yeah. Something like that."

When James asked what the inventions did, Burr said it was easier to show us than tell us. Stopped short, we turned to the next item in our conversational repertoire—girls. We weren't born knowing how to talk about them but did our best to fake it. Big brothers weren't always the best instructors, either. More than one of us had gotten in trouble parroting our big brothers' advice, but not quite understanding what we were saying. Our latest concern was how rapidly girls seemed to be changing, leaving us in the dust. Sidelong glances in the locker room suggested we'd soon change too, and even though none of us were experts in biology, we understood that patience was all we had going for us. Each tuned to an internal clock, some of us appeared to be in different time zones. Even with a mother, sister, and older brother, I was too timid to ask any of the critical questions. If I asked Dad, he'd probably just hand me a book, saying, "Here, read this." Marty thought the Sears & Roebuck catalog was very informative and that all the answers could be found in their swimsuit and lingerie sections.

Surprisingly, Marty showed more interest in Burr's inventions than girls, asking, "Can you make any money with your machines?"

"I never really thought about that."

Just like he did with the blackout patrols, James took over, and even before Burr showed us anything, he proposed a business venture. "Maybe we could form a company. You invent things, we figure out what they're good for, and then me and Scotty could be the salesmen. We'd all get rich."

"Let's just see the inventions first."

Burr's mom greeted us with cookies and looked pleased that somebody besides me was interested in visiting Burr after school. James broke out his adult-sounding manners and thanked Mrs. Boucher, saying they were the best cookies he'd ever had. She scarfed up the compliment like we scarfed down the cookies and went off to fetch us a few more.

"Come down to the basement," invited Burr. "That's where I do most of my work."

The basement clearly functioned as a workshop. It didn't look anything at all like a bomb shelter, and I was curious to see the shelves empty of canned goods. There wasn't even one can of Spam. Like Dad said, maybe the Bouchers thought bomb shelters were a big waste of time.

"Jeez Burr," Marty exclaimed. "Do you get to use all these tools?"

"Yeah, my Dad says tools are the hands of the imagination and imagination is what makes people different from other animals."

"So, show us something inventional," I said.

"Inventional? Is that even a word?" Marty asked.

"I don't know. Sounds like it should be though. That's what messes me up in spelling, words that should be but aren't."

"Yeah, and then there're the words that are and seem like they shouldn't be," James chimed in. None of us knew if inventional was a real word or not.

Burr was getting impatient. "Give it up boys. This isn't an English lesson. Here's something I'm working on now that comes from an old idea. You remember what a catapult is? Well, what if we used a small catapult like this as a pitching machine for batting practice? It's easy to make it throw the ball, but the problem I'm having with it is directing the throw so the batter can hit it. I keep changing springs and the length of the arm, but I haven't found the sweet spot yet. Eventually I will."

James thought a pitching machine could be a real money maker but said Burr was on the wrong track. Hoping to rush our path to millionaire status, he said, "The catapult idea won't work because the ball gets thrown high in the air and then arches down. Pitchers throw directly at the plate. Did you ever see a pitch that looked like a fly ball? What you need to do is shoot it out of some sort of tube pointed directly at the batter. That would be cheaper than hiring a pitcher for batting practice, and teams would probably see it as a solid investment."

Deflated, Burr had to agree that shooting out of a tube might work better. "Where do you think I could get a tube with a diameter the same as a baseball?" he asked.

"I don't know, but I'll keep my eyes peeled."

"Want to see my super saw?"

"That sounds like the sort of thing we came for," Marty cut in.

"Here. This looks like a regular old cross-cut saw, but it isn't. The front of the handle is at a perfect right angle to the straight side of the blade so it can be used as a square to draw a perpendicular line across whatever you want to cut. It even has a protractor drawn on it to measure angles."

"That's genius, Burr," James exclaimed. "That's something we could make and sell right now. Got anything else?"

Confused, Marty asked, "What's a protractor?"

Burr gave him a scornful, exasperated look and quipped, "It's a tractor that lost its amateur status."

Marty and James looked entirely dumbstruck and spouted a confused duet: "Huh?"

I got the dumb joke, and secretly thought it was quite clever. "Did you think that up yourself?"

"Yes. Oh, and I have something else. This is something the Navy might want. You know what a periscope is?"

"I do. My Uncle Ted explained it to me once."

"Well, this is a practice periscope with pictures of enemy ships that you can slide through the viewer to make it look like they're moving. If I could somehow synchronize a trigger mechanism with the moving-ship picture, it would be a great way for submariners to practice launching torpedoes. I'm working on it."

I could see the slide rule in James' head counting away, estimating production costs, and devising a way to make a quick killing. "This is great Burr, but don't you think the Navy must already have something like this? Maybe you don't actually have to make one. We could just sell the idea to the Navy, and they could take it from there."

"Well, I guess that's a job for the sales department," Burr shot back.

Even if there wasn't any possibility of making a fortune from the prototypes in Burr's basement, we were impressed by the fruits of his tinkering brain. Still, there was nothing that seemed to link Burr to the blackout fires, so I prodded him on.

"What's next? This is quite a show."

"How about an automatic door closer?"

"OK, how about it?"

"You just attach this spring to your door, and it automatically closes."

"That's completely dumb. It's already been done," whined Marty. "Scotty even has a spring like that on his back screen door. Lots of people do."

"Yeah, all right. But it works, doesn't it?"

"Anything else?"

Burr nodded and motioned us up the stairs and out into his backyard. Upon seeing the contraption, Marty let fly with his favorite exclamation: "Holy crap."

"It's based on the laws of physics," Burr began to lecture. "They can't be ignored, you know."

I couldn't help making a comeback. "I heard the laws of physics are old and sometimes need a nap in the afternoon. You could ignore them while they're napping."

"Very funny Scotty, but haven't you also heard, gravity never sleeps?"

"No, I'll take your word for it. This giant flinging contraption looks like something from the olden days that can hurl balls of fire over the castle walls."

"People did exactly that. Not with much accuracy, but it was probably very frightening to see balls of fire falling from the sky. I doubt it killed many, but I bet it made them run like hell."

"Well, what are you going to use it for? There aren't any castles around here, and the only forts we know about are defended by the U.S. Army."

"I'm not sure yet. Maybe just for fun, or it might be great for the Fourth of July fireworks."

Burr's use of the word "fireworks" got our attention, and we encouraged him to rattle on. "And?"

"I even made a timed release for it. You can set it, and then walk away and wait for it to go off."

What's in the timer, I asked?

"A spring and some gears from an old clock. With enough discarded parts, there's no telling what you can make if you put your mind to it."

"What would light off the fireworks?" I asked?

"Don't know. I haven't figured that out yet."

"Can we see how it works?"

"Sure, I use big rocks for the counterbalance. Just pile some in that pouch and I'll wind up the release spring. Whatever you want to launch goes in that cup at the end of the arm."

"What shall we launch with it?"

"I used marbles till I used them all up. Now I just get a handful of pebbles."

"OK, let's launch something out over the ravine."

"What if we hit something?"

"Not a chance," I said. "The ravine's huge and there're hardly ever any people at this end."

"Maybe we could launch fruit, or better yet, potatoes," suggested Marty.

Everybody laughed till James reminded us how difficult fresh fruit was to find and what the reaction would be if someone discovered we were using it as ammunition.

"Well, potatoes would probably make better ammunition anyway, and they're way easier to come by," said Burr. "Just dig up any old victory garden and you'll find a few."

"Can you imagine potatoes raining down? The sky is falling, the sky is falling…" teased Marty, and our laughter started up again.

James lobbed his own joke, "I thought those were stars up there, you mean they're actually potatoes?"

Adding my own two cents, I said, "I know people who just blame everything on the Japs and never think about the possibility of friendly fire. They thought Pearl Harbor was bad. Just wait till the potatoes start raining down in the middle of the night."

Injecting a somber note, Burr added, "Well, they already made it across the Pacific, and they weren't using potatoes for ammunition."

"Yeah, and they won't even have any potatoes to throw at us when we get done with them," James said.

A stickler for scientific accuracy, Burr asked, "Do they have potatoes in Japan?"

"I'm not sure," I replied, "but I hear they don't eat cheese."

Skeptical, Marty said, "You've got to be kidding. Who doesn't eat cheese?"

"Well, it's true. When's the last time you had some anyway?" We'd been short on cheese and butter ever since the rationing had upended our diets. My mind drifted, and I enjoyed a brief fantasy about cheesy sauces and melting butter before my stomach grumbled.

Like an army truck towing a howitzer, we wheeled the huge contraption around and aimed it over the sprawling ravine, just behind Burr's backyard fence. We loaded the ammunition cup with an assortment of small rocks and a few hazel nuts the squirrels had passed up. Burr let Marty cock it, and we waited for the spring to unwind and release the counterweight. It let go with a frightening whizz, and we heard the sound of leaves ripping as our scattershot showed no mercy to the nearby trees. The maze of branches made it difficult to tell how far the tiny projectiles went, but it seemed like Burr's gadget could probably launch a potato several city blocks out in the open.

"That could be our first line of defense if the Japanese did invade," I joked. "I can see the headlines now: *Potato Battalion and Their Top-Secret Potato Launcher Save the City*. Or how about this? *Potato Battalion Honored for Their Ingenuity and Bravery*."

We all had a good laugh. If we'd known how much fun this would be, we would've been over at Burr's every day and Mrs. Boucher would've completely used up her sugar ration making cookies for us. In the end, I guess fun was the only thing the contraption was good for, and truthfully, it seemed way too large to make it out of Burr's backyard. If we kept launching things, we eventually would've done some serious damage. Quitting before destruction or injury was something some of us had yet to master, especially when we were all together. A devil force would take over and make us do things we'd never think of doing by ourselves—sort of like a country at war. James and I begged off to do our paper routes, and Marty tagged along.

"Well, what do you guys think? Have we learned anything?"

"That Burr, he's either a genius or completely nuts."

Agreeing, Marty said, "It's hard to tell the difference sometimes."

"What about Burr's nosing around in the ash pile at the garage fire?" James asked. "Didn't you want to ask him what he thought about the blackouts?"

"Yeah, but I just didn't see the point. There's nothing he showed us that makes him the firebug. You couldn't start a fire with those contraptions. You'd be better off using a plain old match. I can still try to get him talking about that other stuff next time I see him."

"But there's nothing he showed us that means he isn't the firebug either," reminded James. "And did you see the jerry cans over in the corner? There were enough to hold at least twenty gallons of gas."

"If that's what's in them," I cautioned. "So, all we found out is that we're right back where we started—in the dark."

"Was that a joke? 'In the dark...' It wasn't that funny if it was. Try a little harder next time, you hankie."

"We can ponder it for a while longer, but I don't think our bug is Burr. If this was a trial, we'd be laughed out of court for our lack of evidence. I don't want anybody to think they can be some kind of hero by pointing the finger at Burr. He gets enough grief from everybody already, just because he's different. Understood?"

"Understood."

"And you, James?"

"Understood."

25. Apology

EVER SINCE THE SHOW and tell at Burr's, I'd felt more than a little guilty for suspecting my friend. Dad and I planned to go salmon fishing on the coming Saturday, and it seemed like the perfect time to fulfill Burr's wish to go along. When I asked him if he wanted to go "rip some lips," he thought I'd gone completely off my rocker. It took a while to convince him that I wasn't going insane. After explaining that it meant "going fishing," Burr cracked up and thought it was one of the funniest things he'd ever heard. He was happy to be invited, and I was relieved, thinking I'd finally be able to forgive myself.

There was no way Burr would be ready to go fishing at four o'clock in the morning under his own power, so he spent the night at our house for the first time ever. Luckily, Dad didn't have to work on Saturday, and he said the tides looked promising. The weight of sleep was many pounds heavier on Burr than it was on me. Announcing it was time to get up wasn't very effective, but when I threw the light switch and jerked the covers off, he went from snoring to bolt upright in less than half a jiffy.

Puget Sound was the catch basin for the water that spilled off the land, and fishing the local waters turned Puget Sound into a magical place. Knowing the waters was one way to understand and connect with where we lived. Erik pointed out that the land controlled the waters just as much as the other way around, but it seemed like a chicken and egg question to me. Plentiful in rivers, lakes, saltwater, and beaver ponds, fish could be anywhere—even, I used to think, in almost any puddle that collected rain.

Knowing where to drop your line was the key to success. Years of experience and tuning in to the local fishing gossip had given Dad the keen sense of thinking like a fish and tipping the odds in his favor. The main trick was a willingness to improvise, he said. A lifetime of trial and error was best avoided by being born into a fishing family. Uncle Ted used to say the luck of a fisherman began before birth. Friends—who only had trial and error to rely on—sometimes returned with salmon smiles too. Accidents happen. In the absence of success, they concocted fishing stories. Fishing also connected us to other fishing fools obsessed enough to get up before the crack of dawn. You could always talk about fishing with someone who spoke the language. For Dad, it connected him to memories of fishing with Uncle Ted when they were young.

Burr lacked the good fortune of being born to a fishing family, and this trip would be his baptism into the realm of the silver horde—his introduction to a world of rippling waters, tidal currents, and fog banks. He'd learn an entirely new language: shakers, lunkers and June hogs; flood tides, ebb tides, and tide rips; mooching, jigging, and trolling; and plugs and spoons. He'd discover how to bait herring so it moved like a wounded fish, and he'd learn how to set the hook but let the fish run and tire itself out, if that's what it had a mind to do. Plumbing the mysteries of the deep, he'd learn the art of a well-placed bop on the head, which, of course, would spawn philosophical questions on whether fish feel pain. If nothing else, Burr would arrive home with herring scales stuck to his fingers.

When he'd first asked about fishing, I'd dismissed him with a vague promise to take him someday. But now I had a reason with legs under it, legs sturdy enough to make it happen. He'd never know this trip was about more than just keeping my promise. I'd broken an unwritten rule of friendship, and my guilt was calling me to account. Whatever I hooked, I'd hand the pole to Burr and hoped Dad would do the same as a courtesy to the novice.

The war wedged its way into salmon fishing just as it flooded everything else we'd taken for granted. The Navy was busier than ever on Puget Sound and planes flocked overhead. Still, once we were out on the water, the war seemed muted and distant. When luck grabbed your attention with a big fish, everything else vanished till you either landed or lost it. Rumor held that the War Production Board would requisition this year's entire commercial salmon catch to can for the troops. Certain areas of the Sound were closed for security reasons, and there was a prohibition against fishing at night. For us locals, the main frustration was gas rationing, which meant some of our more distant fishing holes were out of reach. Traditional derbies, like the ones sponsored by the two Seattle newspapers or the Ben Paris Company, were cancelled in 1942. Dad thought fishing for a prize was an insult to the magnificent salmon, but I was more pliable—who wouldn't like to win a car, an outboard motor, some cash, or even new fishing gear?

We'd saved our gas ration for the car ride to the water's edge. Local boathouses had increased their supply of motorboats in recent years, but without enough gas, rentals were in decline. One thing that didn't require a ration card was catching our own salmon. It only required a salmon license.

Going salmon fishing meant different things to different people. For Dad, it brought escape to a place where he could freely smoke cigars—one of life's greatest pleasures (or so he said) that he self-rationed for Mom's sake and anyone else who had a nose. Once we were calmly settled on the water, he routinely pulled out a stogie and lit up. One look at how his eyes followed the stream of smoke till the last whiff vanished told you he'd drifted away, along with the smoke, from whatever worried him. I wondered if we went fishing as much for cigars as salmon. Privately, I suspected cigar-smelling bait was a sure-fire way to *not* catch fish. Salmon are notorious for their acute sense of smell, but Dad wasn't the only one discouraged from smoking at home. On a calm day, a whiff of smoke might drift across the water from some other guy who didn't want to stink up his parlor either. No stinky stogie today, I hope. There was too much instruction required for Burr's first trip, and it might set a bad example that could get back to the Bouchers, raising tensions between them and Dad even further.

The first hint of the unexpected was Burr finishing his toast and eggs before Dad and I even sat down. He was like a racehorse, "chomping" at the bit. First in the car, he plastered his face against the window, pointing in the direction of Puget Sound like a hound on the hunt. We'd loaded the car with gear the night before. I couldn't imagine trying to lug all that stuff on a bus, not to mention coming home with a big slippery salmon. The driver would probably tell us to walk home, saying, "The bus is reserved for people who respect other people's noses." I loved the saltwater smell of a freshly caught salmon though.

I grabbed the sandwiches Mom made and we piled in the car before the rising sun silhouetted the jagged Cascades. Padded with layers of protection against the elements, Burr and I crammed together in the back seat, and I began answering his barrage of questions, sifting myths from facts. I explained that some things are better shown than told. Off to Ray's Boathouse we went, the car warming to our cause and window fog retreating as the defroster did its job.

"How do you catch salmon anyway?"

"There's too much to tell, so we'll just have to show you. Just relax a bit."

"But how do you know you're doing the right thing if you aren't catching anything?"

"We'll show you. Don't worry."

"Do they have to be a certain size to keep?"

"Jeez, Burr, it's like you have ants in your pants. Ease up, buddy."

Burr pretended to check his pants and announced, "No ants."

At Ray's Boathouse, fourteen and sixteen footers were hoisted onto a rusty carriage hooked to a winch cable and powered by a retired car engine that rattled them down the tracks into the water. The place was already hopping. More than one fisherman did the ants-in-the-pants dance with little containers of herring bait that swayed back and forth while they waited for their turn to launch. The old car engine ran on gas too and I wouldn't be surprised if rationing forced it back into retirement soon. Whenever that happened, the entire launch and retrieve process would be hand cranked using a pulley system like in the old days.

When our turn came, we scrambled over the sides and into the little boat. It was slightly heeled over on its keel, leaning on the two poles that kept boats from floating off the carriage till the occupants were ready. When we returned from fishing, the carriage would be sent down the tracks and submerged so we could float into place.

Sticking out of the water, the poles would help position the boat for the ride up. Today, our ride down was short due to the high tide. Once in the water we used the posts to push clear and gave the signal for the carriage to be pulled back up for the next boat. What the short ride lacked in amusement-park thrill was made up for by anticipating the fish of a lifetime. I never got tired of that wide-eyed feeling and hoped I never would. When the little boat was floating free, Dad took a bearing with his compass. If the fog closed in, the compass would be like an invisible rope pulling us back to where we started.

Suddenly adrift in a world of water, we organized our gear and wondered if it was light enough to legally fish in the morning glow. Synchronizing our trip with the tide and light was Dad's job. Our little boat was as familiar as if we owned her ourselves, and Dad always checked to make sure she was available on the day we wanted to go. We'd even named her. Some years back Dad took a shine to her because of the effortless way she rowed, and he began calling her Lydia. Erik thought he must've had a girlfriend named Lydia back in the old days. "Lydia was all woman," Dad let slip once. Her graceful transom was shaped like a wineglass, in perfect alignment with the rest of her slippery lines. Lydia was made for the water, and it wouldn't have surprised me if she refused to get back out one of these days.

Dad plunked down in the center seat and eased the oars into the locks while I found a safe place for our bag of herring. Scanning the compass, he peered north as the fog bank crept across the water toward the sunrise. He pointed Lydia to a spot about a half mile from the launch and struck up a steady row. Lydia seemed to know just where he wanted to go.

Taking a new person fishing was worlds away from going with somebody who knew what to do. Truth be told, I usually enjoyed someone catching their first salmon more than catching my own umpteenth. I could always go another time, and even though my umpteenth was only my seventh, I prized the rite of passage when somebody caught their first—the precise moment when the longing to do it again took root. Who could tell how those few moments of fishing chaos—the "fire drill" as we called it, when someone yelled, "Fish on, Fish on"—might change someone's life? After a day on the water, you think differently about the land.

"OK, what do we do now?" demanded Burr.

"Just a minute. We need to rig up and I'll show you how the reel works."

"I know how it works."

"Have you ever used one?"

"No, but I can tell just from looking."

"OK then smarty, you get a nasty backlash and you're on your own. Dad, are we going to mooch or troll here?"

"We'll have to troll because there's more than an hour before slack tide. Fish should be shallow this early, though."

"Here's a plug, Burr. It's a good choice for trolling and usually works if there are fish around. I'll show you how to tie it on behind the weight, or do you know how to do that too?"

"Show me."

"Watch closely while I wrap the loose end around the line six times then bring it back though this loop and cinch it tight. Did you follow that?"

"Got it."

"Now just pay out about sixty pulls of line as we troll along and put the pole in that holder."

"Can't I hold it?"

"Sure, but you'll get tired of that in a hurry."

"What's it feel like when a fish hits?"

I took his line and jerked it a few times, making the pole tip dance up and down like a branch waving in the wind. "Like this. Then you set the hook and start reeling, steady like, not giving the fish any slack. If you feel like it's not there, reel even faster 'cuz it might be taking a run at the boat. If you get a hookup, we'll coach you and tell you what to do while you play the fish. Don't worry."

Burr was first in the water. Then I got my pole ready, stripped off a few more than sixty pulls and placed the butt of my pole in a holder. Dad's brand-spanking-new Lucky Louie lure, still glistening in its package, lay patiently in his tackle box. He thought better of tying it on and busied himself instead with cutting the head off a herring at just the right angle to make it spin properly. After carefully inserting two hooks in the herring, he rested his pole on the gunwale with the butt in the bottom of the boat. He paused to examine how our lines were tracking behind the boat and decided that watching his pole while rowing was an invitation for unnecessary trouble.

"You guys catch one. Then I'll take a turn while you two make up a story about how you caught it."

Years ago, I'd learned to identify landmarks as a way of telling where we were on the water. If we caught a fish, knowing where we'd hooked it gave us a chance to find luck again. Who knew when there'd be another hungry fish just waiting for us to come back and feed it? We weren't far from shore, but I'd been on the Sound enough to know how completely disorienting fog could be, and it always unnerved me. There wasn't much when we launched, but it started to thicken up north and drift in our direction, alternately concealing one landmark and revealing another, like in a game of hide and seek. We might get lost in the fog for a while, but with Dad's experience, compass, and some advice from a lighthouse foghorn, we always returned safely. Two of my landmarks were already swallowed up by the fog, and the sun wasn't yet high enough to burn it off.

The tracks for the Great Northern Railway ran along the edge of Puget Sound, probably because it was the easiest place to put them in the days when giant trees ruled the land. We hadn't spotted any trains so far, but the International Limited to Vancouver BC was due a little after nine o'clock. Knowing that Grandpa Johannsen would've helped the passengers board the train at the King Street Station made me smile. It was yet one more connection to place that made me feel like I belonged. Hoping to see the bright headlight of the International snaking along the water's edge as I looked south toward Seattle, I saw Burr's pole take a dive and begin dancing. That kind of dance only comes from the powerful head shakes of a big salmon. Burr had a fish on, and we hadn't even discussed a pool for the first, the biggest, the most, or the weirdest. Dad stopped rowing and I frantically reeled up so as not to tangle lines with Burr.

"I know it hit like a ton of bricks but set the hook anyway. Give it a healthy jerk. Keep the pole tip up and keep reeling, and I'll get the net ready. Dad, will you please take the net? I don't want to be the one who loses his first fish. Jeez, Burr that looks like a good one, maybe it's a lunker."

"A what? I thought we were fishing for salmon."

"We are. That's just a name for a really big fish."

"How big does it have to be for it to be a lunker?"

"Stop talking and just reel. There's no rule for that. What would you say, Dad?"

"Oh, probably anything above twenty pounds," Dad suggested.

"Holy crap, I'm getting tired already and this thing is still running line off the reel."

"That's what lunkers do. Just keep the pole tip up, the line tight, and don't give it any slack."

"I think I'm gaining on it. Nope, there it goes again."

"Keep cranking."

"Jeez, how long is this going to take?"

"Nobody knows. Time stops while you play a big fish. It'll take as long as the fish decides, I guess. There's no point in checking your watch if time has actually stopped."

"Smart ass. Big help you are."

"Watch your mouth. My Dad's right here, you know."

"Sorry Mr. J."

Dad looked stern but didn't say anything. I'm sure he would've at home, especially if Mom was around. We were still within sight of land where moms and good manners held everything together, but rules slackened out on the water. I don't know if it was just that I couldn't help showing off or if I was gripped by a sincere need to be helpful, but in either case, the excitement of the "fire drill" had me barking orders, the same ones I would've silently barked to myself if I was the one with a big fish on.

"Just remember, you're really not in control, even when you think you are. The fish is."

"I think I see it. Did you see that splash? Something's following it."

Dad took charge, holding up the net like it was a rifle, loaded and ready to fire. "OK, Burr. Just keep pressure on the fish and if it wants to run again, don't panic. Let it run. I can tell when it's ready to be netted," he coached.

"OK. There it is again. See it about twelve feet out? Jeez, it looks huge."

"Yeah, it looks huge and it's looking tired. Try to keep it from running under the boat and keep that line tight. It's almost ready."

An explosive splash got all three of us wet and Dad netted what was left of the fish. Burr fell back onto his seat, exhausted more from excitement than from the pull of the fish. He was as puzzled as I'd ever seen him and he looked at both of us, silently mouthing what we knew he was asking.

"A seal got it," I volunteered, "or got most of it, and it was a real honest-to-gosh lunker. Well, it was a second ago."

Burr wondered if half a lunker counted for anything. Dad counseled that fishing was really a quest for the unexpected, even when the unexpected seemed like a sure thing, just inches from the net. I couldn't tell if Burr was disappointed or not, but the charge from this battle fueled a babbling that lasted for the next fifteen minutes. I could tell right then and there that this was a story that wouldn't need any embellishment. It was dramatic and complete— just as it happened.

"So, what do we do with this unlucky lunker now?" Burr asked.

"We keep it. There's plenty of meat on the half the seal let you keep. We know what the seal will be doing with its half, probably already did it."

"What?"

"Chow time."

"We'll dress it out when we get home."

"Dress it?"

"You'll see."

"So, Dad, is it your turn to try to catch both halves of something?"

"You bet." Our captain had decided we should move to a spot where mooching might be more productive than trolling now that slack tide was almost on us. Since he'd already rigged up for mooching, Dad got his line in the water as soon as we stowed Burr's fish and reorganized our gear. My job was to explain mooching and help Burr change his rig, but he was full of questions.

"Well, since I caught the most important part of a lunker, why don't we keep trolling?"

"You want a whole fish don't you, one with both a nose and a tail?" Dad explained that mooching worked best during the slack tide, and we needed to take advantage of it before the tide got running too fast again.

I showed Burr how to cut and hook a herring and how to tell when he hit bottom so he could reel up a few cranks to keep the bait moving and entice another lunker. Lo and behold, Burr was the first one to get a hit. Beginner's luck again, I guess.

"It's not a lunker," he complained.

"Well, with mooching, you never know what you'll get. It might even be a shark."

"A shark…really? How big do they get around here?"

"Not big. Dogfish don't get big, but they can trash your line with their sandpaper skin."

"I suppose there are whales out here too?"

"Yeah sometimes."

"Those killer whales with the giant fin?"

"Yeah, we see some once in a while but the only thing they kill are salmon, I think."

"You think? With a name like that they must go after something bigger than salmon."

"What about it, Dad? What else do they eat?"

"They go after all sorts of things like seals and porpoises. Even baby whales, from what I hear."

"We spotted one or two grays in the early spring. They don't travel in packs like the killers. We've never seen them in here though, have we Dad?"

"No."

Burr reeled steadily during our reminiscing. "It feels different this time."

"The pole looks different too. Maybe it's just a clump of seaweed. Keep cranking though. You never know. As Dad always says, 'You need to be ready when luck comes.'"

"Here it comes. See it?"

"That's the weirdest thing I've ever seen," Burr said, genuinely surprised.

Peering over the gunwale, Dad announced it was a ratfish, something closely related to a shark. If we were the first humans to see one, we'd have called it a ratfish too. Burr asked what other spooky creatures swam the depths, and we both admitted we didn't really know. Puget Sound was a big place. While we were distracted, the fog had snuck up, hiding all of my landmarks. It now seemed intent on coming for us too, making us disappear from everything except ourselves. It slithered across the water in a maneuver so ghostlike, it was hard to tell if it was coming at all. Then, it suddenly swallowed us, boat and all.

We were lost in the belly of the fog bank, and only Dad's compass knew the way home. The doors to our surroundings closed without a sound, and we were completely engulfed, without even the sun to reveal north from south. Up was down, east was west, and our entire world was reduced to a sixteen-foot boat and the three lives it held. I'd been fogged in before and lived to fish again, but Burr hadn't. Fog changes the known into the unknown. It transforms a know-it-all into a no-nothing-at-all and sometimes people even stop

223

believing their compass. I could tell Burr was more than a little uncomfortable.

The air was soft and muted, and we strained our ears though the mist, listening for some sound to poke a hole in the blinding gray. Soon it came. Barely audible at first, we heard the methodical beat of the pistons pulling the International along the shoreline toward the Canadian border. Even though I knew it couldn't be, the train sounded like it was heading straight down the tracks for a little boat trapped between the rails. That's how disorienting fog can be. It was unimaginable, but here I was imagining the impossible collision between boat and train, and Burr's eyes grew wider and wider as the sound of our obliteration intensified. There's no way to explain the mischievous and otherworldly sound to anyone who hasn't experienced it. I've tried. But they just looked at me like I was nuts and looked away when I humiliated myself by trying even harder. I'd eventually give up completely and try to restore my credibility by changing the topic to something more rational.

Burr's knuckles were white from gripping the gunwale as tight as he could. "I know this can't be, but it sounds like that train is going to run right over us."

"It won't. It's just something the fog does to the sound when it takes away your sight. It makes your mind go haywire. It'll pass and we'll still be here waiting for another lunker."

"I know, I know, but it's freaky to not believe what you know is true."

Once the International passed, the only sounds were the honking of the West Point foghorn and a faint warning from a ferry up north. The thing was, nobody ever got run over by a train on the water, but every year several people were hit by large boats doing the business of Puget Sound. The possibility of being overrun by a ferry in the fog was especially worrisome if you happened to be fishing in a ferry lane. The lure of salmon was so powerful that some people lost their heads when the fog settled in and failed to clear out of the shipping lanes. Neither the ferry lanes nor the shipping channels were marked with fencing. Dad had a healthy respect for things that could go wrong on the water, and I can't remember him even having a close call.

We often joked that fish would strike just when you took your mind off trying to catch them. So, I grabbed a sandwich in my left hand and hung onto the pole with my right. Worked like a charm. An unmistakable wiggle on the tip of the pole signaled a salmon, mouthing the bait. All was silent during the breath-holding seconds before I set the hook. The sandwich had done its job and I dropped it into the watery bilge. The fight was on. I'd set the hook according to Dad's textbook advice and after a few head shakes the fish seemed to go dead, but I kept reeling just like it said on page two of the family textbook—don't give it any slack. After regaining its strength, it came alive, pulling off line, and making the pole sashay up and down. Then it paused again like it was teasing—testing me to see how well I'd learned my lessons. I told myself I'd do everything right and if I lost the fish, that's just the way things go sometimes.

Dad came alive, sensing this fish was something special. He knew not to say a word unless I was close to doing something fishingly stupid. Burr reeled up and Dad stood at attention with the net in hand. Most times I never got nervous about losing a fish till I saw that it was within netting distance of the boat. Fishing teaches that too much excitement often gets in the way of good judgment. But with an audience, it's harder to balance excitement with good judgment. Credibility and reputation are on the same line as the fish, and the entire neighborhood will know how you faired by noon tomorrow.

"Dad, how much line is on this reel?"

"About two hundred yards. Why?"

"It's ripped off yards but is still going."

"Just tighten down on the drag a bit and hold on. If it wants to run, there's nothing you can do about it. Wouldn't you want to run if you had a hook in your lip? You've got to respect a fish that can break you off."

"Yeah, I know Dad, but I want this one bad."

I heaved the pole up, then reeled frantically as I lowered the tip back down, and I began to make some progress. Would the knots hold? Was the drag too tight or too loose? Would it rub the line on the keel and break off? Burr watched with his recently experienced eyes and was first to notice the dorsal fin cutting through the water. The fish did a one eighty in the air, splashing down and reminding us the battle was far from over. We shouldn't count our chickens just yet. At that moment I remembered my silent oath to hand over the pole to Burr.

"Here you go," I said, aiming the butt end where I thought his belly button should be. Take it. You need this fish. It might be the other half of your lunker. Same as before, pole tip up, don't give it slack, and keep reeling."

Without saying a word, Burr took over like the pro he'd just become. Dad's calm voice chimed in with sporadic advice but basically let Burr handle his destiny. I grabbed the net and readied my congratulations for when I hoisted the thrashing fish and laid it at Burr's feet.

"This is in your hands, Burr. You tell us when you think it's ready."

"OK. It's still got some fight," he said.

"When it's on the surface, you'll know it's ready, and then you can steer it by the nose to the boat. Don't be surprised if it tries to take off again when it sees the net or the side of the boat, though. They often do that, especially the big ones, and especially if the boat is bright white with the sun blazing on it. It's not a welcoming sight to a fish."

"I can do this," he reminded with a voice of experience and authority.

Dad warned me, like he almost always did, not to stab at it with the net. "That'll spook it. The fish will tell you when it's ready."

"OK, Dad."

The fish lay on its side with one pectoral finning the air. I thought Dad would give me the go-ahead, but he remained a silent observer, figuring I should know what to do by now. Sliding the net under the surface, I smoothly scooped the fish into its braided mouth. I don't know what was louder, the thrashing of the fish or our whooping it up, with Burr still hanging on tight to the pole and me to the net.

"Hey Dad, are we done for the day or are we gonna fish some more?"

"Let's bottom fish for a while, OK?"

By the time we called it a day, we'd made quite a haul, pulling up "half" the creatures that lived in the zoo at the bottom of Puget Sound. Eventually the current became too strong for our bait to reach the bottom. Dad consulted his compass again and teased with one of his often-repeated jokes. "Sometimes people get so confused when the fog closes in that they stop believing what the compass is telling them and row right off the edge of the earth."

Burr gave me a, 'what the hell' look, to which I responded, "Dad likes to scare the hell out of people who think the earth is round,"

227

adding my bad joke to Dad's. Just as I began to think Dad's compass needle had become as confused by the fog as me, the tracks leading up to Ray's Boathouse appeared. The trolley cradle trundled down to get us, and we grabbed on tight to the posts. Up we went to show off our catch. Our time on the water had restored my carefree spirit, holding the blackout fires at bay.

26. *Loose Lips*

THE MORNING BIRDS ACCOMPANIED Greta's thumping as she did her chores, one of which was cleaning the upstairs bathroom. There was no set breakfast time on Saturday, so I put a few finishing touches on the B-17, readying it for a test flight over the English Channel. Greta's ruckus made it all but impossible to concentrate on my flight plan, so I cut it short and headed for the mess hall. I stuck my nose in the bathroom doorway on my way downstairs.

"Why all the banging around today? You upset about something?"

"Yeah, as a matter of fact, I'm upset about you."

"What'd I do now?"

"It's what you *don't* do. How come you never have to clean the bathroom?"

"It's not on my chore list."

"How'd you pull that off?"

"I don't know. I guess I wasn't nominated."

"That could change, you know."

"Don't you remember when we all sat down and divvied up the chores?"

"Sort of."

"Nobody asked me to do bathrooms."

"That's just it. Why do you think it is that nobody asked you? I think it's because you're a boy."

"I don't know why. I have my chores too, you know."

"Yeah, eating cookies and making model airplanes?"

"No, seriously. I have to clean up branches that come down, mow the lawn, and rake leaves."

"With our postage-stamp yard that should only take you about fifteen minutes a year."

"Well, you might think so, but how much time do you spend on the bathroom anyway? Not as much as I do lawn mowing and leafing, I bet. Mowing lasts from April to October, in case you hadn't noticed. And when the leaves start falling, they keep dropping for weeks, because different trees drop at different times. Then, when the leaves get wet, they start sticking together like a big heavy blob. You ever seen how big the pile gets?"

"Yeah, you mean the pile you and your friends spend hours jumping into, pretending you can fly like Superman?"

"Something tells me this isn't about who cleans the bathroom. If I ever join up, I'm sure I'll have plenty of time to make it up to you by doing latrine duty at some military base somewhere."

"Oh great, that'll be a big help."

"So, tell me, what's really on your mind?"

"Mosquitoes."

"What? Mosquitoes? Did you find some in the bathroom?"

"No, I was looking at some under the microscope and got to wondering whether they have a purpose."

"You've got to be kidding me. Why would anybody care?"

"I don't know if anybody does, but isn't it curious? They just don't seem at all useful. In fact, they seem to do more harm than good, spreading disease for instance."

"What should they be doing, fighting the Japs? Can't they just *be*?"

"I guess they could, but everything seems to have a purpose except mosquitoes. They fight everybody."

"Are you telling me this is something you're really worried about?"

"Not worried exactly, just curious."

"And that's what led to all the noise? OK then, I can solve your problem and satisfy your curiosity at the same time. They're bat food, probably dragonfly food, and bird food too. The bat's purpose is to eat mosquitoes and the mosquito's purpose is to be there for the bats when they get hungry. That's how nature works."

"That hardly seems like a purpose, live to be eaten and live to eat. There must be more to it than that."

"There probably is. I don't know. Maybe it's the way everything is connected, how all living beings depend on each other. I just made it up, but it sounded pretty good, don't you think?"

"Not bad for an obnoxious big brother. You're talking about yourself, I assume? You eat to live and live to eat."

"I'm just helping out, giving all those things I eat a purpose."

"You're so thoughtful."

"Thanks. I thought you'd see things that way."

Suddenly spent, Greta absentmindedly wiped the door handle with a rag reeking of ammonia. The conversation may have run its course, but Greta's shoulders told me there was more on her mind than the division of chores and the purpose of mosquitoes. They were clearly just the cover story for whatever she was stewing about.

"Greta, I wish you'd come clean about what's really bothering you. It's not about me or mosquitoes, is it? You're beating the bathroom into submission when all you need to do is clean it."

"Give me a break."

"You know what Mom always says about keeping things inside?"

"I know. Maybe I'm more like Dad and Erik in that way."

"Well, let me know if you want to talk about whatever it is you're keeping inside. I'm going for beans."

"Going for beans?"

"It's a railroad saying I learned from Grandpa. It means I'm going to eat."

When I showed up in the kitchen, Mom was rummaging around but doing it quietly, like she was pretending to look for something.

"Morning, Scott. Get a good night's sleep?"

"Yup. Why? Are you sending me on a mission?"

"No. Just asking. What are you up to today?"

"Not sure. I'll spend some time with Burr, probably in the park, and do my route later this afternoon. Have you talked with Greta yet this morning?"

"Yes. Why?"

"Just wondered. Did she seem OK?"

"She seemed to be. Why are you asking?"

"Oh, nothin'."

Mom always knew nothin' really meant somethin'. After dishing up my oatmeal she hightailed it upstairs for some detective work. She couldn't possibly have missed Greta's loud battle with the bathroom, but all was now quiet, and the smell of ammonia had probably evaporated. Mom would track down whatever was bothering her with some innocent-sounding question, like, "What are you planning to wear to church this Sunday?" She was a human lie detector and could probably get a good idea about what was wrong just by sniffing the air in Greta's room. Finding out exactly what it was might require the third degree, but that wasn't Mom's style. According to Erik, Dad mastered the third degree long before I was born, but he wasn't here this morning. Besides, a heavy hand doesn't always produce the best result. I could see the defeat in Mom's eyes as she returned to the kitchen and asked me what was going on upstairs.

"What were you two talking about? Sounded like an argument."

"Not an argument exactly. More like a difference of opinion."

"About what?"

"Well, Greta seems to think I should be cleaning bathrooms instead of her."

"You certainly could, you know."

"I know, but I've got all my chores, and I don't think Greta would really like to trade."

"How do you know? Did you ask?"

"No, but I just know."

"Well, if you do want to trade, I'm sure something could be worked out."

"OK, Mom. You can be our attorney for the negotiations."

"Attorney for both sides? I don't think it works that way. Finish your cereal and get busy on your Saturday stuff."

"OK, Sarge."

I went back upstairs to get my things and saw Greta leaning against my doorjamb. She pushed inside after me.

"Sit down," she ordered.

I obeyed like the dutiful brother I was.

"Can you keep a secret?"

This was easy. Figuring I'd had more practice keeping a secret over the past number of weeks than I had for my entire life, I said, "Sure."

"Crisscross your heart and hope to die?"

"If that's what you want, but I'm not hoping to die anytime soon, if you don't mind."

"Cut the crap. Don't be smart, OK?"

"Whoa. Are you practicing for a vocabulary test? I've never heard you use that word. So, what's this secret?"

"You know my friend Jen?"

"Yeah, she's kinda cute. I've been waiting for her to grow up."

"I said, 'cut the crap.' She's got an older brother, Arnie, who's friends with that guy you met on the bridge a few weeks back."

"Uh huh, I know who he is. So, what about this Arnie?"

"Last time I was over there, he came home with his face all puffy. It was black and blue, and he had a couple of cuts and a big scab on one of his ears."

"Not surprising for a guy like him. Did the butler do it or did a car run into him during a blackout?"

"Well, Jen and I were talking about it, and it came out that Lashbaugh was the guy driving the car that ran into him."

"Simon doesn't drive."

"You know what I mean. Jen says that's the guy who did his face."

"When did she tell you this?"

"A week ago."

"That's interesting. That's the day after we all went over to Simon's house when Arnie barged in and called Erik the firebug. Simon had been denying everything."

"Think that's why Simon beat him up?"

"That's a pretty good guess."

"I can see your wheels turning."

"Gives me an idea. I wonder if Arnie knows something about the fires and might have a reason to talk now?"

"Even if he does, how're you gonna get him to say anything?"

"Not sure. Do you know anything about what he does when he comes home, where he goes…things like that?"

"Not really, but I suppose I could find out something from Jen. And if I do find out something, can you keep it a secret?"

"Sure, but why should this be a secret?"

"I just don't want to get anybody in trouble, especially Jen or me for that matter."

"Well, somebody may already be in big, big trouble. Not you, of course."

"Don't get me in trouble then."

"You? In trouble? You're never too young to start."

"Just stop it. You're not as funny as you think you are."

"OK. Just see what you can find out about him without being too obvious."

"All right."

It seemed like an entirely new window on things had opened up. At long last a suspect had been revealed and I could barely contain my anticipation about what we might find when we drew back the curtains.

27. A Better Mousetrap

IF CATCHING MICE IS your game, just go to the store and buy an old-fashioned mousetrap. As Burr said, it doesn't need improving. If, on the other hand, you're going after two-legged prey, things can get complicated. The culprit must be enticed, nudged, tricked, hounded, suckered, and sometimes even threatened. I didn't know if Arnie, Lashbaugh's loose-lipped buddy, was the king of culprits, but I was guessing he knew something about the fires and probably knew who'd been setting them. If only we could get him talking. In that never-never land between waking and sleeping, a plan began to take shape, and by morning it seemed like part of a crazy detective show.

We'd try to spook him. That was it. We'd convince him that somebody was on to him and that he was being watched. We'd keep it up till he cracked and have fun doing it. Nothing violent, of course. We'd do it all with paper, slipping notes into his locker and tossing rocks into his yard with notes attached. We could mail worrying notes to his parents and tack them to telephone poles in his neighborhood. Greta could even smuggle notes into Arnie's room when she hung out with his sister at their house. Maybe not though. I did say I wouldn't get her in trouble. No confrontations and no violence, just undercover and out of sight. That was the plan. By the time the sun threw off its covers I'd composed a long list:

They go easier on you if you come clean.

What sort of friend rearranges your face like that?

Just being there makes you an accomplice.

They know you're the firebug.

Not telling is as bad as doing it.

Coming clean could make you a hero.

There might be a reward.

We know more than you think.

What would the neighbors say?

Ever see the inside of a jail cell?

Do you have a future?

Just get it off your chest.

Are you sleeping well these days?

Some people might take things into their own hands.

Make your family proud.

You'll feel a great sense of relief.

"Scott, get up." I was so engrossed with my list that Mom's wakeup warning barely registered. "You'll be late for school."

The storm of ideas pelted my brain as I got dressed and brushed my teeth. The flurry of thoughts made it difficult to match my buttons with the proper buttonholes and didn't even let me crack my soft-boiled egg in peace. I was so distracted that Mom wondered if I was there at all.

"Where's your mind today?" she asked, with a hint of concern.

"Right here behind my eyeballs. Same place it was yesterday."

You wouldn't want to get in even deeper.

The list kept growing with no sign of stopping:

What if your parents find out?

Simon only lives a few blocks away.

How's your face doing?

"I want to look behind your eyeballs just to check," joked Mom.

"Go ahead, here."

"Well, at least everything looks OK."

Do you know a good lawyer?

Don't become the fall guy.

Here's a number you can call.

"Think you're awake enough to find school today?"

"Same place it was yesterday, right?"

"I hope so for your sake. Get going and take your mind with you. I don't want it lying around here all day and gathering dust."

Go to the authorities before they come to you.

Guilty as charged.

Surprisingly, Burr was actually ready when I came by for our walk to school. He must've started eating breakfast right after finishing dinner the night before or maybe his fishing success had reset his internal clock. Catching your first salmon can have that effect on some people, opening your eyes to a completely new and marvelous world.

"Morning, Burr. I've got a job for you."

"A job? I don't work cheap, you know."

"Oh, I think you might do this one for free. Here's the deal. I have an idea that might crack the case for the blackout fires. I think Lashbaugh's buddy, Arnie, knows something about who might be doing it. I've got a plan to smoke him out, and I think he might just be ready to talk after examining himself in the mirror."

"How did all this come about?"

"Never mind. Just trust me on this, OK?"

"Better make it good."

238

"Oh, it will be. The idea is to make him feel like a suspect—like he's being watched and even followed. If he gets spooked enough, I figure he'll start worrying about what might happen if he *doesn't* say something."

"Sounds like a bluff to me."

"It is. But I think we can pull it off if we stay at it long enough."

"So, what's the plan?"

"OK, so we start hounding him with notes—at school, at home, and everywhere we can think of, like places he goes regularly. Here, I made a list of things we can put on the notes, and I know we can come up with more. They just keep coming to me with no end in sight. Feel free to add your own."

"You mean something like this? *Come with us. We want to talk to you down at the station.*"

"Exactly."

"Or how about this, *Scotty Johannsen Wants You.*"

"No, we can't use that. Even if he suspects, we don't want him to know who's rattling his cage. But we could use this: *Arnie Johnson, Uncle Sam Wants YOU!* That would get him thinking. It's even true in a way."

"So, my job is to think more things up?"

"Not exactly. You can if you want, but your main job is to make a contraption to shower him with notes and startle the bejesus out of him when he least expects it. You could do something with trip wires or make a smaller version of your catapult that would launch a blizzard of notes to rain down on him—nothing that could hurt him though. It's sort of like how Tokyo Rose tried to get our troops shaking in their boots. I think he walks his dog in the park, and Greta's going to help figure out some places we could set something like that up."

"Greta?"

"Yeah, she's our insider, but I can't talk about that now. What d'ya think? We could be like the hounds chasing the fox."

"It does sound like fun. I'll start working on something right after school. I don't know why we're even going to school today with such nation-saving work to do."

"I guess that's part of our cover. Nothing to see here, just business as usual, kids being kids."

Burr sidled off to first period muttering something about dressing me up like a G-man so I could hang out under a streetlamp with my hat pulled down so far that Arnie wouldn't recognize me. He made it sound like Edward G. Robinson in a gangster movie, except nobody could carry off playing him, especially me. Besides, it's hard to imagine Edward G. playing a G-man. He's usually on the other side of the law.

Two days after our half-baked plan came out of the oven there was another fire—this one in a row of garages, one of which *The Seattle Times* used as a paper shack. The shack was connected to a real estate office that was hitched to the Tastie Home Bakery. Fire crews put it out before it was able to spread to the attached buildings, but this was a bold escalation that threatened a well-traveled street and could've incinerated an entire block.

Like a mysterious illness, the fires seemed to be spreading, and more and more people were convinced the firebug was setting them as beacons to direct Japanese bombers. According to Dad, the authorities still hadn't made any progress identifying a suspect, despite their stepped-up patrols. This fire removed all doubts that the fires were intentionally set. Some even went so far as to say that our neighborhood had become a second front in the war. Of course, none of us believed that, but the unnerving chatter left us even more worried than we'd been.

28. Deployment

AFTER DINNER, I HEADED upstairs to write notes to mail to Arnie's parents. My crime-fighting career had become an obsession, a nuisance that interfered with my everyday horsing around. I'd hoped that getting the notes out of my head and onto paper would release me to think about something else, but it wasn't working. The ideas just kept coming and coming and coming.

Your friends can't help you now.

We never sleep, how are you sleeping?

Eyes are everywhere.

I wanted my brain to give it a rest, but it just wouldn't stop. Giving in, I decided I'd do just a couple more.

No place to hide.

Fire can burn the firebug.

I had three options for mailing the notes: taking them to the post office; depositing them in the letter box tacked to the telephone pole at the end of our street; or posting them in our personal mailbox and putting the red flag up for our mail carrier to retrieve them. I didn't trust the flag, but the heavy satisfying clunk of the pole-box flap seemed to emphasize that the notes were safe and sound. Even better, using the pole box avoided potential questions from Mom or Dad about why the red flag was in the up position. Our regular mail carrier, Chad, who'd delivered our mail as long as I could remember, might question the increase in red flags too.

Sleepy-eyed, Greta wandered down the hall, giving me a chance to ask what she'd learned about Arnie's comings and goings.

"How's the spying going? Got anything yet?"

"Maybe."

"Let's have it."

"Well, I know the alley he usually uses to go to Simon's house, and I figured out that he often stops by the Shislers to see if the paperboy missed their porch again. When he finds their paper in the shrubs, he steals it."

"I don't think he'll be seeing much of Simon for a while. Anything else, like does he have a girlfriend he visits?"

"I don't know about that, but he does go to the Ice Creamery regularly to hang out."

"That's good stuff. Maybe we can use it. Ever thought of working for the Secret Service?"

"Sounds like I am already."

James knew Arnie's locker number, so today I'd begin my campaign by slipping the first note through the louvers near the top of his locker. I visualized a quick flick of my wrist, fast enough for the note to slip in and fall inside without anyone noticing, even with a hall full of kids. They say good athletes do that sort of visualizing. I picked up my pace, but when I was about thirty feet away, I mentally kicked myself for not practicing when the hallways were empty. Crap. Just like a shot bouncing off the rim, my note struck the fins and fell to the floor. Not wanting to call attention to myself, I left it lying there and walked casually on. Writing the notes on stiff card paper would help me avoid a rim shot next time.

On the way to art class, I reviewed my hallway performance like it was being judged at the Olympics and reassured myself that it was merely the qualifying round. Miss Pershawnsky had a special gift when it came to art duds like me. I'd sit there waiting for inspiration, and she'd cruise by, saying "Just try something." Emphasizing color, line, shape, and texture, she tried to light a fire under all of us, doling out compliments, suggestions, and encouragement like it was kindling. Sometimes we'd catch fire and sometimes not.

If you were doing something, anything—even twitching the fingers of your drawing hand—she'd cruise right on by after dropping her inspirational nugget. If nothing was twitching, get ready to be pestered. By the end of class, I was twitching away, trying to fill out Arnie's note cards without being seen.

At lunch I tracked down Burr. "Hey, mastermind. Got anything yet?"

"Relax, I'll start on something when I get home. I've got some ideas though."

"Like what?"

"We could put a trip wire near the ground where he'd never see it. When he comes along and trips the wire, it'll release a box of notes from somewhere overhead."

"Yeah, that's the kind of stuff I was thinking of. Got anything else?"

"Well, the catapult idea has possibilities too. I could make a small one we could set up without too much problem. We could fold up the notes like spit wads and he'd get showered with them."

"Might be the first shower he's had in weeks. What if the wads don't open?"

"We'd have to experiment with the folding."

"When will you be ready?"

"Probably a few days at most."

"I'll be waiting."

By fourth period I'd recopied several notes onto three by five cards and was ready for another assault. I asked to be excused for the lavatory, which was just around the corner from Arnie's locker. Not a soul in sight and the note went straight in. No muss, no fuss. It was the first shot in a campaign that might drive the fox to ground. Over the next week I managed to get four more notes into his locker. The stiff cards were a big improvement, and like a basketball pro, I got so I could sink the shot without even breaking stride. I assumed that Arnie would see the notes when he opened his locker, but then I started worrying they might pile up with whatever else was composting in the bottom. At least he'd have to see the notes during locker inspections, if not before.

After a few days of this, I had no idea if the locker notes and mailings were having any effect, and I figured we needed a new tactic. Greta discovered that Arnie was a creature of habit. Like most of us, he nearly always took the shortcut through the ravine to visit his friends and traipsed the same alley to and from school. Springing one of Burr's contraptions in the park seemed like it would offer more anonymity than an alley ambush. In either case, timing was critical. Whatever Burr's contraption did, it had to happen to Arnie rather than some stranger or an inquisitive raccoon. We needed the best intelligence Greta could get.

Burr rushed together a mini version of his catapult and took several days to work the bugs out of the trip mechanism before we gave it a go in the park. It required both of us, at full huffing and puffing strength, to roll it out of his yard and hide it in the bushes near the trail. But on our first trial, we knew it was a miserable failure and a colossal waste of time.

Even if Greta was able to pinpoint when and where we were likely to find Arnie, it would be like fishing on dry land. We'd still have to be ready when luck came. I wish somebody would invent one of those Dick Tracy wrist radio thingamajigs for real so Greta could ring me the minute Arnie left the house. Maybe when the war was over, wrist radios would become an everyday thing, and we could talk to anyone anytime we wanted.

After dinner, I kept busy finding ways to avoid my homework and eventually wandered into Greta's room to check on her cure for Polio.

"Any closer to a cure?"

"Cure for what?"

"Polio, of course."

"Who said I was working on one?"

This seemed to irritate her, and she turned away after flashing me a "get out of here" look. I felt invisible just standing there.

"Don't you have something better to do?" she asked, still facing away.

"Yeah, but I'm not doing it very well."

She swung back around and glared.

"What are you talking about?"

"This note thing with Arnie is more difficult than I thought. The notes are easy, but the ambushing is a problem."

"Thought you and your friends were experts at ambushing."

"It's not that. It's setting up in the right place at the right time. It's a lot of work for a small chance of success."

"Know what? You guys are just too smart for your own good."

"What?"

"There's an easier way to do it."

"How?"

"This may sound crazy but aren't these crazy times? Here's what you do. Get a small box and cram it full of notes. Then you can wrap it up like a present with Arnie's name on it and toss it off the bridge right before he comes along. If nothing else, it might unnerve him and get him thinking he's being tracked. Easy, huh?"

"That's good. Really good. But we still wouldn't know exactly when to do it. What would we do, just wait there for days for the wildlife to come into our sights?"

"Well, it would be a waiting game, but it's like science…much patience is required. Besides, you did say you were in it for the long haul. Just think of all the time you'll save not having to haul one of Burr's contraptions around. Arnie nearly always walks his dog in the park after he gets home from school, and I think I know where he goes. That would be the best time to try."

"That's just great, but I have to do my paper route about then. Crap."

"You'd only have to do it once. What about Burr?"

"I don't know if he'd be ready or willing to carry it off by himself. What about you?"

"Me? You've got to be kidding. I thought I was supposed to be working on the cure."

"You could take some time off and work on a cure for the blackout fires."

"Well, check with Burr first, and then get back to me."

Sure enough, Burr balked at doing it by himself. He was worried about getting in trouble for throwing something off the bridge, which was a big no-no. He wouldn't be the first to get busted for that either. Periodically, we sailed our model planes off the bridge to see how they flew. Sometimes, we'd even set them on fire and pretend they were in a death spiral after getting shot up in a dogfight. The neighbors who reported us didn't appreciate how much research had gone into making these spectacles look realistic. Who knew when practice such as this might save a future pilot's life? Burr's refusal to do the deed left few options. I could delay my route or rush through it, risking angry customers who might second guess their decision to give me a big fat tip. Or I could beg and bribe Greta.

"Greta, is there anything I can do for you?"

"Huh?"

"I mean is there something you really, really want?"

"What's with you? It's not even my birthday. Oh, I get it. Burr won't do it, right?"

"Right."

"What's the big deal anyway? Aren't the locker notes and mailings doing the job?"

"I know, I know. I just want to do everything I can to get him to talk. I don't know what his breaking point is."

"Or if he even has one. Maybe he'll think it's some sort of prank by silly fifth graders."

"Maybe, but I still want to try. So, are you with me on this or not?"

"I guess, but you have to make a promise, in case I get in trouble."

"What kind of promise?"

"Repeat after me."

"I, Scott Johannsen, and big brother to Greta Johannsen, promise to do everything in my power to defend, stick up for, and say good things about her, the best little sister in the world. That's what I want."

"Do I have to?"

"You have a problem with that?"

"Can I change something first."

"What?"

"I want a part about being the best big brother in the world."

"OK. Do it."

"I, Scott Johannsen, and best big brother in the world to Greta Johannsen, promise to do everything in my power to defend and stick up for her, the best little sister in the world."

"You forgot the part about saying good things."

"Do I have to?"

"That's the deal."

I filled in the missing part and ended my recitation with a good laugh.

"You have a bunch of notes ready to go? I have a box we can use."

"As a matter of fact, I do. I'll get 'em."

I'd added a few new ones like the one suggesting he apply for a job with the Japanese, and an even better one that included a phone number to call for the reward. The rest were just copies of the ones I'd flicked through the louvers and dropped in the mailbox, a little repetition to drive the point home.

It took nearly a week for Greta, Arnie, and the planets to line up, but when they did, she timed it perfectly, according to her, while I labored under the weight of Thursday's *Seattle Times*.

"You should've seen him. He snatched up the box like a kid in a candy store. He didn't even look up to see where it came from."

"How did you time it right?"

"I pretty much just guessed."

"Would love to have been there. Thanks sis."

"I kind of like this underground resistance stuff. What's next?"

"More locker notes, mailings, and more waiting." Tightening the screws, I figured Arnie's breaking point had to be close at hand.

29. Taking the Bait

"SOUP'S ON," YELLED DAD. Taking my place at the table, I was pleased to see that it really was soup. A hearty vegetable variety of some sort, only Mom knew for sure, and I don't think giving it a fancy name would've made it any tastier. It was warm and filling, exactly the way soup should be on a cool day.

"Either of you kids know anybody who might be crank calling?"

"No, Mom. Why?" My eyes slithered over to meet Greta's.

"How about you, Scott?"

"No, Mom."

"Well, some guy called asking if this was PLAZA 6-6586. He must have known it was since he dialed it, and when I asked who was calling, he hung up. That's happened twice in the past few days."

"Sounds like a prank to me," offered Dad.

"Must've been," said Greta as she slurped her soup.

Both Greta and I asked to be excused as soon as politely possible and charged upstairs almost on top of each other.

Greta turned on me as soon as we were out of ear shot. "You didn't use our phone number on one of the notes, did you?" she hissed.

"Yeah, I did. I wasn't thinking, I guess."

"You guess? I guess not. I thought you didn't want him to know it was you."

"I thought we could trick him with a number to call for a reward. Maybe he won't figure it out. He's not too sharp and it's just a number. How will he know it's ours?"

"Forget that. He'll know as soon as somebody answers saying, 'This is the Johannsens. Can I help you?'"

"That's true. You think it's finally him, though? Has he cracked?"

"No way to know for sure if he won't stay on the line long enough to ask."

It did sound like he might be circling the bait, but like Dad says, "Luring them is one thing, hooking is another, and landing them is a feat in itself."

"Well, do you think we should just keep waiting, or should we try to answer every phone call when we're home?" Greta asked.

"I figure we have another option," I said. What if we confess our scheme to Mom and Dad and let them handle the phone calls if they keep coming?" Mom's friendly voice could turn a gangster into a pile of rose petals and entice him over for tea, and even though Dad might sound gruff, he's as skilled as a surgeon when reeling in a fish. No matter what, it would be out of our hands once we told. "Let's sleep on it, Greta."

"Keep your snoring to yourself, OK?"

"Aw, you know how I like to share."

"Put a pillow over your face and share with yourself."

"How do I do that if I'm asleep?"

The next morning, just as we left for school, Greta grabbed me, forgetting that she was holding all her school things with the same hand. Retrieving her supplies, we flicked off a few wet leaves before returning everything to her bag.

"What do you think?" she asked.

"I think we should tell them, but only if we're sure it's Arnie. Are you going over to Jen's today after school?"

"Yeah."

"Try to find out what's going on with him when you're visiting Jen, OK?"

"Sounds good. We'll meet up and talk after school, OK?"

Preoccupied as I was with the expectation of getting Arnie to talk, the day seemed impossibly long. Was he the lunker or the bait needed to catch the lunker? Just like with fishing though, nothing at all might come of it and we'd come home empty handed.

When I finished my route later than usual, Greta was already home and dinner was almost on the table. Dessert came and went, and Mom asked what we were still doing, sitting at the table.

"You actually find your parents interesting?"

"Not a chance," I said. "Get any more of those prank calls?"

"Why are you so interested?" demanded Dad. "Is it one of your buddies?"

"Just wondered."

"What else could it be besides a prank?" queried Dad.

"It could be somebody wanting to confess about the fires or snitch on somebody who's setting them."

"What the heck made you think of that?"

"I don't know. Can I be excused?"

"Me too please," echoed Greta.

"Uh-huh," agreed Mom. "Make sure you get your homework done before doing anything else."

Greta always brushed her teeth right after dinner, but I barged into her room before she headed to the bathroom sink. "So, any news from the underground? What's Arnie been doing lately?"

"Not much."

"What's that mean?"

"Well, he doesn't go to Simon's anymore, at least as far as I can tell, and he doesn't seem to go anywhere these days. He's always there moping around when I get to Jen's."

"What does she say about him?"

"She says he's been acting kinda funny for the past few weeks."

"Funny how, like telling jokes all the time?"

"No, he's not saying much of anything. He acts jumpy some of the time and like he's in a fog the rest of the time, sort of like he's two different people."

"Do you talk to him when you're over there?"

"No, I never do."

"So, what do you think? Is he our caller?"

"I don't really know."

"Do you have an opinion?"

"I don't really know."

"Well, if you were going to bet on it, what would you say?"

"I don't really know."

"One more question. Does he still go down to the Ice Creamery to feed his Spumoni addiction or whatever it is he likes?"

"I don't think so."

"That settles it. I think he's our man and we've got a decision to make. It looks like it's up to me since you don't have an opinion. I'm betting it's him and I'm ready to tell Dad what's been going on. Are you with me?"

"I guess so."

Settling in for his after-dinner slump, Dad lingered at the table and said something that made Mom laugh. As soon as we came back down to the kitchen, he straightened up and propped his elbows on either side of his placemat. The "no elbows on the table" rule was suspended when dinner was finished. In a few minutes he'd shuffle off to the living room and snuggle up to the Philco for Morrow's broadcast from London.

"Hey Dad, Greta and I have something to tell you."

"Don't 'hey Dad' me. It's not respectful."

"Sorry, Dad."

"What is it? You've captured Hitler and Tojo and tied them up in the basement where Medusa can keep an eye on them? Make it fast. Morrow's on in a few minutes."

"OK. It's something almost as good. Remember when we were over at Simon's and his buddy barged in and accused Simon of being the firebug?"

"Yes."

"Greta found out that Simon beat him up shortly after that. We think it was for spilling the beans and putting holes in Simon's story, so we figured he might know something and be ready to spill some more beans."

"I'm listening."

"We decided to spook him into talking. I've been pestering him with notes to make him think somebody's on to him and that it'll go easier if he talks."

"How've you been doing that?"

"Never mind, it's nothing illegal, I promise. No blood was spilled. It was one of those psych operations. Anyway, I think it might be him that's calling."

"Yeah?"

"One of the notes said there was a reward, and I used our phone number."

"Who told you there was a reward?"

"Well, I just thought it was a gimmick that might work."

"So, what do you think we should do if he calls again, Detective Johannsen?"

"Well, for starters, we need to be sure not to tip him off that he's reached the Johannsens. Then I guess I'd ask if he's calling for the reward, but we need to be sure it's him."

"He might just hang up again."

"He could, but now that you know who it might be you could call him back and talk to him. I bet that would just push him over the edge."

"You're sure he has beans to spill?"

"I'd bet on it."

"Your entire piggy bank?"

"Most of it."

"What do you think, Greta?"

"I'd crack my piggy open too."

"OK. Here's what we'll do next time he calls. If either of you answers, just say, 'Are you calling about the reward?' Then give the phone to Mom or me and we'll take it from there." As impossible as it seemed, I don't think Dad even realized that he'd missed most of Morrow's broadcast.

Nothing happened for four long days. When the call finally came, Greta happened to get the phone and promptly gave it to Mom after the caller asked about the reward. To everyone's surprise, he stayed on the line.

"Do you have a number where we can reach you? Good. We'll have someone get a hold of you. Bye now, thanks for calling." The gangster appeared completely disarmed. I suspect Mom's magic could've talked him into taking ballet lessons.

"That was good Mom, especially that bit about 'thanks for calling.' It's like you gave him some breathing room so he won't panic. Good move."

We began jabbering at Dad about the call as soon as he came home. "One of you has to stop yapping," he said. "I only have two ears." Greta stared at the ceiling as I relayed the details. "I'll give him a call right now," he said. "Strike now while the iron is hot, you know."

"No," Mom and I chorused. "We want to give him time to think about how he'll spend the reward," I said. "We don't want to scare him off."

"I guess that makes sense. I'll call tomorrow then. I'd like him to come clean of his own accord. We can always put the screws to him later if we need to. But I tell you, if there's another fire, I'll look pretty foolish having a suspect that I didn't tell anybody else about. I don't know what my superiors would say."

I'd experienced some long days before, like waiting for a fishing trip or getting antsy the week before my birthday, but this was a whole new theory of time. Minutes took hours and hours took days. Dad finally decided the time was right to call Arnie back on Friday right after dinner.

"Hello, may I speak with Arnie please? OK, I'll call back later, or he can call me at PLAZA 6-6586. Just tell him someone called about the reward."

"Asking for him by name should really give him the willies. You didn't use your name though."

"What difference does that make?"

"No, that's good. I just didn't want you to use our name."

"Why not? You're the Dick Tracy of the neighborhood who may have cracked the case. Wouldn't you like people to know?"

"Not yet. You don't know how things like that work at school. Somebody could get beat up."

"Greta can protect you at school."

"She doesn't go to my school."

"Not funny, Dad," she complained. "How about Dick Tracy here protecting me instead? I'm in this too."

"Yeah, she's our inside person. She's good friends with Arnie's sister who told her about Simon beating up her brother."

I don't know what came over Dad. It was unlike him to joke around like that, especially about something so serious. Dad decided Arnie would be more likely to talk if they met in some neutral place, not Arnie's house or ours. When I suggested the Ice Creamery, Dad lit up. He was known to sneak down there occasionally himself, stopping by on his way home from work. I always wondered if Mom ever questioned him about his pistachio breath, or why he was a half hour late some days.

"Good suggestion, Scotty. I'm going to try to arrange a meeting for the weekend if I can get a hold of him."

"Can I come?" I asked, knowing what he'd say. Predictably, Dad just glared an unspoken 'No.' "Then will you bring me back something? The Creamery was my idea."

"We'll see."

Time started taking even more time to get on with things, and I still hadn't heard anything about Arnie. Even the birds seemed to be flying slower than usual, looking like they'd stall out in the crisp blue sky. We were all waiting for the ending of this story, but nobody seemed to be writing it. Dad didn't like to be peppered with questions, but I was dying for news, and it's not like there was a radio broadcast

I could turn on to satisfy my curiosity. So, after three days without a word, I set my curiosity free and asked what was going on.

"How was the ice cream, Dad?"

"No ice cream."

"How come?"

"We're working on it."

"On the ice cream?"

"I said we're working on it."

What the heck did that mean? I had a right to know, after all. Greta hadn't learned anything more from Jen either, except that Arnie appeared to have lost his sweet tooth and hadn't been to the Creamery in more than a week. I guess I wasn't going to find out anything at the dinner table, but maybe I could catch Dad off guard some other time. A couple of days later, Greta reported that Arnie hadn't come home after school, even by dinner time. Something was definitely up, I thought. The tide must be about to change.

The following day, I caught up with Burr as we headed to our lunch table. James and Marty were chattering away, sharing some sort of exciting news that CBS had overlooked.

"What's the fuss?"

"Oh, Scotty. You won't believe this."

"Try me. I can be gullible when I need to be."

"We heard that Arnie was pulled out of class yesterday and didn't come back. Some kids saw him, along with two big men in dark suits get into one of those government cars."

"What do you make of it, Scotty?"

"I think the game's about over."

"What game?"

"You'll see."

"C'mon, tell us."

"You'll see."

"Know what else?"

"No. What?"

"A little while after that Simon was called out of class too."

"And?"

"We don't know anything more."

There was no clue at dinner that this might be a day to remember. The biscuits were hot and flaky as usual. The gravy was creamy and smooth, despite being made with powdered milk, and there was even a hint of meat flavoring in it. The only unusual thing was that Dad was especially smiley.

Sharing the routine dinner chit chat and business of the day, Mom talked about the scrap drive, Greta chattered about her latest letters to the soldiers, Dad reported an unusually heavy volume of mail at the post office, and Erik expressed his relief at finally hearing from Natsumi, while I had little to contribute. The Philco waited silently for those who cleaned their plates in time to catch Morrow's evening broadcast. The B-17 and a microscope waited upstairs for those of us too excited to even pretend to do our homework. I was sure the news bomb about what had happened at school would soon explode. But the only action was when Dad bounded out the front door as soon as Morrow signed off with his reassuring "Good Night and Good Luck."

Curiosity interfered with my focus on the B-17, and I wandered back downstairs. "Mom, what's got into Dad? It's like he's got ants in his pants."

"Well, I know some biscuits and gravy got into him, but I don't know about any ants. He just went out to check on things during the blackout."

I helped Mom clear off the table and tidy up the kitchen. While drying the dishes, I couldn't help but stare at the clock. It was after eight and Dad still wasn't back, but Mom kept mum.

"Mom, what neighborhood is he checking on, the one in Timbuktu?"

"No, he should be back soon."

About twenty minutes later, in he came, shaking the rain off his coat and laying it over the drying rack.

"Jeez, Dad. We thought you went to join the Foreign Legion."

"I did but they wouldn't take me. You wouldn't believe how picky they can be. They said I was too good looking."

Too weird. Dad was doing comedy now. The world must've turned upside down. Hearing our laughter, Greta had come downstairs to join us. Even Erik was home, wide eyed and ears cocked.

"What are you all looking at, my handsome face?" joked Dad.

Erik responded, "Well, you don't look all that bad for an old guy, but you're still probably ugly enough for the Foreign Legion." Things had thawed between Dad and Erik since our trip over to Simon's, and Erik was home in the evenings more now too. It was Greta who finally came right out and asked.

"Dad, something is going on. You're not yourself." In a practiced, childlike innocence, she asked, "You catch the firebug or something?"

"Well, I think we've got our pyro."

"What's a pyro?" she asked.

"It's someone who lights fires."

"Any fires?"

"No, just illegal fires."

Greta and I let out a satisfied sigh, certain that our stupid plan wasn't so harebrained after all.

"That's great, Dad. How'd you find out?" asked Erik, even though he'd already put most of the pieces together himself.

"So, here's what happened. The FBI decided we should talk to Arnie someplace that wasn't too comfortable."

"Don't tell me. You did it in the vice-principal's office, right? That's not a very comfortable place. Is that where he went when they pulled him out of class the other day?"

"What would you know about the vice-principal's office? Is there something you want to tell us?"

"No. That's just where kids usually go when they get pulled out of class. So, tell us the details. What happened when he got there?"

"Well, first he came down to Mr. Johnson's office and Mr. Johnson was the only one there. He asked Arnie if he knew anything about who was stacking up the lunchroom chairs. Somebody's been stacking them so high that the custodian had to get a ladder to undo the stack. It was that or push them over and cover his ears when they crashed. But that was just a pretext to throw Arnie off and make him relax."

"So, Mr. Johnson didn't ask him anything about the fires?"

"No. They began chatting about sports or something, and once he'd been in there for a while, an FBI agent came in, nice and casual like. He simply sat down with them and smiled. Then another one came in and did the same thing, and after that a uniformed army captain joined them. They all sat there looking at Arnie while Mr. Johnson kept talking about nothing in particular. They could tell that the strategy was working as they watched Arnie begin to sweat and saw his pulse pumping in that big neck artery. They wanted him to feel like there was nowhere to turn except onto truth street."

"Didn't the FBI ever say anything?"

"Oh yes. When they thought Arnie was ready to boil over, they said something like, 'I guess you know why we're all here.' That's all it took. The beans came spilling out, and the FBI took notes on every word and pause. They don't miss much."

"What exactly did he say?"

"He said he knew who it was and would tell them everything. The biggest part of everything being that it's Simon who's been lighting the fires all along. There were times he acted alone and others when he enlisted a buddy or two. Sometimes he used a timing device and others he just tossed a match and ran away, like the Japs were after him." Mom glared at Dad but kept the peace for the time being.

"Arnie ever with him?"

"Only once, or so he claimed."

"What will happen to him?"

"I'll get to that part. "Let me tell it, OK? One thing's for sure. He won't be getting any reward. They might go easy on him for telling us everything though. Anyway, after the story was out, Arnie was taken away by the FBI."

"Yeah, some kids saw that from an upstairs window. We heard that Simon was called out too, but nobody saw him get taken away."

"Well, this is where the story gets more interesting. Simon was summoned from class but never showed up, and as far as anyone can tell, he left school and hasn't been seen since."

"Did they check his house?"

"Not only checked his house, but they've been checking the whole neighborhood ever since."

"So, does anybody have an idea where he might be?" Erik asked.

"I don't think anybody knows for sure, but most of the FBI guys think he's probably somewhere in the park. It's just a natural place to hide. The FBI is coming over tomorrow to talk with you and your friends since you all know the park so well."

Thinking a few of us kids could hide in the park till the cows came home, I wasn't too surprised. "When should we be ready?"

"After you finish your route. Can you get your friends over here then?"

"Yeah, not a problem."

I could see the wheels spinning in Greta's big brain. "I wonder…do they think he could be hunkered down in someone's unused garage or tool shed, or even a vacant house like the Fujikos?"

"Could be," responded Dad. "The park is just one possibility."

Have they found out anything about *why* Simon's been doing this?" Erik asked.

"They asked, but Arnie said he didn't know."

Marty, James, and Burr were all ears the next day when I filled them in and told them what time to come over. When James suggested that we might become junior G-Men and earn our hero credentials after all, I reminded him not to wear his dumb uniform when he came over.

My route took so long that I was the last one to arrive. Grouped around the kitchen table, everybody was sipping tea or powdered milk and munching away on the cookies Mom made for the occasion. The FBI guys acted all chummy with my friends like they were buddies from way back when. Dad introduced me to the two dark-suited FBI guys, Agent Brown and Agent Black, and suggested we get down to business now that everybody was here. He motioned to one of the agents who took charge like it was a regular briefing down at headquarters.

"I think you have all heard what's going on and probably figured out why we're having this meeting. Your dad says you boys know the park like the back of your hands and spend quite a bit of time there. Is that right?"

"Oh yes, Mr. Black," said James. Marty and Burr nodded their heads in unison.

"That's good because you may be able to help us find this Simon. He may be in the park, trying to stay off the streets. Two of you have paper routes, right?" James and I nodded. "Keep an eye out when you do your routes too. Who else besides the paper and mail carriers walk the neighborhood every single day? You know the dogs, I assume. Know what I mean? Just go about your regular business while keeping an eye out for something unusual or out of place—anything that doesn't seem right."

I conjured an image of all the details that drivers missed as they whizzed by. There was a certain value in knowing the dogs and shortcuts, or even the angry people who obsessed over their property lines. Drivers could be in for some nasty surprises if they ever got out of their cars.

"What if we see something?" asked Burr.

"Don't do anything. Just tell us or Mr. Johannsen here."

"Don't do anything at all?" asked Marty.

"That's right boys. Don't do anything except tell us. We'll check things out if you see something. Have I made myself clear?"

"Yes, Agent Black," agreed James.

"Yes, Mr., I mean Agent Black," followed Marty.

Burr chimed in, "Yes, Agent Black."

"What about you, Scotty?"

"Me too, Agent Black."

"All right then. I think we're done here. You boys be careful."

The four of us went up to my room where I showed off the B-17 and we gossiped about this latest turn of events.

30. *Keeping an Eye Out*

EVEN THOUGH IT WAS a quicker way home, the paved streets and cookie-cutter houses held little interest for me. With plenty of time before dinner, I ended my paper route with a walk through the park, keeping my eyes peeled while wandering down the main trail. I didn't expect to see Simon, but the park was the perfect hiding place.

Nothing seemed unusual. Squirrels ran up and down tree trunks, crows argued from their lofty perches, and seasonal birds scoured every nook and cranny for a bug to their liking. Ferns, salal, and huckleberries competed for scraps of sunlight filtering through the trees, while nettles waited patiently for an unsuspecting passerby. High in the broadleaf trees, a squirrel volleyed a nut in my direction, like it was aiming directly at me. Everything appeared as it should, with the park doing what it was destined to do when left to its own devices.

My friends and I had nodded in agreement with everything Agent Black said, but "doing your regular thing" apparently meant different things to different people. James and Marty kept playing secret agents for all they were worth, at least till I reminded them what the FBI said. We eventually agreed that it wouldn't cross any lines if we simply walked more often than usual. We rationalized that a few more eyeballs peering into the neighborhood cracks and crannies was a good thing. Marty couldn't resist joking that Burr's glasses gave him an advantage. Burr shot back, "four eyes good, two eyes bad." We didn't have any special plans, but we did decide it would be better to pair up than go as a group. We figured that Simon would probably hear the four of us coming and be long gone before we were even close. Two years of war games in the park might prove useful. It was our turf, after all.

The four of us met up for the walk to school the following morning and discussed whether any of us had seen or heard anything other than the birds and the bees. Disappointed that we had nothing to report, Marty launched into a crime-stopper theory of how we could trick Simon into revealing his hideout.

"Hey guys. You know Simon's an animal, right?"

"Aren't we all?" Burr emphasized.

"I don't mean like a mean animal, just that all animals need certain things…like food."

James and I understood immediately where Marty was headed and egged him on, teetering on the edge of giggling out loud. "Brilliant," I said.

"I think you're onto something," added James.

"That's right," Burr chimed in. "Animals need to eat."

Marty mistook our interest as enthusiasm, and I felt a twinge of guilt at our deceit. "So, you plan to tempt him with food?" I asked.

"Yeah. We could leave goodies here and there in places he might be hanging out. He must be starving by now."

"You've got to be kidding. You've just got to be kidding." James shook his head as he repeated the phrase. "You have any idea how big this place is? Where would we get all the food? Especially

267

with the shortages and rationing. That would go over real big if word got out. The local wildlife would probably cheer us on though."

Marty looked crestfallen by our rejection of his idea without debate. Nonetheless, he mounted one last defense. "OK. We could package things so the other animals couldn't get them. We could even label them, 'For Simon.'"

James teased that we could take shifts camping out near the food and nab him just as he reached for some meager morsel. Things went downhill for Marty's plan from there, and I wound up feeling even sorrier for him. He was so sincere about the whole thing. The food-trap idea came to a complete dead end when I suggested that we might be mistaken for Simon's accomplices if we left food for him in the park. Even Marty recognized that his inspiration would never see the light of day. It was destined to join the junk pile of "great ideas" we'd racked up through the years.

Before the heavy doors closed behind us, Burr and I agreed to do an after-school walkabout in the park, and James reluctantly partnered up with Marty to scout the neighborhood.

Though the walk home was the same distance as always, it took longer than usual as we scanned side to side like sweeping searchlights. In a neighborhood full of people going about their business, we came across several things that might be out of place and wound up arguing over what was worth reporting. Burr wanted to report everything, but I didn't want us to be like the boy who cried wolf. I'd ask my Dad before reporting anything to the FBI.

Burr interrupted my thoughts. "Hey Scotty, what did you really think of Marty's food idea?"

"Probably a waste of time and good food."

"What if we had some idea of where he might be hiding?"

"It'd still be a long shot. We don't even know if he's in the park."

"He's gotta eat sometime."

"True, but who says he wouldn't steal food? He might even have money to buy something."

"Yeah, I guess so. I'll meet you at the footbridge when you finish your route, OK?"

"Yeah, see you there."

With my route complete, I stashed my newspaper bag on a moss-covered support under the footbridge and waited for Burr to show up. He could be lost in a book or swallowed up by his latest tinkering. Once again, I longed for one of those two-way wrist radios. I'd tell him to wolf down his snack and run out the back door to meet me. As it was, all I had was a tin Dick Tracy ring—free except for the three-cent stamp I used to send away for it. Such a bargain.

Burr arrived shortly after I did. The side trail running down from the footbridge was especially slippery after the recent rain, but we somehow stayed upright all the way to the bottom, skiing though the slick mud on our worn-out shoes. Aside from any hidden critters that might be watching us, we seemed to be alone in the ravine. Several crows tracked us, squawking from branch to branch before deciding we weren't worth the bother. We hadn't seen the dancing man for quite a while and I half expected we'd find him, chanting for the benefit of the trees and critters that probably thought he was as strange as we did. Our walk was uneventful till Burr got wrapped in a spider web suspended between a tree and a girder beneath the Twentieth Street Bridge.

Brushing the webs off his face, Burr pointed at some nearby litter, and I bushwhacked over to investigate. The debris was scattered on the ground and hung up in the bushes, but it hadn't yet melted into oblivion from the rain.

"So, Detective Johannsen, what's all that crap over there?" Burr asked.

"I don't know, Sergeant Smart Ass. Why don't you come over and have a look-see?"

"Somebody must've tossed their homework off the bridge."

I didn't have to investigate any further to know this was where Greta unleashed our present to Arnie. "I hate to see rubbish in the park," I said.

"Can you make out any of the writing? Oh, I know what this is. It's the notes we wrote. Here's one I thought up: *Do right by God and country.*" Moisture had all but disintegrated the notes from the gift box, but bits and pieces were still readable, and we did our best to clean up the mess.

We continued scouting the length of Ravenna and Cowan Parks and returned on the other side of the ravine without seeing anything more unusual than the scraps under the bridge.

"Let's walk up in the neighborhood instead of the park tomorrow."

"Right, Agent Scotty."

It seemed like the only thing we learned was how much litter accumulated along the routes less traveled. I had to wonder what crows did for a living in the places that were garbage free. But the farther away a cranny was, the more trash it seemed to collect. Somebody besides the crows clearly knew about these places.

James wasn't available the next day, so Burr, Marty, and I walked the neighborhood streets and alleys. Even when we were familiar with them, the alleys could be spooky. Shadows lurched there, especially at dusk, dancing and dodging as though in a game of hide and seek.

"You see that?" Marty stopped in his tracks to get a bead on a disappearing shape half an alley ahead.

"No. What did you see?"

"Don't know, looked like somebody ducked behind that garage down there, the one with a door hanging off its hinge."

"So, what if they did?" I probed. "There's nothing that says a person can't cross an alley and go between houses. I do it all the time for my route."

Burr was in an unusually playful mood. "What if it was a yeti or the monster of the ravine?"

"A yeti?" asked Marty. "What's that?"

"It's the abominable snowman of the Himalayas."

"*Abdominal* snowman?"

"No. *Abominable*, like bad or frightening," Burr lectured.

"OK. Don't be such a smarty, you hankie," Marty retorted.

"Are you even sure it was a person, or was it just a shadow?"

"I guess it was probably a shadow," Marty conceded.

"Shadows don't have legs," Burr joked. "We'll just call it the monster of the ravine."

"No monster," I announced. "It was probably just somebody going over to borrow a cup of flour or a *Wonder Woman* comic."

"I'd like to borrow *her*," joked Marty.

Burr snickered. "Try the library."

"Enough of this," I said. "We'll just take a good long look when we pass the spot."

All we saw when we got there was an ordinary garage in the ordinary backyard of an ordinary house on a very ordinary day.

"Now that we've had our excitement and seen the first yeti on this side of the Atlantic, let's go home," Burr said with a sigh.

"Not funny," Marty complained.

"Right, I just forgot to be funny there for a moment."

"Well, try not to forget again, OK? I don't know if I want to keep my eyes out with you two jokers again. I'll hook up with James next time. I don't like being made fun of. I'm probably not the only one who doesn't know what a yeti is."

"Oh no, Marty. We *want* you to go with us when James isn't around. It's just that we've got to keep it down. Six eyes are better than four. No jokes about Burr's glasses, OK?"

"Eight, don't forget Burr's glasses," added Marty.

"Jeez, Marty." Burr called a halt to the joking around. "Stop it and get with the program."

"OK, men. Cut it out. We've got an important mission to accomplish here. How about if we try across on the other side of the footbridge tomorrow, up where my route is? We'll meet at the same time on our side of the footbridge, agreed? Marty, you can do your own thing if you want, or you can come with us."

"Hey Marty, how long has your fly been unbuttoned?" I hadn't noticed at all, but Burr must've been waiting for the perfect moment to spring this on Marty.

"Oh jeez. Why didn't you tell me?"

"I just did. Button up or we'll have to turn you in. We can't be too careful. There's a war on you know."

Burr and I laughed while Marty checked to make sure he hadn't missed a button or two. He joked that he was only trying to fit in with Burr whose left shoelace was routinely untied.

"Enough, OK?"

I got to thinking, if we kept horsing around like this, we'd probably miss Simon even if he was standing right in front of us. Tomorrow promised to be more exciting though as we crossed over into Lashbaugh's neighborhood. The prospect of going past the haunted house was always worth a goose bump or two. Accepting the dare of dares took on a chillier note now that we had Simon to think about. Would one of us finally risk knocking on the weathered front door or peeking in one of the broken windows? Would we discover more than abandoned emptiness inside?

Interrupting my thoughts, Marty said, "I hear it's going to rain tomorrow."

"Jeez, Marty. It's always going to rain tomorrow. We live in Seattle you know."

Burr, who'd read the weather report in the paper, said, "They're only predicting showers."

"What does 'showers' mean anyway?" Marty complained. "Rain is rain."

"Not exactly. There's rain, showers, drizzle, mist, downpours, rainstorms, cats and dogs, torrents, and floods."

"You forgot to mention sprinkles." I added. "Besides, floods aren't even in the same category. They come after."

"Showers mean you might get rained on and you might not."

"That's a big help," Marty mocked. "See you tomorrow."

"Yep, we'll see you then," Burr replied.

The next day, Burr and Marty waited at the footbridge while I finished my route. When I arrived, they were bone dry despite the skies, which threatened any number of moisture options.

"Let me ditch my paper bag first."

"Where do you want to go?"

"Let's start up at twentieth and work our way over a few blocks."

"We could head up to the bakery when we're done."

"We could if we had any money, but I don't think there'll be time."

"Hey Scotty, aren't you the one always telling us about the jar of broken cookies?"

"Yeah, but I never go there just for that. It's only when I go to pick up something for my Mom."

Marty asked where Lashbaugh's house was, and Burr scrunched up his eyes, showing me he didn't know either. Not only did I know where it was, but I'd been inside. While the pair might not be sure about Lashbaugh's house, they were well acquainted with the haunted house—the main attraction, aside from the bakery, on this side of the footbridge.

"Lashbaugh's house faces twenty-second, about three quarters of the way up from the park. I'll show you."

"You think he's likely to be holed up in his own neighborhood?"

"Not likely, but where *would* he be? It's not like he can just hop a freight and go to Canada or join the Foreign Legion." I could see their faces fall as we approached the ordinary house on an ordinary street. "What did you guys expect? That he'd be lounging in his backyard under an umbrella?"

"I don't know," said Marty. "I just thought there might be something more interesting. I guess we should head over to the haunted house. That'll give us a thrill."

"Right. I'm sure he's in there having a grand old time, yucking it up with the crazy lady or maybe the chanting man. Either way, they'd make quite a pair."

"Didn't you hear? Burr asked. The crazy lady got really sick, and they took her away."

"When did that happen?" This was news to me, and I instantly understood that the mission of keeping an eye out now meant focusing on the haunted house.

"About four or five weeks ago, I guess."

"So, the house has sat empty ever since?"

"Guess so."

"Are you thinking what I'm thinking?"

Burr nodded without saying anything and a little wry smile began to distort his face, but as usual, Marty failed to assess the situation. "I am if you're thinking about girls," he said.

"What, at a time like this?" Since I started thinking about girls, I'd discovered that there's really never a bad time to think about them except maybe during a math test, and even then, it's OK if you finish early and decide not to check your work. "God, Marty, you amaze me sometimes. Could you turn them off and stop thinking about them for a minute? Get serious and think about the haunted house instead."

"Turn what off?"

"Girls."

"What if I can't help myself?"

"Then we'll find you some help."

"OK, I turned them off."

"Them? How many were there?" cracked Burr with the wry smile still on his face.

"Never mind, I turned them off like Scotty asked."

It was obvious to all of us, even Marty, that the haunted house might be the perfect neighborhood hideout. Though it spooked us, we knew we'd have to check it out. You'd think the FBI would've thought of that already, but even if they had, I guess there wasn't any harm in checking again. With the crazy lady out of the picture, taking a close-up peek wouldn't exactly be like the dare of dares, and I began mulling over our approach. Should one of us rush up to peek in the windows or bang on the ramshackle front door? Would it be better for two of us to go up to the house while the third kept watch? Or should all three of us charge at once before the spiders and mice realized what was happening? Maybe it would be best to launch ourselves in waves, one at a time, but who should go first? I wondered if we should simply tell my Dad and let the agents in dark suits and slicked-down hair do it.

"How are we going to do this?" asked Burr.

"I know," said Marty. I'll go up to the front and start banging on the house. You two go round back and wait to see what shakes loose—just like shaking apples from a tree."

"Oh great. It would be just our luck to shake loose a hornet's nest. We have no idea what's in there. That idea is just asking for trouble."

"Maybe we should get James involved too. There's strength in numbers," Burr reminded us.

"There's no time to round him up. Besides, we're all here right now." Without any debate or a vote, I made up my mind and assumed leadership. "OK guys, here's what we'll do. Burr, you go bang on what's left of the front door. If he's in there, he'll probably try to make a run for it. Marty and I will go around the back to see if we've got a runner, and we'll try to reach the windows. I saw an old crate up the block that we should be able to use. Sound like a plan? No objections? Let's do it. 'Ours is not to question why. Ours is but to do or die,' as they say in the military."

Burr went to get the crate while Marty and I nonchalantly cased the area. When Burr struggled back with the crate, we made a silent pact to confront our fears.

"Here's one last caution," I warned. "Don't rush the house like it's a German machine gun nest or something. All we need to do is walk quietly up at the same time. If he runs, we'll see him running. And if he's in there, we may get lucky and see him through a window or hear him stumbling around."

Burr handed the crate to Marty, and Marty offered it to me.

At the last minute, Burr said, "I don't want to be the one to go up to the front door," so I passed the crate back to him.

"OK, I'll go to the front and you two go to the back. Ready?"

"Yeah."

"OK."

"Let's go."

Just as Burr and Marty returned from checking out the back of the house, one of the porch boards gave way and I slammed into the front door, knocking it off its last remaining hinge. Just one more misadventure to add to the list, I guess. We braced ourselves for any "reply" from inside the house. When nothing came, we headed for home.

31. Sneeze

BEFORE DINNER, GRETA ASKED me to proofread her next letter for the Red Cross package. It was strange, writing to somebody she'd never met and probably never would, but this little touch of home was intended to keep the fighting men's spirits up, especially if they didn't have family support. Enthusiastic about doing her part, Greta dreamed of a career with the Red Cross. She even thought about the women who served in the military, and asked Mom and Dad if they knew of any she could write to. The letter project was one of the few ways kids could support the war effort, and she was proud to be doing it. Besides, she was a very good writer.

"See anything that needs fixing?" she asked.

"What about this? Is it l-o-s-e or l-o-o-s-e?"

"You might let your dog loose, but you don't want to lose it."

"OK, you spelt it right then."

"You mean spelled it, right?"

"Right."

"Have you and your friends noticed anything over the last few days since you've been scouting around?"

"No. We thought we were onto something when Burr told us the haunted house had been vacant for a while, but we didn't see anything when we looked in the windows except some junk lying around. Here, in this part, should it be laying or lying?"

"If you went around lying and fibbing all the time, like you sometimes do, then there's no 'a' in it. If you're laying something down on your desk, like you do when you get home from school, then there's an 'a' in it."

"That's the kind of thing that drives me crazy about grammar. It's not spelling, it's just memorizing. I'll never get it correct."

"Memorizing is part of spelling."

"Yeah, I guess it is."

"So, you think old Simon has flown the coop? Did you check the haunted house at night or just in the daytime?"

"How am I going to get out during a blackout to investigate at night? You know how Mom and Dad feel about that sort of thing. Marty calls it the 'splat-out' for all the people who run into things and trip over stuff."

"Isn't it worth trying at night though? If he's in there, he might not be so cagey when he thinks nobody's watching."

"Well, maybe, but Mom and Dad aren't going to let me go out for a stroll after dark."

"What if we went together? They're more apt to agree, figuring you're less likely to get into trouble with me along."

"And what about Erik? What if all three of us went?"

"Possibly, but he's so hard to pin down. I don't think we should count on him."

Greta surprised me, but it sounded like she was game for this mission. "How will we explain it to Mom and Dad?" I asked.

"I don't know. Maybe we could go over to Margie's so I can get something for school."

"Wow. What's come over you? It's not like you to lie to Mom and Dad. You're getting to be as bad as me."

"Never. I don't think I'll live long enough for that."

"You're serious about this?"

"Sure."

"When shall we ask?"

"How about tonight, right after dinner?"

"OK then. You do the asking. They're more likely to go for it if it comes from you. Might as well use your reputation to our advantage. Maybe we should wait till tomorrow and ask at dinner though. Wouldn't it seem more natural that way?"

"Anything you say, but that's one more day he has to vanish."

"I say let's wait."

At school the next day, I kept quiet about our plan. It would just cause problems with everybody wanting to join in. On the way home it dawned on me that the advantage of checking out the haunted house in the dark might be outweighed by the disadvantage of checking it out in the dark for the simple reason that it would be dark. With no lights in the house and no streetlights because of the blackout, how could we see anything even if there was something to see? Dad had an extra flashlight that he used for wardening, but I wasn't sure where he kept it, and he might notice if it went missing. He was organized to the point of obsession, and routinely remarked, "a place for everything and everything in its place."

After another long day when the clock seemed to stall out, we finally sat down for dinner. Greta asked about us going over to Margie's as soon as Dad finished the blessing. Neither Mom nor Dad saw a problem with it if we went together, as long as they had

Margie's phone number. Greta jotted down the number, and we cleared out right after the post-dinner cleanup.

"If you're not back in an hour, we're calling the FBI," shouted Dad.

"Not a problem, Dad." At least I hoped it wouldn't be.

The street was about as dark as it could be, but when the moon rose in the east, it etched the familiar rooflines and put some life into the clouds. As I yammered on about the darkness being both good and bad for our little sortie, I soon discovered that "Wonder Sister" had already considered this.

"You're right. The moonlight could throw a wrench in things, but I've thought about that."

"Well, at least the moon will help keep us from falling down a rabbit hole, but what are you thinking."

"We have more than one sense, you know."

"You mean hearing? That would be great if there's a party going on inside but what if it's just quiet snoring?"

"An empty house doesn't snore," she shot back.

Granted, I hadn't taken the moonlight into consideration, but I did notice that Greta was walking funny, like she was concealing something. "Okay, so what've you got under your coat, and what's it for?"

Greta pulled out an object that writhed in the darkness. "I attached two of mom's kitchen funnels to a short chunk of discarded garden hose to help us hear if anything's going on inside. We hold one end against the house and put the other end to our ears. It's like that hard-of-hearing gadget people used in the old days. You know, like what the doctor uses to listen to your chest. Anyway, I figured that the house has so many broken windows that we could probably hear mice scurrying around inside if we held our breath."

"That's genius if it works. Know what else? Maybe we could feel vibrations through the clapboard if anybody's in there clomping around."

"You're probably right. We'll see."

The trickle of moonlight kept us from falling down the stairs to the footbridge and crashing into things on the other side of the ravine. Some blackout-blind cars revved several blocks away, and I imagined their tense drivers breaking hard for every shadow. I guess driving without headlights was fighting the enemy in a home-front sort of way.

The moon was still low in the sky, but there was enough light for someone to spot us if they were on the lookout. "What about barking dogs?" Greta asked. Dogs were the least of our worries, I thought. The only one I knew of nearby was old and arthritic and seldom ventured off its front porch, even to chase a cat.

Shrubs helped conceal our advance as we closed in on the frightening hulk of a house, and the overgrown yard provided good cover for the last fifty feet. A few degrees above the eastern horizon, the moon was primed to throw a little light in the back windows if it found a break in the tangle of branches reaching up from the ravine. The front of the house was shrouded in darkness, but with the trickle of moonlight and my memory I'd be able to get my bearings.

"Careful, Greta, there's all kinds of dry branches and twigs around just ready to snap and give us away."

"At least the carpet of fir needles and rotting leaves will help us be quiet."

"OK, you think you know what to do? There should be a crate by one of the windows from when we looked in earlier. You could stand on it if you need to but be careful. Remember, we're just looking and listening. Don't stay more than a couple of minutes and I'll meet you right back here. We're not *doing* anything, got it?"

"Just espionaging behind enemy lines," she joked.

"Well, if that's what you want to call it. By the way, I don't think that's a real word."

With her two-headed listening snake in hand, Greta silently disappeared around the corner of the house. I approached the front, pushing the tall weeds aside and straining to see any tripping hazards. I froze for several minutes against the side of the house, pressing myself hard to the weathered, rough-cut boards. I listened intently but heard nothing over the pounding in my chest. Splinters grabbed my sleeve as I tried to move silently toward the front window opening. The splinter digging into my jacket made a quiet snap when I pulled away, but nothing stirred inside. The windowsill was about as high as my forehead, and I needed a few more inches for a clear view. A chin-up might snap the windowsill off if it was as rotten as the rest of the place. There was nothing lying around that I could use to stand on, and my only alternative seemed to be jumping up for the brief glance I'd get before landing. My first jump wasn't quite high enough, but the second one was perfect. As I jumped again and again, relief and disappointment blended, and I leaned against the house with my hands on my knees.

My jumps were fruitless, and I tried to catch my breath before slithering off to find Greta. I dodged any number of mole mounds but stumbled over the wreckage of an old chair concealed by weeds and darkness. My surprise at slamming into the ground forced out a muffled "oh shit"—probably the same expression someone inside would use if discovered. Whatever surprise I might have gained by stealthily creeping up to the front of the house was abruptly lost by this little mishap, and Greta still hadn't come out from behind. I froze and pressed hard to the ground in the tall grass. I waited several long moments, then slowly got up and let panic push me along to our rendezvous spot. It was like playing tag and reaching base. I was safe but the game wasn't over. No Greta. Soon the moonlight bounced off the shiny funnel and the snap of a twig announced her arrival. The game appeared to be over.

"I didn't see anything. How 'bout you," I whispered.

"Didn't see a thing."

"No? Nothing? You sure?"

"Yes. I didn't see anything, but..."

"But what?'

"I felt something."

"What? Your heart pounding in your ears?"

"No, I mean I really felt something moving in the house."

"I thought you were going to be listening with your snake thing."

"I did, but that was later. I had to hold onto the window frame for balance while standing on the crate, and I felt some vibrations in the frame. You know that house isn't exactly solid like a normal one. I bet it twists and howls in the wind. Anyway, I put the funnel against the clapboard, and I heard some creaking and something that might've been footsteps. I kept listening, and that's when I heard an announcement—a sneeze. It was unmistakable. There's definitely somebody in there, but we didn't see them because I'm pretty sure they're upstairs on the second floor."

As soon as the words were out of her mouth, both of us heard a second sneeze, and it was all I could do to keep my "Gesundheit" to myself. We looked at each other and mouthed, "An empty house doesn't sneeze."

"All right, we've got something to report. Finally."

"Let's get going. I don't think we made any noise to scare him off, but Dad might want to get some people over here right away just in case."

"You know, I almost feel sorry for him, if it is Lashbaugh. Can you imagine how miserable he must've been these past few days?"

"That's charitable of you but save your sympathy. Do you have any idea how much trouble he's put people through and the worry he's caused?"

"I know, but try imagining yourself on the run, especially in weather like we've been having."

"The weather hasn't been that bad."

"Not if you have a warm bed to sleep in at night."

"He made his own bed, and we found him sneezing in it," she said with a smile.

The moon made significant progress while we'd been playing detective. Now looming higher in the sky, it cast an otherworldly glow, exposing the mole mounds before we tripped over them. Our breath formed little clouds as we huffed and puffed our way across the footbridge. The little creek at the bottom of the ravine glistened in anonymity, staging a private sparkly show just for us.

"Mom, Mom," I called out. "Where's Dad?" Half running into the house, I had to catch my breath from the rush of our case-cracking discovery.

"He should be back soon. He's checking the neighborhood. What's all the excitement about? Something going on over at Margie's?"

"Not exactly, we'll tell you when Dad gets back."

We went upstairs to kill some time while waiting for the slam of the back door announcing Dad's return from his neighborhood rounds. When the slam came, we clomped down the stairs together, making such a thundering ruckus that Dad asked if we were finally having the long-overdue earthquake.

"No earthquake," said Mom. "Just a couple of strange kids excited about something or other."

"What's all the fuss?"

"Wait till you hear this, Dad."

"Let me tell," I interrupted, as Greta opened her mouth to continue. "Remember when we asked if we could go over to Margie's? We never actually got there."

"Don't tell me. You ended up having cookies and milk with Wonder Woman and Captain America?"

"Something better. You know the haunted house over on twenty-third?"

"The one that's only haunted in kids' minds?"

"The one and only. We suspected that Simon might be holed up there, but we wanted to check first, and we just did."

"You had this planned all along and going to Margie's was just your cover story?"

"Let me finish Dad."

"This had better be good. I'm not happy about you lying to your mother and me."

"Oh, it is. We heard somebody in there. Greta felt somebody walking around through the clapboard, then she heard them sneeze, and then we both heard another sneeze. We think they're upstairs."

Dad looked at Greta and waited for confirmation. She knew what big trouble we were probably in but told Dad exactly what she'd told me, adding that maybe somebody like the FBI should get over there right away.

"I don't think we made any noise and they're probably still there."

Erik, who'd just came come up from the basement, had overheard enough of the story to agree, saying, "Yeah, Dad. You should probably call the authorities right now."

I could tell Dad was playing ping pong in his mind—yes, we'd lied, but our snooping might've produced actual results. Nobody likes an "I told you so," especially Dad. And I don't think he appreciated Greta and Erik telling him what he should do either.

"OK. I'll make the call, and I'll deal with the two of you later."

When he got off the phone, he said he was going to meet some men over there right away, and that we'd better stay put. Greta and I began preparing our case for the trial we knew would follow.

"You know, Greta, it's not going to be fun when Dad gets back. I'm hoping he goes easy on us since you're involved. When I last checked, you were nearly perfect, at least in his mind, but there are things he doesn't know about you yet."

"I don't know what to expect now that my halo has slipped a little."

"Well, just try to keep it as straight as you can. Besides, he'll probably be too late to deal with it tonight."

"You mean he'll let us twist in the wind till tomorrow?"

"Probably."

"He knows what we did, and he knows we lied, so the only thing we have to base our defense on is why we did it and how it turned out. I'll bring up the 'no harm no foul' rule."

"If that actually is a rule, I don't think it'll carry much weight with Dad."

"Maybe not, but there's nothing to lose."

"Other than being grounded for six months without an allowance."

"Who knows? He might forget and forgive the whole thing if it actually turns out to be Lashbaugh and Dad gets the credit for discovering him."

"I'm going to bed. You can stay up and consult with the lawyer in your mind if you want."

"What I really want is to find out what happens when they go over there to wake up Mr. Sneezy."

"You'll find out soon enough."

32. Out in the Cold

STILL AWAKE WHEN DAD came home, I heard him talking to Mom with an intensity that said something important had taken place. Just as I drifted off to sleep, I realized I'd have hours to celebrate Lashbaugh's impending capture—perhaps a lifetime even, with no firebug and no bully.

At dinner the next night, small talk was in short supply, almost as though it had been placed on the rationing list. I didn't know if we should ask about the night before or if we should just wait for Dad to tell us in his own good time, but while I was mulling things over, Greta lost her patience and jumped the gun.

"Dad, what happened at the haunted house last night?"

"I guess you two would like to know, wouldn't you?"

"We really, really would," I said. "Please Dad, tell us. Don't you think we should know?"

"Yeah, I suppose you should. Well, things didn't go exactly as planned."

"What do you mean?"

"The FBI sent four agents over there to investigate. Armed with weapons and flashlights, two of them took up positions in front of the house and two at the back. Shouting, 'FBI—come out with your hands up where we can see them,' they waited for a few minutes, but when there wasn't any response, they announced again and waited a bit more. Then one entered from the front and one from the back while the other two waited outside. After they checked out the first floor one of them slowly crept up the stairs. He got as far as the landing when the suspect dove straight out of one of the upstairs windows. He was fast and it was dark, and he made it into the ravine behind the house before the agents could react. Now he's long gone."

"Was it Simon?" Greta asked.

"From the description, it seems like it probably was, but we don't know for sure. After he jumped, a couple of agents looked around in the house and the other two tried following him in the park, but they didn't find any trace of him. According to the agents who searched the house, it was crystal clear that someone had been living upstairs for a while."

"Must've been him that I heard," said Greta with an air of certainty.

"So, what now?" I asked.

"They'll get some tracking dogs tomorrow and go through the park. Meanwhile you and your friends need to stay away. Whoever he is, he's probably desperate, and there's no telling what he might try to do. Is that understood?"

"Yeah Dad," I acknowledged.

"How about you, Greta, now that you've joined the ranks—you understand?"

"Yeah Dad, I won't go in the park either."

"Good."

The news was hardly what either of us had expected, and the ongoing mystery drew me in. If it *was* Lashbaugh and if he *was* desperate, what should we do? We couldn't just stay locked in the house. Without any further discussion, Greta suggested that neither of us should go anywhere by ourselves, even in the daytime, unless absolutely necessary, and Mom and Dad agreed with her common sense. If that was the condition of not becoming a prisoner in my own house, I'd comply as best I could. It really wasn't much of a choice.

There was only one catch, and it involved money and my paper route. I sure as heck wasn't going to get Greta to help me deliver papers, so it was agreed that I'd do my route alone. Collections were a different matter since I had to do most of them in the evening. Even though it was already the twelfth of the month, I still hadn't been able to collect from eight of my customers. I figured I could catch most of them on a Saturday and would run into the others while I was doing my route. But there were always a few that dodged me when I came to collect, and these were the customers that required an evening house call. Even that took several tries and was especially frustrating since the uncollected money came out of my monthly profits. I had to pay for my papers by the tenth of each month, and since I'd sent the *Times* their money last week, I felt like the late customers were living off my money. I wasn't about to consider it a donation. I was in business after all, and I intended to stay in business even after I'd saved enough for a new bike.

The following evening, I was disappointed to find that Dad wasn't home by the time I finished my route. I was dying to know if the search dogs had turned up anything. Where my money was concerned though, Dad's tardiness wasn't reason enough to skip the collections.

"Mom, what should I do about the rest of my collections for the *Times*? I've got a bunch of customers who still owe me money and about the only way they ever pay up is when I do evening collections."

"Why can't you still do that?"

"Because unless they caught that guy, I'm supposed to be with somebody when I'm out."

"Right, I forgot.

"There must be a way to do this. Maybe you could go with me, or how about Dad?"

"I don't know, both of us are so busy and have so much stuff to do in the evening."

Listening, Greta offered up a solution from her stash of common sense. "What about Erik?"

"Yeah, I almost forgot," apologized Mom. "It was for situations like this that we went out and got you a big brother." She tossed me a smile over her shoulder, making sure I got her little joke. "Do you want to ask him, or would you like me to?"

"I'll do it when he gets home."

It wasn't long before Erik wandered in from one of his mystery destinations. I gave him a few minutes to grab a bite to eat before launching in. "Erik, I need your help with something, and Mom said it was OK."

"What is it, calculus?"

"No, I don't even know what that is."

"What is it then?"

"I need a bodyguard."

"Why? Are some girls after you?"

"No, nothing like that. I can outrun most girls."

"Most girls? What about the ones that are faster than you?"

"I'll take my chances. I need you to come with me while I try to collect from my customers. Remember, we're not supposed to go anywhere alone till they figure things out about the firebug."

"You mean Simon?"

"Well, they think it's him."

"OK, but I get half the money."

"No, you don't. You'll do it because you're my big brother and you have to."

"Oh. In that case I'll only take a third."

"No, seriously. Can we do some now before it gets completely dark?"

"Sure. Let me finish eating. How long do you think it'll take?"

"Oh, I don't know. Maybe a half hour, give or take."

There was probably a good forty-five minutes before complete darkness, and it wasn't all that cold this time of year. It would be nice to catch up with Erik while we walked. Doing anything with him was as enjoyable as the thought of counting my earnings.

We headed across the footbridge to Lashbaugh land for my first collection, a few blocks over. "Is there anything special you want me to do?" Erik asked.

'No. Just be here so I can get some of these collections done. On second thought, there is. Since you're my big brother, how about if you try to look as big as you can? There's strength in size and numbers, they say. Maybe it would help just to have you standing next to me all puffed up. But don't look angry. That can set people off."

"What if they aren't home?"

"Yeah, well, that's the problem and there's not much I can do about that."

"Do you ever leave an envelope with a note and our address?"

"I have a few times, but the *Times* doesn't like us to do that. I used to be able to tell if somebody was home if the lights were on, but the blackout curtains make it easier for people to pretend they aren't home. Anyway, here's the first house."

I could never decide if the best thing was to clomp up the stairs, making extra noise to announce my presence or to be as quiet as possible in the hopes of surprising them. Today I did neither and just walked up casual like. I rapped on the door at our first stop and gave my standard greeting when the door opened. "Collect for the *Times*?"

I was in luck. A little kid, just big enough to answer the door, went running off toward the back, yelling, "Mommy, Mommy, the paperboy is here." A woman came out, drying her hands on an apron like Mom does, her face etched in disappointment.

"Can you come back tomorrow?" she asked. "My husband isn't here right now."

"Sure. What would be the best time?"

"Half past six should work."

I turned to Erik, slowly shaking my head as we walked back to the sidewalk. "See how it goes? What can I say? They've got me. Just how angry can I get and still keep them as customers?"

"I see what you mean. I guess that's part of any business, making sure you get paid."

"Well, that's helpful."

"No. I wasn't trying to make light, just making an observation."

"Don't worry about it. Eventually I'll get everybody. Just seems like it's more trouble than it's worth when it takes so long."

I was able to collect from the next two customers, which tempered my frustrations, and our talk drifted to what had happened to Lashbaugh. We hadn't heard anything new since the sneezer escaped.

"You think the dogs tracked him down today?" I asked.

"Don't know."

"He must be a mess by now, hiding out all this time. We've had the usual hit-and-miss rain, and it still gets darn cold at night. How much of that can a person take?"

"Good question. Maybe he's suffering from hypothermia."

"Hypo what?"

"Thermal means heat. Hypothermia is when your body temp drops too much, and things start to go wrong. As your body tries to conserve heat, you get goofy because the brain isn't getting enough blood. Eventually it can kill you. It won't help if he isn't suitably dressed or eating properly."

"Eating properly? He's probably not even been eating *improperly*. Where would he get food anyway? Maybe Mom is secretly bringing him food."

"What?"

"Just kidding."

"He'd have to be stealing food from some place. With the shortages and all, I don't think garbage cans would be a good bet. I don't think he'd try a store either. He probably looks like a mountain man by now."

"If not a grocery store or garbage cans, what's that leave?" I asked.

"What about victory gardens?"

"This time of year?"

"Well, some root crops winter over, and leaf plants like lettuce grow fast in the spring, so maybe so. I don't know what he'd do for protein though."

"He could ask the crows to share."

"You ever seen one share anything?"

The next two customers were both strikeouts. As a last-ditch effort, I suggested we go around back to the alley where I could sometimes tell if someone was home even when they pretended not to be. But Erik had stuff to do, and we decided to head back and face our homework. I was just about to ask Erik if he'd decided anything about the draft, but he tensed, grabbing my arm so hard that it took my breath away.

"You see that? Someone just dashed into that garden shed in the next block and closed the door behind them."

"Yeah, I didn't really register it at first, but yeah. And it's him, Lashbaugh."

"How could you tell?"

"I've been keeping an eye out for him for years. It's like plane spotting—you don't have to see much detail to know who or what it is."

"You're absolutely sure? No question about it?"

"Absolutely no question."

"Well, that answers the mystery about the dogs tracking him down. I don't know if they flushed him out of the park or if he was just up here to raid somebody's garden."

"What do you think we should do, big brother? Go up and say, 'collect for the *Times*?'"

"Get serious. What we should do is call the authorities. But it's almost like he's caged right now, and we're in a position to keep him there."

"Oh jeez, Erik. I don't believe what I'm hearing. That's crazy."

"Sometimes you have to be."

"I think we should call the authorities."

"We will, but not till after we bar the shed door and trap him inside."

"You've got to be kidding. You realize what sort of trouble we could get ourselves into?"

"Only if it's not him or he gets away."

"Oh, it's him alright. Do you think he saw us?"

"I don't think so. It's pretty dark now. So, here's what we're gonna do. See that two-by-four on the ground by the doors? Just like with Grandpa Keister's barn, I'll drop it into the slot, and it'll be strong as heck. We're gonna creep to the back side of the shed and then come around and bar the doors before he knows what's happened. Then I'll stay there while you run up to the Martins to use their phone. I think they're home; I saw a crack of light when we went by."

"Who should I call?"

"Call home 'cuz that's the only number you've got, right? Whoever answers can call the cops, the FBI, and whoever else they can think of. You know the street numbers so you can tell them where we are. Soon as we get the doors barred, take off, okay? I'll stay put. There's not much to that shed. Seems like he could bust right through the siding.

"What if nobody answers?"

"Ask George Martin to call somebody, and then get right back here. You ready?"

"I guess so."

"Let's go."

As noiselessly as in the old silent movies, we crept up to the shed and went around front to reach the doors. I inhaled deeply and placed my foot in front of one door while Erik grabbed the two-by-four. The wood dropped into the brackets with a soft thud that was loud enough to tell the occupant he was trapped. Erik motioned for me to get going, and I took off in a panic. The first loud crash from the shed conjured the image of a trapped animal, thrashing about in terror. The bashing got louder and more frantic as I raced to the Martins. Fearing the shed was no match for its panic-stricken prisoner, I banged furiously on the Martin's front door. A startled Mr. Martin answered with his wide-eyed wife standing right behind him.

"Can I use your phone? I've got to call my house."

"Sure. It's right over there."

Mom answered on the third ring. "Mom, call Dad, the cops, the FBI, anybody. Erik and I have Simon Lashbaugh trapped in a garden shed over by the Martin's house on twenty-first and sixty-second. I don't know how long we can hold him. Hurry!"

I quickly thanked the bewildered Martins and sprinted back to Erik. The frantic blows had intensified while I was gone, but I now heard an answer to every blow. As I got closer, I saw what was happening. Erik had found an old sledge-hammer handle, and for every blow from the inside of the shed, he answered with an intimidating thump. The trapped animal paused every so often, probably trying to figure out who he was tangling with. Already starting to splinter, the shed's siding looked ready to rip completely off the studs. Soon there'd be an opening large enough to offer an escape route, and whatever the occupant was using to bash his way to freedom would still be in hand. Without a word to Erik, I grabbed a fallen branch from the edge of the garden and began banging on the other side of the shed. Blows from the inside became less frequent and more erratic. There was nothing for us to do but answer blow with blow and hope the authorities would show up before the shed gave up its prisoner. Full darkness had arrived, and a few neighbors forgot to turn their lights off before pulling back their curtains to see what the racket was all about.

Headlights soon made sweeping arcs over the rooflines, but the sirens were silent. Several cars came to a screeching stop with their lights pointed at the shed—a temporary exception to the blackout.

Officers approached with guns drawn just as we saw tattered pants and one bare foot break through the splintered boards. Motioning us to step away, the officers removed the two-by-four barring the door. And there he was, crouched at the back of the shed, looking for all the world like an early human from prehistoric times. As soon as the blinding light was on him, he reflexively raised his hands, one of which held an axe. An officer yelled, "Drop it and keep your hands up. Now!" Just that quickly it was over and quiet, and the handcuffs clicked tight around his wrists.

Sure enough, it was Lashbaugh. Not the one from the footbridge and not the one that ruled the school hallways. Absent his intimidating swagger and minus his pack of followers, this Lashbaugh looked timid and afraid—no match for anyone. I knew I'd never have to watch out for him again.

33. Consequences

I HATE IT WHEN adults ask what you think your punishment should be. It seems like part of a grand strategy to make them look good. They expect you to be especially hard on yourself as a show of remorse, and then they get to appear forgiving by lightening your sentence. I don't think Lashbaugh will get that opportunity, but Dad will probably use that trusty parenting maneuver on Greta and me. Even after several days, he hasn't dropped any clues about our punishment. Things hadn't gone according to the FBI's plan either, adding a layer of unpredictability regarding our fate.

Greta was new to the business of awaiting a sentence. Given my experience, I felt it was my duty to provide guidance by example. I kept my mouth shut and listened intently. I wore my remorse like a badge of honor, making sure to look away with shame at precisely the right time while looking Dad in the eye the rest of the time to show that I understood. Above all, I gave no argument, except in the rare circumstance when facts were in dispute. I carefully calculated whether a fact was relevant or mere background noise. It was a delicate balance, and I did *not* want him to think I was trying to throw him off. I was probably a lost cause, but Greta was still in line to become the first woman president, and I'd gone and gotten her involved in something that could be used against her. Some might say that lying to your parents to get out of the house would immediately disqualify you from becoming president. On the other hand, she'd been part of a heroic quest, which would surely increase her chances considerably. It looked like we were in for a game of wait and see.

In situations like this, Dad hardly ever initiated. It was nearly always Mom, who'd say, "Dad wants to talk to you." True to form, that's how it was on the Tuesday following Lashbaugh's departure for three squares and a clean-shaven place of warmth. Even Agent Black joined the kitchen tribunal. I guess he wanted to make sure that the crime of lying to our parents was handled according to FBI regulations. At least he didn't seem to be in an angry mood.

"Hello again," he said. "I wanted to be here when your dad talked to you and Greta about lying to get out of the house."

That didn't sound good. The FBI had never been involved in correcting the error of my ways before.

"Mr. Johannsen, tell them what you decided."

Dad stared at us for what seemed like an eternity before he began. He spoke slowly at first, almost as though he was reading from a script. Then, like the chugging of a heavy train, the beat of his words fell into a steady rhythm.

"Both of you know what we've taught you about the importance of being truthful with us. You know that we expect nothing less, even if you think you might get into trouble." I risked a sidelong glance at Greta, and we nodded in unison, like puppets on a string.

"The fact that you lied to get out of the house was quite a disappointment. We know why you did it, but you're lucky it turned out well in the end. I keep thinking how we'd feel if you or someone else had gotten hurt. Things came very close to not turning out well, don't you think?"

I wanted to remind Dad that Erik's involvement was a hedge against things turning out badly, but I strained to keep my mouth shut. We gave our heads a slight nod and made eye contact to let Dad know we were taking this very seriously, but for the most part, Greta and I kept our eyes glued to the floor.

"Most of our rules are to keep you and others from getting hurt due to foolish behavior. This, however, seems to be a one-of-a-kind circumstance. At least we hope it is. Mom and I have talked about this quite a bit over the last few days, and we've also consulted Agent Black. We're in agreement that what you did does not require any punishment."

Hugely relieved, Greta and I stole a side glance at each other and worked hard to keep our smiles under guard as Dad continued. "But it does require that you understand why we reached this decision and why we feel it was a foolish for you two to go over there the other night in the first place. The purpose of punishment would be to prevent you from doing the same thing again and to remind you that lying will not be tolerated.

"In this case, none of us think there will be a second act. We'd reconsider punishment if you had lied to go out just for fun, like going for ice cream. But you didn't. We don't think that what you did this time sets a precedent for lying in the future, and we considered that you've always been honest with us in the past. Keep that in mind for the future; honesty goes a long way toward building a solid reputation, and there may be times when that's all you've got—your reputation. Does all this make sense to you?"

"Yes, Dad."

"What do you think, Greta? Should there be punishment?"

"Oh no, Dad. We agree with your decision."

"I think Agent Black has some things to say about this too. Agent Black?"

"Down at the FBI we know quite a bit about these things. Some people say the rules are the rules and that's it. That's all well and good for the people who don't have to enforce them. If they did, they'd realize it's a tricky business because we can't make a rule for every situation or a special rule for each person. As a country, we try to make rules that apply the same to everybody. And people need to know what the rules are if we expect them to be followed. Like in your classroom or here at home, you know the rules. They don't come as a surprise, do they? That's not just me talking. It comes straight from the Constitution.

"But sometimes a person breaks a rule for a good reason, or they might be forced to make a choice between two different rules. When I was talking with your dad about this, I reminded him that you didn't lie to get out of the house just because you didn't like the rule that day. You did it because you thought you had a good reason. At the same time, I think the decision you made was very foolish. Something bad could have easily happened and not just to the two of you. You didn't think about what might happen if he escaped, did you? I'll be talking to Erik about that part later. So, if there is ever anything like a next time, don't try to be heroes. Let us handle it from the start, OK?"

Nodding to Dad, Agent Black looked at us intently, saying "I wanted to be here also to give you a personal 'thank you' and let you know that the Bureau plans to do a presentation at both of your schools. I'll be talking with the school administrators about a way to recognize you for what you did. How's that sound?"

"Great," I blurted.

"Gee whiz, that's great. Thanks," echoed Greta.

Talk about an understatement. All I'd said was "great." but the sound I heard in my head was beautiful music. Greta heard it too, and our smiles matched up perfectly.

"But I do have disappointing news," Agent Black added. "There isn't a reward."

I kept smiling even though I knew there wasn't, but I made a list of what I'd do if there had been a reward. Now that our fate was to live another day, I couldn't help but wonder what might become of Lashbaugh, bedraggled as he was. "Agent Black, what will happen to Simon?"

"Well, that's not for me to determine. It depends on his charges. He might get charged with malicious mischief or vandalism, or maybe even destruction of private property, but those would be misdemeanor charges, and I doubt they'd come with any jail time. On the other hand, he might be charged with arson, which is a felony, and that could be five years or more. The most serious charges would be treason or sabotage for interfering with the war effort, and he most certainly would get prison time with a conviction on that. It will also make a big difference whether he pleads guilty or not. They might go easier on him if he does."

"Did he say anything about why he did it?"

"Not much. One of the agents asked him about that and he said that he just couldn't help himself. Hard to say if it had anything to do with the war or not, and hard to believe he wouldn't know why he'd done it. The agent got a sense that he just didn't like the government telling him what to do, especially with all the rationing and shortages. Some people are just like that you know, even when it's for everyone's own good. Maybe it's as simple as that, but I've told you too much already."

It wasn't that hard for me to believe. Sometimes there's an invisible force that makes kids do things they know are wrong. It's happened to my friends and me several times, usually when we're all together. I once talked with Aunt Val about this. She said kids just needed to do more growing up and think what the consequences might be before they did something stupid. I think there's more to it than that. Doing something stupid can be the best teacher, and if it turns out really bad, you probably won't do it again. Besides, it's not always easy to know if it's stupid till you do it—kind of like an experiment. Watching other people do stupid things can be helpful too when you realize you wouldn't want to be *that* dumb. I guess being a firebug didn't seem stupid to Simon till he got caught.

"OK," said Dad, interrupting my thoughts. "The two of you may be excused."

What a relief. The park was back open for business, and I hadn't been branded a criminal. Greta could still become president and there was a rumor that we'd be opening that can of Spam soon. But there was still a war going on, and it had swallowed up Uncle Ted. Several days after my acquittal, Erik filled me in on his talk with Dad about Lashbaugh's cornering and capture.

As might be expected, Dad was displeased about the risk Erik had taken, especially because he'd included me in that risk. Nonetheless, Erik's consequences were limited to his talk with Dad for several reasons. Erik had just turned eighteen which, in Dad's black-and-white view of things, was the first bridge along the way to adulthood and taking full responsibility for one's actions. Both symbol and ceremony, the bridge granted Erik the freedom to make his own decisions—stupid or not. Even if Erik hadn't turned eighteen, Dad was in a squeeze. As word spread about what had happened, Erik was increasingly viewed as a local hero. If Dad were to exercise a heavy hand with Erik, he knew he'd have the community to answer to. They'd have little tolerance for the harsh discipline of someone who'd helped eliminate a major neighborhood concern, especially during this time of global worry.

34. Roses

THE THING I LIKED best about church was the music, especially the pipe organ. Our church wasn't a big cathedral or anything even close, but at some point, the congregation must've decided that a fine-sounding pipe organ would show how serious they were about glorifying God. I wondered if God liked a good pipe organ as much as I did or if he got tired of hearing it every Sunday. An organ solo could shake the church to its foundations, and sound like the engine of the earth itself, throbbing right there in my chest. At other times, it made a sound so small it seemed like it could fit in my pocket. After our organist gave me an up-close look at the console with its three keyboards, foot pedals, and stops, I made a game of trying to guess which stops she was using to make the endless variety of sounds.

I didn't know much about religious stuff even though I went to church regularly. The stories about how to lead a better life and treat people with love and respect made sense. The rest of it just didn't. The business about heaven and hell was hard to picture and people had different ideas about what they were like, almost as though they'd had a tour during their last vacation. Sometimes, I'd make a game of asking people what they thought, but no two answers were quite the same.

Shortly after the war began, our church started a special tribute for families who'd lost someone. White and yellow roses appeared at the back of the church—white for families of those who'd lost somebody and yellow for those wounded or missing in action. We could pick one up when entering the church and hold it during the service or take one when we filed out and shook Pastor Wicklund's hand. If we could produce an endless supply of roses through the dead of winter and beyond, I thought we could surely win the war.

For a long time after the news about Uncle Ted, nobody in our family took a rose. Then one Sunday, without saying anything, Mom picked up a yellow rose and held it tight during the service. Ever since, one of us held a rose each week. For a while, other church members consoled us with encouraging words or hopeful stories about their own loved ones, but as time marched on, more and more held their own roses, both yellow and white.

At first, we'd talked about Uncle Ted, hoping he'd soon be found, but lately the house bulged with silence about what we'd do if he wasn't. Last week, I overheard Mom and Dad discussing what it means if the service person is never found. "I think it's pretty clear that they won't find him," Dad said. "And it's not doing us any good to keep hoping."

Mom understood the grim facts as well as Dad, but she wasn't ready to give up. "I think you're reading a lot into this because he's your only brother, Harlan. I hope you don't feel like you haven't been doing your part while Ted's been in combat." When Dad didn't answer, she continued, "What if he's just been captured?" Mom tried to lead him in the direction of keeping hope alive, but Dad wasn't having it.

"Well, the Red Cross is pretty good about notifying people if someone's been captured, especially after this long."

"Doesn't the War Office have a policy about declaring a soldier dead after a time?"

"Yeah, I think it's a year if they haven't heard anything."

"Shouldn't we wait for that?"

"We could, but under the circumstances I think it's better for all of us if we get used to the fact that he's gone."

"What harm does it do to wait?"

"It only prolongs the hurt."

"Well, I understand what you're saying, but I don't agree," she said in a pleading voice.

You'd think that hope tormented Dad more than the rest of us, but one of the many lessons the war taught us was that everyone responds in their own way, and it's hard to fault anyone. Eventually, the topic of "what if" began surfacing at the dinner table again. Most of the conversation was still between Mom and Dad, but at least they tried to include the rest of us. Mom asked, "How long does the family wait before doing something, and what is the right something to do?" I knew Grandma, Grandpa, and Aunt Val were having similar conversations, but nobody told me much of anything directly. They probably thought they were looking out for my feelings, but I knew my feelings were old enough to take care of themselves.

Secretly, I thought the rose idea was nice but kinda pointless. After all, a cut flower is already dead. But I guess it was something people could do when nothing else could be done. With my turn to hold the rose, something unexpected came: It soothed and comforted me with its sweet smell and delicate petals.

I wasn't accustomed to this feeling at church, where even after all these years, I was nervous about doing the right thing. Mostly though, all I needed was a sidelong glance to see that I was doing what everybody else was doing. Like a school of fish or flock of birds that twists and turns as one, I took my cue from others and did as they did.

Holding the yellow rose did make me think about Uncle Ted, but not in a sad way. It got me thinking about how funny he could be, talking so loudly it was embarrassing. When I was younger, he'd pick me up and swing me around, threatening to let go and fling me off to one of the four winds before I yelled, "put me down, put me down." Even without words, he'd managed to say so much, just by jostling my hair. He always smelled of Old Spice, a smell that was probably lodged in my brain for all eternity.

I'd held the rose on two different Sundays, when, without warning or explanation, Dad took a white instead of yellow rose. Mom held it on the drive home and Dad glanced over at it every time he stopped for a red light. They hadn't simply run out of yellow ones, and I knew the white rose was not a mistake. The lack of chit-chat on the drive home told us we'd have to wait for the explanation. Greta and I went straight up to our rooms and waited for the call, "Soup's on."

Erik, who'd been helping Mom in the kitchen, called us for lunch when everything was ready. Our small talk was smaller than usual. Dad seemed to be in no hurry to tell us anything, and for a while I thought I must've completely misread the situation. I wolfed down my food but didn't ask to be excused. Neither did Erik. Finally, Dad reached into his breast pocket, took out a little brown v-mail envelope and carefully unfolded its miniscule contents. Nobody interrupted.

"This letter from one of Ted's shipmates was sent to Grandma and Grandpa, and they wanted me to read it to all of you."

Dear Mr. and Mrs. Johannsen:

I don't know how to start this letter, as letter writing is a hard thing for me to do—especially this kind of letter. What I am trying to say is I was with Ted when his ship was sunk and I am one of the crew members that survived from the ship when it went down. I thought you would like to hear from someone that was with him. He was one of the best friends that I had on the ship. Him and I was always setting around talking about our families. I am deeply sorry he didn't make it and I hope you accept my sympathies. Hope to hear from you.

—Willis J. Granison

Having no words, tears were our only response.

35. Memorial

AT LUNCH THE FOLLOWING Sunday, Dad announced he was arranging a memorial service. Still without official word of Uncle Ted's death, we'd received the letter from Willis and had no doubt that he was gone. Greta and I were spared the family discussions about a memorial, for which I was thankful. While each of us, in our own private way, had been saying goodbye to Uncle Ted for weeks, the memorial service was a way of confessing it to the world. I wondered if it was also a way to tell God, "You can have him—we'll get along without him." But I didn't really believe that's how things worked, and the thought vanished as quickly as it appeared.

Though I'd never been to a memorial service, I figured there'd probably be rules, especially since it would be held at our church. It wasn't something I could take a class in, but I reckoned there'd be some sort of printed program and I could follow along with what everyone else did, much like a regular Sunday. Mom and Dad would be there to nudge me toward correctness.

When Mom asked if I wanted to say anything when Pastor Wicklund gave the call, my gut clenched, and I thought there was no way I'd want to get up in front of all those people. But ever since she'd asked, I wondered if Uncle Ted would appreciate it if I did. Mom said I was free to think about it till the time came and that nobody expected me to do it, but I knew Erik was planning to say some things and assumed he could speak for us kids.

The service was held in the middle of the afternoon on a weekday, making for an unusual time to be in church. A few people talked quietly in the lobby, and I recognized some from church and others from the neighborhood. Erik chatted with a few of Ted's friends, two of whom wore military uniforms. Dad explained that since this wasn't an official military funeral, it wouldn't include Taps or the presentation of the flag. In fact, the only military present were Uncle Ted's uniformed friends. I wasn't sure whether they were on leave or hadn't yet deployed.

The background organ music sounded timid, like it didn't want to offend anybody by letting loose with how it really felt. Gradually, everybody drifted into the sanctuary and found a place to sit, some with friends and family and others by themselves. Grandma and Grandpa Johannsen sat with Ruthie, who they'd arranged to bring up from college in Arizona. As the organ stopped, Pastor Wicklund stepped forward.

As his words, "Let us pray," broke the stillness, I sent up my own prayer: "Please God, let Pastor Wicklund not say anything about going to a better place." I couldn't imagine anywhere better than living next to the park with my family and good friends nearby, especially with a war on. I wished I could ask Uncle Ted if he was in a better place.

The soloists stood up and everybody glanced down at their programs. The duet turned out to be what Mom called a comfort hymn, one that all of us knew and could easily find in the Common Service Book if we wanted to follow along. The hymn was one I would've picked, given the choice, and I mouthed along while the duet did the work of lifting the words up to wherever Uncle Ted might be. The singing was beautiful, even if the reason for it wasn't.

Pastor Wicklund stepped forward again, saying, "Please be seated." He took a very long pause and looked us over like he was stumped for the right words. Like most of us, he believed that the Common Service Book contained the perfect sentiments for occasions such as these—words that evoked truth if you were a believer, and comfort even if you weren't, especially when the entire congregation recited them together. He gathered a copy of the book and held it overhead. "Let us recite the Twenty-Third Psalm."

Like the hymn, the Psalm was comforting in that nearly everybody knew it by heart, and it gave us the feeling that whatever it was we were in, we were all in it together. I was torn between thinking the words might open the gates of heaven for Uncle Ted and the feeling that he was probably on his own right now, wherever he was.

When the recitation was finished, Pastor Wicklund moved from the lectern, still appearing to struggle for the right words. I recognized this must've been especially difficult for him because he'd grown up with Ted, and they'd remained friends all these years, but as he stepped up to the pulpit to deliver his message, he seemed to regain his pastoral composure, like he was calmed by the familiarity of his role.

"I see many familiar faces and some new. Some of you, like Ruthie, have come quite a distance to be with us, and I welcome you all. Today, we'll remember and offer up Theodore Johannsen—a son, brother, friend, and patriot who gave his life just as Jesus did. "Ted," as most of us called him, and his family have been members of our church since before I became a pastor. The Johannsens have always been willing to do whatever needed to be done and give whatever needed to be given. Now they've made the greatest sacrifice of all, and we grieve alongside them. But that's not the only reason we're here. We're gathered also to remember a life well lived—a man full of enthusiasm, smiles, and humor, who chased down the answers to all his questions, and sometimes crashed into things along the way.

"I can still picture those Saturday work sessions when we cleaned the mortar off the bricks from the old part of the church to use on the new addition. Ted must have been about eight then. At first, little Teddy had no idea how to clean bricks. Then several parishioners—after seeing him repeatedly bash his thumbs—showed him how to use the chisel to pop the mortar off with one or two blows. He got good at it and was so pleased with himself that the rest of us thought about leaving for the afternoon and coming back when he was done. We didn't. We worked even harder to keep up. That's the kind of person Ted was. Not only was he a quick learner and a hard worker, but he was also the kind of person who inspired those around him to step up and find out what they were capable of.

"As Ted grew older, he became a bit of a nuisance with his non-stop questions. One Saturday during confirmation class he asked why we used real wine for Holy Communion when drinking wasn't supposed to be good for us. I don't know if my answer satisfied him, but I told him that we didn't drink enough for it to be a problem and besides, there were stories of people drinking wine in the Bible. He wanted to know what page those stories were on and wondered if many people came to church just for the wine. I have a rich store of personal memories, but I know others of you have your own stories to share, and I want to make sure there is plenty of time for that. We'll start with Ted's older brother, Harlan Johannsen."

It seemed rude to look around to see who might be crying. Besides, seeing or hearing someone else crying was a surefire way to set me off. If there was any place where crying in public might be acceptable, and perhaps not even noticed, it was here, but I didn't want to be viewed as out of control. I knew what seeing Grandma's face would do to me, and I vowed not to look. But just thinking about what she must be feeling started my lower lip quivering. Dad rose slowly and approached the lectern. I hoped his steady, booming voice would offer the protective shell it always had.

"Teddy was quite a bit younger than me, and when we were growing up, I thought it was my job to keep him in line and out of trouble. That proved impossible since I couldn't be with him all the time, run as fast as he did, or keep him on a short-enough leash. Perhaps it's a good thing I couldn't. He didn't always take well to his bossy big brother. They say some of us need to get in trouble from time to time to learn how to stay out of trouble and become the people we're destined to be. That's the way it was with Ted. He had an enthusiastic wild streak and didn't always think before crossing a creek on a log, if you know what I mean. That impulsive wildness was balanced by a sense of fairness that served as his rudder.

"The first time I remember seeing it at work was in a baseball game when he was about nine. His friends were trying to organize a game, but the teams were uneven, so Teddy volunteered to solve the problem by playing center field for both teams. That was the key to getting the game going and everybody agreed since he was pretty good with his new birthday glove. During the second inning a high fly ball came his way, and he dropped it. The team in the field razzed him and gave him a hard time. So, in the interest of fairness, he decided the best thing to do was to promise to drop a fly ball when he was in the field for the other team as well. This virtually guaranteed they'd try to hit in his direction. Sure enough, after a few feeble hits, along came the fly ball and Teddy did drop it. I never did find out for sure whether he dropped it on purpose or simply missed it.

"My favorite story about his sense of justice was when two of his high school friends, unbeknownst to each other, fixed him up on a blind date with two different girls at the same time. When Teddy found out, he fretted over how to make a choice without hurting the girls' feelings. Taking them both to the dance probably wasn't in the cards, so he decided the best thing to do was to get both girls together, tell them what happened, and then flip a coin. Both girls agreed and it seemed like the perfect solution. Teddy knew which one he wanted to dance with, but he didn't let on and vowed to go with the decision of the coin. You guessed it. The girl who lost the coin toss is the one he got engaged to before going to Officer Candidate School. He couldn't resist sending her flowers on behalf of the coin. Maybe that's what got things started between them. Neither of them ever said. Melissa gave me permission to tell this little story and my heart goes out to her. She will always be part of our family."

This was about as much as Dad could say without breaking down himself, and I could tell he was fighting to keep that from happening. Pastor Wicklund announced Aunt "Rosie" next using her real name, Velma Johannsen.

"Harlan is the oldest and I'm the youngest. It's strange and tragic to think that someday I'll be older than Ted. Whenever I start thinking that way, something kicks me in the butt and reminds me that even as I pass him in age, he'll keep leading the way, like he always did. When he became valedictorian of his high school class, he told me I could be the first female to do the same at West Seattle High. I didn't make it, but I did come close, a lot closer than I would have without Ted's encouragement. He was outstanding at track too and when I lamented that girls weren't able to compete, he organized some parents and a few members of the track team to see what they could do about it. He convinced the boys that the more students who were interested in track, the better off they'd all be, getting more people to pay attention.

"He didn't talk much about the war, but I do know he wasn't gung-ho about it. He sometimes said we should make the old men who started it go and fight. That way, he figured, the war would be short so they could get back in time to take their afternoon naps. He was joking, of course, but he made his point nonetheless, and it makes you reflect on all we've lost, when it's the young that do most of the dying. Even though Ted was in the Navy, and I work on the planes down at Boeing, every rivet will seem more like a bullet now—not the random and ruthless bullets of revenge but those that are fired for only one reason, to end the war as soon as possible and bring servicemen like Ted home to family and country."

One of Ted's buddies got up next. The uniform did little to conceal his nervousness, but he conquered his fears enough to speak. "Ted didn't have to enlist you know. His job down at the Port of Seattle was considered nationally important, so he was draft exempt. But when his friends started enlisting or being called up, that didn't sit right with Ted, especially while he had a comfy job at home. In the end, he said he enlisted to 'shorten the war,' and I believe that Ted accomplished his goal even if those he saved will never know his name."

For some reason, maybe because I didn't know her all that well, I didn't expect Melissa to get up and say anything. She had a piece of paper with her, so I thought she'd written out some sort of speech. Probably a good idea and maybe what I should've done. Turned out, it was a personal letter to her from Ted's shipmate, Willis Granison.

318

Just like in the letter to us, he apologized for not being a good letter writer. No need for apologies, I thought, especially for letting his words flow like tears. When he expressed for the second time how much Ted loved her, Melissa couldn't finish reading. She beckoned to Mom who came to Melissa's side to finish reading the letter. If there was ever a time for an intermission, I thought, this was it.

From spying on him over the last week and side glances down the pew, I knew Erik had written some things out. I hoped he wouldn't get up and just read something. That didn't seem right. I was glad to see his hands were note free when he came forward and began abruptly without introducing himself.

"Ted once told me I tied my shoes incorrectly. I thought, how can that be? As long as they stay tied, and I don't trip over the laces, what the heck difference does it make? After he showed me how I should be doing it, I got up the courage to ask him why it was so important. He explained that my fumbling method made it look like I didn't know what I was doing and that if people saw that, they'd assume I was tentative about other things too. 'Confidence starts with the way you tie your shoes,' he joked. At the time I thought it was completely ridiculous. But later on, I understood that it wasn't meant to be taken literally and that the point was to do things like you know what you're doing. That way, it will usually turn out that you do.

"Those of us who knew him, know he was an avid outdoorsman, and those of us who knew him well, remember how he took a special pleasure in sharing his love of the outdoors. He sometimes teased about our family being an 'indoor' family, and he figured it was his job to make sure that I got some exposure to what lay beyond the city limits. He bought me a fishing pole and began taking me fishing long before I knew the difference between a perch and a trout. Every outing was filled with lessons about the outdoors.

319

"The trips I remember best were our annual steelhead trips. I wasn't exactly sure why he chose New Years Day at first. Maybe it had something to do with the fishing seasons, or maybe it was just Uncle Ted's private tradition. However, because it was New Years Day, the drive to the river was sometimes more interesting than the fishing itself. Ted used the drive as an opportunity to point out vehicles by the side of the road that hadn't made it home from their celebrations the night before. What he was really looking for were tire tracks showing where a vehicle might've gone off the road or down an embankment. He explained how a car could be so easily concealed by the underbrush that nobody would even know it was there. He'd seen it happen, and if someone was still in it, they might be injured or trapped and freezing to death. On our third year, Uncle Ted found someone in a pickup who was badly injured, and he probably would've died of hypothermia or injuries if we hadn't come along. It was like our annual fishing trip was just an excuse for a rescue mission."

It seemed like Erik had said all he wanted to say but he hadn't.

"Since before I turned eighteen, I've been thinking about the draft quite a bit. I've also been thinking about whether to enlist and have tried to hide my frustration when people keep asking me what I plan to do. With Ted in mind, I've finally made up my mind and have decided to enlist in the United States Navy."

I've never known people to stand up and clap in a church service, but that's what we all did. Erik walked back from the lectern to take his seat, and a few people at the end of the aisles reached out to shake his hand. Pastor Wicklund asked if anybody else had anything they wanted to share.

Greta looked straight ahead as she shoved a folded-up sheet of paper into my hand. In her perfect printing I saw the words, "Please read this for me." A hot flush of surprise singed my face, but there was no time to think and no time for practice. Nobody else accepted Pastor Wicklund's last offer, and, like an auctioneer, he seemed ready to bring down the gavel and declare the bidding closed. There was no reason for anybody to stand up after Erik had stood up for all of us, but I looked down at Greta's paper and realized there was something she needed to say but couldn't find the courage to voice. As I stood up, Pastor Wicklund made clear the bidding was still open, and he motioned me up the steps to the lectern.

"I'm Scotty Johannsen, Ted's nephew, and my sister Greta has asked me to read this to you."

> *Uncle Ted, I'm mad at you...*
> *For riding the wind and waves*
> *To wherever you are.*
> *We said, "take care and come back"*
> *And you promised you would.*
> *I won't be waiting, though.*
> *I'll be off living the life*
> *You died for.*
> *Uncle Ted, I forgive you.*

Greta was immediately smothered between Mom and Dad, who'd scooted down in the pew so I wouldn't have to inch along in front of them again. Dad had never looked at me so approvingly, and the soft spots he was riddled with were all on display. The closing hymn was one of my favorites. I never paid much attention to the words of *A Mighty Fortress Is Our God*, and if you asked me to recite them, I wouldn't get past the first line. For me, the song's power wasn't in the words but in the melody—a magnificent march that swept up everything in its path and carried it along, especially with the entire congregation singing and the organ covering up whatever failings we had as a concert choir. It seemed like a victory march.

Pastor Wicklund closed the memorial with the Lord's Prayer and the Benediction. The organ hummed its goodbye as people slowly stood up and began filing out the back of the church. Conversations sprang forth from those who hadn't felt like speaking in front of the congregation. Erik was swallowed up by Ted's Navy buddies who weren't afraid to get their dress whites rumpled by hugging him. Greta wiggled her way into the huddle of manly affection, grabbed Erik's hand, and said, "Let's go home. Mom made spam fritters and your favorite cake."

Afterword

An Empty House Doesn't Sneeze takes place in Seattle in 1943—the year my father was killed while serving as an Ensign aboard a U.S. Navy minesweeper in the Mediterranean. I was only a few months old. My mother told me that prior to joining up, he was a conscientious objector. It was many years before I understood how ironic his transformation from an objector to a Navy officer was. While working on the story, several years after my mother passed, I realized that I didn't know whether he'd received formal conscientious objector status under the Selective Training & Services Act of 1940 or if the family lore meant simply that he was sympathetic to these views. This question remains unanswered, but his college papers suggest that he largely agreed with the conscientious objector position. In the end, and with the convincing of his friends, he felt that the threat from Nazi Germany and Japan could only be met with military force and so he signed up for Officer Candidate School.

Growing up in the 1950s, I developed an interest in WWII. Perhaps I would have even if my father hadn't been killed in combat. Initially, my interest was limited to battles, strategies, and armaments. Later, during the 1960s, I found instruction in TV programs about the war. Walter Cronkite narrated *Air Power* and a related program, *The Twentieth Century*. Since my father served in the Navy, *Victory at Sea* was my favorite. I often wondered if my mother let me watch during Sunday suppers just because she liked Richard Rogers' theme music and Cronkite's voice as much as I did. The real reason for her accommodation was probably because she understood what it might mean to have a father killed in combat.

Fascination with the machines of war eventually gave way to more thoughtful reflections on how the war came about and imagining how I would have viewed it, had I been of draft age in the early 1940s. I wondered too about how I would have responded in pre-war Germany—a curiosity that never quite leaves me. I never pursued WWII as a formal field of study, and life carried on, but often when I least expected it, my questions rushed back, fracturing into a diverse array of answers, and eventually, even more questions.

Relatively late in life as careers go, I became a public-school teacher. Faint echoes of WWII lingered outside the curriculum and periodically bubbled up in the form of student questions or sometimes, a disturbing remark about Jews, suggesting that the vaccination of the war hadn't been completely effective. Even though a few students had read *Anne Frank: The Diary of a Young Girl* or *Maus: A Survivor's Tale*, most knew nothing about the war. Few had any idea of what Adolf Hitler represented and even fewer could fathom shortages that led to rationing in America. After all, sixth graders are eleven and twelve years old. Not even Vietnam is in their living memories. Even so, a surprising number of students were curious once the subject came up. Very few, it seemed, had ever talked about WWII with an adult.

Young people aren't typically endowed with an appreciation of history, and, as a young country, many Americans seem unaware of how we got where we are today. It's appropriate that the young are looking forward, but there's a balance to be achieved between blindly forging ahead and reading the charts drawn by those who've navigated before us. In fog-shrouded waters, it's difficult to decipher rocky shorelines. Some basic understanding of history is the keel that keeps us upright in heavy seas.

In *An Empty House Doesn't Sneeze*, I wanted to keep some of this history alive and present it in a way that younger readers might relate to, hence the mystery format. During my teaching career, those who remembered WWII firsthand began passing on, and their children, like me, were getting on in years as well. Thinking a work of historical fiction held some promise, I focused on the home front, hoping to forge a connection with those who were more than a generation unborn when the world went to war.

In part, *An Empty House Doesn't Sneeze* pays homage to all who lived through the war, not just the ones in uniform, but the tens upon tens of millions who were affected in ways they may or may not have understood. After reading a draft of the story, the real Aunt "Rosie" speculated that the memorial for Uncle Ted was really a memorial for my father. Perhaps it was.

No matter how much history is written, no catalog is large enough to grasp the human tragedy that was WWII. It fades, but it is not forgotten.

I often wonder what my father would say if he was asked, "What did you die fighting for?" When I was younger, I thought he would have replied that he was fighting against the horror of the Nazis and to preserve democracy. During the 1960s, he might have answered that he fought and died for me personally, given that his death resulted in my exemption (sole surviving son) to the Vietnam draft. Would he have said he died to preserve freedom and the American way—even knowing how tainted it still was by the legacy of slavery and Jim Crow? Perhaps he died for his fellow shipmates that served on the YMS-30. Or maybe for the marines who survived the landings at Anzio, Italy, precisely because the YMS-30 did its job of sweeping some of the mines away—before it was sunk by one. What did my father and many others fight and die for? Now I tell myself that he died for his dreams and the dreams of countless others, but maybe the real answer is, "All of the above."

Appendix

The entries below are intended to help the reader better understand the historical context for the story, both locally and in the wider world. A complete chronicle of the war and life on the home front is available online and in print.

1911: Ravenna Park is purchased by the city of Seattle. Cowen Park, located at the west end of Ravenna Park, also comes under city control after being deeded to the city by Charles Cowen several years earlier.

1913: The steel girder bridge on Twentieth Avenue NE is constructed across the main Ravenna Park ravine.

November 11, 1918: This is the date most commemorations use for the end of WWI, and why Veterans Day is November 11. World War I is also called "The Great War" and "The War to End All Wars." Over 35 million combined military and civilian casualties resulted from WWI. Of those, 15 million died, and 20 million were wounded. Historians have argued that the seeds of World War II were sewn into the Treaty of Versailles (the formal end of the war on June 28, 1919) by the restrictions placed on Germany, which eroded Germany's self-esteem.

1918: The worldwide influenza pandemic takes hold in the United States as soldiers began returning from WWI in Europe. It is also called the "Spanish Flu" and "The Forgotten Flu." The War didn't cause the flu, but close-quarter conditions during the war and an increase in worldwide travel enabled it to spread more widely and quickly than it otherwise would have. It is alarmingly different from the usual outbreaks of influenza because most of the victims are young, healthy adults. It is estimated that 50 to 100 million people, or 3% of the world's population, died because of the flu. It has been described as the greatest medical holocaust in history.

1920s: Commercial radio begins to develop in the 1920s, but it isn't until the 1930s that it starts to rival newspapers as a major media. The development gives rise to the national networks known as NBC, ABC, and CBS. Early home radios are bulky wood cabinets that use vacuum tubes and occupy a central place in the home. Popular brands of these console radios include RCA, Magnavox, Philco, and Zenith. The commercialization of radio revolutionizes access to information and entertainment. Home radios are later replaced by television beginning in the 1950s.

1921: Franklin D. Roosevelt is diagnosed with poliomyelitis and becomes paralyzed from the waist down. Even after becoming president in 1932, much of the public is unaware of his disability given the absence of a 24-hour news cycle and the limited use of cameras at the time. Polio had been around for centuries, but major epidemics hadn't begun to appear until around 1880 in Europe. Polio epidemics peaked in the U.S. in the 1940s and 1950s. Effects of the disease range from mild paralysis to death, but media coverage makes it seem like the epidemic is more widespread than it actually is. Some ineffective vaccines are tested in the 1930s and 1940s, but it is not until the 1950s that an injectable one developed by Dr. Jonas Salk and an oral one developed by Dr. Albert Sabin are effective enough to all-but eradicate the disease in the U.S. The fight to find a cure gives a major boost to medical philanthropy, and polio survivors become instrumental in securing rights for the disabled years later, which results in The Americans with Disabilities Act, enacted in 1990.

1922: King County leases 268 acres to the Navy and development begins at the Sand Point peninsula on Lake Washington. There had been talk of turning it into an air base since before WWI. In 1940 Congress approves a four-million-dollar expenditure to improve Naval Air Station, Seattle. During the war years, the work population of the base rises to more than 8,000. The base serves various Navy functions and is even used by commercial sea planes for a time. It is officially deactivated as a Navy base in 1970, after years of negotiating the details, when the property is returned to King County and becomes the site of Magnuson Park.

1922: The original Rin Tin Tin appears in a 1922 silent film as a wolf. Rin Tin Tin was a German Shepherd puppy rescued from a WWI battlefield in France by an American soldier named Lee Duncan. Portrayed as having unusual physical prowess and human-like characteristics, his popularity in films grows. One fanciful story claims that when the original "Rinty," as he was nicknamed, died in 1932, it was in the arms of actress Jean Harlow, who made arrangements to have his body returned to France. German Shepherds were subsequently trained to star in other films as well as a TV series that lasted until 1959.

1929: The Third Geneva Convention establishes guidelines for the treatment of prisoners of war. Not all countries involved in the war sign the treaty, however, including the Soviet Union and Japan. Generally, prisoners had to be treated humanely—they were not to be sent into battle, nor used as a human shield, and they were not to be used as slave labor. Countries differed in their compliance and interpretation of the guidelines and did not treat combatants from different countries equally. Germany treated British, French, and American prisoners in accordance with the convention, but non-western prisoners were dealt with more harshly. Japan, a non-signatory of the Third Geneva Convention and a non-adherent of earlier international agreements such as the Hague Convention, treated most prisoners very harshly. In the United States, prisoners were treated well as a rule. This became controversial as the American public grew to resent favorable treatment toward soldiers who'd been in recent combat against American soldiers.

1930s: Comic strips become a regular feature in most major newspapers. During and preceding the war years, most comic strips incorporated a war theme into their presentations. Two of the best known were *Blondie* and *Tarzan*. In both cases, their popularity and that of many other cartoons was reflected in films, radio, comic books, and eventually television. In various forms they remain accessible today.

November 1932: Franklin D. Roosevelt is elected to his first term as President of the United States.

March 1933: President Roosevelt gives his first radio address directly to the American people. The radio talk begins a tradition known as "fireside chats," that comes in the form of a weekly radio address. During the 1930s, topics deal primarily with the Depression, but they gradually turn to war preparedness and eventually the war itself. The "fireside chats" garner more listeners than the most popular radio shows.

1934: Following groundwork laid in the 1920s and his pivotal appointment as Germany's new chancellor in 1933, Adolph Hitler becomes head of state in Germany.

1930s: "G-Men," a slang term for special agents of the U.S. Government, particularly the FBI, are popularized in books, movies, and radio programs.

1935: Strombeck-Becker Manufacturing Co., who, along with its predecessors had been making toys since the late 1800s, begins manufacturing a line of pre-carved, solid-wood model kits. Initially most of the kits are steam locomotives. Later the kits include airplanes, ships, and other military weapons. The B-17 Flying Fortress, like the one Scotty builds in the story, is one of these, but it was apparently released after WWII. Today, these kits are true collector items.

July 1935: The first Boeing B-17 prototype is flown. The "Flying Fortress," or the "Fort," as it comes to be known, first sees combat in 1941 for the British Royal Air Force and begins daylight bombing missions over Europe. Boeing plants build 6,981 of these aircraft and other manufacturers build another 5,745.

November 1936: Franklin D. Roosevelt is elected to his second term as President of the United States.

1936: Fifteenth Avenue NE (the Cowan Park Bridge) is upgraded to reinforced concrete.

1936: *Flash Gordon and the Witch Queen of Mongo* is published as a Big Little Book. Big Little Books were text and graphic novels that were lengthier than comics and published in a unique format. These hard-bound books measured one and one-half inches thick, were about three and one-half inches wide by four and one-half inches tall and were published by the Whitman Publishing Co. of Racine Wisconsin.

1936: American Jesse Owens, an African American athlete, wins four gold medals in track at the summer Olympics in Berlin, Germany. Hitler hopes to reveal the inferiority of African ethnicity and show off German athletes as a demonstration of their superior Aryan ethnicity. He also sanitizes Germany, particularly Berlin, to rebut fears that the German state had become oppressive to many minorities. Whether Owens was snubbed by Hitler when he failed to acknowledge or congratulate him after his victory remains in question. Owens, who never received a congratulatory telegram or invitation to the White House did say he felt snubbed by President Franklin Roosevelt. Eventually, his accomplishment is formally acknowledged by President Dwight D. Eisenhower. The University of Washington eight-man crew beats the Germans in the 1936 Olympics. The summer Olympics of 1940 and 1944 as well as the 1940 winter Olympics were canceled because of the war.

December 11, 1936: King Edward VIII of England abdicates. Edward has difficulty following court protocol and constitutional conventions. His proposed marriage to American socialite, Wallis Simpson causes a crisis that results in his abdication. He is succeeded by his younger brother, Albert, who chooses the regal name, George VI. George VI reigned until the accession of Elizabeth II on February 6, 1952.

March 1937: A U.S. Gallup poll reveals that 94% of Americans wish to keep the U.S. out of foreign wars.

1938: Partly because of President Roosevelt's struggle with poliomyelitis, a campaign to find a cure begins. It is called the National Foundation for Infantile Paralysis and acquires the name March of Dimes from Vaudeville performer Eddie Cantor.

1938: Sky Bars are manufactured by Necco and introduced with a sky-writing advertising campaign, for which they are named. They sell for five cents in 1942 and consist of four milk chocolate sections, each with a different filling—caramel, vanilla, peanut, and fudge.

Unique, given their four different fillings per bar, they're still available today in limited supply online and in heritage candy stores.

October 30, 1938: The Orson Welles' broadcast of "The War of the Worlds" rouses panic in more than a million across the country as listeners confuse the radio play with a real news bulletin. Just as listeners hear that New York has been destroyed by a Martian invasion, a thunderstorm and power outage descend on Concrete, Washington, where a surge of panic inspires many residents to believe the world is coming to an end.

November 9, 1938: Nazi gangs terrorize Jews in Germany, Austrian cities, and elsewhere. This date becomes known as "Crystal Night" (night of the broken glass). Many homes, businesses, and synagogues are looted and burned. Ninety-one Jews are killed and 20,000 are taken to concentration camps.

February 1939: The World's Fair in San Francisco opens in February, closes for the winter, and then runs through September 1940. The fair is called the "Pageant of the Pacific," and features goods from around the Pacific. It also celebrates the dedication of the Oakland Bay Bridge (1936) and the Golden Gate Bridge (1937). Several railroads run special trains to the fair, but railroads serving Seattle directly are not among them.

August 1939: England begins Operation Pied Piper, a voluntary evacuation of children from major cities that authorities expect to be bombed by the Germans. Over 1,500,000 people are relocated from urban centers, 800,000 of whom are children. Evacuations from cities are remarkably smooth, given the numbers, but receptions in the countryside, as managed by local authorities, are met with mixed results. Some children are placed with friends and relatives, but this isn't an option for many. Complications include a clash between urban and rural cultures as well as religious and ethnic ties.

1939: Edward R. Murrow and the CBS team begin regular radio broadcasts from Europe. These broadcasts inform Americans about what is going on in Europe, providing insight into a war most don't want to be involved in. European broadcasts continue through the war and cover the liberation of the Nazi concentration camps in 1945.

1939: Todd shipyard in Tacoma reopens after being closed since the end of WWI. The Tacoma yard launches its first "Liberty Ship" freighter in 1940. The Todd shipyards in both Seattle and Tacoma build and launch many ships for the war effort.

September 1939: Germany invades Poland. Polish forces hold out till October 6, but eventually fall to the onslaught of the German army. Germany and the Soviet Union divide and annex Poland. Most historians regard this as the beginning of the war. Britain and France declare war on Germany.

1940s: Launched in the early part of the nineteenth century, A.C. Gilbert Co. is best known for its Erector Sets and model trains. In the 1940s, the company begins producing chemistry sets and microscopes like the one Greta receives from her aunt in the story. One of the company's advertising slogans is, "Developed at the Gilbert Hall of Science."

April 1940: Germany invades Norway and Denmark.

May 1940: Winston Churchill becomes Prime Minister of the United Kingdom.

May 1940: Germany invades Belgium and the Netherlands.

July 1, 1940: The Tacoma Narrows suspension bridge opens to traffic. The bridge later collapses during a windstorm on November 7, 1940, and the undulating motion of the bridge deck is captured on film. People who see the newsreel of the collapse begin calling it "Galloping Gertie." The two towers, which were left standing, were dismantled about ten years later when a new suspension bridge was built across the Narrows.

July 2, 1940: The Lake Washington floating bridge connecting Mercer Island with the city of Seattle opens. It helps the war effort by providing quicker access to Seattle and is named the Lacey V. Morrow Bridge after the older brother of journalist Edward R. Morrow, who attended school in Washington. Built on a series of floating pontoons, it is the first of its kind for a major highway. Before the Interstate Highway System, it is part of U.S. Route 10. It later becomes part of Interstate 90 and is expanded to include a parallel floating bridge.

July 1940: Germany begins bombing Britain. Brits use the subway tubes in London as bomb shelters.

July 1940: Green Lantern first appears in *All-America Comics #16*.

July 1940: Appointed Army Minister in Japan, Hideki Tojo is involved in the ongoing plans to attack Pearl Harbor. In October 1941 he becomes Prime Minister. Serving as War Minister, Home Minister, and Education Minister, he ultimately becomes the face of the Japanese war effort. A supporter of fascist ideas, his power and influence are roughly comparable to Germany's Adolf Hitler. After the war, he is tried for war crimes and executed in 1948.

September 1940: Germany, Japan, and Italy agree to a military alliance and sign the Tripartite Pact. They become known as the "Axis Powers." Several smaller countries join and withdraw from the pact during the course of the war. Countries at war with the Axis, such as the U.S., Canada, Britain, and Australia are called the "Allies."

September 1940: The U.S. Congress passes the Selective Training & Service Act. This creates the first peacetime conscription (draft) in the U.S. Men between the ages of 18 and 45 are liable for military service and all men between 18 and 65 are required to register. The Act also provides a way for persons who object to the war or military service to apply for conscientious objector status through their local draft boards. The application can be based on conscience or religious grounds.

A nondiscrimination clause was inserted in the 1940 Selective Training and Service Act. Most African Americans who served were designated to support/non-combat roles and the racial discrimination they hoped to escape followed them into the military. Nonetheless, non-combat troops often served at the front lines and suffered many casualties. African Americans that did see direct combat served in segregated units and were not given their due even when they served with distinction and honor. The Black Panther tank battalion and the Red Tails/Tuskegee Airmen are probably the best known. A slogan and sign called the Double V emerged to signify their desire to defeat the enemy abroad and racism at home. The U.S. military was not officially integrated until 1948.

The draft did not apply to women. Though women did volunteer for service, none were allowed to serve in combat roles. The Women's Army Auxiliary Corps (WAAC) served with the Army but weren't part of it and therefore not entitled to military benefits. Women Accepted for Volunteer Emergency Service (WAVES) served as part of the Navy. In 1943 two separate groups of women pilots were combined into the Women's Airforce Service Pilots (WASPS), but they were considered civil service, so they were not entitled to military benefits even though they were controlled by the military. Filling non-combat flying roles, they ferried planes from factories and towed targets for gunnery practice to free more male pilots for combat. Their service records were sealed for many years and only released in 1975. The story of their contribution and struggle to earn recognition is an important chapter in the expansion of opportunities for women.

September 1940: The differences between British and American fastening systems cause problems that need to be overcome when the Packard Motor Car Company agrees to manufacture the British-designed Merlin aircraft engines under license from Rolls Royce. The Merlin engine powers some of the most effective aircraft of the war, perhaps most famously the American P-51 Mustang. Packard agrees to use the British Whitworth system of bolts and threads so the project can go forward. This engine powers the P-51 Mustang, the British Mosquito, and some British Lancaster bombers. After the war, a common thread system called the "Unified" was adopted by the British, Americans, and Canadians. It survives to this day and is primarily used in aircraft engines. Many of these engines power racing hydroplanes developed after the war.

The bore of American guns is expressed using both the conventional and metric systems. Small bore guns are expressed in a decimal fraction of an inch, called inch caliber, and larger gun bores are expressed in millimeters, called millimeter caliber, generally 75mm and larger.

The metric system had been used in Germany since 1872. Japan replaced its traditional system of measurement in 1924 with the metric system. Some of the old units are used until 1966 when they are forbidden for official purposes. Russia also adopted the metric system in 1924. Currently, the United States uses the U.S. Customary System for some things such as carpentry and some hardware applications but uses the metric system for most manufacturing.

November 1940: Franklin D. Roosevelt is elected to his third term as President of the United States. This is the first time a U.S. President serves for more than two consecutive terms. To manage the isolationist sentiment in the U.S. while helping Great Britain and other nations through the Lend-Lease Program and preparing for the war he feels is inevitable, Roosevelt tells the American people (several times during the presidential campaign) that he won't send American soldiers to fight in foreign wars.

1941: The British Mosquito aircraft enters production in 1941 and sees widespread service in 1942. The aircraft becomes known as "The Wooden Wonder" because it is constructed primarily out of wood. The design saves strategic material such as aluminum and employs many skilled woodworkers. The British Mosquito aircraft turn out to be among the most successful and feared aircraft of the war because of the many different roles they effectively fill.

1941: Farm labor shortages begin to appear because so many are serving in the military and many others are moving from farms to cities to work at higher paying jobs in military factories. To compensate, farm families work harder, often receiving draft deferments, some prisoners of war are offered farm labor on a voluntary basis, and immigration of foreign labor is encouraged. The use of war prisoners is controversial for several reasons and union supporters insist that farmers pay for this labor. Ultimately, increased efficiencies due to new mechanical farm equipment probably had the greatest impact on production, resolving the shortages.

March 11, 1941: Congress passes the Lend-Lease Act which gives the President almost unlimited power to send war material to countries fighting the Axis powers. The primary recipient is Great Britain, but the Soviet Union, China, and France also receive equipment. The U.S. is compensated through various agreements for rent of bases and promises for return of the equipment. Lend-Lease significantly expands the powers of the presidency and effectively ends the pretense of U.S. neutrality. Authority under the act ends in 1945.

March 1941: Captain America first appears in *Captain America Comics #1* from Marvel Comics' predecessor, Timely Comics.

June 1941: Germany invades the Soviet Union.

December 1941: Wonder Woman first appears in *All Star Comics #8.*

December 7, 1941: Japan bombs the U.S. Naval base at Pearl Harbor, Hawaii and destroys much of the U.S. Pacific Fleet.

December 8, 1941: The U.S. declares war on Japan. President Roosevelt announces the declaration in his famous "Day of Infamy" speech. After Pearl Harbor, Winston Churchill worries that America will adopt a "Pacific first" policy and Lend-Lease supplies destined for Britain will be diverted. Churchill believes that a "Europe first" policy is most likely to win the war.

December 8, 1941: Blackouts begin along the entire West Coast of the United States, but some lighthouses are left on to protect shipping. Windows in homes and businesses require coverings at night. Some people still drive, but with their lights off, thus causing numerous accidents. Outside lights must be turned off. An amateur radio blackout is also put in place. Commercial radio stations in the Northwest, west of Boise, are silenced at seven each evening. Blackout measures are intended to make it difficult for Japanese planes or ships to locate targets.

December 11, 1941: Germany and Italy declare war on the U.S., saying that the Tripartite Pact they signed with Japan obligates them to do so after the U.S. declares war on Japan. The U.S. declares war on Germany and Italy.

1941: Nearly everything needed to fight in Europe and the Pacific, as well as everything needed to support the British must be transported across an ocean. The vast bulk of the tonnage is transported by sea using the United States Merchant Marine. Members of the merchant marine are not uniformed military in peacetime, but in wartime they are considered military personnel.

This effort becomes the largest sealift in history, but losses of personnel and equipment are staggering. Overall, 733 cargo ships are lost, and an estimated 9,300 people are killed. The death rate was about one in 24, which makes it the highest casualty rate of any service. This casualty rate is kept secret, so the enemy won't realize how effective their efforts are. Not until 1943 did the ships built exceed the ships sunk. This was, in part, because the range of air cover eventually extended to close the "air gap" in the middle of the Atlantic, where ships were previously defenseless against German U-Boats.

1941: After America's entry into the war, journalist Ernie Pyle becomes a roving correspondent for the Scripps Howard newspaper chain. He gains a wide following, is known for his engaging folksy style, and writes from the perspective of the common soldier. He gains stature as more than just a war correspondent. Many people feel like he is a friendly uncle looking after their loved one in the field, and his columns are as welcome as letters from a soldier. He dies in combat on an island off Okinawa, Japan after being hit by machine-gun fire.

January 31, 1942: The Navy Department calls on high school students, initially boys only, to turn out 500,000 scale model airplanes by June 30. Fifty different types of aircraft are modeled on a scale of one inch per six feet, or 1:72. A scale model at 35 feet looks the same as the real thing at half a mile. Standards for dimensional accuracy are strict and the models are used to train pilots and gunners. With women working in aircraft factories, the program is also opened to girls, and there is no color bar.

1942: "Tokyo Rose" is the name given to women who are the voice of Japanese propaganda aimed at allied soldiers. The intent is to taunt and mislead them and thereby hurt morale. One of these women, Toguri D'Aquino is an American citizen visiting Japan when the Pearl Harbor attack takes place. She is pressured into participating, and is later tried and convicted in 1949 after she returns to the U.S. She is pardoned by President Gerald Ford in 1979.

1942: By the time the U.S. enters the war, there are over one hundred boat houses and resorts around Puget Sound where sport fishers can rent small wooden boats of various styles. Some also rent motors. Fishing derbies are very popular, but most are suspended after 1942. However, many resume after the war. Over the years these facilities disappear, primarily due to the availability of small, affordable, trailerable boats and the depletion of salmon stocks. Due to dams, overfishing, pollution, and habitat destruction, salmon stocks significantly decline after the war years and Puget Sound Chinook salmon are listed under the Endangered Species Act. There are many efforts to reverse this trend, but no consensus on how effective they will ultimately be.

1942: "Final Solution" is the name given to the German plan to exterminate all European Jews. Even though the Germans have killed approximately one million Jews and others prior to 1942, the Final Solution is a plan to speed up and industrialize the process in "extermination camps." The precise number will probably never be known, but historians usually refer to six million Jews having been killed by the German Third Reich before it was defeated.

February 1942: By executive order of President Franklin D. Roosevelt, approximately 110,000 Japanese, the majority of whom are American citizens living along the West Coast are ordered to "War Relocation Camps," where they are detained for the duration of the war. They aren't called "concentration camps," but the Japanese are indeed prisoners, confined by barbed wire and guards. The official term for the relocations is "internment" but many called it "incarceration." Conditions are harsh and the disruption of having to leave homes, businesses, and community is painful. Many are given only one week's notice to pack up and be ready to leave.

What is now known as the Puyallup Fair Grounds, near Tacoma Washington, is used as a relocation processing center for Japanese from western Washington and Oregon. From there, Japanese are sent to one of ten encampments, most of which are located inland in desolate areas of the western U.S.

Later in the war, some second-generation Japanese, or "Neisi" as they called themselves, volunteer for combat and the Military Intelligence Service of the United States to prove their loyalty to country. They serve with distinction. Long after the war, the U.S. Government offers an apology to the Japanese who suffered this relocation and in 1990 authorizes $20,000 to each internment camp survivor. Neisi service members were also honored. It is still debated whether this relocation was necessary, but most now believe it was an overreaction to the panic caused by the attack on Pearl Harbor.

April 18, 1942: Lieutenant Colonel Jimmy Doolittle is the mastermind behind a daring raid on Tokyo. Sixteen B-25 medium bombers, which were never intended for carrier operations, take off from the USS Hornet. Pilots know they won't be able to return and will be lucky to even land on the Chinese mainland. Damage to the Japanese is minimal but it is a great morale booster. Though the planes are lost, all but three crew members out of 80 survive. It is estimated that 250,000 Chinese are killed by the Japanese while they are searching for the crews. The Japanese recall some fighter squadrons to defend the homeland, thereby weakening the forces available to engage the Americans in the South Pacific. The raid may have goaded the Japanese into an attempt to destroy the U.S. Pacific fleet, which erupted in the battle of Midway. The raid is dramatized in the movie *Thirty Seconds Over Tokyo* in 1944.

May 1942: U.S. Office of Price Administration (OPA) freezes prices on practically all everyday goods. Many of these items require ration cards to purchase. Gradually, items are added to the list as scarcity becomes a concern. Affected items include sugar, coffee, gasoline, rubber, silk, meat, shoes, and nylon. Each person in a household, including babies, is required to have a ration book. To conserve gasoline, a maximum speed of 35 mph is established, and carpools and driving clubs are encouraged.

May 28, 1942: Even though individual Seattle schools have been conducting air drills for some time, there is an unannounced city-wide drill on May 28. Most school officials don't know it's a drill until right before it's announced. This causes quite a controversy. Some people likened it to the "boy who cried wolf," claiming it would make school personnel take the real thing less seriously.

June 3, 1942: Six months after Pearl Harbor, the Japanese bomb Dutch Harbor, Alaska. On June 6, a significant Japanese invasion force invades and occupies two small islands in the Aleutian chain. A series of air raids on Japanese positions and numerous naval battles persist until late 1943. The miserable weather and remoteness of the area make it difficult for the U.S. to quickly repel the invaders. The Japanese strategy seemed aimed to discourage a U.S. attack across the North Pacific and possibly divert attention from the South Pacific. The U.S. launched a counterattack in May 1943 and took the islands back in late August after the remaining Japanese abandoned their positions.   Often referred to as the "Forgotten Battle," it is overshadowed by the battles of Midway and Guadalcanal.

June 4 – 7, 1942: The Battle of Midway is a turning point in the war. It is the first major defeat for the Imperial Japanese Navy.   The Japanese plan to attack the Midway atoll and use it as a base to attack Hawaii.   They hope to draw the U.S. Pacific Fleet out from Hawaii and ambush them.   Instead, the Japanese fleet is discovered in route to Midway Island and U.S. forces ambush them.

June 1942: On the nights of June 22 and 23, a Japanese submarine surfaces and shells Fort Stevens, on the Oregon side at the mouth of the Columbia River. The Americans are instructed not to return fire because that might help the Japanese better locate their target. The Fort suffers only minimal damage and there is no loss of life. Around this time, several ships are torpedoed as far south as San Diego. Oil fields near Santa Barbara are shelled. On September 9, 1942, the only aerial bombardment of the U.S. mainland takes place. The Japanese drop incendiary bombs on a forested area in Oregon in an attempt to start a forest fire. The bomber is a small float plane with wings folded up and carried across the Pacific in a large submarine. It drops two bombs near Brookings Oregon, but they fail to ignite the anticipated fires. Later in the war, the Japanese send approximately 9,000 bomb-laden balloons across the Pacific via the recently discovered jet stream. This is another attempt to start forest fires, but only about 300 reach the U.S., and they do little damage. Knowledge of these events fuels the West Coast "invasion scare."

1942: The song *Rosie the Riveter* is released. "Rosie" becomes a symbol for the increasing number of women in the workplace, and the can-do spirit of the home front. During the war, many women take jobs formerly held by men as increasing numbers of men join the military. "Rosie" is eventually featured in the famous "We Can Do It!" poster, which is reprinted to this day.

July 17, 1942: The Battle of Stalingrad (now Volgograd) is fought from July 17, 1942 to February 2, 1943. It is one of the fiercest, bloodiest battles of the war with approximately two million killed, mostly Soviet civilians. The Germans suffer a major defeat, which marks a turning point of the war in Eastern Europe.

September 21, 1942: The Boeing B-29 Super Fortress takes its maiden flight. It has been called "the weapon that won the war in the Pacific" because it made the long-range strategic bombing of Japan possible. Because it is so revolutionary, it has significant "teething" problems and American pilots are reluctant to fly it until several WASP pilots demonstrate that they can fly it.

1943: American-style recipes are adapted for rationing and shortages in the wartime edition of *The American Woman's Cookbook*. This cookbook classic contains numerous substitutions, enabling scarce food supplies to stretch further.

June 13, 1943: A mock air raid is conducted at the University of Washington's Husky Stadium. Its purpose is to demonstrate what citizens could expect from an air raid and show how the Seattle Civilian Protection Division would respond. A mock neighborhood with businesses is assembled on the playing field and P-38 fighters simulate the attack. Anti-aircraft gunners fire blanks at the attacking planes. Incendiary devices are set off to simulate bomb strikes and their aftermath. Volunteers then extinguish the fires and tend to the "wounded." The stadium is filled to its seating capacity of 35,000.

July 24, 1943: This day marks the beginning of Operation Gomorrah, eight days of bombing the German city of Hamburg. Although many cities on both sides were bombed, the bombing of Hamburg is noteworthy for the level of death and destruction. Estimates are that

35,000 died and 135,000 were wounded. The resulting firestorm was so intense that some reported people being lifted off the ground as the fire sucked in oxygen to feed itself. The extreme devastation has prompted several writers to call this the Hiroshima of Germany.

1943: Zoot Suits come into style. The flamboyant outfits featuring broad shoulders, ballooned pants, long coats, and broad-brimmed hats were favored by various ethnic groups and made popular by jazz musicians. Because of their extravagant use of materials, they generated resentment among some, and wearers were sometimes accused of being unpatriotic, given the rationing and shortages. Some went so far to say that Zoot Suiters were draft dodgers. An altercation known as the Zoot Suit Riots erupted in Los Angeles when some service personnel and civilians came to blows over the suits. The race of many zoot suiters was often cited as a flashpoint.

September 3, 1943: Italy signs an armistice with the Allies, but the agreement is kept secret for several days. German military units in Italy fight on until finally surrendering in May 1945.

1944: After the attack on Pearl Harbor, many plants manufacturing war material are covered with netting. As bombing accuracy improves, more sophisticated camouflage techniques are employed. Boeing's Plant #2 where the B-17s are built is covered with an entire fake neighborhood. Fake houses, streets, and trees are constructed on the plant's roof and designed to blend in with the surrounding area. The camouflage looks fake at ground level, but from 5,000 feet up, it is quite convincing. A fake village is built on the roof of Boeing's Seattle plant to disguise it from the air. Called "Wonderland," the village features fake cottages, streets, and lawns.

June 6, 1944: Known as "D-Day," this is the date that Allied forces, who had been amassing in England, cross the English Channel and land on five beaches in Normandy, France to begin their final drive to defeat Germany. It was and remains the largest amphibious invasion of all time. It involved 160,000 landing troops, 195,700 navy personnel, and 5,000 ships.

June 22, 1944: The Russians launch Operation Bagration against Germany on the eastern front. They use several times the number of ground forces used for the D-Day invasion of France.

November 1944: Franklin D. Roosevelt is elected to his fourth term as President of the United States.

December 15, 1944: Glenn Miller's plane disappears in heavy weather over the English Channel as he is on his way to entertain U.S. troops in France. One theory holds that his plane was the victim of friendly fire. Glenn Miller joined the Army in 1942 and was eventually placed in charge of the Army Air Force Band. Of all the bands and orchestras of the swing era and war years, The Glenn Miller Orchestra is among the most closely associated with the music of that time.

February 1945: Dresden Germany survived most of the war without significant damage. That changed in February 1945 when the Allies began a bombing campaign that destroyed most of the city. The city was so devastated that it was difficult to tell how many died. Estimates vary from 25,000 to 135,000. The bombing of Dresden was controversial then, and debate continues as to whether there was a military justification for the raids. The bombing and resulting firestorm became the backdrop for Kurt Vonnegut's novel, "Slaughterhouse Five."

March 9-10, 1945: "Operation Meetinghouse" is the name given to a series of air raids on Tokyo, Japan that are regarded as the most destructive bombing raids in human history. Because of the dramatic impact of the atomic bombs dropped on Hiroshima and Nagasaki, the bombing of Tokyo is often forgotten.

April 12, 1945: President Franklin D. Roosevelt dies while still in office and Vice President Harry S. Truman becomes President.

April 15, 1945: The Soviet Army enters Berlin from the east.

April 30, 1945: Adolph Hitler commits suicide in his Berlin bunker.

May 7 & 8, 1945: The first of two German Instruments of Surrender is signed in Rheims, France on May 7. The second is signed in Berlin, Germany on May 8.

July 26, 1945: The United States, along with several allied nations issue the Potsdam Declaration, in which they call for Japan to surrender. Japan ignores the declaration.

August 6, 1945: The United States drops an atomic bomb called "Little Boy" on the Japanese city of Hiroshima. The bomb is dropped from the B-29 "Enola Gay." Although Boeing did build B-29s, this specially equipped version was built by the Glen L. Martin Company in Nebraska. It is estimated that by the end of 1945, there were between 90,000 and 140,000 casualties from the blast and radiation, with 69% of the buildings destroyed.

August 9, 1945: The United States drops the atomic bomb called "Fat Boy" on the Japanese city of Nagasaki. It is estimated that there were between 60,000 and 80,000 casualties from the blast and radiation by the end of 1945.

August 15, 1945: Japan unconditionally surrenders and documents are signed on the deck of the USS Missouri. The Missouri is commissioned in June of 1944 and is quickly nicknamed "Mighty Mo," or "Big Mo." It is decommissioned on February 26, 1955, and mothballed at Puget Sound Naval Shipyard in Bremerton, Washington where thousands of visitors come to view the "surrender deck." It is reactivated in 1984 and finally decommissioned again in 1992. In 1998 it is donated to the Missouri Memorial Association and taken to Hawaii where it remains today as a museum ship.

World War II is and remains the deadliest military conflict in history. It is estimated that 60 million people are killed. Forty to 52 million are civilians and 22 to 25 million are military casualties. The United States recorded 416,800 military deaths and 1,700 civilian deaths.

Acknowledgements

Writers sometimes write themselves into a corner and might remain there if not for an excellent editor. A good editor is not just someone who knows the language. They also have the intuition to decipher the subtleties of the story. These skills would be all but meaningless if your editor isn't also someone that's easy to work with and with whom you can develop a rhythm for moving the story forward.

I was so pleased with Sally Jo Martine's editing of my first book, *River's Reach: Coming of Age Amid the Fish War*, that I didn't hesitate to enlist her help on my second, *An Empty House Doesn't Sneeze*. I can only assume that her experience working on this book will have sharpened the skills she brought to the project and that she will be even more successful with future endeavors. I consider myself lucky to have had her technical assistance and thoughtful advice throughout this project.

Many thanks also to Beverly Gilyeart for her eagle eyes and last-minute proofing.

Biography

David Scott Richardson's new work of MG/YA historical fiction, *An Empty House Doesn't Sneeze*, explores life on the home front during WWII. Drawing from two decades as a sixth-grade teacher, Richardson recognizes history as the keel that keeps us upright in heavy seas and aims to forge a connection with those who were more than a generation unborn when the world went to war.

Richardson's characters convey nuanced and diverse perspectives as they work to unravel ethical knots—from the origins of war to the meaning of a promise—and shed light on how beliefs and fears influence one's choices. His themes probe father-son conflicts, grief, and ethical dilemmas, all while invoking an innate connection with nature, compelling the heart as much as the mind.

Richardson's first MG/YA historical novel, *River's Reach: Coming of Age Amid the Fish War*, was published in September 2023.

Please help this book reach the people who will love it!

Now that you've finished this book, it would mean the world to me to receive your honest review. Please kindly leave a review wherever you bought the book.

Thank you!
David Scott Richardson